Also by Jay Magidson

Shira's Wish

Colors

Madness of the Muses - the Art of Ingrid Dee Magidson

The Crystalline Sword (coming late 2013)

THRESHOLD

of the

MIND

JAY MAGIDSON

Stratumentis Publishing
www.Stratumentis.com

August 2013 ISBN 13: 978-0-9840213-7-6 (Paperback)

FICTION/Science Fiction/Hard Science Fiction

Also available in
Hardcover and Ebook versions

Stratumentis Publishing
www.Stratumentis.com

Cover illustration: agsandrew/Shutterstock.com
Cover design by Gessocat

for Eva,

Thank you for your friendship
and sharing *The Supreme Effort*

1

THE EARTH IS crowded, 17 billion men and women crowded. At the end of the 21st Century, people desperate for space have sprawled onto every available sliver of land, squeezed into every crack; even the most difficult and remote areas have succumbed to their insatiable need for land. Mankind has trampled the vast forests of North America, scraped the tundra of Asia and crawled up and over the mountains of every continent. Every acre of arable land has been farmed and every mountainside terraced to create more. Not a rock has been left unturned or a tree standing that could provide sustenance or shelter for the teaming masses of humanity.

With one exception.

The Grand Canyon in the Southwestern United States has repelled the onslaught. Two billion years of history have shrugged the human lichen off its towering walls and expansive gorge, like a slap in the face of the desperate overcrowding. Even the ancient dwellings of aboriginal cultures and the ugly tourist structures of the 20th Century have been wiped clean, returned to their natural state of barren rock and sage native to the Arizona desert. It was not nature that won this battle, however. It was a strength far greater than any natural force – the will of single man. A man so powerful and so wealthy that he could afford to buy the very wind that whipped through the time-carved gorge.

⸻

Dr. Alexia Serguey was awakened by some bump, or movement of the jet aircraft. She blinked a few times to regain her surroundings, glancing at the time readout on her VR glasses, 04:30. Could it be only six hours since she had boarded in Reykjavik? Weeks of frenetic planning and effort has left her a shell of exhaustion. Once on the jet, she had only the energy left to collapse into her seat, snap the buckle and fall asleep. Alexia scanned the dimly lit cabin, the windows shining black against the night sky; the interior whispering the vast wealth of its owner. The walls of the cabin glowed with the deep warmth of real wood, not the geneered junk that was supposed to look like wood, but never quite did. The latches and handles gleamed of polished brass. Alexia looked down at her stockinged feet, where someone had done her the courtesy of removing her shoes. She dug her toes into the thick carpet, enjoying the sensuous pleasure. The large cabin was arranged more like a private club than a jet. Tall, soft leather seats were set in groups of four around short round tables. On her table was laid a set of exquisite china, delicately filled with red grapes, cheeses, warm rolls, jam and butter. Next to this, a crystal goblet with ice water and a carafe of coffee. She didn't recall ever seeing a server, yet the ice in her water had not melted and the rolls steamed with fresh warmth. Her favorite breakfast, how did they know?

Alexia filled one of the carved glasses with water and drank deeply. It lacked the steely taste of antibacterials that municipal water required. The coffee was rich and mild and made her sigh with each sip. The rest of breakfast was more flavorful than anything she had tasted in years. It had the complex richness of non-modified food. Geneered food always went too far, fruit was too sweet, bread too bland and butter too rich.

Finally satisfied, Alexia peered again into the dim cabin. She realized she was not alone. The three other seats in her small sitting area were empty. But there were three other seating areas identical to her own. These were full. To her left, four large men sat rigidly straight staring directly ahead. Their table was empty. They looked alike, hard chiseled faces and overly developed bodies that seemed to be stuffed into identical black suits, their muscles threatening to tear through the expensive fabric. Clearly they were security.

Alexia looked to the next group. Two men, two women, all of indeterminate age. They had the generic good looks of geneering, gene manipulation that could give a 60 year old the skin of a twenty year old. All of them stared into their VR glasses, hypnotized by virtual reality. Each was in his or her own unique world. It could be work, an imaginary office, or recreation, rock climbing the icy slopes of Mount Everest, or the sweaty warmth of a virtual sex room. Their arms and legs twitched with the false reality of a world which didn't require limbs.

Alexia quickly looked away, to the final group. Two men were conversing in the loud whispers of a scientific argument. Alexia smiled with recognition. They were bent close to each other, oblivious to the rest of the world. The third, a stern looking woman, shot back a look at Alexia, pinched her lips tighter, then glared back into space. Alexia felt her own face. "Do I look like that?"

Next to the pinched face woman was a soft pudgy man perhaps in his late sixties. He had either chosen not to alter his genes, or had altered them to look like this. He smiled gently at Alexia. She was reminded of her grandfather when she was a child. But her grandfather was long gone, everything in her past was gone. She looked away, letting her mind wander, something she hadn't done in a long time.

A moment later the elderly man was standing at her table. "I hope you had a pleasant rest. May I sit down?"

Alexia motioned to the empty seats with an open hand. "This is not my jet, sit where you like."

The older man dropped into the chair directly across from Alexia, reached his hand out. "My name is Horace Spartan. I live, well I used to live in London. Where I was head of neurosurgery at..."

"Oxford." Alexia interrupted. "The Doctor Spartan. The doctor who removed the first fully intact neuron from a living brain? That Doctor Spartan?"

Spartan's smile seemed to freeze on his face. "Yes, but that was some time ago. Unfortunately, no one found any use for a brainless brain cell." His smile thawed at his own pun. "That was the last publicly funded project at Oxford. Our team separated, going off to pharmaceutical labs or to corporate R & D. I stayed at Oxford to teach. Not much money in that, but it keeps food on the table. Not food like this, of course." He gestured at the table, "but I stay alive."

"But your work was brilliant; no one has been able to repeat it." Alexia said.

"And why should they? It was dead-end research, the frivolous meanderings of mad scientists. No financial rewards in it, so it was dropped. Rightly so." He leaned toward Alexia, melting into her grandfather again. "But what about you, Doctor Serguey, a brilliant career in neuro-biology. Too many successes to count. Why are you here?" He gestured around the cabin, "You don't need to revive your legacy, you're living yours."

"Very presumptuous of you to think you know me." Alexia's voice was ice.

He laughed. "We all know you, of you I should say. It is why we are here. Your reputation is a beacon to research scientists. How else could we be convinced to leave our lives to join...well you know." His voice dropped to a whisper.

"No I don't know. Now if you'll excuse me, I'd like to wrap up a few personal matters before we arrive." Alexia adjusted her VR glasses on her face to give the illusion she was plunging into virtual reality.

"Of course doctor, my apologies for disturbing you." Dr. Spartan rose, bowed and returned to his previous seat.

Alexia glared out the broad window into the blackness. Why did Spartan seem to know more about their destination than she did? But how could he know, no one could. Her mind drifted back to her conversation with Tatsuo Hamachi only a month ago. Tatsuo Hamachi, the man who owned this jet and now everyone in it.

"I'm still not sure what you mean by 'project.'" Alexia had said.

Hamachi's expressionless face hovered large in the void of virtual reality. "I understand your trepidation doctor. Unfortunately, I cannot say more over a live connection. It is simple. We are doing primary research on brain function and connectivity. We are nearing a breakthrough and I want the best person to lead my teams." His face grew implacable. "You are the best Doctor Serguey. My financial offer has demonstrated that, has it not?"

"Yes, yes. Your offer is more than generous, Mr. Hamachi. That is not the issue. You are asking me to leave everything behind, my career, my home. To be cut off from everything I know. You won't even say for how long. You ask a lot, but you reveal very little. How can I make such an important decision with so little data?"

"The way you make all your decisions, doctor. I have looked deep into your career. You have an uncanny knack for making things work when everyone and everything points to failure. You use intuition, a rare quality in the late 21st Century. I want that quality leading my project." His face remained smooth, but his eyes sparkled with excitement. "Think of the rewards, doctor. Of being part of something extraordinary." Hamachi sighed then continued. "It is so frustrating to speak this way, but I cannot reveal what is happening in my research facilities. You must trust me. Would you hesitate to lead the team that first sequenced human DNA, or the one which pioneered genetic engineering? What we are doing is as important – if not more so." Hamachi's voice went flat again. "I am sorry doctor, but I can only give you another 24 hours to decide. Then I will be forced to accept second best. Doctor Spiro has accepted pending your decision."

Alexia clamped her emotions. "You will have my answer in 24 hours. Thank you for your generous offer Mr. Hamachi." And she severed the connection.

Doctor Spiro, Alexia fumed. He was all show. Spiro had clawed his way to prominence on the backs of talented research scientists with no talent of his own. She knew at that moment she would take the job, she was too competitive to do otherwise. "Damn, Hamachi knows how to manipulate me."

Alexia's mind returned to the present. She found herself looking down at the dark earth gently sliding by. A string of headlights marked the roads. Transport trucks loaded with supplies for the insatiable cities. Ants carrying grains of sugar back to the colony. The smaller lights seemed to feed the brilliant spread in the distance – Las Vegas. The modest sized city of 25 million had prospered as a hub for the vast solar farms of the Southwest. It had been founded on decadence a century and half ago. But that had become irrelevant with the advent of virtual reality. Why travel for what you could have anytime with a blink of your eye. So the city, like so many, had reinvented itself. Successfully, if the intensity of light was any indication.

They were close. Las Vegas was only 200 miles from the Grand Canyon. With that thought, she felt the engine noise decrease and the jet begin its descent. Her heart skipped a beat. Close to the unknown, her decision was about to reveal itself as foolish caprice, or brilliant intuition.

Alexia shifted her gaze to the brightening sky to her right. The dull gray night sky was being replaced by turquoise and hints of pink against the pitch black of the earth. She couldn't remember when she had last seen a sunrise, a real sunrise. At least not as an adult. "It's lovely." She whispered to herself.

As the jet banked to the left, her view became an empty sky. Alexia turned her head to look out the other side of the cabin. And she gasped. There below was the deep gash of the Grand Canyon delineated against the high desert plan. The deep cut in the earth was a black void against the brightening greens and grays of the desert. As beautiful as it was, that wasn't what had caught her breath. Floating in the blackness of the canyon was an enormous golden sphere. The sunrise reflected off the smooth surface creating the illusion it was a second sun rising inside the Grand

Canyon. "Stratumentis." She breathed. Hamachi's floating city, her destination and her destiny.

Hamachi had purchased the Grand Canyon for the sole purpose of building his enormous floating city, Stratumentis. At over 3,000 feet in diameter, more than half a mile wide, it was suspended by impossibly strong nanofiber cables strung from towers placed along the rim. Two towers on each side of the canyon, over one mile high were anchored into the ancient rock to hold the enormous weight of the spherical city. The suspension system was invisible to Alexia from this height and gave the city the illusion of floating. The golden surface was made from Crystaleen, a synthetic polymer grown in high earth orbit at enormous expense. It had extraordinary properties. It was as light as plastic, as strong as steel, as transparent as glass with the added ability to turn opaque with a small electric charge. But most important, it was an excellent solar collector, capable of powering the entire city.

Stratumentis was self-contained and self-sufficient.

The jet continued its slow banking turn, straightened and came to a landing on a private runway on the north rim of the canyon. A beautiful woman in a blue and green uniform led them to a small adobe building. The interior was not as richly appointed as the jet, but it was comfortably understated. From there, the nine passengers and their guide sped through a glass lined tunnel to the transport station. The young woman simply gestured to the private tram, where only the jet passengers boarded. The interior again spoke of Hamachi's vast wealth, plush leather seats, thick carpet, wood and brass trim. Alexia didn't notice any of these however; she was mesmerized by the incredible views. The sun had risen now and the steep walls of the canyon had turned to fire. The sides of the tram were nearly all glass, Crystaleen to be precise. One could watch the sides of the canyon, or even the bottom, 6,000 feet below, the river a ribbon of blue just now visible. Stratumentis had seemed large from the jet, but it was enormous from the tram and grew larger with their approach. No one spoke.

Alexia had been briefed on the design of the city, she supposed they all had. Stratumentis was laid out like an inside-out globe, using longitude and latitude for direction, with the additional dimension of depth. Logical enough, she grasped the concept without understanding its scale. The sphere was two hundred stories high and fifty rings deep at its equator. The interior spaces were used for mechanical rooms, offices, storage and most important, research laboratories, hundreds of them. The outer rooms were living spaces, apartments, restaurants and meeting rooms.

Alexia thought of her own apartment in Reykjavik. Windows were dangerous and wasteful amenities in the northern latitudes. Exterior walls were coated with insulation and solar collectors. But Alexia had chosen her apartment in the expensive high rise because it had a view. A few square feet of glass that looked out over the dense city of Reykjavik and to the bleak landscape beyond.

Stratumentis grew larger until it filled their entire view, then swallowed them whole. The tram slid quietly into the city station identical to the one at the rim. Four guides met them, two men and two women, all in the now familiar blue and green uniforms of Stratumentis. One of the male guides, the leader, waited while they gathered in the terminal. He was impossibly good looking, as if carved by a Greek artisan.

"Your attention, please." His voice a silky tenor. "Thank you. Before we continue, please turn on your VR glasses, you will not need to search for an address, there is only one. Good. Mr. Hamachi will now speak with you."

Alexia's view changed from the plush interior of the tram terminal, to an expansive canyon view, similar to the one on the tram ride, but closer, somehow grander. She staggered, then caught herself. The human race had developed an additional sense with the advent of virtual reality. One could be fully immersed in an illusory reality, yet keep an unconscious hold on the physical world. This second sense kept people from stumbling or falling over when encountering contradictory input. This developed sense was known simply as "grip."

"Welcome to Stratumentis." Hamachi slowly resolved into the view. He was sitting behind a heavy wooden desk where only his upper body, face and arms could be seen. Behind him, the walls of the Grand Canyon flamed red and orange with the rising sun. "Each of you has been invited here to share a vision, a vision of possibility." His hand swept across the view. "Look around you. Impossibility becomes reality here. Open space, pristine nature in a crowded world. You have all been invited here to be part of a grand project. But there is a cost. And that cost is no communication outside of Stratumentis. None." His eyes narrowed. "Think carefully, that includes virtual clubs, entertainment, even banking. All of your work and socializing will be done here, and only here."

Hamachi's eyes seemed to bore into her head. Alexia wondered if it appeared that way to the others as well.

Hamachi continued. "Each of you has signed a non-disclosure agreement. You have promised to give your best effort and skills to the tasks ahead. But that is not enough. You must also pledge your loyalty to an ideal you do not even know yet. Consider carefully one last time. If you hesitate, or have doubts, remove yourself now. There will be no consequences. Simply tell one of the uniformed guides and you will be returned in the same manner you arrived. There will be no cost, no retribution; your former job will be waiting for you. This door does not swing both ways ladies and gentlemen." The VR screen went blank.

Alexia let out the breath she'd been holding. She nodded toward the lead guide. "Let's go, I'd like to get started."

2

ZEKIEL MALAFFAIRES ENJOYED looking at his city before he had his eyes removed. The crumbling infrastructure of New Denver appealed to him. He vaguely remembered the intense blue desert sky above the city; now blocked by massive conduits crisscrossing the space between buildings like giant spider webs, their bulk threatening to tear the cornices off the ancient structures and fill the streets with rubble. Somehow they stood, while every year, more were added, until they filtered so much of the bright sun that the ground was only stippled with light – a gray jungle floor. And at night, if there was such a concept anymore, it was neither quite light nor dark enough. The weak colorless glow of low intensity diodes, ubiquitous to everything electronic, gave the gray world a macabre, nightmarish quality. The city was everything Ezekiel loved, anthropomorphized gloom.

Deep within the decaying wood and stone walls of New Denver, were the distinctly 21st Century inhabitants; teaming hoards of sleepless men and women sardined into cramped apartments. They toiled endless hours to pay for the electronic addiction that made their lives bearable – virtual reality. A man would work at midnight in China, 6:00 a.m. in London, and 3:00 p.m. in New York, all without ever leaving his room. On his VR glasses, he would see the projected reality of a large modern city with chrome office buildings towering into a cloudless sky. He would be one of the handsome executives in a perfectly tailored suit flirting with the buxom receptionist. And he would overhear the excited conversations of deals being made, the promise of inclusion and reward in this synthetic world. Cardboard flavored food, over chlorinated water, roving power outages and advanced sleep deprivation were not allowed in this manufactured world. And those who could afford it, never took their VR sets off, not even to sleep.

Reality wasn't that interesting anymore, so Ezekiel had his eyes removed, replaced with high-speed network connectors linked directly to his optic nerves – prosthetic eyes with a plug where the pupil would have been. The worm colored network cable plugged directly into his eye-jack. It bounced when he blinked, and shuttered when his plastic eyes wandered. But instead of the imperfect projection of a VR set, he was immersed, fully bathed in synthetic reality. If he chose to see businessmen as man-sized banana slugs in suits, and their arrogant assistants as vertical centipedes, that's what he saw. But more than saw, he smelled their earthy decay, and felt their slimy skin. virtual reality was not virtual for Ezekiel.

Ezekiel had not left his windowless apartment for years, had not even looked around without the enhanced vision of virtual reality. If he had, he would have seen the standard 20 by 20 foot cell of the single male. The apartment came furnished and he had changed nothing. Near the entrance sat a single plastic chair and a cheap synth-wood table, its top delaminating into sharp splinters. Lined along the adjacent wall sat narrow fiber-foam bed, darkly stained and sagging in the center. Beyond that, a wall unit housed a food storage and prep station where piles of empty containers spilled over and onto the floor. The far corner formed an exposed bathroom. Over the stained sink hung the room's only mirror. If Ezekiel had bothered to look at himself, he would have seen a fleshy 35 year old man with thinning, greasy brown hair, tangled beard, broken yellow teeth and plastic eyes.

But on *the I*, the virtual network, Ezekiel chose who he would look like. Sometimes he was an immaculately dressed businessman, other times a muscular bronzed model. He could be a child, a woman, anything he desired. It depended only on his effort and skill to create new avatars. If nature had not been kind to him in reality, luck had blessed him in virtual reality. Ezekiel's job was reaching into the network day and night stealing his way into secure sites, testing them for hardness. It was the perfect job for a misanthrope.

Ezekiel slid into the global satellite feed again this evening. He'd been snooping around banks and investment cores for days. His mind was spent and the view from space helped him relax. He knew the danger of breaking into the main link, but that only applied to the losers that got caught.

He felt like a space eagle from way up here, peering down on his prey. Ezekiel swooped around like this for a while, mindlessly looking at the brown and black tangle that was New Denver. His eyes wandered to the varying shades of green rectangles that surrounded the dense city. They extended into the distance, dotted only by the occasional farm depot then stopped entirely by the white caps of the Rocky Mountains themselves.

Ezekiel zoomed in and out, letting his imagination and the freedom of flying guide him. He'd seen all this many times, but he still relished the primal feeling of flying in his earthbound body. It was power and freedom from even the mundane laws of physics. Then something caught his attention. "What's that?" He focused on a large brown area in the sea of variegated green. "Interesting, maybe a failed crop, or a genetic line gone wrong. Let's take a closer look." He muttered.

It was a barren field. That shouldn't be strange in itself, it was winter after all. Perhaps they had simply harvested whatever crop had been growing. What was strange, was that there were small buildings scattered about the farmland. "Houses?" Ezekiel pondered. "Impossible." A quick increase in magnification showed him that they were indeed houses – with smoke coming from their chimneys. They were burning something, perhaps wood! Ezekiel glanced at the longitude and latitude coordinates of this strange place and made a mental note of them.

The winter scene splintered into a flash of orange brilliance. "Shit!"

The proximity alarm. Ezekiel had stayed too long inside the satellite's computer system. Their anti-body software had finally sniffed his presence. Their counter measures were slow, but effective. If he couldn't outrun them now, he'd be burning his system, changing eyes, and looking for a new place to live within the next few minutes. The penalty for breaking into the Global Satellite alliance was death. Getting caught was not an option.

Ezekiel blasted virtual flak into the air around him. It should give him the few precious seconds necessary to back out of the system, sweeping his tracks as he did. He froze as the anti-bodies surrounded the black nodes of software flak, licked one or two, then moved away. They hadn't been fooled. "Damn, it's not working. Time for more drastic measures." Ezekiel cradled a small metallic sphere pulled from his jumpsuit. He gave it a quick twist, setting it for 400 milliseconds, then tossed it into the air. Simultaneously his other hand, the one in real space, yanked the cables from his prosthetic eyes. Ezekiel glimpsed an instant of the destructive flash of the system bomb before he jacked out of virtual reality.

"Damn, that was close, too close." He muttered in the twilight gloom of his apartment. He knew that damaging their system was not an elegant way to escape. They couldn't ignore sabotage, and they'd be looking for him. But not for a while, not before they got their satellite back online.

Ezekiel untangled himself from the jackchair, that all important piece of furniture that allowed him to lie comfortably prone for hours, even days if necessary, taking care of his bodily needs. He slapped a mobile VR set into his eyes so he could tap into the local VR. The filthy gloom of his apartment dissolved into an expansive south facing penthouse. The greasy jackchair became an elegant leather sofa, the rest of the furniture changed to match. It was the default setting that came with his apartment. Ezekiel groaned, he'd never gotten around to fixing it. Way too corporate wet-dream for his taste.

"Record location notes." Ezekiel monotoned into the air. "Lambda negative 107 point 598 by Phi 38 point 865." He knew his tired brain would lose the coordinates of the crazy farm houses if he didn't note them. He tossed his exhausted body onto the crumpled bed. Tossed for a while, but was far too keyed up to sleep. "Solve the mystery, then I can sleep. OK, locate note coordinates on standard map." Instantly his vision filled with a bird's eye view of Western Colorado. The brown spot was green on the old satellite photo, now marked with a red pin. "Zoom 25%." The field resolved into building roofs and wheat fields.

Ezekiel stared at this for a moment. "Location name?" A label appeared at the top of his virtual screen: Paonia, Colorado, population 0. "No, no, that's the abandoned city. What is the name of this group of small houses?" "No data found" popped onto the screen. Ezekiel scratched his beard. "Research land records, use note coordinates." "Match found" showed on his screen. He blink/clicked the hyperlink. The old county records filled the screen. Scanning through the legal mumbo-jumbo, Ezekiel finally came to the name of the land. "Gaialandra."

"What the..?" A quick search of Gaialandra came up with very little, but enough. Gaialandra was the name of this bit of land or enclave held by the cult group called The Anti-Techs. Apparently they'd been in this spot for more than 50 years. Only a few hundred miles from New Denver, and he'd never heard of them. He must have flown over the area a dozen times. They blended perfectly during the rest of the seasons, but Anti-Techs wouldn't use 'geneered crops. And nothing else would grow in the winter.

More research revealed what little was known about the Anti-Techs. It was a small private group who lived 19th century lives. Their fields were tilled by horse and ox and their homes were heated with wood or dried manure. "Lovely." Ezekiel mumbled. They only ate what they grew and made their own clothes. They didn't even have electricity, and definitely no VR. "Idiots." The mystery was solved, and not a very exciting one at that."

Ezekiel lay on the lumpy bed still fuming about his clumsy escape. It would be weeks before he could back into the global feed. Someone had to pay for this inconvenience. He glared at the shingled roof tops of the Anti-Techs filling his screen. "Who would give a shit about these culters and their mangy bit of land." The corners of his mouth broke through the tangle of beard into a cruel grin. "Maybe there is someone who would be interested. I think it's time UnitedFarms met its gentle neighbors. I'll bet they could coax a few more stalks of wheat from that sleeping soil."

3

FROM THE OUTSIDE, Stratumentis appeared completely uniform. But the bottom ten stories were unique, as separate as they were impenetrable. These were the private floors of Tatsuo Hamachi. The very bottom floor housed his luxurious office with its towering views of the Grand Canyon walls, and unobstructed views of the river below. Layered above this impressive room sprawled the expansive living quarters, meeting rooms, kitchens, exercise facilities, and guest apartments Hamachi seldom used.

Hamachi sat behind the rare mahogany desk meditating on the rising sun. The transparent floor and walls revealed it blazing its way down the canyon walls. In the center of this fiery brightness a perfectly round shadow blotted the sunshine, a man-made eclipse.

A glint of reflecting blue caught his eye, and Hamachi peered down into the canyon floor, more than 4,000 feet below. He felt a strange kind of satisfaction that the very river that had carved the canyon for millions of years - would never reach its destination - would be sucked dry by man long before that.

His mind was wandering today, one thought leading to another. Power made him think of his father, the great Akio Hamachi, founder of Mitasashi Corporation. He had never seen the great city of Stratumentis and its god-like views. Hamachi had accomplished so much, built Mitasashi into the world's largest corporation, far bigger than any government left standing. But he was most proud of his spherical city in the sky. Would his father have been impressed with even this great achievement, or would he have asked in his inimitable way, "What will you do now Tatsuo?"

Hamachi shook the thought away, there was much to do, and his visitors would be here momentarily. He stole a glance at the round shadow, then spoke into the air: "Floor full opacity, windows half, lights daytime normal." The floor became dark and solid, and the walls, ordinary windows with only a muted hint of their incredible views.

"Doctor Alexia Serguey, Doctor Lani Smith, and Doctor Horace Spartan have arrived sir." The virtual attendant monotoned into the air.

Hamachi rose and walked to the center of the room. "Send them in."

Doctor Alexia Serguey led the group into the room. Her sharp features and statuesque form belied her age; 56, Hamachi knew from his records. She could have used 'geneering, or even traditional surgery to tighten the fine lines around her eyes and mouth, but somehow, it seemed out of character. They were the hieroglyphics of her life, ones which a careful observer might learn to read. Hamachi smiled to himself, here she was at last, the great Doctor Serguey. Behind her, Doctor Lani Smith, the brilliant nanobot designer, her Nordic featured pinched into a permanent scowl, suspicious. Beside her, the soft form of Horace Spartan. The genius neurosurgeon and throwback who would rather waste his great talents teaching pimple-faced students at Oxford than use his great skills. Hamachi held his gaze on Dr. Serguey, "Welcome to Stratumentis."

Hamachi ushered them into a seating area facing the South Rim. The brilliant reds of the canyon reflected on their faces and hands giving them all a ruddy, healthy looking complexion. "I know that you are here because of my coaxing and financial rewards. Beyond that, you know little and have probably speculated much." Hamachi turned his gaze to Spartan. "Perhaps you have committed yourself to working here for a few years. Placate the mad caprice of an eccentric trillionaire and gather a neat pile of gold to spend in your waning years." His eyes shifted slightly, boring into Smith. "Or maybe you could use this as an opportunity to gain access to original research and apply it to future technologies; making yourself the most knowledgeable human asset in your field." His eyes returned to Alexia, "Or maybe you came here to feed a deep fantasy that you would be part of something important, unique, that would change humanity profoundly."

Hamachi looked away from the three. "Madman, eccentric, visionary. Perhaps I am all of these. You decide." He spoke into the air. "Windows full opaque. Lights, theater." The main interior lights went dark, leaving only small floor lamps under the chairs and tables for orientation. A holographic image of a man wearing a large clumsy looking VR set appeared in front of them.

"Virtual reality doctors, has changed everything. The antique looking device on this man's face was the first modern VR headset. It was designed by my father, Akio Hamachi. Before this, VR was an entertainment novelty, flat images were projected separately into each eye. The wearer experienced headaches, nausea, disorientation. It was a toy. My father discovered how to feed information directly through the eye onto the optic nerve itself and virtual reality became real enough to gain wide spread acceptance." The holographic image morphed into newer and sleeker VR sets, until it reached the ubiquitous modern version each in the room was wearing. The modern VR set was little more than a titanium bar emanating from the user's right ear and hovering an inch beyond the wearer's eyebrows. "Improved, perfected, unobtrusive, and most important, effective. A person using the latest version of our VR sets is fully immersed in virtual reality. Or partially immersed if so desired."

"And no one has been able to replicate it." A voice said in the still darkened room.

"That is correct Doctor Spartan. Mitasashi Corporation has held the design since my father created the company."

"And the all-important data links to *the I*." Spartan added.

"Yes doctor, without the connection to the vast network of interlinking computers of the Internet, or *the I* as it is colloquially known, virtual reality could not exist. It requires a tremendous amount of data, moved at great speeds to make all this work. Mitasashi provides this as well. And yes doctor, we charge for all of these things. It is why you are here today, working for me, and not feeding at Oxford's public trough. The same trough that is thoroughly and utterly dry. May we now continue Doctor Spartan?"

"Yes, of course Mr. Hamachi, my apologies for the interruption."

"As I was saying, VR works, and it works well, but it is communication that is filtered in too many ways. The computer link, avatars, synthetic voice, body language constructs, virtual settings. It is all in the way. When we speak, we communicate with much more than just words, there is tone, inflection, facial expression, eye movement, body language, and other subtle things we can't explain." The hologram of the man wearing a modern VR set was replaced by two figures reclining in chairs, a bundle of thin wires grew from the side of each man's head. The wires merged into a cable which plugged into a metal box between them. The two figures lay quietly, except for their eyes, which jumped rapidly as if in wild dreams. There were audible gasps from Spartan and Smith. Alexia remained still.

"Filters, doctors. That is what separates us. But what if we could communicate without them? Imagine speaking to a colleague across the world with a thought. No lies, no innuendo, no misunderstanding, only pure clear information. Thought.

"Ask yourselves, what is reality?" The hologram changed again. Now a disembodied brain appeared, incredibly detailed and several times larger than life. It rotated slowly in the dark room. "The human brain doesn't feel, see or hear anything. Without our external senses – the filters that connect us to the world – the brain would be alone, isolated like this projection. If we found a way to crosswire our sense of touch with our eye sight, we might see with our fingers, hear with our eyes. The brain doesn't know anything, unless we tell it what to know. Reality is mutable, because the sensors are mutable.

"In virtual reality we can fly, jump over buildings, do impossible things that break the laws of physics. What is physics anyway, imaginary laws and constructs created to match the limited experiences of our senses.

But our brains don't have these limits. What I propose doctors, is that we remove these limits, remove the filters standing in our way."

The hologram faded and the lights came on. Everyone sat quietly for a moment.

Spartan was the first to speak. "Have you done this? Successfully connected brains together?"

"No doctor, that is why you and many others like you are here."

"How close are you? What needs to be done?" Alexia spoke this time.

"We've connected to living brain cells, but we get too much interference for the data to be useful. We need to isolate a single neuron using Doctor Spartan's expertise, and keep it alive long enough to process the experiment."

"Yes of course, but micro-leads will need to be connected using hyper-photonic nanobots with..."

"...if we can separate the dendrites. Those were the hardest to disentangle during removal from the..."

"...the nanobot motility affect in glucose can be nullified using..." Doctor Smith and Spartan were talking over each other excitedly.

Alexia stood and moved over to where Hamachi was standing and smiling. "What do you think, doctor?"

"I think I know very little about your project. But I think with minds like these and others, if it is possible, they'll find a way." Alexia said.

"And what about you Dr. Serguey, do you think it is possible?" Hamachi's smile was gone now.

"Yes Mr. Hamachi, if you have enough money and patience, I think it is."

4

ALVAR TERRAHAUTE GAZED out over the acres of pristine snow, ashamed of the secret it hid. He used to love the winter, its pure quiet beauty, its message of rest and rejuvenation. That was before the stranger had come, before the terrible compromise. Now, he was just like the rest of world, a human shell without a soul.

For decades the Anti-Techs had been left alone, their rich little slice of earth overlooked, or more likely ignored. But they'd been found and their winter rest disturbed. UnitedFarms had thrust a stranger onto them. Was it only a month ago? He had come unannounced, because he had no way of communicating with the Anti-Techs, they had no computers, no VR sets, not even an ancient telephone or radio. If the situation weren't so serious, Alvar would have laughed at the memory of his clumsy arrival.

The tiny commuter vehicle had slipped its way up the snow covered farm road, finally smashing into a pile of snow that had slid off one of the high roofs. An ordinary-looking man pried himself out of the car wearing just a thin, shiny business suit and no hat. He trudged to the nearest door and pounded on it, then waited. Rubbing his arms and hands together, he soon began to shiver. He did this several times before two men heard his pounding from a nearby house. The man had been knocking on a storage shed.

He was led to the central hall, the large building where the Anti-Techs held their group meetings, dances or entertainment. They revived him with hot tea and a blanket. The big fire was lit, and a call sent out to all the families of Gaialandra for a special emergency meeting. It took two hours for all the families to get settled in. The teenagers watched the young children, the grandmothers made food and hot cider, the grandfathers sat in the large hall speculating and arguing over what the stranger had come to say. Everyone else brought chairs, candles, blankets for the cold ones, plates and utensils for the food. It was the most exciting thing they'd seen in years, and everyone was in a festive mood anxious to hear the stranger's words. Only Alvar was quiet. He had seen the "UF" logo on the frozen car.

The Anti-Techs led themselves by a loosely knit council of leaders. "The Committee" it was called. Each year two representatives were replaced by random draw from able adults in the community. They made all the major decisions about planting, seed storage, and settled any disputes. Anyone could challenge their decisions by calling for a vote from the entire Anti-Tech community at their biannual meetings. The leader of "The Committee" was chosen by a simple vote from its members. This year it was Alvar.

"OK, everyone, settle down, settle down." Alvar called into the noisy crowd. Eventually the talking quieted to a murmur, then to silence as curiosity took hold. Alvar and the visitor exchanged a few whispered words, then Alvar led him to the makeshift stage in front of the crowd.

"This person," Alvar gestured to the stranger, "has come to us as a representative of UnitedFarms."

The room erupted in exclamations and shouts of: "Throw him in the snow." And "Smash his car." And "No engineered crops on our land."

"Quiet!" Alvar shouted over the crowd. "Quiet. We are men and women, not jackals. This man has come to us to speak. We'll listen to him as we would to any of you. The next person who speaks out of turn will be escorted back to his home. If you want to stay, you will sit politely while this man speaks. There will plenty of time for questions." The room settled into whispered grumbles. "Thank you." He turned to the stranger who had continued to smile blandly through all the shouts. "Friends of Gaialandra, please hear the words of Mr. Bennett Bannock of UnitedFarms."

Alvar recalled the moment with a clenched gut. Perhaps it had been a mistake to listen to Bannock, maybe they should have let him freeze to death pounding on the storage barn. But he knew UnitedFarms would have sent another, or several next time. At the time, Alvar had been just as curious as the others to hear what Bannock had to say. The winter was long, it was an exciting break from the routine. Their mistake had been their arrogance he realized now. They had felt immune from the outside, from the techies. But they'd simply been lucky. His mind went back to that moment when Bannock stepped to the center of the makeshift stage. Alvar remembered the suit, so unnaturally smooth and elegant, so sharply contrasting the rough thick wool of those in the crowd.

Bannock began, his voice a beautiful opera tenor, sensuous and captivating. "Ladies and gentlemen, people of Gaialandra, thank you for listening to me this day. And thank you for your hospitality, your warmth and kindness to a stranger." He gestured to the small table with hot tea, jam and a misshapen loaf of bread. "I came here alone, unprepared, not knowing what to expect. Like you, I question and suspect the unknown. Look at my clothes. I am naïve, unprepared for winter. Yet you did not leave me in the cold. Your natural inclination is to help a stranger. Thank you." And he bowed his head in gratitude.

Alvar narrowed his eyes suspiciously, then scanned the crowd of Gaialandrans. They were suspicious but warming to his charms.

Bannock continued. "And thank you for taking the time from your busy lives to listen to me. I'm sure in your world as in mine, it is impolite to ask a group to gather and listen without an appointment or schedule. But I was unable to reach you by ..."

The crowd shifted uncomfortably at the high-tech reference.

"But never mind that. We are here now together, and you are curious to know what I have to say. Let me begin with the basics. As Alvar so graciously introduced me, my name is Bennett Bannock, and I represent UnitedFarms." He waited patiently, never losing his smile as the crown grumbled and muttered. Bannock waved Alvar aside. "I understand your discomfort at the name. UnitedFarms is gigantic, one of the largest and most powerful companies in the world. It sounds frightening, overwhelming, crushing. It is none of those things. But before we discuss my employer, let me share a little about the world of 2080."

Bannock, his smile now gone, scanned the crowd, seeming to look at each and every man and woman directly in the eye. "The world is crowded my friends, very crowded. There are now seventeen billion of us. Children, mothers, fathers, grandparents, brothers and sisters, friends, and neighbors – just like you. They want the same things as you, a warm place to live, education for their children, lights to see by, clean water, and food, safe nutritious food.

"Which brings us back to UnitedFarms. We manage billions of acres of farms on every continent. Even on Antarctica! Though I admit that kind of farming is more than a little challenging. It is our job, no, our duty to bring food and energy to those who need it. And because of what we do, everyone gets enough to eat, all seventeen billion of us. Don't take that lightly, because we don't. Did you know at the beginning of this century, millions died each year from starvation. Ask your grandparents, they'll remember. And what a cruel waste that was."

Alvar pulled his eyes away from the crooning Bannock and to the men and women in the large room. He knew everyone in here by name. He grew up with most of them. Others had joined them more recently, but he knew them too. Men and women trickled in to their enclave hoping for a way out of their struggles. Gaialandra had become a kind of living myth attracting the disaffected. Some stayed on, but most left after a year or two. The work was too hard, the entertainment too bland. The Anti-Techs were an anachronism in this world, only existing by going unnoticed, but apparently no longer.

Alvar's attention returned to the man on stage and Bannock continued. "Please don't misjudge me by my clothes, by the way I speak. I am just as human as you. And I do understand what you are creating here, separated from the teaming millions. I understand why your parents and grandparents came to this slice of remote land to settle it, to work it with their hands. I understand why you stay. We all do, all seventeen billion of us. But the world is full, and it is hungry. We make incremental improvements in productivity, plant yields, but there is little or no room for error. If we waited for the caprice of rain or sun to coax the fragile plants to grow, if we ignored the scourge of insects and plant disease, if we relied on the inconvenience of changing seasons – billions will starve, billions.

"You are probably asking yourselves, why should our few acres of arable land matter in this giant world. There are hundreds of billions of acres on the earth, much of it better than this, more accessible, with longer growing seasons. But it does matter. No one lives in a vacuum, we are all intertwined, depending on one another. So, while you quietly work this land, producing just enough food to feed the 300 or so living here, your neighboring farms produce enough food to feed thousands. Where you coax one, sometimes two crops from your fields each year, they produce 8 or 10. While you allow your fields to lie fallow all winter, they continue to produce. When your ancestors settled this land, it was a different world, and the idea was a good one, perhaps even noble – now it is a danger, a risk to the lives of thousands."

Bannock paused, looking around at his audience. Alvar could see this man had done this before, perhaps to small farms just like his own. He wondered how many were still out there, or were they the last? He knew what was coming, the others had probably figured it out too. The serious faces confirmed it. But they let Bannock go on, they were all too stunned to stop him.

Bannock smiled again. "Let us not dwell on the negative. Let's discuss the future. Work with us, share your land with us, so we can bring about its true potential. We're not your enemies, not even your competitors.

We're farmers, just like you. UnitedFarms is a reasonable company to work with. The little you need will be yours. We're not even suggesting you change your lifestyle. Remain isolated as you wish, away from the corruption of technology, communication, outsiders. All this is possible, just let us help you do it - only better."

The room started murmuring and Alvar knew he had to speak, that they were waiting for their voices to be heard. His voice for theirs. Alvar stood up next to Bannock. His voice rough from years of calling in the cold mountain air, but it was strong in a way Bannock's never could be. "Mr. Bannock has reminded us of the outside world, the world we've chosen to be separate from. We didn't ask him to come here, to tell us of farming at the South Pole. We ask only to be left in peace. Fifty years ago when we came here, when our parents and grandparents bought this land, they were able to do so, because no one wanted it. It wasn't good land, the soil had been depleted from years of over farming and too many fertilizers and too many pesticides. The nearby streams were polluted, undrinkable. They worked the land, cleaned the streams, helped nature rebuild the damaged soil." Alvar turned to the still smiling Bannock. "And now it seems, this land we've worked so hard to make fertile again is suddenly too valuable to ignore. I doubt these few acres are going to make a difference to the hungry billions you talk about. And what, Mr. Bannock, are you going to do if we simply stuff you and your shinny suit back into your little car and send you back to your hungry world?"

The room erupted in voices and the scratching of moving chairs. Most had risen to their feet. The room was energized with Alvar's plain speech. He had given voice to their feelings. Yes they were simple and peaceful, but strong from years of physical toil. One didn't just walk away from one's birthright.

Bannock stood there unperturbed. He glanced at some electronic device in the palm of his hand, then covered his right ear, carefully listening to something over the roar of the large hall. Bannock leaned over to Alvar and said several words that wiped the smile from Alvar's face. A moment later, he nodded to Bannock.

Alvar waved his arms for attention. "Quiet. Quiet everyone. Mr.

Bannock has something else to tell us. I think it is important." Alvar stepped away from the stranger when it was quiet enough for him to begin.

Bannock's face had gone serious. "Thank you for allowing me to continue Alvar. As you've said, there's always a choice, sometimes many. But I haven't come here as your first, or even your best choice, I've come here as your last choice. What you say is correct. Your ancestors bought this land legally. You've worked it and paid your taxes on time, done everything right. So ask yourselves, why am I here if you don't need to cooperate with me?"

The men and women in the room murmured a bit, but the simple logic gripped them. This man spoke from the great unknown that surrounded them. They joked about it, derided the technological world outside their fields. But they also cowered in the shadow of its intimidating power. For those who joined the Anti-Techs, this subtle threat was a stark reminder of why they had left. For those who had never lived that life, it rang of a strength far greater than their own. They were both drawn and repulsed by this power, and definitely afraid of it.

Bannock continued, "UnitedFarms is not the only one who has become aware of your little farm." He glanced at Alvar. "Your government, the one you've paid – no let me be blunt here - bribed to leave you alone for so long, has also noticed you. Oh, this lumbering bureaucracy is clearly inefficient and annoying. And if that's all they were, yes you could pay them off, and yes you could stuff me and my shiny suit into my transport, and we'd be done here. But we all know that's not all they are." He paused for effect as he looked calmly around the room, clearly holding their attention. "They are also corrupt."

Bannock unrolled a panel that quickly stiffening into a computer screen. It filled with lists of number. "It is always important to be prepared. I see that you've paid your ever increasing taxes on time, and more interesting, at arm's length. Which means to me, you may not realize what your government has become. Huge companies, such as UnitedFarms have the resources to outmaneuver the government, to literally move out of their sight. One day we're a Dutch corporation, and the next Japanese. We can move daily, hourly if necessary. And why? To avoid the taxes and capricious restrictions of these meddling entities. But you, ladies and gentlemen do not have that choice, nor those resources. So they'll come right in here and confiscate your property under some newly written law, ordinance or rule that gives them the right. You'll end up walking away with just the handmade clothes on your backs. And we'll end up farming your land as if you were never here."

Bannock spread his arms wide. "But why should it be that way? UnitedFarms can be your ally, no, your protector. If the government has already decided to confiscate your land, let us deal with them. We'll tie them up so tight, they'll forget which continent they govern."

The room was numbed into silence. Alvar turned from this outsider to his cowed neighbors. He was witnessing three generations of effort slipping away in front of him.

"OK Mr. Bannock. You say you'll be our ally. How does this work? Tell us what you plan to do with our land?" Alvar asked.

"Good man, let's talk specifics. It looks like a lifeless snowfield out there, doesn't it. But your region offers something very special, even in the winter – lots of sunshine. We have machines that can work the frozen soil, and plant soy beans, corn, wheat, the same plants you are familiar with..."

An old woman in front interrupted him, her voice cracking with anger. "You mean 'geneered plants, hybrid freaks of nature." The crowd mumbled agreement.

Again Bannock stood calmly waiting them out. And when there was a drop in sound, he spoke again. "Please, please, there is a lot to discuss and I'll explain it all. But shouting over each other won't get anything accomplished." He moved closer to the old woman, lowering his voice so everyone craned their ears to hear. "I'm not here to lie or fool you. I'm here to work with you. So, yes, that's right, we will plant genetically modified strains. Plants that can grow in the winter, in the frozen earth, turning ice into water and using it. They're stronger, grow faster, are more nutritious than the plants you use now. They're more disease and insect resistant too. They even produce their own fertilizer. Why does that sound bad to you? Look around yourselves, aren't you the product of genetic modification? Haven't years of evolution turned you into a more efficient version of your ancestors? We've simply sped up the process."

The old woman stood now, her face red and her lips so tight that she could barely speak. "You said you wouldn't lie, but you just did. What you do is not a quickened version of nature. Nature doesn't combine species the way you do – putting animal DNA into plants. What you do is an abomination. It is against everything we stand for, against life." The veins on her neck stood out and her face was beet red. She sat down, unable to continue.

Bannock spoke up quickly before the room could erupt again. "She's right, we do those things. And what of it." The room, ready to burst again was suddenly quiet with his admission. "And what of you?" Bannock waved his arm derisively across the crowd. "You preach your anti-technology rhetoric, but is it? You are not against technology, just against some of it. You are capricious and random about your choices. Look at this room. Did you forge the nails that hold the wood together. And what about your clothes, how did you weave the cloth? You had to use a loom. Technology. And your food is cooked, preserved and stored – all technology. And when your children get a serious infection you use antibiotics rather than watch them die." He lifted the thin computer tablet above his head, tapping roughly on the screen. "I have a record of it right here. A record of all the things you buy, all the technology you buy from my world – that you shun, but use. You've chosen to draw an imaginary line: this technology is OK and this is going too far. We at least are not hypocrites."

And then the room burst into a chaos of voices too loud for anyone to get control of. Alvar pulled Bannock aside and shouted into his ear, "I think you've said enough for now, don't you?"

Bannock shouted into Alvar's ear. "I'll write up the terms so you can present it to your people when they're ready to listen again."

Alvar looked from the angry group, to this man he despised. He closed his eyes and slowly nodded his head. "We'll cooperate."

5

EZEKIEL SCRATCHED HIS prosthetic eye in frustration. He'd been off *the I* for two weeks, an eternity. He jacked in cautiously, staying as low and quiet as possible. The system bomb he'd released into the Global Satellite Feed had caused a lot more damage than he intended. The connection sputtered when he touched it, they were clearly looking for him. Damn, that meant wannabes sniffing around for a reward. And sometimes, one of the bumblers gets lucky.

Ezekiel burned the next two days wiping the tracks and trails he found. He cringed at his sloppy exit every time he found a telltale he'd left behind. If it was a financial or data system instead of the global feed, he'd have been melted by now. Lucky, he whistled.

Finally it was done. Ezekiel slept fitfully that evening, tossing and dreaming of thousands of little men dressed like Sherlock Holmes. Each with a magnifying glass looking at the ground for clues. "I see him!" One shouted. Ezekiel woke, drenched in sweat.

He gazed around the gloomy apartment too nervous to sleep, too exhausted to work. "What a mess. I've got to get a hold of myself." Ezekiel played a game to calm the paranoia, a fantasy of what chaos he might have created for others. He replayed his discovery of Gaialandra and the Anti-Techs. After a few minutes of visualizing the scurrying farmers, curiosity took over. "I wonder what really happened to them?"

Ezekiel plugged the cables into his eye sockets, then broke into the main computer systems at UnitedFarms. The system was huge. He floated down canyons of data, the synthetic sky blotted by skyscraper-high file cabinets. Ezekiel yanked one open at random. Yawn. Soybean production in Mozambique. "Search assistant." Ezekiel called into the imaginary canyon.

A man appeared in front of him smiling. His suit was perfectly tailored and his jet-black hair combed with a neat part on one side. "Oh brother." Ezekiel breathed. "Find reference to Paonia, Colorado" The canyon walls shifted and several drawers glowed red. Still too much data. "Refine. Gaialandra." The canyon disappeared altogether, leaving just a small box in the middle of an empty street. "Search complete." The search assistant evaporated.

Ezekiel pulled up his virtual sleeve to reveal a series of wristwatch-like devices. He checked the first one, the proximity detector. Pale green, still OK. Paranoia was his friend when he was hacking. Ezekiel lifted the lid gently off the data file. "Altitude, climate, contracts," there - "employee notes." And inside that, VR recordings of Bannock's presentation. Damn, too long to watch in here. "Copy." Ezekiel whispered then looked around uncomfortably. His proximity watch had turned yellow. "OK, time to go." He checked the copy, slid the cover back on the file quietly and slipped out of UnitedFarms.

Adrenaline cranked his nerves. Now he was definitely too agitated to sleep. "What the hell. Bannock's presentation to the Anti-Tech should bore me right to sleep." Ezekiel made some popcorn and blinked the play button on his VR set.

Ezekiel was transported to a stomach churning ride on a snowy road. He fast forwarded through that and some other garbage with old ladies poring tea and a lot of people moving chairs. "Did I get the wrong recording?" Ezekiel muttered. Finally, Bannock began his presentation. "Jesus." Ezekiel groaned. The Anti-Techs were amazing. This gaggle of bumpkins had somehow managed to stay unnoticed all these decades by sheer luck. He listened to a bit, then sped through the recording, bored by Bannock and his 'geneered voice. How could anyone have the patience to talk to these idiots? It was like watching a kindergarten class.

"Wait, what's that?" Ezekiel froze the screen and worked his way back frame by frame. There, two rows into the crowd was a woman that caught his eye. Not just a woman, a goddess. Ezekiel zoomed in as best he could, but the damn recording had been compressed for their archives. Corporate idiots. He ran through the rest of the recording slowly several times, trying to catch her again. But she was only in that one passing shot. The recording was what Bannock saw from his VR set mounted just over his eyes. This Bannock must be a homosexual to miss this beauty. Ezekiel enlarged and stared at the few frames of this dark haired woman for a long time. He clearly saw she was angry, but that only made her green eyes flash. Ezekiel thrilled to think how different she was from anyone he'd ever seen before, well at least on *the I*. She was solid, real. Ezekiel pondered this, she wasn't 'geneered, probably had never heard of it. "Nice, a truly natural woman. I've got to have more of this."

Ezekiel ran several face recognition programs. Useless. He twanged the cable coming from his eye in annoyance. This was a unique kind of problem. These morons were Anti-Techs, off the grid. Was it possible this was the only recording ever made of this woman? The concept itself was hard to hold onto. Everyone, everywhere left traces of themselves, no matter how careful they were. When they went outside, they were picked up by security cameras. Any financial transaction left identity logs, whether virtual or not. V-mail, virtual reality conferencing, security cameras on every form of transportation, every store, every restaurant. It was impossible to be unrecorded. But here in front of his eyes was a completely unknown woman. Ezekiel felt his crotch warm with the challenge.

But how? Ezekiel flicked the cable from eyes. Then, he did what always worked when he faced an impossible challenge, he closed his eyes and fantasized. It was easy with the fresh memory of this mysterious beauty. The answer danced around the dream, so obvious, so frightening, yet just out of reach. With every thought, she became more alluring, more beautiful.

He embraced, then ravished the green-eyed seductress. He ached for her.

Wet release in his crotch snapped him from his fantasy. With the tension gone, the answer revealed itself. So obvious, so frightening – he'd have to go there in person. It was easy, right? He'd just get up and go, leave the apartment he hadn't stepped foot out of in years, hire a driver to take him to the Anti-Tech farm. Then he'd just walk up to her and say, "Hi, my name is Ezekiel, what's yours?" His skin went cold with the idea, every aspect of the journey was terrifying.

Ezekiel lay like this for hours, vacillating between lust and fear. An interesting idea finally came. Didn't the Anti-Techs take in outsiders. He recognized them in the VR recording. They were different from the others. First, he could easily look them up on *the I* using face recognition software. And second, they had a different look in their eyes. Hard to describe, he just recognized his own. He'd convince the group he wanted to join them and then he could talk to her, record her, maybe more.

Emboldened by his plan, Ezekiel dove back into *the I* and into United-Farms. He quickly discovered the deal the Anti-Techs had made with the giant farm company. The corporation would farm 50% of their land using 'geneered seeds and modern techniques. In exchange, they would leave the Anti-Techs alone, along with a few e-dollars for their trouble. Ezekiel could see this one playing forward. Fifty percent would become seventy-five percent, then one hundred percent. It just worked that way. They'd already made this naïve group compromise, the rest was detail.

The long drive from New Denver gave Ezekiel far too much time to think. *The I* connection sputtered between good and bad, too insecure to do any serious hacking and too annoying to get lost in sex rooms. He finally dropped it all together and stared out of the window of the speeding vehicle. Ezekiel had never been out here, never this far from the city. He'd only ever seen it from the safe height of a satellite camera. It was too big, too real. The green fields spread endlessly in every direction, stopping only when they reached the white capped Rocky Mountains in the distance.

With clock-like regularity an enormous truck would rumble by nearly shaking the tiny passenger vehicle off the road. Ezekiel gripped the torn seat beneath him as the UnitedFarms logo filled his view for a terrifying instant. Other times the view would turn suddenly claustrophobic as enormous plants blotted their view completely. Strange woody things with trunks the size of trees and thin spiky leaves as long as a man's body towered 40, 50 feet above the road. Ezekiel stretched his prosthetic eyes to see the bulbous fruit swelling sexually at the very tops of the plants. And then just as abruptly, the field would be open, flat, tiny shoots poking through the dirty snow.

Ezekiel's curiosity quickly dried. He turned his attention to the reflection of the driver in the rear view mirror. His eyes were unnaturally round and the conjunctiva flamed red around the cloudy pupils. Ezekiel recognized the signs of long term synthadrene addiction. A man who never slept made for poor conversation. So as long as he stayed between the white lines of the highway, Ezekiel wasn't going to interrupt his waking dream, not at 80 miles per hour. So he opaqued the windows and drifted off to sleep.

A leathery hand shook Ezekiel awake. "Destination. Destination." The queer voice kept repeating.

"Yeah, yeah. Give me a second." Ezekiel pulled himself back to full consciousness. The open door framed the driver in bright daylight and cool air. Ezekiel dragged himself out of the car and stood looking around. A handful of wooden buildings dotted the area. The ground was hard, frozen, with traces of snow in the cracks. "I'm not sure how long I'll be here. Can you hold the vehicle for a while, maybe a few hours?"

The driver shifted his eyes nervously, focusing, trying hard to understand the question. "Possible, yes that is possible. Set the alarm, you must set the alarm." His voice rose unnaturally on the last word. "You must pay. You must pay the amount shown."

Ezekiel didn't argue. He punched in four hours, scanned his thumb for payment. He backed away from the vehicle. The driver stood by the front door staring straight ahead his wide eyes darting nervously, but unblinking.

The sun was high and it wasn't really that cold despite the frozen ground. Ezekiel heard the sound of children talking and playing not far off. Let's start there. They'd be easier to talk to and maybe they would know the green eyed goddess.

The children stopped their play when they saw Ezekiel approach. They were clearly curious, whispering and laughing as he neared. "Snot-nosed brats, what are they laughing at?"

But their laughter froze when Ezekiel was close, only their curiosity keeping them from scattering. Six boys, none of them older than 10, had divided themselves into two groups. Each had piled a rude shelter of snow and were forming and stockpiling snowballs for the upcoming battle. Ezekiel looked at these elements without comprehension.

He spoke to the tallest boy, "You recognize this woman?" He held out the glossy holo-print of the green-eyed woman.

The boy held his ground, trying to impress the other boys who cowered behind their snow forts. His face glowed pink under cropped blond hair. The torn hand-knit sweater, two sizes too large hung heavily to one side. He radiated health and energy, which annoyed Ezekiel greatly. He glanced quickly at the picture, then said, "Yeah, I know her. That's Alvar's friend, Chloe. They're always holding hands and stuff."

"You know her last name?" Ezekiel asked, with growing excitement.

The boy cocked his head. "Hey mister what's wrong with your eyes?"

Ezekiel blushed deeply. "My eyes? Nothing's wrong with my eyes. I can see your ugly face well enough. Little bastard."

One of the boys shouted. "Jack, run! He's a cyborg. He's gonna' put a computer in your head!" And in a second, faster than Ezekiel realized boys could move, they scattered into the buildings beyond.

Ezekiel looked around dazed. Well, he'd at least gotten her name. And wasn't Alvar the one he saw in the recorded holo-vid, the leader Bannock was talking to? Good, he was on the trail now. Just like searching *the I.* Ezekiel smiled as he contemplated his next move.

"Did you just call my son a bastard?" A gruff voice called from directly behind him.

Ezekiel turned around to face a large clean-shaven man about his own age. But age was the only thing they shared. The other man was thickly muscled from a life of physical activity. His closely cut hair was neat showing a deep tan beneath. His clothes were coarse and simple, but immaculately clean and carefully fit. Ezekiel looked at the man's arms bulging beyond the rolled up sleeves of his plaid shirt. They were as thick as his own legs and capable of great harm. Maybe this wasn't as easy as searching *the I.*

"I, uh. I'm new here." Ezekiel choked out. "I don't know your jargon, maybe the boy misunderstood my way of speaking. I was just asking him if he knew a certain person I'm looking for."

The boy's father clenched and unclenched his fists. "Yeah he said that too. Must be a misunderstanding. I know we take in freshies. But that don't mean I have to like it. Now listen carefully," The man's voice dropped to a whisper, "Stay away from the kids. You got a question, you ask an adult. There's a lot going on right now and the kids don't need any more surprises." The man squinted at Ezekiel's eyes. "Let's get this over with."

"Uh, get what over with?" Ezekiel stuttered.

"Just follow me."

Ezekiel stared at the man's broad back as they wound through a clump of buildings that must be the central part of the community. The buildings were made of wood in varying states of repair. The paint was bright and fresh on this one, then peeling or missing on the next. Their steps crunched on the packed gravel walkways. Ezekiel kept silent.

They stopped at a small white building, perhaps a house. "Come on. This is the place, let's see if they have time for you." Ezekiel hesitated at the entrance. "I thought you were here to join us?" Ezekiel could only nod his head. "OK then." The man grabbed Ezekiel's arm nearly lifting him into the foyer.

Ezekiel's mind was racing. "Oh no, am I going to have to join these fools just too meet Chloe?"

An inner door opened and a tall woman entered. It was Chloe. Ezekiel could barely breathe. But he managed to blink the record button on his VR set. Then he just stared, she was far lovelier in reality.

"Good day miss Chloe. I found this man wandering around the residences looking for you, talking to the kids." The large man paused. "But if you don't have time for him," he turned and gave Ezekiel a cold smile, "I'll be glad to show him back to his vehicle."

Chloe considered Ezekiel carefully, then sighed. "I can spare a few minutes."

"Then I'll stay right here while you do."

She gave the man a warm smile. "That won't be necessary Robert. I know you have a lot of work to do and I'll be fine."

Robert nodded, then turned to Ezekiel. "Mind your manners when you speak with Miss Chloe. Understand?"

Ezekiel nodded vigorously.

"Good." Robert gave Ezekiel a hateful glance then left.

"Don't mind him. He's a big bear, very protective, but wouldn't hurt a fly." She gave Ezekiel a warm smile. "Please sit down. Robert said you just arrived, let me get you something to drink."

"I'd like that." Ezekiel squeaked.

He watched her leave. Her lithe form was clearly outlined in the thin wool dress and her tan legs tapered sensuously to bare brown feet. Ezekiel scanned the brightly lit room. Flowered curtains framed the windows and crude drawings and paintings covered the wooden walls.

"The children give me these. I can't take them down. Sweet, aren't they." She handed Ezekiel a glass of water.

Ezekiel concentrated on her hand. She had the long delicate fingers of a musician, but deeply tanned and calloused from outdoor work. The contrast thrilled him.

"My name is Chloe." She offered her hand.

He took it shyly, then squeezed it quickly, memorizing its roughness against his own soft hands. "Ezekiel Malaffaires."

She smiled. "Tell me about yourself."

"I came from New Denver this morning to join your group." He sputtered.

"That's a long drive. I mean tell me about yourself. Your life, why you're here. How you discovered us. I'm always curious about that."

"I live and work in New Denver, and I heard of you, your group through *the I*, uh, the computer network we all work under, the Internet. We call it *the I*."

"Go on." She urged.

"Well I discovered your place while doing some work with United-Farms." Ezekiel hesitated when she frowned.

"They promised not to speak of us. That was our agreement."

"No. No one told me. I sort of stole it from them. It's definitely a secret. That's what I do. That's my job. I break into networks, so I can test their security. That's how I found out about you, about the Anti-Techs, I mean."

"Hmm. Doesn't sound great, but it serves them right." She snickered. "But that doesn't explain why you came all the way out here."

"Well, I'm kind of burned out on life. I'm looking for something more..." Ezekiel let the words hang, hoping she'd fill it in for herself.

But Chloe didn't, instead waiting patiently for him to find the words.

"Real?" Ezekiel looked away with his eyes, careful to keep the VR set pointing at her, still recording. "You see, I'm a little lost. Have you seen my eyes?" He looked back at her.

"Yes, they are a little different. What did you do to them?"

"I had them replaced with these, so I can plug directly onto *the I*. I still can see through them right now, more or less the way I used to. But when I'm connected to *the I*, it's amazing, fast, real, brilliant. It is magnificent, more real than..." Ezekiel stopped.

Chloe stood up and walked to the window. "Do you know what we do here Ezekiel?"

"Grow food, I guess."

She turned, her face serious. "Yes that's right. But it is much more than that. We take time to live. Our parents and grandparents decided the world was trading efficiency, convenience for the important parts of life. Those things that can't be experienced electronically or anyway but in person. They settled here in this valley and called it Gaialandra – land of Gaia. They wanted to create a place that was closer to the earth.

"A hundred years ago, this area was a thriving farming community with rich soil and close knit neighbors. But large corporate farms took over the land, demolished the little houses. In a few short years they overworked the soil, squeezed out what they could, then left it for dead. Our ancestors acquired the worthless dirt and brought it back to life, brought themselves back to life. We don't shun high-technology just to be different, we shun it to live."

Ezekiel watched the passion move across her face, forcing his own to remain impassive. "Thank god I'm recording this, she looks so good right now." He thought.

Chloe continued. "You came here because you felt something is wrong, maybe missing in your life. But you can't know what's missing if you've never had it. So you ran to the first thing that seemed to fill that void. I have to be honest with you Ezekiel, it's not right for most people, maybe not right for you. You have to think about it harder than anything you've ever thought about. You'd be giving up everything you know, not just the bad stuff, all of it. This precious I that you connect with, the conveniences, the millions of things that you take for granted would suddenly become real effort. The clothes on your back, the food you eat, the bed you sleep in, everything has to be created from your effort, with your own hands. Sometimes it's cold outside, raining or snowing, but animals have to be fed, land has to be tilled, fruit canned. A million little things that you push a button for now. And it isn't just your own life that depends on it. Each of us depends on the other. Do you understand?"

Ezekiel nodded. This was great stuff and he wasn't going to interrupt for anything. "Go on," he said weakly, his mouth dry with lust.

She walked over to him, leaned over and took his hands. "I understand you left a car here waiting for you. Does that sound like a commitment to a group of people you don't know?"

Chloe was so close he could smell her clean earthiness, see the swell of her breasts beneath the rough wool as she leaned forward. A few strands of her thick brown hair fell across her cheeks framing her smooth tanned face. And her eyes, the green eyes he'd barely captured on the holo-vid, here they were, just a foot from his own, beautiful, clear. And her full young lips were moving, speaking to him, but he couldn't hear over the rush of blood to his ears. Ezekiel sat frozen in his chair, his eyes wide, not willing to move lest he scare her away.

Chloe released her touch, then moved away. "Look around, meet our people, see how we do things. Then go home. Think about what you've learned here. Maybe take a little of our family back with you. See if you can bring it to your own world. But if you decide one day to give it all up, let me warn you, we don't just accept strangers on faith. You can try to join us, but only if we accept you. And we might not. Do you understand?"

Ezekiel just nodded, not trusting himself to speak.

"Good." She smiled, taking his hand again and leading him to the door. "Now take a look around and remember what I said, take a little of us back with you."

Ezekiel had been in the hired car on the way back to New Denver for 30 minutes before he realized where he was. He stared absently at the towering stalks of wheat ripping by the window. "Good God, she's lovely." He felt the wet release fill his crotch and orgasmic warmth radiate out to his legs and up his chest. Ezekiel sighed. He still had the long ride ahead to watch the recordings of Chloe on his VR set. Again and again.

6

THE MONTHS OF work had taken their toll on Alexia. Irritation and failure seemed to be her standard mood these days. Hamachi had made her the head of his secret project without giving her a full understanding of was expected. He had warned her that they were doing primary research, that some of it would surely fail, but that all of it was necessary. She had hoped to have something to show for it by now, but so far little or no progress had been made. She was expected to solve an enormous puzzle with her eyes closed.

Ong, Alexia's assistant, materialized beside her. The woman had the annoying ability to move around silently, then simply appear when least expected. Alexia called her "Ong" not knowing if that was her first or second name, nor caring for that matter.

"Ong what is my schedule for today?" Alexia asked the air.

"You have a progress meeting with Mr. Hamachi with the executive board at 10:00. At 11:15, you have…"

"Oh damn, I completely forgot about that." Alexia looked at the time readout at the lower right corner of her VR screen. It was only 7:00. But that also meant spending time preparing a presentation, ignoring other experiments.

"Ong, what is the status of the manual neural output reader experiment?"

There was a slight pause as Ong looked up something on her VR set, "No additional progress, Dr. Serguey."

"Oh, damn their incompetence." Alexia grumbled. "Are they working on it?"

"Yes doctor. They're just making the final connections now." Ong replied in her characteristic monotone.

"Tell them not to proceed beyond the connections until I arrive." Alexia barked.

On the way to the special lab, Alexia thought of the problem. It was monumental in so many ways. They were trying to feed and receive information to and from a single living human brain cell, a neuron, but in vitro, outside of the brain. This meant removing the still living cell intact from its living host brain. The dissection itself was a herculean task. A neuron was not like other cells in the body, discrete, compact. A typical neuron has thousands of dendrites, tiny fibers emanating from the cell to receive signals from other brain cells. From its main body it sprouts a single axon, a long fiber that branches over and over producing thousands of endings or synaptic buttons, each connected to other cell dendrites. A single axon might be several feet long, winding and threading itself around and through the billions of other axons and neurons in the brain. To remove a single cell with all these thousands of microscopic fibers intact was a daunting task indeed. But thanks to the extraordinary skill of Dr. Spartan, they had done it several times now. "Well," Alexia thought, "at least that is a great accomplishment."

But to keep it alive, the cell had to be fooled into thinking it was still communicating with its companion cells. That meant attaching microscopic leads to each receptor and transmitter site. Thousands of them. And all of this accomplished before the cell died. Most cells could easily be kept alive in a nutrient solution for an extended time. But neurons were different, without the steady input of connecting brain cells, something triggered their death after only a few hours. Hundreds of hours of microsurgery were lost with each failure.

And all this effort was only the beginning of the experiment. The goal was to send a simple bit of information to the neuron's receptor sites, then read what came out from the transmitter sight. It was all designed to discover the actual mechanics of how a brain cell worked with data, how it stored it, manipulated it. To keep the data at its simplest, they'd used the number "2," a commonly reoccurring number in all of nature. But each time they sent the single number, the cell returned volumes of garbage data, yottabytes, numbers too high for normal computers to work with.

All this data from a single cell didn't make sense. It was obviously an error in the experiment or the process. But as yet, they hadn't found any source of contamination or interference. The lab and equipment had been shielded for electromagnetic frequencies. The technicians were screened for implants. Maximum clean room protocols followed. But all with the same results: the number two went in, a trillion trillions came out.

Ong and Alexia arrived at the lab a few minutes later. Both were rushed through the decontamination chambers. The lab itself was not that impressive. It was a dimly lit windowless room about 30 feet on each side and 10 feet high. Machines lined every wall, covered in translucent red sterile plastic. In the exact center of the room sat the cellular nutrient metabolizing chamber, the device that kept the cell alive. It looked like an ancient washing machine with too many water lines coming into it. The top of the device formed a flat working surface, except for a four inch indentation in the center. There lay the curved glass dish that held the nutrient solution and the still living brain cell. From this dish emanated the thousands of gold threads of the receptor leads. These microscopic wires were so fine, that all of them combined would still be thinner than a single strand of silk. All of this was covered with a glass dome to protect cell and leads from contamination and air movement.

Dr. Spartan stood between Alexia and the neuron protectively. "Dr. Serguey, the final leads have just been connected. We're sending minimum signal pulses to the neuron simulating a deep sleep state. We're ready to proceed upon your direction."

"Thank you doctor. I'd like to inspect the cell please." Alexia's voice was slightly muffled by the surgical mask. Dr. Spartan moved reluctantly out of her way.

Alexia peered down at the glass with its thousands of connections. "Was it really possible to bridge the gap and communicate with this tiny cell. It's time to find out." She thought.

"Dr. Spartan, how long can we leave the neuron in this state?"

"Unknown. But I don't advise waiting to initiate the experiment. Some neurons have lived days, others only a few hours."

Alexia peered deep into the small nutrient dish for direction. "Ong, how much time do I have until the board meeting?"

"One hour, 17 minutes, doctor." Ong answered without hesitation.

"Not much time. I have two choices, let the scientists in this room do it again without me, with the same failed results. Then wait another week for another living brain cell. Or I can do it myself now and risk being late to a meeting with Hamachi." Alexia shuddered involuntarily, but made her decision.

"Ong, if I'm late, contact Mr. Hamachi and tell him I'm in the middle of an important experiment that couldn't be stopped."

"Yes doctor."

Alexia looked around the room at the waiting faces. "Each of you is the best at what you do and I have no doubt of that. But something is being overlooked, some small flaw, perhaps something too obvious for expert eyes. I don't expect you to understand what I'm going to ask of you now. Please leave the room, all of you. I'm going to perform this connection alone."

"But doctor Serguey," Dr. Spartan protested, "you don't have the experience in this particular set up. Hundreds of hours could be lost over a tiny mistake. Please. You perform the experiment, but keep us here, ready to assist."

Doubt crept in, but she held firm. "No. This one needs to be done alone. Stand by in the sterile waiting area. You can be here in a moment if I need you. But precious time is slipping away. Please leave the lab."

The finality in her voice ended the protests and they all left. Alexia felt the weight of her decision, her foolishness descend on her in her isolation.

If the experiment failed, they would have simply done it again. But now, she had taken this gamble. If it failed, her actions would be questioned, the responsibility on her shoulders alone. And to make it worse, Hamachi would be kept waiting, perhaps embarrassed in front of his board. She forced the doubts away. "Damn it! We've worked on this long enough. I know it will work. I know it." And with the thought, she flipped the switch from sleep to active signal. The number two was sent to the cell.

Nothing dramatic happened, only the output on the cell transmitter monitor changed from "nominal" to "overload."

Alexia stared at the word. The same as every previous experiment. She had failed. "No, I don't believe it, there's something there." She switched the view from status to raw data. The monitor went to static. "Computer, analyze the data." She spoke into the room.

"No coherent pattern. Data not analyzable." The computer voice droned.

"Computer, analyze all connections to and from the cell."

"Connections nominal." Was the terse reply.

"Computer, check for all known interference." Alexia said.

"No electromagnetic frequencies above normal earth emissions found."

"What. Repeat." She said.

"No electromagnetic frequencies above normal earth emissions found." The computer repeated.

"Frequencies, that might be a clue." She thought, then aloud she said, "Computer, analyze data for interlaced frequencies. Use maximum reduction."

Several seconds elapsed. "Extremely weak correlation found. Maximum frequency demodulation of 65,536 applied."

"Show data of first frequency." Alexia said excitedly.

The monitor changed from static to a kind of jerky static, flashing and popping occasionally.

"Computer, analyze data." Alexia said.

There was a brief pause this time, "Patterning random, analysis failed."

"Computer, run demodulation program on this single frequency."

Again, several seconds passed.

"Correlation found. Maximum frequency demodulation of 65,536 applied."

"Display data of first frequency." Alexia was nearly shouting now.

The static was replaced by something almost recognizable. Images running too fast to separate, almost like a video running at some ridiculous speed. "OK, now we're on to something. If I can find out what this garbage is, I'll find out where it's coming from and we can isolate the interference."

"Computer, analyze data." Alexia said.

The delay was long enough that Alexia was ready to repeat the command, when the computer voice finally answered, "Significant patterning. Data analysis failed."

"What kind of patterning?" She cried. "I mean, Computer, describe patterning."

"Patterning discernible, but unrecognizable Data analysis failed."

"OK," Alexia thought, "let's do it again." Then aloud, "Computer, run demodulation program again, using this single frequency."

The seconds ticked away as the computer performed its analysis. Alexia turned away from the monitor, grabbed a plastic bottle of water from its sterile receptacle. She slid the thin tube under her mask and pulled a long swallow. This would surely show the source of the problem. They might even be able to isolate the interference and run the experiment again on this same cell. She glanced at a time readout. "Good, I should still be able to make it to the meeting on time, or only a few minutes late. This was well worth the delay."

"Strong correlation found. Frequency demodulation stopped at 1,834 discrete channels. Data analysis successful." The computer voice droned.

"Good, now we'll see what's ruining my experiment." Alexia looked at the output monitor as she spoke the command, "Computer, display first frequency."

The thin plastic water bottle slipped from Alexia's hand, smashing on the tile floor and splattering cold water on her legs. She didn't even notice.

Several hours later, Alexia was interrupted by a tap on her shoulder. "Not now. Whatever it is, tell Ong and I'll get back with you."

"I'd rather speak with you now."

"Mr. Hamachi!" Alexia turned in surprise. He was wearing standard white clean room gear, but his ridged figure was unmistakable. Alexia glanced at the time readout in the corner of her translucent VR screen: 14:35. The board meeting, she'd missed it by hours. "Mr. Hamachi, I'm terribly sorry. But we've made a major breakthrough and I just couldn't stop."

Hamachi put his hand up. And though she couldn't be sure, she thought she saw a mischievous glint in his eye through the plastic goggles. "Tell me about this breakthrough that is more important than the executive board." He said dryly.

"We've done it. We are communicating with a single neuron. But it is nothing like what we expected. Each cell is an enormous storehouse of data, memories, I should say. The memories are tangled and fragmented, difficult to access directly, but it appears everything is there, every experience, every thought. All of it." Alexia said excitedly.

"Interesting, but I find this hard to believe. And you're able to view these data?" Hamachi asked.

"In a way. Our first mistake was ignoring the enormous data, assuming they were garbage. But equally important was our poor choice of input. Neurons are not little microchips with gates and switches, they are far more complex and different. They communicate with images, we should have been using one." Alexia turned back to the output monitor. "Look at this for example." She brought up a large fleshly image. It was blurry and difficult to discern. It looked like skin, but it was hard to be sure.

Hamachi peered at the image, then at Alexia. His face went serious.

This was not what he expected from the director of his most important project.

Alexia was too absorbed in what was in front of her to sense Hamachi's impatience. "It is crude, but watch a moment. The data are interlaced, fragmented. I have to get it from several areas to play it back in sequence. We'll get our computer techs to look for a pattern, but for now, I've created this simple program. Here it is. Now watch."

Alexia was clearly excited. Hamachi watched sternly from just behind her. The screen started to change images, jumpy, like a damaged film. "Keep watching." She urged. The flesh shifted angles somewhat, then began to pull back in jerky segments. It continued and a deeply pink area formed at the bottom of the monitor, then grew larger until it filled the screen. Then backed out further, now clearly discernible. It was a nipple, still wet from suckling, tiny drops of milk showed as large as marbles on the screen. The scene continued to move out, until the entire breast was visible, fabric showed around the edge and a woman's hand moved, jumping with the irregular scenes. It closed the fabric over the breast and the screen went blank.

Hamachi spoke evenly. "And this isn't some kind of interference, a holo-vid you picked up accidentally." Hamachi hesitated a moment, "or some kind of joke placed on the core by one of the techs."

Alexia shook her head slowly. "No, Mr. Hamachi. I've checked for all that. This room is completely isolated from all but minimal electromagnetic frequencies. We don't even have VR access in here. And the scene you just saw is not on the core, it is running live from that cell over there." She pointed to the metabolizing chamber in the center of the room. "No Mr. Hamachi, this is no joke. What you just witnessed was the actual visual memory of this subject as a baby feeding from his mother. I checked the records of the cell's host and he was indeed breast fed."

Hamachi's mind reeled with the implications. This changed everything. The entire project would evolve, grow from this amazing discovery. His disciplined mind held the thoughts in check, put them into the appropriate folder for later. "You'll need to verify the data, repeat the experiment. Find ways to record and access the data more efficiently." He said quickly.

"Of course." Alexia smiled broadly. "With pleasure."

"Very good. I'll leave you to your work then." Hamachi turned to look at Alexia as he moved out of the room. She had already buried her face in the computer readouts. He noticed a wisp of blond hair that had slipped from underneath her sterile cap. Suddenly, he was overwhelmed by a desire to walk over and tuck it back into place. Hamachi stood staring at that wisp of hair for a long moment, then turned and swept out of the lab.

Once out of the clean area, he barged into the nearest office. It was occupied by three women speaking noiselessly on VR sets. They all froze in mid-sentence as they recognized Hamachi.

"I have need of this office. Leave now, come back in 10 minutes."

The women nodded, jumped up, tripping over each other to escape the room. Hamachi closed and locked the door. He spoke into the air. "Computer, this is Tatsuo Hamachi speaking, secure this room for access code."

"Room secured. Computer ready." The computer voice replied.

"Computer, Tatsuo Hamachi, accesses code Alpha, lambda, seven, seven, zero, semicolon, asterisk, eight."

"Secure code recognized. Computer ready."

"Computer, initiate security protocol alpha." Hamachi called into the air.

"Stratumentis lock down protocol initiated. Maximum security procedures now in place at all loading docks and transport terminals. External Internet access terminated. All wired, wireless and satellite communications terminated. Maximum encryption on all internal communication systems." The computer droned a long list of security measures.

When it was done, Hamachi said, "Computer, begin and analyze for communication transmissions on all known frequencies. Begin monitoring internal voice conversations. Key phrases: neuron, brain cell, cellular memory and associated terminology."

"Analysis program running. Voice monitoring and pattern recognition programs running."

"Computer, Tatsuo Hamachi, security access, log out."

"Security access, Hamachi logged out." The computer voice replied.

Hamachi relaxed imperceptibly. Only then did he allow Alexia's recent discovery to sink in. This was astounding. He wasn't taking the chance some greedy fool would try to leak the discovery beyond these walls. "Father will be proud." He whispered.

7

ALVAR SHOVED A boot into the man's chest as he started to rise. "Lie still until someone gets here."

"Look. I don't have a problem with you or your people. But if I'm not back in that machine in a few minutes, there's going to be hell to pay. A whole lot of people are going to be here to find out what's wrong." The downed man said, not trying to get up any longer.

"That's what I'm counting on." Alvar replied. "Just stay down there in the dirt. I'm not sure what I'll do if you get back up."

The complaint had come in a few hours ago. A UnitedFarms machine, Alvar guessed it was some kind of giant plow and seeder combination, had begun tearing up the Anti-tech fields. It was no mistake and the driver only stopped when Alvar managed to pry him from his seat and throw him to the ground.

"Come on, let me up. I can't afford to lose this job, I got people to feed. Have a heart." He pleaded with Alvar. "You don't understand who I work for. First, they'll send an inspection team to find out why the combine stopped. If they see you standing on my chest, they'll call the Cor-police. Look, it's not too late, just let me up. It'll look like I took a break, or checked the machine for a jam. I won't say nothing." He sat up hopefully. "What do you say? I won't tell no one."

Alvar shoved him back down with his boot. "You're the one that doesn't understand, I want them to come. Your company has crossed the line too many times. This contract is broken. I want this whole damn deal ended."

Over the past several months UnitedFarms had pushed and pushed. The boundaries had been encroached a little, a storage shed destroyed from the bump of one of their monstrous machines. It was clear what they were doing and what they were planning. If they weren't stopped now, they'd plow their homes into the earth.

And worse, high tech was bleeding into their world. Children had been playing around with VR sets, jumping into virtual reality. The new arrivals had pointed out the devices, Alvar wouldn't have recognized them. How the VR sets got into Gaialandra was never known, but Alvar was sure it was no accident.

They'd made a pact with the devil and it was time to admit their mistake. If this was the only way to get in front of a court, then so be it.

The first team arrived as the driver had promised. They didn't bother to inspect the machine, simply communicating to their superiors in the strange silent way the VR set allowed. An hour later, three more men arrived, in uniforms. Dull black articulating armor covered them head to toe. The helmets had smoked face shields that hid their faces. On each of their right shoulders, burned a stylized logo, Alvar didn't recognize. They were clearly the Cor-police the downed man had warned of.

Alvar watched patiently, his foot gently resting on the worker's chest. The black figures stood very still, probably communicating with a supervisor. "Good. Let's get on with this." Alvar thought, wiping sweat from his forehead. He squinted at the afternoon sun, grinning to himself. "If I'm hot in this thin shirt, those goons must be broiling in their toy robot gear.

"Is your name Alvar Terrahaute, residing at the compound known as the Anti-Tech community of Old Paonia, Colorado?" One of the uniformed men spoke.

"Are you talking to me?" Alvar replied. "Who are you?"

"My designation is Officer Donnely, badge number A-2948 of the 18th rural precinct, region five, corporate alliance of the Colorado sub-district." He motioned to the other uniformed officers. "This is Officer Longey, badge number RT-8993, and this is Officer Samton, badge number B-2571, of the same jurisdiction. Once again, is your name Alvar Terra-haute, residing at the compound known as the Anti-Tech community of Old Paonia, Colorado?"

"Yes, that's me." Alvar nodded.

"Remove your foot so this worker may stand."

Alvar reluctantly removed his foot and the man scrambled to his feet. He was clearly terrified of the dark suited men standing there. He brushed by Alvar as he stood, "Let it drop man, let it drop. It ain't worth it."

Longey separated the two. "We've recorded your conversation. Now be warned everything from the moment of our arrival has been and will continue to be recorded and entered into evidence. Virtual council has been assigned."

Donnely turned to Alvar. "Will you cooperate, or must we use restraints to continue this hearing?"

"I'll cooperate." Alvar nodded. "But what hearing? You just got here."

"We are authorized by jurisdictional authority of the Colorado sub-district to perform virtual court hearings in situ." Donnely answered.

"What!" Alvar's face burned with anger, but held himself in check. "You don't even know what's going on. This man is trespassing on our land, destroying our property. He wouldn't stop until I pulled him from this machine. UnitedFarms has broken its contract by farming our lands. Until that is heard, none us will let their machines destroy our property."

"Breach of contract is a civil matter, Mr. Terrahaute. You will have to take that up in a civil court. Interfering with an authorized UnitedFarms worker in the course of his assigned duties is a class 4 felony as described in section 301b, subsection 81, of the Southwest States penal code. Do you plead guilty to that offense?" Donnely droned from under his helmet.

"I'm not pleading anything to you goons. I'll speak in front of a proper court, in front of a judge, not here in a potato field." Alvar spat.

He watched as the one called officer Longey spoke to Donnely. Then Longey reached into a compartment on the front of his chest plate and pulled out a plastic wrapped VR set, then handed it to Alvar. "It has come to our attention that it is the nature of your association not to wear technological devices. So you are likely not aware of the proceedings underway. Please put on the VR set so you may properly participate in the hearing."

Alvar was reluctant to break his long standing resistance to technology, but his serious disadvantage in this circumstance overcame it. He looked at the UnitedFarms worker to see how the device fit, then looped it over his ear and across his forehead. Instantly, the world changed. Alvar stumbled and almost fell. The sunny field in Colorado was gone, instead he was standing in a wood-lined courtroom. The illusion was fantastic, perfect. Alvar turned in wonder, forcing his reeling mind to remember that he was still standing in a freshly plowed field. Where the combine had been, a judge now sat, a court reporter busily typed on a device off to his left. Alvar glanced down at a high table in front of him, real and solid. To his left, a man in a blue business suit stood stiffly by. To his right and behind sat the forlorn looking UnitedFarms worker. But instead of the dusty blue uniform, he was wearing a neatly pressed brown suit. His hands and face were clean and his hair now neatly combed.

"Mr. Terrahaute. Mr. Terrahaute, over here" The man in the blue suit next to him urged. "It is very good you decided to join the proceedings. Now I can better assist you. My name is Councilor Sebarsky, I'll be your defense council throughout this hearing."

The judge, from the front of the room barked sarcastically. "All settled in, Mr. Terrahaute? May we now proceed, I have a full docket today."

Another man suddenly appeared just to the right of the judge. His suit was identical to Sebarsky's, except that it was deep red instead of blue. "Mr. Terrahaute, you are accused of criminal malice to an authorized employee of UnitedFarms. How do you plead?"

"Who's that?" Alvar whispered to Sebarsky.

Sebarsky turned to the Judge, "A moment to explain the defendant's options, your honor."

"You are granted two minutes." The judge grumbled.

He turned back to Alvar, "That's the prosecuting attorney. You must enter a plea of guilty or not guilty. But be warned, either plea will not delay the case. And you are already on record stating that you pulled the man out to his machine. If you plead guilty, there is a chance of leniency. Probably a fine and one year's probation. A not guilty plea will bring the full wrath of the court down on you. Judge Franklin is a very impatient judge, as you can see."

"But I'm not guilty, the man was clearly trespassing. If I plead guilty, will I be able to enter the contract as evidence?" Alvar was beginning to feel the weight of the situation.

"No. A guilty plea will begin the sentencing hearing immediately, no new evidence will be allowed."

"Then not guilty." Alvar said firmly.

This time, Alvar did stumble to the ground. He could feel freshly plowed dirt under his hands and knees, but his eyes reported a different reality. He was looking down from a great height at the UnitedFarms machine tearing up their field. Alvar watched as he saw himself waving frantically in front of the vehicle, the worker ignoring him. He saw himself crawl up the ladder, open the door and pull the man from the vehicle. It was the same as he remembered it, though it was strange to watch from above. Alvar thought to himself, "Where are these cameras that can record so much detail, satellites? They are watching everything we do; I must remember to warn the others."

The scene changed back to the courtroom and Alvar stood back up. "Do you deny the validity of the recording you've just witnessed?" The prosecuting attorney shouted at Alvar.

Alvar cocked his head in wonder. He leaned over to Sebarsky, "Why is he shouting?"

"Oh, just ignore it, it's just something he does to sound more intimidating." Sebarsky whispered back.

"Answer the question, Mr. Terrahaute." The judge sounded.

"It looks the same as I remember it." Alvar answered.

"No more questions." The prosecuting attorney said. Then grinned at Alvar and disappeared from the room.

"Defense?" The judge asked.

Councilor Sebarsky looked over at Alvar sadly and shrugged.

Alvar said, "Your honor, I pulled the man from the vehicle because he was destroying our property. If I hadn't..."

"Objection. Improper form. What question is the defendant answering?" The prosecuting attorney had reappeared and shouted into the room.

"Sustained." The judge said. "If you have evidence to support your innocence you may present it now."

"I don't have it with me, but there is a contract that designates the boundaries of our property. UnitedFarms is trespassing, and..."

"Evidence, Mr. Terrahaute. Documents, recordings, affidavits, testimony, witnesses, Mr. Terrahaute. Do you have any of those things?" The judge smiled cruelly. "If there is a contract for us to see, retrieve it and enter it into evidence.

"I was just dragged in here a moment ago, how could I have any of those things." Alvar argued.

The judge spoke to the prosecuting attorney who had remained visible in the courtroom. "Apparently, the defendant has no evidence to place before the court." He focused on Sebarsky. "Does the defense have anything more to add?"

"Damn right I do..." Alvar's voice was cut off in mid-stream. He was still shouting, but no sound was coming from his mouth.

Sebarsky shook his head, "Nothing to add, your honor."

Very well. Prosecution, do you have anything else to add?" The judge said, ignoring Alvar's desperate plea to get his attention.

"Nothing more, your honor." The red suited prosecuting attorney said and vanished.

"What!" Alvar mouthed to Sebarsky. "This is not a court. This is a..." But he was still inaudible.

"This hearing is now complete. The defendant is found guilty of the charge of criminal interference of an authorized worker. Maximum sentence is hereby imposed. Five years at a work facility, to be designated by the offending party. Court dismissed." A gavel was sounded, and everyone disappeared except for Alvar and Sebarsky.

"I warned you. This is bad. Any questions before I leave?" Sebarsky asked.

"What just happened here?" Alvar asked, his voice now returned.

"You've been sentenced to five years at a work camp. That could mean anything. But they usually take your skills into account. Which probably means a farm facility somewhere."

"What! But surely I can speak to the judge, appeal my case, prepare, explain this better."

Sebarsky cocked his head in a questioning way. "There is no judge to speak to, no appeal. Don't you understand where you are? A judge is only here for trials."

"Yes, I'm not that naïve. I know he was not actually standing here, that I saw only a virtual image of him."

"No Mr. Terrahaute. He is only here for trials, as am I, the prosecuting attorney, the court reporter and the bailiff. We are smart programs, not people." Sebarsky said blandly.

Alvar's eyes widened. "You're not real, not even alive. I was just sentenced by robots." Alvar whispered.

"Not robots, smart programs, designated by the court to be impartial and fair. I am sorry I wasn't able to help more. Now Mr. Terrahaute, both of us must go." Sebarsky and the courtroom disappeared. Alvar found he was standing in the field again. It was like waking from some kind of strange hyper realistic nightmare. Alvar remembered the VR Set on his face and ripped it off with a savage slash of his hand.

Except it wasn't a dream. The worker was still there, his head bowed sheepishly, as were the Cor-police. "You." They gestured back to the worker. "Get back into your vehicle and continue working." The worker ran to the enormous machine, stumbling on the loose dirt in his rush.

"Hey wait a minute. He can't just continue destroying our property like nothing happened." And Alvar moved towards the vehicle. But the three officers immediately moved into his path.

"You will be coming with us. A transport vehicle is on its way. You still have a choice. To wait here calmly, or..." Officer Longey's voice trailed off ominously, "we can quiet you."

Alvar fell back a step. "I'm not going anywhere."

All three of the officers pulled pistol-like weapons from their holsters.

"You're not going to shoot me. Not over this. Even your corporate masters don't have the power to murder people." Alvar turned his back to the black clad men and began walking toward Gaialandra. Alvar shaded his eyes from the bright sun. He saw the clear blue sky and the snow-capped mountains in the distance. The cluster of faded wooden buildings that was Gaialandra, his people, his home stood only a few hundred yards away.

Alvar took a second step, then felt three sharp pinches, two in his back and one in his leg. The mountains, sky and buildings turned gray, then black. Alvar fell face-down in the soft plowed earth.

———

Consciousness came back in painful waves. First, Alvar felt an aching in his joints, then a tight pressure on his head, like someone was sitting on it. Alvar pried his eyes open and felt the cold panic of waking in a strange place. It was a small room with two rows of steel benches on each side, six men occupied each. He looked at each man quickly in turn, hoping to recognize a compassionate face or at least one that wasn't outwardly hostile.

Alvar stayed on the floor for another moment, giving himself time to clear his mind. He felt a sideways pull, then back, sliding on the hard steel. He realized they were moving. This wasn't a room, but a vehicle. He peered through the gloom more carefully trying to understand where he was. The walls, floor and ceiling were made from some kind of dull metal. It was about eight feet wide and maybe twice that long. The ceiling was low, barely tall enough to allow an average man to stand upright. Tiny lights littered the roof giving off a feeble light, adding to the claustrophobia.

He thought of Chloe, beautiful, Chloe. What would happen to her, who would protect her? No one saw him in the field. "What a fool I was to stand up to these people without a clue." And what of the others, and Gaialandra? Would others stand up to the machine, be taken one by one.

Or would they watch as their homes were plowed under?

Rage welled in Alvar and it was difficult to remain sitting. He wanted to move, no he wanted to smash the steel walls that held him in here.

Alvar snarled at the other men in the vehicle. He recognized their type easily enough – the unemployable, the discards of an ultra-efficient society. He recognized them only because they were the same men who'd come to the Anti-Techs sometimes looking to join, or for temporary work. But it was unlikely that men so badly beaten down would fit into the tightly knit society of a commune. And with no exceptions, they'd always been turned away. Alvar winced now, remembering that he had never thought about what would happen to those men when they were refused by the Anti-Techs.

"How long have I been out?" Alvar said to no one in particular.

"Who knows? They took away my fancy new watch." A man said. He had an angry looking purple bruise covering half his face, one eye swollen shut.

Alvar turned and looked directly at another man staring at the floor. "How long do you think I was unconscious?"

The man looked up uncomfortably, obviously trying to avoid being noticed. "I, uh, I'm not sure. A few hours, I guess."

"And do you know where we're going?" Alvar asked.

"No."

"Were you here when I was brought in?"

"No."

"Do you think there is a way out of here?" Alvar lowered his voice.

"Ha, why don't you just smash the steel with your thick skull." The man with the bruise spat.

Alvar locked eyes with the bruised man. "It looks like you already tried that."

The bruised man jumped up in anger, but was pulled down by the man sitting next to him. "Cut the crap, assholes. As soon as the guards hear a scuffle, they'll fill this shithole with gas. And I'd just as soon stay awake."

The man who'd pulled bruised face down, hadn't even looked up. But there was something in his body language that demanded caution. There was a tired kind of authority about the man. Alvar spied a dull gray metal collar around his neck. He also noticed something unusual about his skin. It was hard to see in the dim light, but it was slightly iridescent and strangely textured. Above the metal collar Alvar could make out folds of skin, almost like gills. And then Alvar realized the man was a 'geneered amphibian. He'd heard of this, but discarded it as fantasy.

Alvar worked over to the 'geneered man. "Do you have any idea where we're going?"

"Wrong question Einstein."

"What's the right one?" Alvar asked.

The man uncocked his heavy head and Alvar could see that his eyes also had the square pupils of a reptile. "What are they going to do to you?"

The other men in the vehicle turned to this man in fearful curiosity.

"What do you mean?" Alvar said.

"You think I did this," The man pointed to his gills, "to myself to attract girls?"

"Maybe a pretty gecko." A man in the corner snorted.

A few men chuckled.

The amphibious man got up slowly and strolled over to the joker and sat down next to him. Alvar watched him whisper something into the other man's ear. The comedian's face went white and he nodded. The amphibious man got up and returned to his seat.

He turned back to Alvar. There was no anger in his voice, only tired resignation. "I've seen so many of you idiots come and go. And you're always the same. Boo hoo, why me? Where are we going? What's go to happen to me? I'll tell you what's going to happen to you – whatever the corporate fucks want. If they want you digging for worms in solid rock, that's what you'll do. If they want you breathing underwater caring for their fucked up eight-headed fish, then that's what you'll do. And don't think they can't change you into anything they want, whenever they want. What you see on me is nothing. I've seen men that don't even look human anymore." He looked around slowly at the scared faces. "Welcome to hell boys."

The bruised man stuttered fearfully. "But you're not taking care of fucked-up fish now, are you? You must have gotten out. Or maybe you did this to yourself and you're just trying to scare us. That's your plan, to scare us. But I'm not scared. I heard lots of people get out, pay their time and get out, maybe even get a job afterwards like they promise."

The amphibious man raised the corner of his mouth in a sardonic smile uncovering a few pointed teeth. "Sure, plenty of people get out, rich ones. They just buy off their sentence. That is if their contract is for sale. But that ain't you, or you wouldn't even be in this van. A job? That's a laugh. You think they'll give you rat-eaters a job later. Why should they, when they got you for nothin'. You been watching too many corporate holo-vids. And me, who said I got out. How do you think you sleeping beauties got in here? Dreamed your way in? But I guess you'll find out if I'm lying soon enough, won't you." He spat on the floor in front of him and looked away. After several minutes of silence, it was clear he wasn't going to speak again.

Alvar got up and sat down in the only spot available, next to the man who'd made the joke. After several quiet minutes, he asked the man, "What did he say to you?"

He turned to Alvar, still pale. "He said he'd bite my eyes out if I didn't shut up. Did you see his teeth, I think he would have."

Alvar shook his head, trying to shake off the terror the amphibian had instilled. He'd been foolish, arrogant to fight a battle where the rules, even the players were unknown. "What was I thinking?" Alvar mentally kicked himself. Then calming himself, he thought, "Careful, think, use your brain. Keep your eyes open for opportunity. Learn."

But there was nothing to be done now but wait. And for hours nothing interrupted the silent men from their terrified thoughts. Then the vehicle stopped. The men stirred in growing anticipation and fear.

"Knock it off. We ain't there yet. It's just a shift change or food stop for the drivers." The amphibian said.

His statement was punctuated by a scraping metallic sound, a small panel that had been invisible previously, opened at the rear. A pile of plastic wrapped items tumbled forward into the room and the panel slammed shut.

"Food. If you can call it that." The amphibious man got up and grabbed one of the packages and sat back down with it. The rest of the men quickly followed his example.

Alvar opened his package suspiciously. It could be loaded with drugs. But if they wanted him unconscious, why bother with his food. So he might as well eat, his stomach ached with hunger. Inside was a single block of something about the density of stale bread. It didn't taste like anything in particular, neither bad nor good. Alvar finished it quickly and emptied the water container too. In a few minutes he felt drowsy. The food was drugged after all. Before Alvar lost consciousness, he looked over at the amphibian. He was smiling sadly with his needle-sharp teeth.

Alvar was jolted awake by a jerk of the transport vehicle. Then everything was still again. About half of the men were still lying unconscious on the floor. The others were sitting on the benches, their eyes dull from drugged sleep.

"What happened? How long have we been out?" Alvar asked.

No one answered. Alvar looked around for the amphibian, but he was no longer in the room.

Alvar felt more movement of the vehicle, then another jolt, then the clang of metal against metal. After a long pause, the rear of the transport slid to one side. Alvar's heart raced in anticipation. This could be a chance to escape, maybe his only one. They had to transfer them from the truck to a prison or camp or wherever they were going. It was this transfer that would be the most vulnerable part of security. Alvar moved to the door, ready, his mind on fire and his body poised looking for any hint of an opportunity. But instead of the light of day or night, all he saw was more gray gloom and felt a blast of frigid air. The receding door revealed a steel hallway made of the same material as the inside of the vehicle.

"Move forward." A mechanical voice boomed in the small space.

Alvar looked back at the other men. The benches had disappeared into the walls and he could just make out some movement at the far end of the transport – the rear wall was sliding toward them.

Alvar walked out of the transport and into the corridor. The others followed. When they were all out of the truck, the rear wall had slid completely forward and another panel moved into place in front of it. Alvar's hopes of escaping during transfer evaporated and he walked forward with the others.

The air was cold and the men wrapped their arms around themselves. Alvar noticed white patches of frost on the dull gray walls. Where were they? It must be very cold outside.

"Move forward." The mechanical voice sounded again.

A panel about 50 feet ahead slid open and the rear panel began to push toward them. This process repeated several more times, forcing the men forward down the gloomy corridor. There was no choice but to comply. Eventually they ended up in a larger chamber lined with doors. The entrance panel slammed shut behind them.

"Stand directly in front of the door marked with your name. If you cannot read, speak your name and the appropriate door will respond by repeating it. Do not attempt to use the incorrect door, it will open only by gen-scan. Disobedience will be punished." The mechanical voice droned.

Alvar saw a door with his name written on the screen above it. He hesitated as the others moved in front of their doors.

"Move to your door now. Delay will be punished."

When everyone was in front of a door, the voice sounded again, "Place both thumbs on the gen-scan on the door in front of you. Delay will be punished."

Alvar watched as one by one the other men placed their thumbs on the gen-scan and were whirled into the next room. There was a reason the gen-scan required both thumbs. This kept the men's arms close to their bodies. Otherwise, the motion of the revolving door would surely have severed their arms like a guillotine. Alvar held his breath and placed his thumbs on the scanner. The force of the revolving door threw him to the floor in the next room. He looked back quickly, but the opening was gone.

The new chamber glowed brightly with no obvious source of light. In the middle of the room stood a metal platform – maybe a table or bed, but with absolutely no detail. It was little more than a slab of steel raised off the floor. "Take off all of your clothes and lie face up on the table." The voice ordered.

"Now wait a minute. First I need to know what is happening to me and..."

"If you do not comply, you will be rendered unconscious and an assistant will undress you. Then you will be punished. You have 60 seconds to remove your clothes and lie face up on the table." The finality of the voice did not invite further discussion.

Alvar hesitated the briefest moment, then thought better of it. This was not the time for conflict or resistance. They had the upper hand and would likely keep it. If there was opportunity for escape, it was not here and not now. He'd just have to keep alert and ready. Every security has its flaw. He'd always believed the more technical and complicated a system, the more opportunity for error, it was just less obvious. But doubt filled him, the eternal seed of hope in the back of his mind was under heavy assault.

In a moment he was undressed and lying naked on the table. It was cold and it took an effort of will to lie still. Suddenly, curved restraints emerged from somewhere under the table and closed over his arms, legs and the top of his head with a dull "click."

The voice droned. "Do not be alarmed and do not attempt to move. The restraints will only tighten under force. This may become uncomfortable or painful. Remain still and you will not experience unnecessary pain." Alvar watched anxiously as a mechanical arm emerged from a ceiling panel. A blue light scanned his body, for implants, he speculated.

"Continue to lie still. You will not be harmed, but it is very important you do not move during the next procedure."

Alvar discovered he couldn't move more than his eyes anyway and didn't resist.

"Your brain will now be scanned and mapped. A sample of your fluids will be taken and your DNA sequenced. General drugs will be injected, but customized drugs will be introduced later. You may experience intense anxiety, but continue to lie still and the feelings will subside quickly. Resistance only makes the process more difficult and lengthy."

Alvar winced with the sharp poke of the needles going into his arms, one to inject drugs, the other to remove blood. A moment later, as the voice had warned, anxiety intensified to a frightening level. Had he not been immobilized so quickly and effectively, Alvar would have been clawing the steel door for escape. He did his best to stay calm and push the fear down and breathe normally.

Eventually the panic subsided as whatever tranquilizer they had given him took hold. From that point on, he found he was only superficially interested in the rest of the procedures performed on his trapped body. They cleansed him, took more blood, injected him several more times, then ended by shaving his head. It was their body now, it must be in their interests to keep it healthy. A nagging memory hoped their drugs would allow him to keep his own mind, but through the fog he realized he didn't really care anymore.

8

"**WHAT IS THAT** damned buzzing?" Ezekiel grumbled. It was disturbing his concentration and he had been frustrated all day trying to crack into the National Commerce Bank of New Atlanta. It was boring work, but he didn't get paid if he didn't get in. How was he supposed to think with that damned noise.

Ezekiel disconnected from the bank portal and connected to his living space. Now he recognized the sound. It was the door buzzer. Someone was trying to get him to answer his door. Ezekiel transferred his view from inside his apartment to the hallway scanner. The blurry image from the damaged camera showed a fisheye view of the hallway. Men, women and children crowded the corridor with their piles of boxes, makeshift kitchens, folding beds and portable toilets. Residents who couldn't afford rooms, but at least didn't live on the streets.

In the middle of this rabble was a tall dark haired woman leaning on his buzzer. The image was too poor to see who it was, but it was interesting enough for him to let this stranger in. He voiced the code for the door release.

"Come in and shut the door behind you." He said into the system.

The interior lights were still dim from traveling *the I*, so Ezekiel could not immediately recognize the woman who entered. She had a distinctive way of carrying herself, as if she was trying not to touch anything, including breathing the air. Ezekiel spoke into the room, "lights normal." The room lit, revealing Chloe standing in Ezekiel's chaotic apartment.

Chloe put her hand to her mouth and gasped. Ezekiel was facing her, sitting up in the jack-chair, still connected to *the I*, long silvery bundles of wires sprouted from each prosthesis, shifting and vibrating with each movement of his eye.

Ezekiel was just as shocked as Chloe. He had spent hours manipulating the recorded video and sound from their meeting two months ago. Under his digital skills, she had morphed from a 28 year old farm hand into a virtual sex fantasy willing to do and say anything Ezekiel could imagine. Chloe standing here in his apartment was as strange an event as if the table unfolded its legs and began to walk.

Chloe looked away from Ezekiel. Her eyes scanned the tiny cluttered apartment. "I'm sorry to bother you at home. I didn't know where else to turn." Her words trailed off, then she continued softly, "Maybe this is a bad idea after all, I'd better go." And she turned towards the door.

Ezekiel realized he was still connected to *the I* and pulled the wires from his eyes with an audible "click." He jumped from the jack-chair, across the tiny room until he stood between her and the door. "No, no, don't go." He swept a pile of computer parts and paper off the table and onto the floor. "Here, we can sit here and talk."

"OK, thank you." Chloe said mildly.

Ezekiel sat at the other chair, more than a little overwhelmed. He looked around at the chaos of his apartment, then back at this perfect being. The contrast unsettled him. Ezekiel stared at her, waiting for her to speak, unable to say anything himself.

"I didn't know who else to come to." Chloe said, avoiding Ezekiel's eyes. "Alvar's been taken, but there seems to be no way to find out where." She was unable to continue.

"Alvar?" Ezekiel feigned ignorance.

"Of course, how could you know. Alvar is my...how do I explain?

We grew up together in Gaialandra. He's a friend. Only lately..." Chloe blushed, "we've become more."

Ezekiel's face remained nearly impassive, except for his bunching jaw muscles. "I see. And what is Alvar's last name?"

"Terrahaute, Alvar Terrahaute. No middle name."

"Tell me what you know."

"That's the thing, we know nothing for sure. There was a United-Farms worker who operated one of the large machines that's tearing up our fields. He was leaving one day, said he'd been transferred and wanted someone to know what happened. I guess he didn't have much time, so he grabbed the first person he saw, a 10 year old boy. He told the boy that Alvar had pulled him out of the cab of the machine and was arrested."

"Damn kids again" Ezekiel thought, then aloud, "were you able to find the worker?"

"No, he'd been transferred that day and the new person won't talk."

Ezekiel nodded. "If it won't disturb you too much, I need to jack into *the I* to get more information."

"Anything, if it can help." She nodded vigorously.

"Amazing how their anti-technology philosophy goes out the window when they're in trouble," he scoffed to himself. Ezekiel discovered Alvar in a few seconds, then spent several minutes adjusting sensors and software so he could scan Chloe better. His prosthetic eyes came with infrared scanners and coupled with the right software could virtually peel the clothes away from a person. He set software and sensors to work in the background so he'd have it for later. It would be too distracting now. Anticipation warmed his crotch.

A few minutes later, Ezekiel was disconnecting the wires from his eyes. "It's what the farm hack told you. Alvar was arrested and convicted of interference with an authorized employee. But I wouldn't doubt the whole thing was a set up. It makes no difference, though. UnitedFarms got what they wanted. He was sent to a prison farm in the central province of Incorporated Canada to serve out a five year sentence plus fees."

Chloe was clearly crushed by this news, but managed to speak, "Is there any way to appeal his sentence or reduce it?"

"Appeals are a waste of resources. They'll just stall you forever, longer than the contract in any case. But normally you could just buy his sentence and..."

Chloe brightened. "We'll do that. Tell me how much they want, we'll get the money together and we'll send it to them."

Her face was lovely with the hope of saving Alvar. Ezekiel almost forgot they were talking about her boyfriend. "Uh, yeah, normally it is simply a matter of paying the value of the convict's contract. If it's for sale, that is. Unfortunately, this one's not. Which means they want him, more than they want the money."

"This is a nightmare." Chloe whispered. "Where is he? What's happening to him?"

Chloe was looking down at her hands and Ezekiel took the time to look her over carefully. He realized what made her so lovely were her flaws, not her perfection, though she was both. He'd seen plenty of perfect women. Well, not exactly real women, but scans and holograms. But Chloe was real. Ezekiel saw a small mole on her cheek, something one would never see on a simulation and small creases and tiny blond hairs on her neck and arms. All these small things would have been removed genetically from living women, or left off in holographic simulations. It drove him to distraction. Concentrate. What had she just asked? Oh yeah, about Alvar.

"He's at a work camp, a farm in Canada. So he'll uh, be farming." Ezekiel stumbled.

"Oh, he's a farmer, it won't be that bad then, will it?" She said, hopefully.

Ezekiel shook his head. "No it's nothing like what you do on your farm, or on farms here. We still have some minimum human rights. Incorporated Canada is owned by the corporations. They have only one rule – maximize profits. It's cold up there in the winter and difficult to grow crops at night in near arctic conditions. The crops, machines and men need to be adjusted for the environment. They wouldn't hesitate to manipulate Alvar's body and brain to suit their needs." Ezekiel stopped when he saw Chloe's look, her eyes moist.

"I need to know. What does that mean exactly?" She asked staring at his plastic eyes.

"Oh they can do a million things with the human genome. Amazing things. They can change almost any system, even combine species, or introduce plant or insect traits into a system. But those are not used so much, they don't combine as well as basic mammal traits. And that's what they'll probably work with. You know, obvious things like, thicker skin, an added layer of subcutaneous fat for warmth, probably thick hair or fur all over. Then they can do strange things to a person's metabolism, selectively slow it down to retain warmth, but increase it in other areas to create heat. They're also likely to add plenty of psychotropic drugs to control his thoughts, keep him docile. Without looking into it further, I can only guess, though."

Chloe was crying freely now. "You just listed these horrible changes like he's some kind of stock animal. No that's not true, animals would be treated better. Good god, why did I come here." She looked around the apartment horrified. "This is your world. What can I do?"

"Let me look into it."

Chloe nodded numbly, stood up and stumbled to the door. "I'm sorry to have bothered you." She pulled on the locked door. "Can you release the door? I'd like to leave now."

Ezekiel's eyes narrowed a fraction. Did anyone know she was here? But the thoughts of force quickly passed. His flabby arms were no match against a woman who worked outside on a farm. "Uh, just a second." Ezekiel squeaked. And the door released with an audible "click."

"Wait!" He blurted as she yanked the door open. How do I reach you, when I have something?"

Chloe avoided his eyes. "The same way you did before." She sped down the crowded hall, bumping carts and boxes.

Ezekiel closed and locked the door when she'd moved out of sight. "Alvar. Sounds like a new word for obstacle." He flipped the replay button on his X-ray program and watched Chloe's naked buttocks sway as she rushed down the hallway. "Alvar's going to have to wait a bit."

9

THE SUN DIPPED below the rim of the Grand Canyon leaving the sky a riot of orange, pink and blues. Visible far below the semi-transparent floor, flowed the ribbon of flame that was the Colorado River. Alexia ignored the extraordinary scene before her and turned back to the stoic Hamachi.

"There is too much we don't know before we can just start cutting into a living brain. It is butchery to go in blind."

"Dr. Serguey" he began calmly again, "you've connected to dozens of brain cells now. Each successfully, each with the same results. What is the purpose? It is time to move forward."

"The purpose, Mr. Hamachi, is to learn what all this data coming from a neuron is and how to communicate with it." She hissed.

Hamachi shook his head. "You can't communicate with a single cell, any more than you can read a single word from a book and know the story. It is time to move forward. I understand your reservations, your reluctance as a doctor. But you are also a scientist. The data we are receiving is being filtered a dozen ways, machines, computer programs, monitors, our own eyes and ears. A brain cell is designed to communicate with other brain cells, not computers. We need to connect to a living brain, or we will be stuck here indefinitely." Hamachi watched Alexia closely. She had dropped her eyes in agreement, but she was still hesitant.

"We have volunteers standing by. They'll be pioneers in this uncharted country. Think of it Doctor Serguey, communication at the most primal level, brain to brain. And what else will we learn? What else can the brain tell us about itself? Are there pockets of potential locked in the brain we've only dreamed of? We'll be the first to find out. The first to reach into the depths of stored knowledge."

Alexia continued to look down, but Hamachi saw that he had indeed plucked the right cord.

"What do you mean by volunteers?" She looked up at Hamachi.

His voice hardened. "The project is moving forward doctor, you will find the subjects available as needed. Ong has been briefed."

Alexia stared into the canyon floor, unseeing. "Very well, Mr. Hamachi, we'll begin immediately. Is there anything else?"

A smile flashed at the corners of Hamachi's mouth. "Yes. Keep me closely informed of the progress. I think it is going to move very quickly now."

Alexia nodded stiffly and left his office.

She'd come around, he thought. It was good to push people beyond their scruples, to a point. He wanted Doctor Serguey pliant, but still in full control of her intelligence and creativity. It was a subtle and dangerous game. Push too hard and he would create robots, not hard enough and they would dance around the goal without touching it. Yes, she would come around, she had to.

Alexia whipped into the lab amidst a flurry of activity. Machines of every variety were being dragged in, a nanobot generator, electron tunneling microscopes, several sterile chambers and multi-processor computer blocks. She wove through the chaos nearly colliding with Ong.

"Why do you insist on sneaking up on me like that!" Alexia shouted.

"I don't know what you mean doctor. I just arrived to update you on the progress of stage two of the experiment." Ong answered in her customary monotone.

Alexia recovered her calm. "Yes, go ahead then."

"The surgical team is assembled and ready. It is assumed the surgical site on the skull will need to stay exposed for an extended period, so self-replicating, sterile nanobots have been designed and stand ready. The implant team has been moved from the cell lab and is also ready. The computer team is working on details, but should be ready for implant tomorrow."

Alexia interrupted, "What do you mean should be ready. What details?"

"We expect much larger volumes of data from a living brain and as such, it will be difficult to capture all of it, they are considering ways of selective or compressive storage." Ong paused.

"I need to talk to them." Alexia commanded.

A moment later they were standing in the doorway of a small room off the main lab. Five software engineers were arguing over an arcane set of symbols on the digital whiteboard on the back wall.

"Excuse me. Quiet everyone. What seems to be the problem?" Alexia shouted over the arguing in the room.

Hockman, the lead engineer spoke first. "These morons want to use standard compression algorithms to save all the data. I've been trying to drill through their thick sculls that we'll use up all our storage blocks in the first 15 minutes of the link."

"Not if we use multiple paths to eliminate the duplication, Einstein." One of the other engineers shouted back at him.

"Hold on everyone." Alexia interrupted. "Mr. Hockman, explain the problem to me, in layman terms please."

Hockman let out a long sigh. "The problem is non-trivial. The data coming from the single cell in the previous experiment was a huge amount of data. We were able to store it using standard compression techniques. But that was a single cell. We can expect data trillions of times greater. We are simply trying to capture it. But at the rate it will come in, storage blocks will fill faster than the computer can feed them. There will be no time for change out. The computer may go into a locked state if it tries to feed data with no blocks to accept it."

Alexia nodded thoughtfully. "Perhaps the brain can give us a clue."

"What do you mean?" Hockman asked.

"Well the brain doesn't store information sequentially like a computer. It holds it associatively and in clusters." She paused, literally watching the ideas sink in to the engineers' minds. "Perhaps we can store it the same way, or at least in a similar way."

"We could use parallel self–checking packet routines that..."

"Are you nuts? The processor overhead will bring the data stream to a crawl..."

"Not if we added Seinlan routines..."

"Don't bring up that outdated garbage again..."

Alexia shut the door softly. "They'll have it worked out by morning." She smiled to Ong. But the other woman's cold face quickly dried her enthusiasm. "Show me the surgical room."

"Yes doctor."

They eased into the outer chamber of the surgical room, not wishing to disturb the sterile environment on the other side of the glass. The room was typical of a surgical chamber: bright overhead lights, stainless steel tables and wrapped instruments. A plastic encased bundle of wire at one end of the room was the only clue as to its real purpose tomorrow.

"What's on the other side of that door?" Alexia asked, pointing to a large red sign that read, "Authorized personnel only, absolutely no entry."

"The prep room, Doctor." Ong answered.

Alexia narrow her eyes, "Why the warning signs then?"

"The volunteer is in there."

"What?" She spun around to face Ong. "When did he arrive? On whose authority?"

"Mr. Hamachi contacted me several hours ago and I simply followed his instructions." Ong said patiently.

"Show me. I want to meet this volunteer."

Ong raised her eyebrows slightly, at least enough for Alexia to notice.

This was the equivalent of a verbal protest by anyone else. But Ong quickly complied by placing her thumb to the door lock.

The two scientists entered the bright room. It was about the size of a large bedroom and there was indeed a bed and nightstand at one end of the room. Sitting on a chair facing the wall was a thin woman with her head recently shaved.

"It's a young woman. Why did I think it would be a man?" Alexia thought, then aloud to the woman, "What is your name?"

The woman didn't move or respond in any way. The two scientists edged closer so they could face the woman. Alexia guessed she was in her twenties, but something in the hard face suggested someone much older. Her cheeks were gouged with deep scars that came together into intricate patterns.

"We don't know her name and she will not speak to us. One of the technicians named her Bertha." Ong said.

"Where did she come from? If she won't give us her name, how did she come to volunteer?"

Ong shot Alexia a sharp look. "Dr. Serguey, this young woman has been brought here on the specific orders of Mr. Hamachi. Do you suggest he is capable of such a mistake." Ong placed a hand on Alexia's forearm, gently pulling Alexia toward the exit.

Alexia pried Ong's hand away. "I don't doubt Mr. Hamachi's instructions Ong. I just want to learn about the person sitting here."

"It is not likely you will Dr. Serguey." Ong said quietly. "Bertha, or whatever her name is, was brought to us several days ago, addicted to synthadrene. We've been administering anthidrone, the counteracting agent. She hasn't slept, but she appears stable. We cannot force her to speak."

"What!" Alexia shouted. "What kind of volunteer is this. An addict with brain damage?"

"Please, Doctor Serguey. Synthadrene does not affect brain function beyond over stimulation of the adrenal glands. Otherwise, the subject is relative healthy and average. Average is what we want Dr. Serguey. But I suggest we have this conversation elsewhere." Ong spoke as if she were reading the label of a food package, without emotion or inflection. It was strangely calming.

Alexia nodded.

Once outside the prep room, Alexia confronted Ong. "What kind of volunteer doesn't speak or react."

Ong remained impassive. "Dr. Serguey, I am confident Mr. Hamachi has worked out all details correctly. If you disagree, please speak with him. Now if you'll excuse me, there is a lot to prepare before tomorrow's surgery."

Alexia was left standing alone. This was wrong, yet as she allowed the thought to bubble to the surface, she also knew she would not call Hamachi, nor would she do anything else about it. "We are connecting passive receptors to a brain. If we don't get a response, what harm can it cause?" Alexia thought to herself. This girl was likely to kill herself with drugs anyway. Then she hurried off to prepare for tomorrow's surgery.

The next morning was a blur of activity, final preparations, rechecking equipment and surgical pre-op. But finally, they were ready.

The operation was a relatively simple one and minimally invasive. Dr. Spartan, the master neurosurgeon, would remove a small section of bone for access to the right frontal lobe. Dr. Smith would unleash her swarm of pre-engineered nanobots into the area, which would then connect the thousands of fine leads to a single neuron in the patient's brain. Then they would watch the results. In many respects, it was less risky than working with a single cell removed from the brain. The elaborate dissection was no longer necessary, nor was there the need of the many machines and fluids to keep the cell alive. The brain would do that. And if the cell died while being connected, it was irrelevant and they could move on to another. They had planned for such contingencies and would try different connections, even moving to different sites on the brain if necessary.

"Surgical ready." Dr. Spartan's English baritone announced in her earpiece.

"Computer ready." Hockman was next. She smiled to herself, she knew they'd do it.

"Nanobot team ready." Smith droned.

And so it went through the many systems and teams, until there was nothing left but silence and anticipation.

Alexia peered through the observation window into the surgical room. It was packed with surgeons, technicians and engineers. They all turned expectantly to her after the final ready signal.

"Very well, all teams have reported ready. Dr. Spartan, please begin." Alexia spoke to all teams.

Doctor Spartan was quick and efficient. The opening to the brain was small, about the width of a pencil. Spartan backed out of the way and the nanobot team began. In a few minutes, they too moved away. Now all eyes watched the monitor.

"Connection complete, Dr. Serguey. Ready to initiate computer link on your word." It was Dr. Smith.

Alexia glanced around. They were about to make history, or add another scar to this young woman's head. It was time to find out. "Begin."

An instant later the monitor filled with the intense stream of data similar to the single cell.

"Software." Alexia called. "How's the stream? What are we receiving?"

"The data stream is nominal and we are keeping up." Hockman said.

"No. I mean what is the data?"

"How should I know? It looks like the same garbage as before."

"And the rate. Is there more?" Alexia asked.

"No. About the same. Looks about the same. Kind of busy here Doctor Serguey." Hockman barked.

Strange. A whole brain connected and it was the same as a single cell. Of all the things they had expected, this was not one of them. "Dr. Spartan." Alexia called on his private channel.

"Yes, Dr. Serguey."

"Check the physical connection to the cell. Be sure we don't have cross over or multiple neurons."

"Certainly." Spartan answered.

Alexia waited as Dr. Spartan donned the thick headset that connected him directly to the tunneling electron microscope. With it, he could look at each microscopic link.

"Checking." Spartan said. "Checking - "Dr. Spartan's voice was choked off. His back stiffened and he stood up suddenly, his body completely ridged.

"Spartan, what is it? What do you see?" Alexia called.

There was no answer. The others nearest Spartan watched him intently, but still he didn't respond.

"Dr. Spartan. What is it, what did you see?" Alexia was moving to the door when she felt a strong hand on her upper arm.

"Doctor, the room is sterile. You mustn't go in there." Ong said.

"Spartan, answer me." Alexia shouted.

And then, as if he were moving in some heavy liquid, Spartan reached up and yanked the bulky headset from his face. Alexia could see his eyes through the thick observation window. They were wildly dilated.

"The...connection... works." Spartan managed. Then he collapsed to the floor in a heap.

10

I T WAS A moonless November night in central Canada. And it was dark. If not for the feeble light of the threshing machine, one would get lost two feet from the enormous vehicle. Alvar peered dully though the great windscreen of the control room. The headlights were absorbed by the thick forest of wheat, doing little to illuminate their way. In their path, the great stocks towered 20 and 30 feet high, with stems as thick as trees. Giant seed pods hung ponderously in fat grape-like clusters, each berry the size of a coconut. The machine itself was more than two-stories high and over 100 feet long. It chewed through the tall stocks as if they were blades of grass.

Alvar had been picked for this duty for his above average intelligence and his pliable mind. The great machine was automated, guided by GPS and could run for days without stopping. It not only harvested and separated the wheat, it also plowed the field, replanted new seeds and then covered the fresh soil with mulch made from the ground up stocks. The harvested wheat was fed into a large trailer attached to the rear of the machine which was periodically replaced by another robotic machine. But it needed a pilot, someone to be there if anything ever went wrong. It was Alvar's job to stare at the instrument console.

He sat there, half in catatonia, half in concentration. He was pumped with drugs that enhanced his ability to focus on such mundane tasks without getting bored. The corners of his mind were free to roam however. Like clouds drifting into a clear sky, he would dream of his home and previous life. But the thoughts were too difficult to hold onto and like clouds, simply drifted past.

Alvar had been molded into a perfect worker with drugs and genetics. He resisted at first, as all the inmates had, but that was futile. They manipulated his body with genetic engineering, or "'geneering" as the others called it. His skin was thickened with added layers of fat and a lush pelt of fur to keep him warm in the arctic winters. They enhanced his muscles and improved his night vision. The mind alterations took longer, but Alvar was hyper aware of every change as it progressed. He was like a passenger on a train heading for a crash, unable to do a thing about it. His mind was taken from him, transformed into something else, something docile and obedient. But by accident or design, they left a small part that was still him, a kind of trapped observer, a watcher that could do nothing but hate.

If there was a weakness to their system, it was that the subject needed a steady flow of engineered drugs. The titanium collar wrapped around his neck accomplished that, as well as gave his captors constant information on his whereabouts, health and even mental attitude. It was all carefully planned and executed. And no one ever got out.

Alvar noted the time readout, 03:00. Some dull part of his mind told him he'd been out here 11 hours and that there were still 5 hours left in his shift. The machine would stop then, but only long enough for refueling and a shift change. A flash of thought reminded him of his abuse. His mind roiled like a storm cloud on a clear day. But the thought was quickly countered by a squirt of some drug and he went back to dully staring at the gigantic wheat in front of him.

"Base 22 to worker 791. Why have you stopped?" The radio sounded into the cabin.

Alvar looked forward and only now realized the giant stocks of wheat were no longer being pulled into the machine. He also noticed a slight leaning of the entire vehicle. He had no idea how long he'd been staring at this now unchanging scene.

"I don't know." Alvar managed to say.

"Well get outside and find out what's wrong, idiot. And don't touch anything, just get back here and report." The radio voice replied.

Alvar didn't bother with a winter coat. The thick fur covering him was better than any coat. And it wasn't that cold tonight anyway, a mild 10 degrees above zero, Fahrenheit. He walked along the machine on the driver's side, careful to stay clear of the plow blades, mesh and other machinery jutting from underneath and sides of the great beast. He came to the enormous drive wheals at the rear of the main machine. They lurched sporadically continuing to dig themselves into the soft loose soil. There was no hope of going forward. Alvar immediately recognized that a second vehicle would be needed to pull this one forward. A pinch of anger broke through the drugged fog. He'd be blamed, punished and likely forced to pay for the delays. It was how they kept him and the other prisoners here. You were expected to pay the debt of your prison sentence, but every possible expense was piled on to the total. Any crime that got you here, no matter how petty, was in all practicality a life sentence.

Alvar's attention was brought back to the erratically spinning drive wheels. They were indeed digging themselves deeper into the soft soil, but why wasn't the excess dirt piling up behind the giant wheels. As he stared at the strange scene, the giant machine suddenly lurched, but not forward – down. Alvar's drugged-numbed mind tried to understand what he was witnessing. Something far older than thought or drugs took over – the instinct to survive. Alvar leaped back barely in time to avoid the falling of the great machine.

A hole. His mind reeled with the realization. There must be some void or cavern under the field that the great machine was being drawn into. The ground shifted to sand under his feet and the giant stocks of wheat vibrated, then tumbled like toothpicks as everything poured into the growing hole. Everything moved in slow motion as his mind sped forward, desperate to find a way to save himself from being crushed by a thousand tons of grating steel. The path away from the machine was an uphill flow of sliding soil and broken wheat stocks. His racing mind saw the only possibility of safety – the wheels.

The enormous drive wheels were designed to traverse rugged terrain without effort. Each was about 8 feet high and half as wide. There were two at each end of the axle. But to allow for maintenance and keep debris from accumulating, they were mounted about 18" apart – just enough space for a man to crawl between. Alvar dove at the small space between the wheels. The still spinning wheels burned the fur from his left arm. Ignoring the pain, Alvar grabbed the thick greasy axle and pulled himself into void between wheels. At the same time, the entire machine lurched hard toward him. The rough hardened steel of the axle smashed along his face, neck and shoulder. His sight exploded with a flash of pain, then all was black.

Consciousness came back in waves of pain. The side of his face and shoulder felt like a burning fire. And the back of his neck throbbed deeply with each beat of his heart. Alvar, peered into the gloom, fearful of falling into the sharp edges of the broken machine. It was quite dark, but his improved night vision helped him to make out the slow turning of the inner drive wheel. Good, that meant he could have only been only unconscious for a few minutes. He listened for the sound of debris or settling, but all was quiet. Whatever was going to fall, must have fallen.

Alvar dragged himself to the edge of the wheel and looked out. Pain shot through his face and neck, making him gasp. A rare thought bubbled up, I've got to get out of here, maybe there's time to make a run for it before the repair crews come." With that thought, realization that he could even think of escape flashed in his mind. Something had happened to the drugs. Alvar reached up to his neck. The collar was gone! The fall into the axle must have broken the collar away from his neck. Freedom. Every second was precious now. The broken collar would send a signal to base. They were probably on their way already. He felt the dull tug of the drugs still holding him hostage. He'd have to keep moving, burn the chemicals out of his brain with the metabolism of his own body.

The throbbing pain helped. Alvar crawled from his capsule between the wheels and looked at the wreckage before him. The enormous harvesting machine lay on its side in some kind of cavern about 20 feet below the fields. He could see the stars through the break in the ceiling. But it wasn't a cavern, it was man-made. He saw ancient heavy beams running across the width of the open space, broken where the machine had crashed through. The metal beast had landed onto the side where he had been standing moments ago. If he hadn't jumped between the wheels he would have been crushed. Alvar smiled. Maybe the investigation crew would think the same thing. He had to move quickly.

First the collar, he had to find it and stuff it under the wheel. He forced himself back under the threshing machine to feel for the collar. Precious minutes passed as he felt around for it. Nothing. Alvar rubbed absently at the throbbing pain at the back of his neck. There, he felt a smooth bit of metal poking through the matted fur and skin. He grabbed the slick metal and pulled hard, searing pain threatened to take consciousness from him. But he held on. The sharp, broken end of the collar had embedded itself in the thick muscles of his upper neck and shoulder. The collar had come free, but so did a steady stream of blood.

Alvar shoved the broken metal under the tire, all the while allowing the dripping blood to pool there. It would help tell the same story. Done, it was time to leave. Alvar pressed his hand to the wound to staunch the bleeding. But as he suspected, it had slowed to a trickle. The improvements to his body included enhanced healing.

He rubbed his hands in the loose dirt to dry the blood and cover his skin. Then hand over hand, Alvar scaled the machine itself, doing his best to avoid leaving foot and hand prints. He imagined they would have infrared sensors or some other device that could search for his heat signature. But that couldn't be helped. Perhaps they would be fooled long enough for that to dissipate.

Once on the surface, he jumped to the torn ground and faced the forest of enormous wheat. A dread filled him. How could he beat a path through this jungle? In despair he walked up to the torn edge of stocks. They were even larger up close than they appeared from the control window of the threshing machine. Each stock of wheat was as thick as a young tree. Up close, he realized the stocks created gaps in the same way a forest full of trees would. It would never be straight, but there was plenty of room for a man to run between the towering wheat.

And Alvar ran. He ran not as a man escaping the pursuit of his captors, but as a man who enjoyed the movement of his own body. He hated the insult of changing his body to suit their needs, but he loved the feeling of its increased strength. Now that he tested it and controlled it for the first time; it was a magnificent feeling. He was strong and agile. The towering stocks slid by in a blur as he ran and ran, enjoying the steady rhythm of his pumping legs.

The constant movement and flowing of his blood continued to clear his mind. Though he still felt the residual fog of the drugs, he was almost himself. He stopped. It felt good, but it was foolish. Where was he going? He might be headed directly for the main base. He had to find out where he was and where he was heading first.

He climbed a giant stock with ease; the thick branching leaves created a natural ladder. At the top he looked around. He was even with the top of the wheat, not above it, so he couldn't see far. He used his improved night vision to look for movement or man-made lights. There! It must be the repair crew. He could only see the glow of some movement. But it must be where he'd left the threshing machine. But there was no way to see more.

Now time was against him. How long before they discovered his ruse and how much more before they began tracking him? An hour, maybe less. The scenarios ran through his mind. If they thought he was crushed under the machine, there would be no hurry. They would wait until morning or longer to extract the machine. If they thought he escaped, they would begin searching immediately. Or would they?

Alvar looked away from the glow and off into the distance. It was all wheat and dark. How big was this farmland? Miles, certainly. But could it be more. Could it be hundreds of miles of wheat? He combed his drugged memory for clues, but nothing came. He realized he had no idea. But what was the alternative? Alvar peered down at the stocks of wheat below, thick with their grapefruit sized pods of seeds. He would not run out of food, but what about water? It had snowed lightly some days ago and he had walked through some dirty patches. Alvar snatched a final look at the glow in the distance before he descended. He was sure of only one thing, he wasn't going back to that.

11

I T WAS SAID that no one travels *the I* alone. It was an old saying and no one remembered its origin. But everyone knew its meaning – whatever done or said on *the I* was permanent. A drunken picture at a party, a recording of an angry message to an ex-girlfriend. It all stayed in the virtual ethers forever. It might sit unobserved for years, but eventually the evidence was there for anyone who knew how to find it. But most people didn't take the statement literally – that you were being watched during your travels, or shadowed as they used to say. Certainly someone as competent as Ezekiel would never allow such a possibility.

Ezekiel had finally located Alvar again after many weeks of failure. His last meeting with Chloe was a challenge that he couldn't decline. And it was a grand challenge. It was one thing to find out that Alvar was a prisoner and a farm worker, it was quite another to track him within their system. The prisoners became numbers, the numbers became statistics and the statistics became profit and loss statements.

But finally, Ezekiel got a break. And there was Alvar - a green blip on the dispatcher's tracking terminal. Worker 791 was commanding a class 3 threshing machine in the heartland of Incorporated Canada. There wasn't much to watch. The blip moved slowly, the fields were immense and the shifts were long. Ezekiel took pleasure in his success, but quickly became bored with the result. Sure he found him and he was probably trans-formed into some human hybrid, but without video, a picture, or even a printed description, what did he have to show Chloe. He couldn't just go up to her and say: "I found your boyfriend, he's working in Canada. What, how's he doing? I don't know, all I have is a tracking blip." Not a good dating line. So he waited.

A week after Ezekiel's initial discovery of Alvar, he stared at the track-ing blip on the dispatcher's terminal. He could read the tiny number next to the dot: 791 as it moved imperceptibly in the coded rectangle that meant wheat. It was tortuously boring. Ezekiel put the tracking on auto - to alert him if there were any changes, or when Alvar got off shift. Maybe there would be a surveillance video or monitor that he could capture, though after a week, he didn't have much hope of this either, but still he had to try. Might as well get some sleep he thought. Ezekiel simply closed his eyes, as he was already comfortably lounging in his jack-chair.

Chloe danced seductively in his dreams, slowly peeling off her rough, hand-made cloths. Each layer revealed yet another underneath. Each pro-gressively rougher: cotton revealed wool, then burlap, then hemp. The luscious curves of her body were increasingly hidden with each succeeding layer.

The auto alarm buzzer was a welcome relief from the frustrating dream. Ezekiel was still jacked into *the I*, so he only had to think himself awake. It was like imagining opening one's eyes, but not actually doing it. Alvar's blip had disappeared from the dispatcher's tracking terminal. Ezekiel gave a mental shrug. He's off-duty, so what. "I guess I'll watch for a while, see if I can catch a glimpse of the ghost." Ezekiel thought, still shaking off the cobwebs of his dream.

Ezekiel moved his attention to the bleak prison housing units. But he found he couldn't enter here any longer. The security screens had been raised and everything was off-line. Interesting. He moved back to dis-patch to find out what was happening. It didn't take long to learn the details. Ezekiel sighed heavily – the moron had gotten himself crushed under a million pound threshing machine. Would it free Chloe from her idiot boyfriend or make her hate the messenger. Hard to say.

Crews were dispatched over the next several days to assess the damage. They had removed the receiving chamber at the back of the machine, but pulling the actual threshing machine from the collapsing cavern had proven difficult (expensive, Ezekiel translated to himself). Except for the initial report, no further mention of worker 791 had been given. But that wasn't surprising. Still something nagged at Ezekiel's mind, no remains were found, only that the collar had transmitted a catastrophic failure signal at the same moment the thresher had fallen. It was logical that he was dead, but not conclusive. Alvar was a wily character; Ezekiel had seen the reports regarding his psychotropic drug therapy. It had taken three times as long to control him compared to the average prisoner. Ezekiel just couldn't shake the feeling Alvar was alive. So he watched, occasionally tapping into the satellite feed to look at the wheat fields. He gave that up quickly. If Alvar was out there, he was far smaller than a needle in a haystack.

<hr>

There was another who didn't give up so easily.

A woman, 1,000 miles away who had been piggybacking Ezekiel's signal for months. Watching him, trailing him, following his bizarre behavior. Ezekiel was legendary among those with similar skills. The woman's name was Sigé. And she was Ezekiel's equal, if not superior in skill and talent. But she traveled *the I* differently and was thoroughly intrigued by his strange methods. Where Ezekiel was reckless, she was cautious, where he was arrogant, she was humble. Nothing on *the I* surprised her of course, she was no stranger to virtual sex rooms, corporate firewalls, or breaking into government facilities. But Ezekiel's choices were strange, not random exactly, but inexplicable. One day he would crack into a bank site and another he would be watching a low tech group from a GSA satellite. She couldn't find the pattern and that fascinated her.

She'd learned about Alvar through Ezekiel's wanderings. A man who shunned modern technology, who had no trace on *the I*. Sigé was drawn to his simplicity, the driving goal to be apart from everything modern, to plow the fields by hand, build houses out of wood, read books made from paper. It was silly and somehow so charming that she couldn't put him out of her mind. She had seen only one image of him before his genetic modifications, taken during his capture. Sigé's chest flushed with the memory.

Since then, she had followed Alvar continuously, only losing his signal after the crash of the thresher. She had been frantically trying to find him since. Like Ezekiel she didn't believe he'd be killed, not because of a hunch, but because she couldn't believe someone so vital could be killed. She broke into the UnitedFarms' satellite feed as easily as opening an unlocked door. She placed her anxiety into a container in another part of her mind and started the slow process of scanning the fields.

The satellite was equipped with the most advanced sensor equipment. It could pick up a wide portion of the electromagnetic spectrum: visual light, ultra violet and most important, infra-red. But by the time she'd gotten into the satellite it was morning, the heat of the warming fields hid the subtle detail of a man's heat, especially one covered in insulating fur. Those hours had been the worst of her life, scanning the fields over and over, looking for movement or some sign of life. Doubt and fear filled her and yet she refused to go back to the prison dispatcher's feed, superstitiously afraid she'd be betraying Alvar if she did.

During that torturous day, every movement of every stock of wheat made her heart jump. But it was a just a breeze or some super genetic rodent chewing on the grapefruit sized grains. Sigé did the calculations, how fast could an uninjured man run. The search area grew exponentially with each agonizing hour. "Oh Alvar, I don't have to find you, just be alive." She cried in her head.

Finally, night came on and the advantage of the infra-red cameras returned. The area to scan was vast now. If he had gone 20 miles, which was entirely possible, the area to scan was over 1200 square miles – and growing 200 square miles every hour. If he was injured, he might be only a hundred feet from the crash site, so that couldn't be dismissed either. All the while she ignored her nagging doubts and refused to tap into the prison dispatcher's feed. She was convinced he was free and that she would find him.

Providence was being kind to her, it was a cold clear night and the wheat stocks gradually lost their stored heat of the day. Unfortunately, it wasn't as simple as looking for a large heat signature in the vast area. The enormous height and density of the stocks diffused anything warm that was on the ground. However, Sigé began to grow encouraged when she was able to find the nests of a number of super rodents. Their combined heat signatures were about as large as a grown man, which sent her on many false leads. Sigé also knew this would thwart UnitedFarms if they were looking for Alvar too. "Run Alvar." She mentally urged. "I'll find you anyway."

Deep into the night, nearly 30 hours since she'd begun her search and more than two days since she'd slept, Sigé stumbled upon an unmoving heat signature. Her weary mind and heart sighed, probably another nest. But she zoomed in to investigate. It was blurry through the wheat and she could only guess its size. She watched for several minutes while nothing moved. "Do something, kick each other, scurry away you filthy creatures." Her mind screamed. Then a long thin shape emerged from the mass – could it be an arm or leg! It had to be. It was a man, it was Alvar. And her eyes blurred with tears as she sobbed silently.

Her fatigue evaporated. Sigé watched the still mass for the rest of the night, mentally hugging and caressing it. He was nearly 25 miles from the crash site. A long distance for a man on foot, an impossible distance for an injured one. She zoomed out to see where he was and more important, to see where he was heading. The fields were vast, spreading in every direction for at least another hundred miles. There was the occasional equipment outpost, but there were no cities for hundreds of miles. And worse for Alvar, he was heading north. It was early winter now. If he did remain free, how long could he stay out there without shelter when the real cold came on, 20 and 30 degrees below zero.

In that moment, she made up her mind to help Alvar. She would either rescue him, or if that became impossible, she'd report him to UnitedFarms – but she wouldn't let him die out there.

Ezekiel watched the clumsy retrieval of the giant threshing machine. Apparently, it was valuable enough to warrant its recovery, or perhaps it wasn't damaged as bad as it looked. Ezekiel was watching from the UnitedFarms' Satellite feed. They controlled it, he only had to piggyback their signal for a fabulous view. He munched buttered popcorn as the cranes connected the heavy cables to the thresher. The enormous machine shuddered once, then began to rise. A cable must have been fastened poorly, or broke loose and the thresher smashed to the ground with a puff of dust. "Ooh Alvar, that's gonna leave a bruise." Ezekiel laughed at his joke, spitting a cloud of popcorn into the air.

Soon they fixed the cables and added others and the behemoth began to rise again. Ezekiel held his breath watching for the crushed mess that would be Alvar. Ezekiel had tapped into the audio feed of local crews on the ground.

"Steady, steady." A man said. "Another five feet and she's clear. There. That's it, now swing her to your left. Slowly, slowly, this bastard's heavy, don't give her any momentum. A little more, we want to be completely clear of the hole. That's it. Now set her down, but not all the way, let's see if we can right her at the same time."

The dialog went on like this for a while as they tried to right the thresher. Ezekiel watched and listened impatiently. There was no mention of a prisoner, not even if there was anything stuck to the wheels. "Come on guys, I ain't got all day." Ezekiel barked at the video feed.

Finally the thresher was righted and he heard one of the voices chime in.

"Tony here. Come over here, look what I found."

Ezekiel grew alert, anticipating the smashed and frozen carcus. He watched as the satellite view swung around to the center the cavern.

The man called Tony held the broken collar above his head. "Sonofabitch got away."

Ezekiel frowned, "for now boys, only for now."

12

AFTER THE SUCCESS of the experiment the previous night, the lab was frenetic with activity. No one wanted to risk missing anything new. There was a great deal of information that had to be analyzed from the brain connection with Bertha, but much of the work was tedious and routine; not deserving the kind of excitement that was evident now. Alexia shrugged, the initial excitement would wane. They were all professionals and would recognize the amount of work to be done and pace themselves accordingly.

Dr. Spartan was not doing well after collapsing following the connection with Bertha. He may have simply been ill, but nothing showed up on tests. There was some speculation that he had some kind of synthetic or geneered virus, or that the nanobots had gotten into his brain, but they had yet to find any evidence. He was resting in his apartment in a near state of catatonia.

Alexia made time the following day to see him. "Dr. Spartan, are you feeling better?" He sat on the edge of the bed, simply staring at the far wall.

Spartan turned slowly toward her voice, but not quite far enough and stared without focus at a point a few feet to her right.

"Dr. Spartan, it's Dr. Serguey. We are all quite concerned. Is there anything you can tell us that might help?"

Very slowly as if moving through a think fluid, he turned and focused on Alexia's face. "I...am very tired."

"Please, Dr. Spartan, it's very important. Can you tell us what happened to you?"

Alexia looked at Spartan closely now. The top of his bald head was shiny with perspiration. His clothes stuck to his body in great dark spots, and his face was red and blotchy. Alexia feared that he had a dangerously high fever. She was about to call in a medic, when Spartan began to speak.

"...must have...brain implant. I..." His lips kept moving, but his voice simply stopped coming out of his mouth.

"Dr. Spartan, you're very ill, you have a fever and we must get you to the infirmary. I'll call..."

"Not sick!" He shouted. "Must have...brain implant. My mind... altered...by experiment. Please...not delay." And he stopped, exhausted by the effort.

"What! Your brain was altered by the experiment? But that's impossible, you were only looking at the connection through the electron microscope..." Alexia cut herself off. That must be it. Somehow, the link that should have only affected Bertha, affected his mind too. The optic nerve is the most direct external sensory connection to the brain. Alexia linked to her VR set and contacted the neuro-science section. "Lurst? Good, I want you in Doctor Spartan's apartment immediately. Bring a hyper-encephalograph."

Then she turned back to Spartan. "I have a neurographist on his way to measure your brain waves. If there are any measurable changes, we'll find them. Now please help me understand. Tell me what happened."

Spartan's face contorted with the effort. Alexia waited while he forced the words out.

"The connection with Cory...not called Bertha...triggered...stimulated...dormant brain center to activate. Center is for...connection to...others. I...not connected. Pressure building. Cannot think, cannot think.

Must have implant...for normal brain function. Must have implant...relieve pressure." And then Spartan stopped, exhausted.

"Dr. Spartan. Will it help if I speak and you just nod or shake your head?" He nodded quickly. "Good. Are you sure about this brain center?" He nodded, then shook his head. At that moment the neurographist had arrived with his equipment.

"OK I want you to rest a moment. Mr. Lurst is going to measure your brain for any anomalies. As you know this process is completely painless and will only take a few moments." Spartan nodded.

Alexia watched as Mr. Lurst connected the leads to Spartan's head and plugged them into the machine. In a moment, they had several images on the screen. One was a three dimensional picture of the brain with changing colors representing blood flow and electrical activity. Another screen showed the workings of the lower brain centers, such as the brain stem, cerebellum and thalamus. A third screen monitored isolated activity of the cerebral cortex by individual lobe. A long narrow monitor tracked the individual brain waves.

Mr. Lurst looked nervously back and forth at the monitor, adjusted some leads, then turned to Dr. Spartan intently. He moved close to Alexia so Spartan would not hear what he was saying. "Dr. Serguey, there is something very strange about the readings I'm getting." He gestured to the agitated figure of Dr. Spartan. "I think we should speak in private."

Alexia looked at Spartan and then thought of herself in his position. Would she want technicians whispering about her condition behind her back, speculating in private about her brain. "No, whatever the results, we'll discuss them here. Dr. Spartan is a scientist, an expert in brain function. If there is something anomalous, he should hear it as we discover it. He may be able to help."

Lurst nodded, then turned the monitors so that they could all see them, he began pointing at specific regions. "Dr. Serguey, I can't explain what I'm looking at. Dr. Spartan's entire forebrain is active."

"He is obviously quite agitated and perhaps is searching his memory or other such..."

"No Dr. Serguey, you misunderstand – the entire cerebrum is active.

That just doesn't happen. The brain uses areas for certain functions, but it doesn't use everything at once. In fact, the brain uses very little of its capacity at any one time. But look, here and here, every part of Dr. Spartan's cortex is on - fully on. It would be like plugging in and turning on every appliance, every light, every computer, everything that required electricity in an entire city. The strain on the power grid would cause it to overload. I cannot imagine what he is going through. It must be a terrible effort just to stay conscious."

"Thank you Mr. Lurst. I don't think you need to speculate on Dr. Spartan's mental state. Let's concentrate on the facts."

Lurst reddened. "Of course, Dr. Serguey."

"And perhaps there is something wrong with your equipment, or it is calibrated improperly." Alexia said.

"No." Spartan blurted. "Equipment is right." Then he crumpled again.

Lurst said. "Look here Dr. Serguey, at the bottom screen, the EEG readings are...My god! There's an additional brain wave pattern. But that's not possible. Dr. Serguey look at this!" He pointed excitedly at the little squiggles of the graph plotting the brain waves. Alexia followed his finger and indeed there was a new and unique frequency emanating from Dr. Spartan's brain.

"Yes Mr. Lurst, we've seen this pattern on Bertha, I mean Cory." She nodded to Dr. Spartan. "It is some kind of echo, or error with the machine."

They both turned and looked at the contorted form of Dr. Spartan on the bed. Lurst spoke first. "Dr. Serguey, I am not a doctor, but I've scanned a lot of brains. This man cannot remain in this state for long, just the energy demand alone must be staggering." As Lurst said this, he walked over and felt the top of Spartan's bald head. By the way he pulled his hand away, it was obviously very warm.

Alexia turned to Spartan, "And this happened just by witnessing the connection of the brain implant on Cory?"

Spartan nodded jerkily.

Suddenly Alexia's eyes went wide. She linked on her VR set. "Ong, emergency connection."

"Dr. Serguey, this is Ong." Ong replied over the VR terminal.

"Stop the second implant on Cory!"

"Cory?"

"I mean Bertha, just stop any brain implants until I..."

"It's already complete Dr. Serguey. Dr. Smith just finished the second implant a few minutes ago."

"What!"

"We ran the experiment as you directed Dr. Serguey. Dr. Smith ran it herself. She just went back to her quarters, she said she was suddenly quite tired. You can probably call her there right now."

"Damn!" She shouted and pulled the headset off, disconnecting the communication.

Lurst stood there quietly staring at his monitors, trying not to be noticed.

"You...must...implant module...now." Spartan struggled to say.

Alexia looked at the monitors and back at Spartan. If she didn't do something right away, Spartan might have brain damage or worse. There appeared to be no choice. "OK. Mr. Lurst, pull your leads we're moving Dr. Spartan to the main surgical room."

Ten minutes later they were preparing for surgery. A dozen technicians moved furiously around Dr. Spartan. The biggest delay was the nano team. They had to synthesize the DNA-specific nanobots that would manipulate the connection of the tiny brain module. Everything they had done was geared to Cory's specific micro-anatomy. Alexia took the initiative to have them begin the fabrication of nanobots for Dr. Smith as well. She was resting in her apartment, but it was obvious she was now going through the same hell as Spartan.

A flashing red light in the corner of her vision alerted her of an emergency call. Alexia had turned off her VR set to keep from being disturbed.

Hamachi! In all the frenzied activity, she'd forgotten all about him. She mentally kicked herself as she established a link. "Serguey here."

"I expect to be informed when one of my top scientists suddenly becomes part of an experiment." The semi-transparent form of Hamachi's face filled her vision.

"I'm sorry Mr. Hamachi, we're in an emergency situation, there was no time to explain. Spartan has been...infected by the...by whatever happens when viewing the live implant. Dr. Smith has also succumbed to this effect. The remedy appears to be actually implanting the module into their brains."

"Dr. Spartan was exposed two days ago and now you determine this miracle cure in...what, ten minutes?"

While Alexia bristled at the insult, she knew better than to acknowledge it or become defensive. Instead she patiently described the extreme brain activity and additional brain wave pattern - that Spartan's brain was literally cooking inside his head.

"You have done every conceivable test on the original subject, why didn't you discover this additional brain wave pattern in her readings?" Hamachi questioned.

"Well we did see them, but ignored them. Brain wave patterns are ancient technology without a lot of information. They are too general, more like noise than data."

"Perhaps you shouldn't have ignored them." Hamachi hissed.

"It would have made little difference. But yes, you're right, we won't anymore. Which leads us back to the problem at hand. Now that you know what I know, may we proceed with the implant in Dr. Spartan?"

"And Smith?"

"Yes, and Smith if it works." Alexia said.

"There seems to be no choice. But this time, measure every possible reading and please don't let anyone else become infected." Hamachi paused. The audio was muted as he turned to one side. His mouth was blurred, but he appeared to be speaking with someone in the room. A moment later he was facing Alexia again. "Dr. Serguey, perform both implants simultaneously."

"What! Why? That is just bad..."

"Do it." And before she could protest again, Hamachi's virtual form evaporated.

"Damn. That just doesn't make any sense." She thought. "If something goes wrong, we won't be able to avoid the problem on the second subject." But it was clear, if she didn't do as Hamachi insisted, someone else would.

"Ong, retrieve Dr. Smith and prepare her for implantation. We're doing both procedures simultaneously."

Ong raised her eyebrows, but simply nodded.

In a few minutes, Dr. Lani Smith was lying next to Dr. Spartan. And like him she was sweating profusely. Her eyes moved about erratically.

"Dr. Smith, can you hear me?" Alexia said.

After a long pause, "Yes."

Dr. Spartan insists that the only way to help you, is to perform the brain implant. Do you agree?"

"Yes. No other...way. Must hurry...brain not..." Smith trailed off.

Alexia walked away from her two patients, over to the scanning station. There Lurst and others were watching the brain activity.

"Dr. Serguey look at this." Lurst pointed at one of the screens. "It's impossible. It has to be impossible."

"What's impossible, I don't understand what you're looking at." Alexia was tired of surprises.

"The new brain waves, they're identical."

"What do you mean, identical, you mean they both have them."

"No Dr. Serguey, they are the same, exactly the same." Lurst manipulated the screen, until the two new brain patterns of Smith and Spartan filled the screen. Then he slowly superimposed them. "See. They're identical."

"Impossible. Wait, put Cory's pattern up there too. See if hers is also the same?"

In a second, Cory's additional brain wave was superimposed onto the other two. It was clearly identical.

"And these are current readings? And you're sure we're not just reading some kind of interference, radio transmission, something like that?" Alexia's asked.

"No. We've tested everything, there is no mistake. I can't explain it. But there's more. When we brought Dr. Smith into the room, the amplitude of the new wave increased. This would be normal for a sound wave or radio wave in the open. Identical frequencies multiply in amplitude. But brain waves are so weak they are not in the open, they don't influence each other."

"Until now." Alexia interrupted. "Continue monitoring. Let me know if you find anything else."

"Dr. Serguey. The nano team is ready and standing by." Ong said.

"What about the recording teams, are they ready to monitor two patients now?"

"Yes. Everything is ready on your approval."

Alexia felt the weight of the decision as they all stared at her for direction. "OK, then let's begin."

The sterile nanobots were applied to the incision areas and the two doctor's skulls were opened. The implant nanobots were introduced through the opening, alongside the microscopic leads coming from each doctor's head.

"Nanobots inserted and working." The nanobot technician toned into Alexia's ear. "Connection complete." He added a moment later.

"Very well, activate the link." Alexia directed.

She watched Spartan intently during the activation. Suddenly all the tension and pain left his face. She shot a look over to Dr. Smith, and she too looked relieved. "Lurst, What's happening?"

Lurst's face was buried in the monitors. "Aside from the additional brain wave, all three have normal brain activity. They appear to be...sleeping Dr. Serguey."

13

HAMACHI DIDN'T LOOK up from his desk, "Come in Dr. Serguey."

Alexia strode across Hamachi's large office, fighting vertigo, as she attempted to ignore the transparent floor and the 4,000 foot drop beneath her feet. Hamachi could have easily turned the floor opaque to make it easier on his visitors, but he preferred the view to their comfort.

"Sit down doctor. There is much to discuss." He directed her to a sitting area off to the side of the main office. The floor was solid there, and he saw the relief in Alexia's eyes.

"Please update me on the progress of the recent brain implants on doctors Spartan and Smith." Hamachi said.

"They're still sleeping, as is the original test subject." She said perfunctorily.

"Yes, I know. And their brain patterns?"

"Hard to explain. We are monitoring the brain waves of all three continuously. We are watching and recording the new pattern, which we've named omicron waves." She looked up at Hamachi, who nodded to continue. "These ultra-high frequency brain waves are likely an artifact, or even interference. It is possible the implant changes something in the brain to create the waves. We can't read them on any other subjects. But it is also possible the wave is already there, just too weak to read until the connection is implemented. However, I am not convinced the new brain wave is not interference. That all three are identical certainly points that direction.

"Perhaps, but let's not jump to conclusions too rapidly. What about the heavy brain activity that led to the implants?"

"Brain activity in all three subjects has dropped to..." Serguey hesitated, "normal levels."

Hamachi stared hard at Dr. Serguey, frustrated with her evasiveness. "Doctor, there is no normal any longer. Explain what you mean clearly, or I will speak with one of your staff who will."

Serguey reddened. "I am not trying to avoid an answer, there just isn't one. The overall level of brain activity is the same as any other sleeping subject, it is just that it seems to move more. In other words, while we are dreaming, certain areas of our brain are activated, while others are quiet. This is the same in the three subjects. But it tends to shift a bit more than average. It is subtle. It was only noticed when one of the technicians put all three scans on the monitor simultaneously. He found the movement to be the same in all three subjects."

"And you find this normal doctor?" Hamachi said. "Three individuals with an additional identical brain wave pattern, and brain activity that moves in concert. You call that normal?"

"No." She blurted. "I only meant normal for a sleeping person. Everyone's brain is different, there is no standard amount of activity."

Hamachi raised his hand for her to stop. Dr. Serguey was brilliant and competent, but could be defensive when challenged. He looked off into the distance, to the extraordinary view of the canyon valley. It was winter on the canyon rim, snow covered the brown leaves of the scrub oak. But down below on the canyon floor, it was still late autumn, golds and reds swarmed the river banks. The canyon was so vast one could see more than one climate zone at a time. Large events were that way too. And he understood Serguey's hesitation. Many employees had this flaw, they were terrified of being wrong, stumbling in front of the boss, afraid of punishment. It was tedious, like working with children.

It made him think of his father, the ancient founder of Mitasashi Corporation. As no one had heard from him in so long, they assumed he had died years ago. But he lived on in a care facility in Phoenix, Arizona, not that far from Stratumentis. Hamachi had visited his father several months ago. He returned cursing the biological advances that could keep a man alive for 140 years but not sustain his brain function. Hamachi's father, the tower of strength and creativity that had single-handedly brought virtual reality to the world, was now a living, breathing vegetable. All the gene manipulation in the world wasn't capable of saving a rotting brain.

Thinking of his father reminded him of his childhood. A childhood very different from any other. Of course, he hadn't known that at the time. He had been named Tatsuo after his grandfather. Hamachi's mother had died in an accident shortly after his birth. As a child, he called his father Kyo, or sir, and knew no other name for him most of his life. The elder Hamachi trained him from birth to be the independent man that he is today. But it had been hard for the young Tatsuo Hamachi to live up to the old man's standards. There was never time for play, everything was training. Hamachi recalled analyzing financial reports when others his age were learning how to count; or learning about management styles when others were playing sports.

When he was old enough, he began working at the mighty headquarters of Mitasashi Corporation, not as a manager or executive, but as a clerk. He worked his way up from the bottom, advancing quickly. Everyone knew he was the son of the great founder, Akio Hamachi, but instead of helping, they were told to judge him harsher than his coworkers. So when he became vice-president of manufacturing in his mid-twenties, it was because he had thoroughly earned it. Hamachi was never bitter about the way his father had made him struggle, how every advancement was a towering wall. He had learned to relish challenges, embrace them.

But something happened when he reached the management plateau of senior vice-president. The mechanical challenges of advancement were understandable, even calculable. But there was the ultimate challenge that he knew he was not ready for - unseating his father, yet he must scale this wall too. For the first time in his young adult life, Hamachi experienced doubt.

Hamachi worked in his job as senior vice-president of manufacturing for several years. He became very good at it, bringing advance after advance to the company, performing better than anyone in the position had ever done. But when he would meet with his father, though the old man would say little or nothing, Hamachi would read disappointment in his eyes. Hamachi knew his own obstacle was not fear, or even ability, but lack of experience. He had learned about business from the moment of his birth, but he had not learned about people. He was an alien on his own planet.

Hamachi placed three of his underlings in charge of his job, then took a leave of absence.

"How long will you be gone?" They asked. "As long as it takes," was his reply, "but be ready for my return, because I will be back when you least expect it."

He bowed deeply to his father when he told him of his decision to leave Mitasashi for a time. The old man did not say a word, but the hint of a smile was all Hamachi needed to know he had made the right decision.

Eight years later he returned - a different man. Blind arrogance had been replaced by confidence born of experience.

"I can see by your face Tatsuo, that you are changed. Will you tell me of your experiences?" Akio Hamachi asked his son.

Hamachi looked at his father for a long time. The elder Hamachi looked young and healthy. His body was constantly replenished with gene therapy and implants, but the eyes were old, frail, tired from the years of work, of struggle. Hamachi felt a deep respect for his father, the man who had never shown him a moment's affection or undeserved kindness. But deep down, Hamachi realized a certain feeling had left him– he realized he was no longer afraid of his father. "Yes, father, I will tell you everything."

"I started at the bottom as you taught me. At the lowest dregs of humanity, those who have little right to call themselves men. There is much

I am not proud of, but I am grateful for everything that happened." His father gave a subtle nod of understanding. "As I said, I began at the bottom. It is indeed a cruel world to those who do not have the drive to pull themselves out of the gutter. But I was on a quest to learn about my fellow creatures. The question that I never answered was why? But I'm getting ahead of myself.

"They live in the shell city that surrounds this one, that surrounds all cities, the abandoned buildings and homes that are too decrepit to house anyone with a shred of dignity. I lived with them, ate their rotting food, slept in their louse infested beds with their filthy daughters. I drank their homemade alcohol that blurred their world into something bearable. I didn't stay long. The only lesson worth learning from these people, was that humanity without drive, is the basest thing on earth. Animals are higher beings, at least they have a purpose and use in the world. These men and women only take up space and consume resources that they cannot replace. What little pity I had for them turned to revulsion. It was soon time to move on."

Hamachi remembered the look on his father's face. He was old and perhaps no longer capable of hiding his emotion. Hamachi saw a shadow of regret pass over his father's face. For the old man must have realized the danger Hamachi had faced among those people. He was a stern teacher, but he was also a father.

Hamachi continued, "So I cleaned myself up and used my money to enter the opposite end of society – the levels at the very top closed to all but a handful of men. You are wealthy enough to join these men and women, father, but you never did, did you? I wanted to learn why. So I joined them, the so-called elite. I joined their clubs, went to their dinner parties and listened to their stilted conversations. And I admit, at first I was charmed by it all. It was so comfortable and stimulating next to the drab existence of the filth I had just left. I had nagging doubts, however, but I thought, 'perhaps these are my peers.' I dug deeper, wanting to know more about them too.

"I learned the real meaning of decadence. The real purpose of life was pleasure, they told me – in all its forms. I tasted their food and wine, some delicacies so rare, only one man in the world was trusted to its preparation. I tried their designer drugs tailored to an individual's DNA; drugs that would give them the confidence and arrogance they needed to carry on in their lives. I joined in their sexual fantasies, some so elaborate it took dozens of people and weeks to prepare. They've created a special class of prostitutes genetically altered to fill every desire – no matter how perverse.

"But beneath it all, the parties, the travel, the sex, the fantasies, I realized that they were bored of life. Oh, not all of them of course, but those that weren't bored, didn't stay at the parties, they returned to their work, something drove them away. It wasn't hard to understand what it was, they had purpose in life and all the money in the world would not have kept them from it, they needed to create. And I understood that and longed for it myself. You taught me that.

"When I realized this, I knew there was nothing more to learn from these people, but also that I was not ready to return to my world, not yet. Because there was a great mass of society I knew nothing about, the teaming billions who work every day, because they have to."

Hamachi looked hard into his father's eyes.

The senior Hamachi interrupted for the first time. "These are the people who need Mitasashi, who make our company what it is. You learned why this company exists and thrives, didn't you?"

"Yes father. I learned that, but much more." Hamachi paused, collecting his thoughts. "I joined the mass of society so stupidly labeled the middle class. A moniker that means nothing. There was far more variety and detail than I was prepared for. And certainly, I'm not so naïve as to think that meeting a few thousand individuals qualifies me for knowing the billions, but I saw enough to understand mankind deeply. As you said, to know the men and women that Mitasashi serves," and Hamachi paused, "and more important, who serve it."

"Men live by our products, which have changed the very fabric of society. Man is a social animal and he must communicate with other men, or he will shrivel and die, this is nature. But it was harder than I realized to get to know these creatures. They are hidden, huddled in the dark honeycombs of the city. Some don't come out for months – living alone, meeting others only on the overly lit streets of virtual reality. The few like this I was able to get to know are damaged beings, crippled from lack of sleep and real interaction with others. They work hard and perform their jobs well enough, but they are hollowed out shells – robots.

"But those are not the majority of mankind. I was still on the fringes, still hacking my way into the heart of the jungle. Of course they were not hidden, or even difficult to find. It was my own blindness that kept me from the men all around us. They were beneath my very nose, they are the men and women who work right outside these doors, in this building, on the VR sets that plug into our many virtual satellite offices. But because these men are so ubiquitous, they are also invisible.

"Once I realized this, I joined them. I entered their lives, lived in their crowded apartments, ate their synthetic food. They are the model of adaptability and when jobs are scarce, two or three will share one. Time zones and work hours have long since become illusions. One can as easily work in New York as New Singapore. With some simple software, two men can pretend to be one man working a 24 hour job without sleep. But they pay a price for their cleverness. Many are addicted to cheap stimulants, like synthadrene to stay awake, or tranquilizers like somnadrone to sleep. Their homes are crowded and they breed too fast, so when disease flares, it spreads like a plague.

"Their sleep-deprived brains have induced many to modify their bodies to reflect their strange images of themselves. I've seen men and women with gills, additional limbs, or insect-like eyes. Some have experimented with plant DNA, growing flowers from their skin. I saw many who were so deformed, nothing could bring them back.

"But through all this, one thing remains, their insatiable desire for virtual reality, where they can still be anything they wish to be. It is the power of a dream, without the necessity to wake up. And they are all addicted to it. Those are the people we serve."

The elder Hamachi was the first to break the long silence that followed, "Yes, son. It is good you left here, left the womb, so you can see what mankind has become. I am proud of the products we make, not because of the money or the illusion of power it gives us, but because it had to be this way. I did not create virtual reality, nor did I invent the VR glasses that makes all this possible. But I did perfect these products and make them available to the men and women who demand them. Addiction is a choice, always a choice. They choose to travel *the I* as avatars that are inhumanly beautiful, or unnaturally strong. Mitasashi does not create these illusions, it simply produces the means. If reality is too dull for a man, then let him choose the brightness of virtual reality. If reality is too dangerous, let him choose the safe, risk-free world of *the I*, where he can fly through the clouds, or swim at the bottom of the ocean without fear. We are not gods Tatsuo, standing atop Mount Olympus, judging their choices. We are men and we create what other men demand."

Hamachi nodded. "Yes father. But I learned that I am one man and that I must live my own life, not yours and not theirs. And father, you are wrong about one thing. Not all gods stand on Mount Olympus."

His father narrowed his eyes.

"I shall take over this company, father. I will take your position and make Mitasashi Corporation what it was meant to be: the largest and most important company in the world. But father, with all due respect, I will do it my way."

The elder Hamachi sighed, the strength of will that had sustained him all these years suddenly left him. His body sagged, revealing the weariness of time through his artificial youth. "Then it is done. My body is young, but my spirit is old and tired. You will begin today." He bowed slightly to his son, not lowering his eyes, the way one does with an adversary – or enemy. Then the elder Hamachi left the office that had been his for so many decades. Father and son never spoke again.

Hamachi looked away from the spectacular view of the Grand Canyon. He brushed off the cobwebs of his past and looked back at Dr. Serguey. She had been staring at him, frightened by his prolonged silence.

"Speculate." Hamachi said. "Why are their brains harmonizing?"

Serguey frowned. "I think they're preparing to communicate with each other."

"Interesting." Hamachi urged, "go on."

"Smith and Spartan only witnessed the connection, but it activated something in their brains, something dormant. Whether we are evolving toward some kind of...communication, or have evolved away from it. The fact remains, it is within us – all of us."

"Telepathy doctor?" Hamachi asked.

"I didn't say that. But there appears to be some influence, a subtle kind of communication that keeps the brains moving together. We've watched their REM sleep, the dream state and recorded their eye movements. After slowing them down – they too are identical. You asked me to speculate and I have no other explanation."

Hamachi sat back in the thick leather chair and thought to himself: "Was it possible, human communication without sound or sight. It had been a myth for so long, no scientist could possibly take it seriously, but maybe here it was, right in front of them." Then he spoke aloud to Dr. Serguey, "How long have they been sleeping?"

"A little over 10 hours."

Hamachi's eyes burned into Alexia's. "Wake Spartan. It's time to find out what's happening."

14

ALVAR HAD BEEN heading north for weeks. He considered turning around several times, making his way south out of the Corporate Provinces of Canada. But he'd gone so far already, he wasn't sure his spirit could take it, repeating all those miles. And this would be the last direction his pursuers would expect. He was certain they had discovered his escape by now. The real problem was staying alive until he found some kind of civilization and ultimately a way back to Chloe. But so far, he had found nothing but geneered wheat.

It was deep winter now and the long nights had turned bitterly cold. The genetically altered wheat grew slowly up here. He sometimes trudged for days without finding mature seeds. The immature wheat berries caused intense stomach cramps. But Alvar kept at it, hoping his body would adapt. It was that or starvation.

Alvar lay on his back on this clear cold night staring up at the brilliant stars seemingly close enough to touch. He was under no illusions now, he would not make it through the winter, perhaps not through the month. It was beautiful here, the sky, the stars, the bright moon when it was out. He had learned to love the sky. He wasn't sad about himself, everyone died, but he wondered about his people, the Anti-Techs. If UnitedFarms had gotten rid of him so easily, what would happen to the rest? And dear Chloe, his lover, what would happen to her? She was always on his mind, the beautiful doe who would rather help a stranger than herself. How would she fare in the technological hell that was crowding in on them? When Gaialandra fell would they arrest her, modify her body too. But into what? A love slave, a doll that served bored laborers. Alvar ground he teeth as his imagination tormented him, but also kept him going.

Though exhausted, sleep refused to come. Alvar rose slowly, brushing the leaves and stocks off his body he used for insulation at night. And there he saw it, a bare spot on his right forearm. It was the third spot he'd discovered in the last several days. Alvar had cursed the genetic modifications they had made to his body, then marveled at his own ability to stay warm in these arctic conditions. But something was going wrong. Perhaps it was the poor steady diet of raw wheat berries, or maybe the genetic modifications didn't last, or maybe, he smiled wryly, he was molting.

Alvar had lost any real hope of escape and the long miles were counted off simply as a job each day. At first he traveled into the night, but an ancient memory warned him about being tracked. He wasn't so naïve about technology as to not know what infrared scanning was. He realized he would be a beacon at night, his warm shape and movement would glow brightly against the frozen backdrop. So he carefully covered himself with leaves and dead stocks each night and slept as best he could.

But thinking about Chloe and his impotence shattered his spirit. He was a man, born stronger than Chloe, to be a provider – a protector. Instead, he had been a fool, standing in the way of that giant beast that was UnitedFarms, tossing himself under their great machine, churned and shredded as easily as the wheat all around him. And for what? He had thrown his life away. He no longer cared whether he lived or died, whether he was captured or free. It was all the same. The only thing that mattered was walking. So that's what he would do until he could walk no more.

Sigé watched the sudden flare of heat on her satellite feed. It was Alvar, she was certain of it. The heat signature glowed bright orange against the cold blackness of the ground. She had been tracking him steadily since his escape. Though she was diligent, she sometimes lost him for days. Alvar was clever, he must have known about the infrared and hid himself very well. What was different about tonight? She was worried. Sigé searched the weather readings. It was bitterly cold, minus 25 degrees Fahrenheit. Her heart tightened at the thought of Alvar stranded out there in this cold. It was late December, January would be worse. How long could he last?

"Why is he getting up now? He has been so cautious, something must be wrong." Her mind cried.

Sigé reduced the infrared feed to a small window on her VR screen. Then she tapped into the UnitedFarms prison computer system. They had set their scanner to automatic search after they had discovered Alvar's escape. The program was still running, but they had never sent out an actual search team. They probably ran some kind of cost/benefit program and determined it was cheaper to let him surrender, or die in the fields. His escape was so old now, perhaps the program would ignore something so far away. She could only hope

But she knew that programs didn't care about hope as she watched their computer feed. Sigé saw the program status turn from passive monitoring to active tracking. They had discovered him, Sigé realized anxiously. If Alvar was captured now, she would have no chance to help him. She knew what she had to do.

Sigé moved her attention back to the satellite connection. She marked Alvar's location, then zoomed out. "Oh thank god." She thought. Alvar was only a few miles from the border of the vast farm lands. And beyond that, the lights of a small city burned white hot on the infrared screen. "If only he'd slept tonight, just one more night." She cursed his bad luck. "Run Alvar, oh please dearest, start running."

But Alvar didn't run. He trudged on numbly, step after frozen step through the thin wheat stocks barely taller than a man. And that's when his bleary eyes saw it – the distant glow of light. He stopped and stared, not sure what he was looking at. The sky was lighter straight ahead, but not like the glaring lights of the threshing vehicles he sometime saw. He had learned how to avoid those easily enough. This was large and still. It took his brain a long time to understand, but he finally realized what it had to be – a city.

All the fatigue and despair of the last few weeks drained away in a flood. He wasn't going to die out here after all and he wasn't going to get captured either. He was going to escape and he was going to go back and be with his lovely Chloe. Alvar started walking faster, then slowed himself. "Steady Alvar, there's still a long way to go, save your strength." A few minutes later he would find himself nearly jogging again.

The going was getting easier too. The wheat struggled in the frozen soil. Sometimes he would reach barren patches with no plants at all. But why wasn't there snow on the ground? He'd gone through several storms recently, it was cold enough, but it never seemed to stay. He gave a mental shrug and kept going. The ground was hard and rocky beneath his shredded shoes. At least he wasn't leaving tracks. "I'm at the end of their farmlands. Apparently, their genetic alterations can't make plant grow in solid rock."

Alvar continued like this for some time, continuing to gain hope as the distant light of the city grew stronger. He stopped, held his breath and listened. "What's that sound?" He strained to hear over his own heartbeat. It was so cold and quiet out there, sound traveled for miles. It wasn't a threshing machine, he recognized that sound and why would they harvest this pathetic stuff? This was different, deeper, a kind of wump, wump sound. "Turbo-copters. They'd found him!" His mind screamed.

He began to run. The fields continued to thin, helping him move quicker, but also exposing him completely. There was nowhere to hide in this rocky wasteland. Alvar had to reach the frontier of the farmland before the turbo-copters reached him. The sound grew and Alvar pushed harder. Weeks of poor food and freezing conditions had sapped his genetically mutated stamina. His heart beat sickly in his chest and the frigid air burned his lungs. Ice built up on his beard and mustache bouncing painfully against his face.

"Wump, wump, wump," the sound of the turbo-copters filled his ears now. They were nearly upon him. The occasional sprig of wheat disappeared and the tilled soil changed to frozen rocky dirt, then to fields of river stones. He must be on the edge of a very broad river bed. Alvar was forced to slow or risk breaking an ankle in the dark. "Damn my luck, I'm so close." Alvar cursed.

"Whoosh." Alvar felt a rush of air past his face. "They're shooting at me!" His mind screamed. Possibly a tranquilizer dart, but maybe that was worse than a bullet. He pushed his aching body harder, moving side to side to keep from being an easy target. Then he saw it in the darkness – an irregular mass blacker than the surrounding area ahead of him. Trees, maybe a forest. The turbo-copters would be useless in that, they'd have to land. "Let's see if those soft bastards can follow me on foot in this cold." He grimaced, then pushed himself harder. His lungs burned in agony, freezing him from the inside out.

"Thump." And he felt the sting of a dart stick in the back of his left shoulder. Alvar yanked it out as quickly as he felt it. Was it too late, had it dumped its poison into his body? He didn't feel any different, but he knew he'd better move quickly or they'd surely hit him again.

The pain in his chest lifted and Alvar felt light, apart from the world. But some far-off part of his mind held firm, "It's the drugs, don't give up. You have to stay with it. Do you want to be a zombie again? Run Alvar, damn you. Run!"

Alvar stumbled forward, falling, picking himself up, staggering drunkenly on. He'd forgotten why he was moving. His mind screamed for sleep, but a distant, implacable voice drove him on. Suddenly he was upon it and stupefied, he stopped. A deep black mass at his feet bared his way. It took eons to understand what it was. Then finally realization broke through, it was a river.

"Stop. Stop, you fool!" He heard voices shouting over the roar of landing turbo-copters.

Alvar turned slowly. He saw three men puffed ridiculously into dark green parkas and fur hoods. "It's so warm out here, why are they dressed like that?" Alvar snickered, barely awake now. A gun pointed at him, then, "Whump," he felt a distant pinch as the dart hit him in the chest. He stared at it uncomprehendingly. Then the voice, the iron voice that wouldn't let him sleep, so quiet now, so distant, gave its last shout. "Don't let them capture us, anything is better than that."

Alvar turned back to the slowly moving water. Black and thick as death. He was like a child raising his hand in class, "If it's so cold out here, why isn't the river frozen? Where's the ice?" And with the question, he stepped forward, into the river.

The cold of the water was unlike anything he had ever felt. It bit into his skin like a hundred thousand razor blades. Alvar's mind cleared slightly from the pain as his breath rushed from his chest with a gasp. His burning lungs protested, unwilling to take another breath. Alvar bent his head back and looked up at the sky, the beautiful stars, close enough to touch. Then he sank beneath the thick black surface of the water and even the persistent voice that wouldn't let him sleep, spoke no more.

15

"YOU'RE WASTING YOUR time and effort." Spartan grumbled at Alexia.

"You've said that. But I assure you doctor, we're going to do it my way, not yours." Alexia replied.

"I know." Spartan hissed. "But you would learn so much more if you just connected us directly."

Alexia turned her back on Dr. Spartan, tired of arguing with him. She surveyed the room. It was much larger than the one used for the implant, a square about 60 feet on a side and 15 feet high. Despite its size, technicians swarmed the many machines making it feel crowded. The three subjects, Dr. Spartan, Dr. Smith and Cory (formerly Bertha), lay on hospital beds spreading outward, feet first, like spokes of a wheel. At the hub of this wheel lay the four quantum computers, their small glass housings swathed in tubes and pumps. Quantum computers worked by cooling helium until it reach a liquid state at − 455° F, a point at which sub-atomic forces became manageable. Adjacent to each computer sat a stainless steel rack lined carefully with graphite data cubes, so black they seemed to absorb light. Twelve technicians stood by, three for each computer and its associated data cubes, unattended the machinery with god-like reverence. They needed only hooded robes to complete their role.

"The computers are too slow doctor. They'll just get in the way." Spartan called across the room.

"Ong!" Alexia called.

"Yes doctor." Ong said, suddenly standing next to the surprised Alexia.

"I wish you wouldn't do that." Alexia said.

"Do what?"

"Sneak up on me."

Ong only raised an eyebrow in response.

"Go over and tell Dr. Spartan, that if he doesn't stop complaining and shouting, we'll gag him."

"Yes doctor." And Ong slid silently away.

After implanting connections in Spartan and Smith, the three subjects had slept for 12 hours, until they were awoken on Hamachi's orders. They all pleaded for food, sweets with glucose to feed their brains. Even Cory spoke, who up until then had not uttered a word. Repeated inquiries into their experiences yielded nothing. Alexia couldn't say they were hiding anything, but they certainly weren't helpful. Perhaps it was simply too different to explain. Either way, they were going to find out what was being shared and this was the only way they knew how.

"Ong." She called, not surprised this time to suddenly find the slender woman standing next to her. "How soon until we can begin?"

"Within the hour, doctor."

"Very good. Keep me posted." Alexia moved off spending the next half hour checking stations for problems and readiness.

Finally it was time to begin. Alexia broadcast her voice through her VR set to all technicians and assistants, "All stations report ready. Computer link, initiate the connection." Alexia watched the faces of the three subjects go from alert curiosity to bland relaxation. One might think they were resting or meditating.

"Computer capture nominal." A voice toned in her ear piece. "Sixty-five percent of capacity, rising at expected levels."

Previous experiments told them they couldn't keep up for long, they were just hoping to get a piece of the communication, to learn what was worth capturing and what wasn't. It was clearly impractical to capture communication on this clumsy scale in the future. But it was necessary for now.

"Eighty-seven percent of capacity." The computer station reported in her ear.

It was going faster than expected. Alexia looked from Spartan to Smith to Cory. They all had bland uninterested expressions. They were apart from the world. "What is going on it your heads?" She wondered.

A flashing red light interrupted her reverie. "Computer number three unresponsive, switching to backup." Alexia heard the flat voice of the computer.

She switched her VR set off so she could see what was happening in the room. Smith and Spartan continued to lie still, but their faces were twisted with pain. Cory's body was convulsing, her back arching terribly. "Medical!" Alexia cried, "Get to Cory."

Alexia clicked her VR set back on, switching her view to vital signs. Cory was going into cardiac arrest. She glanced at the other two subjects' readings. They were high, not dangerous yet. "Computer capture." She barked. "Keep the other computers running."

She ran over to where the medics were feverishly working on Cory. They had torn her gown open. She looked even more childlike with her pale skin and tiny breasts exposed. An IV was quickly inserted in her neck and a breathing tube into her throat. A heart compressor was slid over her chest and under her back. Alexia checked her vital signs again on her VR set. Still no heart activity. "Come on Cory." She whispered.

Alexia turned to Spartan, then Smith. Their heart and respiration rates had returned to normal and their faces back to their bland relaxed state. "Damn them, what is going on?" She turned to the computer read outs. Computer number four, the backup connected to Cory, was reading zero, the others at 90 percent capacity. If it was the computer crash that had caused Cory's heart failure, the other two were in extreme danger. "Computer capture." She bark at the computer team. "Can we use the backup computer to assist the capture of Smith and Spartan?"

"Negative, doctor. The computers must gather the data directly, we have not been able to increase capacity with parallel..."

"Then begin shut down procedures." She interrupted.

"Yes, doctor." The voice toned dully in her ear.

Alexia had moved over to Spartan and bent to whisper in his ear. "We're going to shut down the computers Dr. Spartan. Do you hear me? We're shutting down the connection. So whatever it is you are doing in there, prepare for disconnection."

"Computer link severed." A voice droned in her ear. It was done.

"Medical. Check on Spartan and Smith." She had already seen their vital signs, but she wanted the physical check regardless. They were fine. If it was the sudden crash of the computer that had caused Cory's heart failure, it hadn't happened again. Perhaps the girl's heart was weak from her drug addiction and chose this unlikely time to fail. Alexia didn't believe in coincidences.

Dr. Spartan was beginning to stir. Alexia shook his shoulders gently. "Dr. Spartan, what's going on? What happened to Cory?"

Spartan took a deep breath and squeezed his eyes open and shut, like someone forcing himself out of a deep sleep. He pushed himself up to a sitting position and shook his head, wires and leads rattled from the movement.

"I think you can safely remove all these wires now. I'll tell you anything you want to know. I don't think you'll see much excitement coming from my brain now." Spartan said. His voice was quiet, rough from being unconscious, but not halting as it had been before the implant.

"Yes, we have already confirmed that. But we'll leave them on just the same. I'm sure you understand."

"Fine, fine, they're only slightly uncomfortable, nothing more."

"What happened to Cory?"

"You know what happened, she died when the link was severed."

"She's not dead. There are doctors working hard right now to revive her."

"No Dr. Serguey, I assure you she is dead and cannot be revived."

"You don't know that. We'll keep trying." Alexia said.

"I'm sorry doctor, I do know it."

Alexia frowned "Was it because of the computer failure?"

"Yes." He answered simply.

"But you and Dr. Smith didn't die when your link was severed."

"You gave us warning. Centuries of time in relation to the speed of the mind. We were able to prepare, to pull back."

"I still don't understand, why would she die?" Alexia pressed.

Spartan was thoughtful for a moment. "It's difficult to explain. You see, our minds were communicating, but slowly. It's the cumbersome nature of the quantum computers that caused the drain. I know this doesn't make any sense. Let me try to explain another way. It would be like breathing underwater through a snorkel, then suddenly replacing the pressure of air in the tube with an infinite vacuum. You would exhale into the vacuum, quickly emptying your lungs with no possibility of ever filling them again. Without the pressure of the connection – the connection of the other minds, our minds – her mind was sucked out of her brain, pulled into the infinite vacuum of the missing computer link."

"Then there can be no reviving her. She's dead." Alexia said quietly.

"Oh no. Only her body can't be revived. She's quite alive." Dr. Smith interrupted. She was now sitting up stiffly to join the conversation.

"What…how?"

"She's in here." Dr. Smith pointed to her head.

Alexia stared at Dr. Smith, using every ounce of will not to sound patronizing. "Yes, you had the chance to get to know her and now she'll be with you. The rest of us didn't get to…"

"No, no! Not that melancholy nonsense. In here, really in here. All of her. Her memories, her experiences, her emotions, everything. It's all here." Smith tapped a bare spot on her crowded forehead, which sprouted wires like a porcupine.

"What? How can that be possible? You were linked together for only a few minutes. You're telling me her mind was transferred to yours in that brief time. That would be an enormous amount of data to transfer. No, I don't accept that."

"What Dr. Smith says is true." Dr. Spartan said. "She's here, inside both of us. I can have a conversation with her right now, the way I'm speaking with you." Dr. Spartan hesitated, gathering his thoughts. "Dr. Serguey, it's not like a pipe that can only feed so much water at a time. The mind doesn't work like that. Concepts, ideas, associations cross and re-cross creating an infinite variety of mental…textures or thoughts. It's not just a matter of recording data. Thoughts and information are not interchangeable. Information is capable of being quantified and digitized, thoughts and concepts are not. Information is only a symbol for our minds. The picture of a lake is not the lake, no matter how precisely rendered. We can describe the color of the water and sky in the photograph. We can go on and on about smells and sounds and the movement of light on the water, but never come close to the infinite subtlety of the place. The information we store in our computers is the same way. It is not the thought itself. The reason we are able to use information at all, is because our minds recognize the symbols and translate the shorthand back into thoughts and concepts. That's why your computers are useless, they will never capture our thoughts, even if you put one thousand of them in parallel"

Spartan watched Alexia frown and continued. "Let me try to give you an example. If I say the word 'apple' to you, your mind fills in the concept of an apple, but not necessarily the one I have in my mind. Yours could be large, red and sweet, mine small, green and tart. Just this one simple word produces an entire concept. The word 'apple' takes only five bytes of information to store in a computer memory, yet the concept would take billions of bytes to describe and still be imprecise. Now multiply this inaccuracy by the subtle differences between people, cultures and languages, then add in the infinite number of words, thoughts, impressions, memories and concepts and you far surpass the storage capacity of the world. But you and I can share concepts so much quicker and more efficiently than this. You understand 'apple' because we have a common reference – a reference all human beings are capable of – designed for."

"What do you mean designed for?" Alexia grew angry at any implication of metaphysics or religion. She was a scientist, such things clouded ones logic – mere excuses to avoid mysteries that simply needed more research.

"I'm sorry Alexia, I can't properly explain. The connection Lani, Cory and I experienced was the most natural thing imaginable. Our minds are made for this kind of communication. The very structure of the brain is designed for it."

Alexia was becoming frustrated with the turn of this conversation. When things shifted away from provable, hard science, she quickly lost interest. "Let's go back to Cory. So Dr. Smith is holding her mind…"

"Both of us are." Spartan interrupted.

"Both of you are holding her mind, inside your own. It must be very crowded in there. Why not each other's minds, won't it fill up soon. How many minds until you can't hear yourself think?" Alexia said facetiously.

Spartan didn't pick up her sarcasm, "It's not crowded at all. I don't see why there would be a limit, or if there is, it might be thousands of minds."

"I see. And what about this design that you just implied. How could a biological structure a million years older than any man-made technology, require a technological trigger to reveal this undiscovered ability? If it's so natural to communicate directly through the mind without words, then why can't we all do it?" Alexia spat.

Dr. Lani Smith smiled sardonically. "But doctor Serguey, Horace and I are doing it. Right now."

16

EZEKIEL HAD LEFT a tap on the UnitedFarms satellite feed. When Alvar's heat signature flared on the tracking system, Ezekiel jumped onto *the I* and zoomed in. He munched popcorn as the turbocopters chased Alvar, laughing as the furry figure stumbled along the riverbed. "You'll be caught now, monkey-boy." Moments later Ezekiel's jaw dropped as he watched Alvar step into the river. "You stupid fool. It's 20 below zero out there. You'll die if they don't fish you out quickly." Ezekiel expected the uniformed men to dash after Alvar and drag him out of the river, revive their precious company property. Instead the three men just stood alongside the river for a minute or two, then turned and left.

"What the hell." Ezekiel snickered. "I'm not spending my vacations in Canada if that's how you treat your guests." Ezekiel turned off the feed. "Sorry Chloe, your boyfriend's a popsicle." He wasn't sure how he would play this with her. It would be easy enough to lie, tell her he was recaptured. But that would give her hope. If he told her he was dead, then she might hate him for telling her. The best thing to do in cases like this was to go back to work. Soon he was off to hacking banks and insurance systems, causing generals discomfort to anyone in his way.

Several days later, Ezekiel found himself in a foul mood. He couldn't get Chloe off his mind. He bailed out of SecureTrans Bank & Trade and slid over to Sticky, Wet & Wild, Virtual Sex Club. But instead of finding a room full of strangers, he was greeted by dozens of naked, writhing Chloes, just the way he had hacked it. The oiled beauties closed in, tugging at his leather suit, "Come on lover, show us what you've got." Ezekiel grew quickly bored and logged off. Nothing was easing his frustration, or his infatuation. He needed the real thing. "Damn her idiot lover for getting himself killed. And damn me for needing Alvar to get to Chloe. There had better be more to this story than just a frozen farmer."

With a twang of his optic cable, Ezekiel jacked back onto *the I*. Quickly the stream of data enveloped him, sliding by like water over a dolphin's skin. In a moment he was staring at the portal to the Global Security Alliance, the GSA. He ignored the public information area and jetted right to the secure area. A towering steel door loomed high in front of him. At its base an angry looking attendant sat stuffed in a glass booth. A sign overhead read: "Authorized Personnel Only." Framing the high door were floating skulls and crossbones, warning that unauthorized access would be met with swift and fatal punishment – no exceptions. Ezekiel ignored all this and floated over to the side wall, staying close to the tall concrete barrier topped with razor wire and gun turrets. Every so often he would pause at a small steel door and try a security code. These side portals were for authorized programmers. They represented the most obvious source of attack and consequently were the most reinforced. Ezekiel tested them only as a burglar would jiggle a lock or try a window. If you can walk through the front door, why crawl through the basement?

Ezekiel rounded the back of the fortress and paused thoughtfully in front of a small crevice in the concrete. He zoomed into the crack and saw a tiny communication jack. It might be a forgotten high speed node for linking to mirror sites. Typically such ports were fused shut until needed. But as Ezekiel suspected, this one had not been fully shut down, the likely result of a lazy or overworked programmer who forgot to close the leak.

He felt around with his virtual fingers to determine connectivity type.

Ezekiel reached into a simulated pocket on his vest and pulled out a tiny adapter, then plugged it into the port and waited. Working in the background, one of Ezekiel's many custom programs tested the link, probing and massaging until it found an opening. A small light on the port turned green indicating a successful link. "And here we go." Ezekiel shrank to the size of a flea, paused an instant at the base of the enormous wall, then whipped through the cable itself. He squirted out onto the hard stone floor inside of the fortress. Picking himself to his feet, he regained his full size and looked around. He estimated the cavern to be about 1,000 feet wide and so long that the file cabinets lining the walls blurred into darkness in both directions. "OK, I'm in." He sighed. One could never be relaxed while breaking into a secured site, especially not one where the punishment for getting caught was death.

Ezekiel spoke directly into the air, "Satellite backup, position lambda negative 104 point 8332 by phi 53 point 1443 degrees. Time index, 67307.1." Instead of feeling himself move to the appropriate file, the millions of cabinets slid alongside him. The movement was a momentary blur, just an illusion to occupy the viewer as the computer searched its records. The cabinet opened to reveal four large bound volumes. He pulled the first from its shelf and opened it, but instead of pages, his view was filled with the high definition satellite images of the area during the time Alvar stepped into the river.

Ezekiel had seen all this from the UnitedFarms satellite, zoomed in as far as their cameras would allow, but it wasn't enough. UnitedFarms was known for its ability to make fat profits for its shareholders. But they didn't waste money on ultra-high def cameras or recordings. The images he saw of Alvar were grainy blobs, he wasn't even completely sure it was Alvar. So Ezekiel broke into the GSA's satellite system.

The wars of the 20th and early 21st Centuries were unprofitable affairs, sucking valuable resources into their vacuous maws. In 2050, the great corporations of the world formed a pact, to compete on every conceivable level, but not allow war to break out anywhere. There were plenty of examples to support their model. One they most closely related to, were the great gang feuds of the early 20th Century, where organized crime groups struggled for dominance. They murdered each other until they became weak enough to be crushed by local law enforcement. They founded the Global Security Alliance and gave it world power to squelch any violence above a fist fight. It was great at first. Cruel dictators and despots toppled like dead trees. Their oppressed people soon felt the surge of abundance and wealth that flowed into new markets. The giant corporations patted themselves on the back for their genius; they had ended war and made themselves great piles of money for their efforts.

But ultimately man had traded one despot for another. Mass violence was exchanged for complete and utter corporate control. Mankind's 50,000 year philosophical struggle to create a better world for oppressed individuals ended in a single decade. The GSA watched the world with its ubiquitous eyes and ears, crushing all who threatened the dominance of those in power. There was only one penalty for breaking in to one of their satellites, computer systems or many smart programs – death.

Ezekiel shifted nervously as he zoomed into the crystal clear image. Alvar's furry face filled his view. One foot was raised as he readied himself for the icy plunge. "Forward five seconds." He spoke to the air. Instantly the scene changed to the overhead view of Alvar's half submerged body. "Switch to infrared." The scene turned white and green. Warmer images showed whiter against the dull green of the ground and river. The water was nearly black indicating its extreme cold. Alvar's upper half glowed brightly, his lower half dark green, clearly beginning to cool. He had moved about 10 feet downstream from where he had entered. "Forward five seconds." The image now showed Alvar's body fully submerged and the bright gray green turning darker. His hands and feet now barely registered against the frigid water. "Forward five seconds." The river was solid black, no heat signature.

Ezekiel zoomed in and out scanning images up and down the river, but there was no sign of Alvar's body. "He couldn't have cooled that fast." Ezekiel muttered to himself.

"Reverse three seconds." Again, Ezekiel saw the cooling shape of Alvar in the river. "OK, forward two seconds." Again the same thing. "Forward one second." Again the river was empty. Ezekiel repeated this process, using smaller time units until he was looking at two sequential frames of the recording. The first showed Alvar's submerged body and the next showed an empty river. Impossible, but there it was, Alvar disappearing from the river.

Ezekiel spoke to the computer, "Zoom out 1,000 feet, focus north 100 feet." The view changed to the area of the far side of the river. Nothing but a thick stand of trees. "What the hell. Where did he go?" Ezekiel loved and hated the mystery. He loved the challenge of solving the puzzle, but hated not knowing and so was driven to find out. It was what made him so good at what he did, but also what caused him so much anxiety.

"Someone must have doctored this recording." Ezekiel zoomed in to the micro-pixel level. These were the very tiny elements that made up the picture itself. It was nearly impossible to hide changes at this level. Ezekiel began the tedious task of following the hyper zoomed image of Alvar in river at this detailed level. It was like looking at a mountain through a microscope and one could easily get lost.

An hour later, Ezekiel's eyes watering, he thought he saw something strange, a micro-pixel changing color, which was impossible on a still image of a recording. It might just be his tired eyes. He moved back and waited. There it was again, a single micro-pixel had changed from white to green. "I got you shit-head." Ezekiel swore into the room.

Ezekiel ran his stealthiest personal program. There was a ghost in here, right now: another person in the very same place as he, one that had not noticed Ezekiel yet. He pulled back from the magnified image and looked around the cavern. Nothing. Different filters still revealed nothing. He had to hurry, the ghost wouldn't stay around any longer than necessary. And what about GSA security? He'd been in their system way too long for comfort. Anxiety cramped his stomach. "Show yourself, damn you." Ezekiel scanned again, every frequency, every variation, still nothing. How could anyone hide like this? Several seconds passed, he was out of time.

Low level detection was the last resort. It would reveal everything about the area. But it would also expose him to the ghost. It was like taking a flash picture in a pitch black room. You'd capture everything, but just as surely give yourself away in the process. There was no choice. Ezekiel pulled the device out of his pocket, paused, then braced himself for a struggle or a chase. Whoever it was would fight or run, he'd be ready. And if it was a GSA smart program...well he'd better not to think about that right now.

FLASH. A tiny area of the cavern lit up as if by the sun. And there, no more than three steps in front of him a cloaked figure hunched over one of the maps painting carefully with a tiny brush. Ezekiel ran toward the crouched figure hoping to pull back the hood before he ran, but was a second too late. The figure jumped up and ran right through the wall as if it weren't there. Ezekiel ran right behind him. In an instant they were out of the GSA and into the heart of *the I*. The figure darted in and out of chat rooms and virtual retailers trying to lose him in the crowds. But Ezekiel held tight. Had he not been so near from the first instant, the ghost surely would have lost him by now. But he was close, so close he could feel the rough fabric of the cloak brush against his fingertips as he repeatedly tried to grab the hood.

The ghost made a sudden turn and headed for the Grand Cayman Financial Clearing House, one of the busiest sites on *the I*. Ezekiel knew he would never be able to follow him through the enormous volumes of data. With a last surge of speed, he pulled close enough to push a note into one of the folds of the cloak covering the ghost. The next instant they reached the entrance of the clearing house and Ezekiel lost the figure in the chaos of the site.

He tried desperately for several minutes to pick up the trail of the other, but knew it was useless. Whoever he was, he was good. Better than good. Ezekiel felt the sting of jealousy. "No one shows me up and gets away with it."

Ezekiel left the financial clearing house, slowly, methodically. The ghost would definitely find his note. Ezekiel reread the copy. "Alvar is mine. Interfere again and I will erase you."

17

LVAR AWOKE LYING on his back on a hard bed of some kind; a low dirty ceiling filled his view. The room was too bright and he had to blink several times to adjust to it. "Where am I?" He croaked, his voice raw and strange, like he hadn't used it in a long time. Alvar shook his head to clear the heaviness. His neck was stiff and sore, but he managed to turn it to the left. There he spied a heavy metal door with a frosted window. To the right the wall was lined with metal shelves rudely stacked with cardboard and plastic boxes, nothing discernible.

He was very weak, and it took a great deal of effort to raise his head to look over his body to the far wall. There were a few unrecognizable machines, again giving him no clue to his circumstances or to the nature of the room. But something peculiar caught his eyes. His body was covered with a gray blanket that went all the way to the foot of the bed he was lying on. That was not strange, it was the way it lay on his body that made his heart freeze in his chest. The outline of his thighs was clearly visible, but they ended at the knees.

In growing panic, Alvar reached up to throw the blanket aside. The covers tangled in his arms and he couldn't make his hands grasp anything. It took every ounce of will to stay calm as he worked the blanket slowly from his chest. Finally he got it free. Horrified he stared at his arms – the right one ended at about the elbow, the left midway up the upper arm. Morbid fascination flooded him as he turned his arms as best he could. Each ended in thick white bandages, sprouting a cluster of tubes.

He wriggled himself up to a full sitting position, feeling the pull of tubes on his lower legs. Alvar fought an overwhelming need to vomit. Cautiously, he pulled on the blanket that covered him with his two shortened arms. This was difficult enough, but the added tangle of tubes made the process agonizingly slow. Eventually he let the weight of the blanket pull itself to the floor. And there he saw the full extent of his injuries. Both legs ended above the knees and were wrapped in the same white bandages and tubes as his arms. His skin was blotched dark purple and red, most of the fur was gone, leaving only sorry looking clumps here and there.

He tried desperately to recall what had happened, how he had gotten here, but the last thing he could remember was the sound of turbocopters and running on the rocky ground. There was something about a tranquilizer dart, but the rest was blank. Alvar looked around for a clue as to where he was. It did not look like a hospital room, more like a storeroom. UnitedFarms, if they were going to fix him and he doubted that they would, would not put him in a makeshift room like this. He thought back to his time there with hatred. "They would have kept me full of drugs and locked up tight" he thought.

He grimaced at his missing arms and legs, the full impact of his mutilation hitting him. He was useless now. Everything he had done, worked for, was out of his reach. Instead of a leader, he would be a burden to those who needed him most. Forgetting his missing hands and forearms, he reached up to cover his eyes. The sudden movement and surprise of the missing appendages threw him severely off balance. His natural instinct was to put a hand out to catch himself as he tumbled toward the side of the bed. But instead of stopping his fall, his momentum threw him fast toward the floor. The full force of his falling body landed onto the stump of his right arm. Alvar mercifully fainted, but not before unimaginable pain shot up to his brain.

———

Alvar was awakened by an unbearable itching sensation in his wrists and ankles. He tried to reach over to scratch his right wrist, but was unable to move either arm. He attempted to move his legs, but they were equally immobilized. Only his head was unrestrained, so he was limited to a view of the dirty ceiling. He guessed he was still in the same room. Someone must have found him on the floor and placed him back onto this bed. There were crude looking straps binding his shoulders and midsection. They looked like twisted linen. This was definitely not UnitedFarms or a hospital, but who and where then?

Alvar sighed deeply in despair, he still couldn't remember anything about getting here. All he kept seeing were his shortened limbs mocking him. He fought his restraints, but they held tight. He remembered the pain of his landing and gave up. Even if he got free, how could he leave? At least his mind felt clear. He would have to trust the intentions of his benefactors.

Alvar must have dozed off, when the whispered sighs of breathing whipped him awake. His eyes shot open. There, hovering over him was the most beautiful woman he had ever seen. Her wheat colored hair was pulled gently back to frame her exquisite face. Her skin was pale, almost translucent against her full red lips. But it was her eyes that made Alvar's heart skip. They were a deep clear blue and seemed to sparkle from a light of their own. Alvar noticed just a hint of mischief dancing about the corners.

"Hey who are you? What is this place? How did I get here and what happened to my..? The words trailed off.

The woman raised her hand anxiously, putting a finger to his lips urgently, insisting on his silence. Alvar couldn't help noticing her long elegant fingers moving with an ethereal grace. A pang of longing and loss flowed simultaneously through him. Was this more of their torture, to show him something he would never have? How he would be nothing to Chloe, only a burden, a source of pity. The blunt image of his missing limbs burned his eyes like acid and he had to look away from the ethereal beauty before him.

She seemed to sense his despair and frustration and touched his cheek gently to face her, as if to say, "it'll be all right, trust me." The mischief was gone from her eyes, replaced only with concern. "Why won't you talk to me? Just tell me what's happening."

She shook her head sadly covering her mouth. Then her eyes widened as an idea came to come to her. She raised one graceful finger as if to say "one minute, I'll be right back" turned and glided out of view.

She returned shortly. Again, Alvar was mesmerized by her lithe beauty. Before he could open his mouth to ask the many questions he had, she pressed her hand to his lips firmly and shook her head emphatically. It was clear he must not speak, or perhaps not make noise. He didn't know which, he'd have to trust her.

In the woman's other hand was a set of VR glasses. Their design was different from the ones he wore at the virtual reality court hearing. This one was larger with tiny wires and connectors exposed, perhaps handmade. She placed them gently over his eyes and touched a sensor on the temple.

Alvar's vision suddenly filled with disjointed color. Soft static filled his ears. After a moment the screen focused and the sound quieted. The scene resolved and he was looking at an enormous expanse of wheat and snow from a great height. The camera zoomed in until he was looking at the indistinct outline of a man making his way through enormously high wheat stocks. "It must be me." Alvar realized. "She is telling me she was watching me."

The scene changed, now replaced by a fur covered Alvar running toward a stand of trees. There was a turbo-copter chasing him. The figure slowed his running, began to stagger, but continued deliberately to the edge of a wide black expanse – a river. Then it all came back to him. He'd chosen the river over capture. A tiny child's voice came back to him, as if asking a teacher in a classroom, "Why isn't the river frozen when it's so cold outside."

As if to answer his silent question, the scene changed again. This time he was looking at the inside of a research lab. Every shelf and table were crowded with computers, machines, microscopes, glassware, test-tubes and beakers. Two men were discussing something very important. One wore the ubiquitous uniform of the scientist, the white lab coat; while the other the standard uniform of the businessman, a suit.

The sound rose and Alvar listened in on their conversation:

The scientist was speaking, "...won't do it. The risk is too great. Can you imagine if we are unable to control it? Whole environments would change. Successful crops might be changed in ways we can't reverse, whole species pushed out of existence. We might alter the very climate as a result. It's madness to begin without years of further testing."

"Like what changes?" The businessman said, "Trees that grow in the winter. Useless plants disappearing. So what. Maybe they'll thrive along with everything else. Think about it. We'll be able to grow crops in the dead of winter. While all of our competitors are selling stored grains at high winter prices and correspondingly high costs, we'll be harvesting and selling fresh crops. Low inventories, high margins. We can cut the price just enough to force them into selling at a loss or give up their markets completely. Hell, maybe we'll push them out of business. We're going to make a killing!" His voice rose with excitement.

"I have no doubt of its commercial potential. We're talking about eco-systems here. There are a lot of unforeseen consequences to such a discovery. We must think beyond profit for once."

The businessman scowled, "You mean beyond the profit that pays for all your research, beyond the profit that pays for this equipment, your salary? Is that the profit you don't want to think about?"

The scientist said nothing, his face a mask of anger.

"OK, OK, calm down, no one's threatening you. Just be logical for a moment. You've just invented something worth billions, maybe trillions. And you want to shelve it, wait for someone to steal it. Why invent it if you can't use it. You know how fast discoveries are being made. I wouldn't be surprised if another scientist is close to the same discovery. Then what? You and me get nothing and still the stuff gets out there. Same scenario, just no money. It's not like we're trying to change the laws of physics or something, we're just keeping water from freezing at 32 degrees that's all. So what? Besides, you'll be doing a lot of good. We'll be able to grow food almost all year long. Think of it. We'll be able get staples like wheat, rice and soy inexpensively to tens of millions of people who are on the verge of starvation. It's just good business. Starving people don't make anyone any money."

The scientist stood there with a thoughtful look on his face. "Well, it is likely someone else is working on this. It has always fascinated me how ideas come to several people at once. Besides it will only give us a short term edge anyway. Our competition will learn how to make the stuff soon enough or steal the formula outright." The scientist said.

"They always do. Secrets don't last long anymore. Now tell me more about this super-water, how cold can it get before it freezes?"

"At sea level, -10° Fahrenheit before it starts to freeze, a little lower if it's under pressure or moving rapidly, like in an aqueduct or a fast river."

"And could you drink it? Now, that's an idea, maybe you could keep people from freezing in cold environments."

Alvar watched the scientist roll his eyes in irritation. "Plants are very different from animals. If anything that cold touched any part of you it would quickly cause frostbite and cell death. Just because it's water doesn't mean it isn't cold. And God help you if you fell into the stuff."

"No wonder the river wasn't frozen, it was filled with that, what did he call it, super water." Alvar thought. He remembered his shortened arms and legs. "The greedy bastards, they'll do anything to increase their profits, destroy the whole planet if they have to."

His thoughts were interrupted as the scene changed from the scientist and businessman to the interior of a large auditorium. It was filled to capacity with purple robed figures. Alvar was not able to understand what was happening until the camera view panned over to a lone speaker on the expansive stage. He was an ordinary looking man, probably in his late fifties with dark short hair with a touch of gray at the temples. He was clean shaven and had a kind, intelligent face.

The sound came up and Alvar was able to hear what this gentle looking man was saying to the large robed audience:

"We've come a long way my friends. Look around, you see hundreds like yourselves, your friends and neighbors who are also finally ready to lead worthy, truly productive lives. You're about to embark on the most important journey in man's history. We are pioneers. We will transform the wasteful ways of our ignorant cousins into the crystal-like purity of intellectual pursuit. While they use the gifts of technology to craft sturdier yokes around their own necks, you'll be forging keys to unlock the secrets of the human mind. You will be the first, finally free to explore the infinite landscape of the mind unfettered by material restraint."

The speaker's eyes blazed with passion as his voice boomed through the quiet auditorium. Alvar was captivated by the man's raw charisma. "At last we are breaking the cycle of the master slave relationship. No longer must you use your precious talents and skills paying homage to an insatiable overlord, forced to pursue your intellectual gifts as some kind of secret hobby, hidden from view, ridiculed for its lack of commercial uses. No longer will you spend the majority of your productive lives working for greedy strangers who squander your priceless efforts on quickly forgotten trinkets – pearls before swine. No, my friends, we are just moments away from the final freedom, to expand our minds and knowledge the way nature intended from man's inception – without limits.

"Our new home in the north is ready and awaits us. You'll want for nothing. All of your material needs will be provided for, or you'll create different ones if it pleases you. Bring only your imagination and your thirst for knowledge. The rest is already there.

"As I said, we are very close now, but we are not totally free yet. As long as there are some out there who would destroy or enslave us for our knowledge, we are in danger. Yes, we have mastered our material desires, but we have not mastered ourselves. The human ego is weak, it needs constant reassurance of its worth. There are great temptations out there, even in the seclusion of the north. Some of these temptations are subtle and insidious and some are very seductive. You may not believe me now, but many of you may one day turn from the righteous path."

The audience filled the room with a chorus of "No, no, never." And it was several long moments before the speaker calmed them back to silence.

"No, you can't imagine it now. But yes, it's true, some will be seduced by the charms of the world, perhaps it will come from a misguided sense of pity for your ignorant cousins, perhaps you'll want to feel superior, or perhaps you'll just long for companionship. And if just one of you strays, we are all in danger.

"My brothers and sisters, we can never let this happen. We must not let temptation conquer us. Never! You don't realize now what a great threat we will be to our ignorant cousins. They will want to destroy us, or worse, control us. They will claim their need is greater than our freedom and they will enslave us. We must bind ourselves together with a universal symbol. One which will not only make it difficult to share our secrets, but one which will always remind us of our commitment. One which can never be broken, one which will separate us forever from the others. A symbol as powerful and lasting as the one Jehovah gave to Abraham over five thousand years ago.

"I see the fear on your faces, the resistance to the unknown. Don't be ashamed, you are logical, intelligent men and women and you understand the risk. That is normal. But to begin this journey, we must not only bring down the bridge that lies behind us, we must destroy the very tools that built it in the first place."

The speaker's voice had risen to a shout. And Alvar was barely able to make out the next words over the cheers of the crowd.

"And so, without hesitation, childish longing, or nostalgia: We relinquish our voices – forever!"

The speaker paused while the crowd shouted and cheered, finally quieting down enough for him to continue.

Alvar watched in anxiety as he was caught up in the frenzy of the crowd. "What is he talking about, 'give up our voices?'" Alvar thought.

Finally, the audience was quiet enough for the speaker to continue.

"The chatter and babble of the ages will finally succumb to a glorious, everlasting silence. Soon we will each be able to hear our own divine voices without the inane cacophony that has drowned it out for countless millennia."

The densely filled auditorium was hushed to silence. Alvar scanned the crowd as the camera moved around the room. He was not used to large numbers of people, but estimated the group at many hundreds, perhaps thousands. Each face stared enraptured at the man on the stage, tears streaming from many. What kind of cult is this? Why is this woman showing me this? Alvar's musings were interrupted as the camera swung back to the lone man on the stage.

"Volunteers are passing cups among you now. Each is filled with a genetically engineered drink. The drug inside will erase the speech center of your brain. It will also free this enormous area of the brain for any purpose or knowledge you may choose. But the real strength of this formula is that it also alters the gene for speech. Our offspring will never be burdened with the clatter of voices again. Though we will always remember the sounds and distractions of speech, they will never know it.

"So raise your cups high. And for the last time aloud, toast our rebirth:

"To the Children of *the I*." He shouted. And the crowd shouted in response, "To the Children of *the I*."

Alvar watched in horror as the multitude of robed figures drank the concoction. Every muscle ached to reach out and throw the cups from their hands. He wanted to shut his eyes, hide from this horror, though he knew that he was probably watching something in the distant past. This lovely girl was trying to tell him about herself. She must be part of this strange cult. And by her youth, she was likely a child of these fanatics. She probably had never known speech. No wonder she wouldn't let him speak. The sound of a voice in this place would be a hideous outrage and the mark of an intruder.

His eyes were uncovered as the VR set was removed. The strange woman rested her delicate head on his chest. He would have embraced her, even with his lowly stumps, but he was still restrained, unable to move.

She must have felt his muscles tighten in his effort, for she raised her head and looked into his eyes for a long time.

Then she stepped back slightly from the table, enough so he could see all of her at once. She reached up and pulled the white dress slowly over her head and let it drop sensuously to the floor. Alvar gasped. She was even more lovely naked. Her body was the very essence of sexuality, as if all the great sculptures, paintings and memories of Venus had been distilled into this one perfect creation. The hint of mischief around her eyes returned as she watched his reaction to her display. She stood there utterly confident, no hint of modesty or self-consciousness tainted her expression.

She glided over to Alvar, bent down and kissed him roughly on his gaping mouth. He could feel an erection pushing achingly against the cover. She looked down and opened her mouth in silent laughter. Alvar felt a pang of sadness, her voice would have been as clear and lovely as her body. He smiled shyly, hoping to hide his passing melancholy.

Before he realized what was happening, she had swept the covers away. He was completely naked as well. It was not in Alvar's nature to allow himself to be out of control like this and he was surprised how aroused he was by it.

As if reading his mind, she began exploring his body with her sensuous mouth. Alvar closed his eyes. It felt like she was everywhere at once with her probing lips, tongue and dancing fingertips. The nerve endings of his skin came alive. He ached to roll on top of her and thrust himself upon her as she continued her sweet torture. His longing grew until it felt like it couldn't continue without release. Then with some masterful intuition, she slowed her caress, or moved to a less sensitive area, allowing the tide of passion to recede – but just enough. Then with renewed vigor, she would begin the process all over again, bringing him just to the edge of climax, then pulling back, over and over, until Alvar's mind was awash with passion and desire. All his chattering thoughts, fears and doubts were supplanted by waves of pleasure.

Alvar was surprised and delighted to look up and find her mounting him. She thrust herself upon him, her head thrown back in abandon. Her hands fondled and caressed her perfect breasts for the captive Alvar. She was consumed by the same passion she had evoked in him, completely awash in wave after wave of climax. Her face and chest grew flushed with the heat of orgasm after orgasm. Seeing her so aroused and excited was too much for him to hold back. Alvar's last thread of restraint shattered as he succumbed to a climax intense beyond his imagining.

And then it was over. Alvar opened his eyes slowly. The head of his silent goddess was lying on his chest and she was breathing quietly. Her hair flowed languidly down his neck and shoulders. Again he ached to hold her, stroke her hair, or at least whisper his gratitude. But he dared not disturb his gentle fawn for fear of scaring her off. He pulled the warm memory of their lovemaking back into his mind. He gave the top of her head a soft kiss, then let his mind roam, finally drifting off to blissful sleep.

When Alvar awoke, he found her gone. He also discovered he was dressed. As he strained to look down below his chest, he discovered his upper body was no longer restrained. He tested his arms and found them also released. He sat up, grateful for the freedom. He attempted to move his legs, but quickly discovered they were held by wide straps.

Alvar bent awkwardly to the side to see if there was anything interesting by the table. One side was empty, but on the other was a tall packing container stacked with various types of partially opened packaged foods and several large containers of water. Alvar frowned at this. It appeared his benefactor might not be able to come back as often as she'd like. Perhaps not for days by the quantity of the supplies.

Also on the crate were the VR glasses he had previously used. Alvar squeezed the glasses between his two stumps, pressing firmly, knowing that if he dropped them to the floor they were lost. It took several frustrating minutes to get the glasses onto his face. There was a moment of static, then the colors of the screen cleared to a single blue. Hopefully they worked like the game consoles his friends had sneaked into school when he was a child. He found the familiar red circle in the lower left part of his vision. When he looked straight at it, it doubled in size. He held his focus and blinked twice rapidly. The screen was instantly alive with text and symbols. This must be the main menu. Alvar scanned through the mostly incoherent items, titles like: Planar Dynamics, Technological Ontology, sub-photonic computing. He made sure not to stare long at these items, for risk of activating them.

Alvar continued to scan the screen for something familiar. About three quarters of the way down the massive list was a simple phrase that caught his attention, Northern Prison Systems. It was so out of character with the rest of the list that it must be meant for him. Alvar starred at the item for a long moment, then blinked twice. His view filled with the face of his benefactor. Her mischievous expression warmed his heart. Text appeared just below her face and it began to scroll down as he read.

"I'm glad you found my message, I wasn't sure it would be obvious enough or that you would even try the VR terminal. I know about your group, the Anti-Techs and I was not sure you would use our technology. There are so many things to explain and our different worlds make it very difficult. We rely completely on technology, while you abhor it.

"I'm sure you have many questions. They will all get answered in time. I will just tell you my story in the order it happened, then you can ask anything I have left out another time. It is important that you know this is live. I composed this message some time ago as I did not know when I would be free to communicate with you, or if that time would be during your waking hours. In our lives, we are not allowed to keep secrets from each other. We do not even have the concept you so proudly cherish, called privacy.

"You must know that I rescued you and perhaps that I followed you after your escape. But cannot know how I discovered you. It was through a man named Ezekiel Malaffaires. I have known of him for many years and learned a great deal from him as well. He is an I-surgeon, that is the popular name of someone who is expert at breaking into sites on *the I*, or Internet as it was once called. I do not know why Ezekiel was tracking you, but I cannot believe it was for good intentions. I have watched him for a long time and I know that he is not capable of good.

"I learned of you, because I too travel *the I*, but to learn the mechanics and subtleties of its network. Ezekiel and I share one trait, which is curiosity. So when he was so intent on finding you, it raised my interest. It may sound foolish, even childish, but the more I got to know you by tracking you, the more I came to admire your courage and uniqueness.

"I fell in love with you.

"You also know that I tracked you after your escape from UnitedFarms and followed your long horrible journey through the wheat fields. My love for you was a fantasy and you were someone I could never meet. But when I saw you heading for the river, I knew that you would not surrender, but you would try to cross it. I knew of the super-water, that you would die if you entered that river. I had to take a chance, I had to do something that defied all my teaching from birth. I had to rescue an outsider.

"I was waiting on the far bank. I pulled you out after only a few seconds in the river. I had to wait until those horrid guards turned their backs. It makes my heart tighten to think how close you came to dying. The genetic modifications they did to you saved your life. But the cold of the super-water froze the ends of your limbs and destroyed the cells, they could not be saved.

"I brought you here, barely alive and was caught by my people immediately. We are strangers to you and your world and we must not ever be discovered, but we are not murderers. So we used our knowledge to save you. The tubes you see coming from your limbs are feeding them the drugs and genetic material necessary to regrow your arms and legs. It will take some time, but you will have your hands and legs back my love.

"I love my people and would never do anything to harm them. But I have endangered them by bringing you here. Fortunately, you do not know where we are, so you are safe. But when your limbs are returned you will be a danger to us. I can't say how that will unfold. In the meantime, I can only come rarely to help with your healing. If I show unnatural interest in you or your condition, I will be separated from you. It is such torture to know you are here and I can see you so little. Rest and grow strong, we will find a way."

It was signed, "Sigé"

Alvar had to look away from the text. This girl, a stranger, had risked so much. But what did she mean, "...how that will unfold?" regarding his mobility. They would protect their secrecy in any way they had to. But how? Was he to be a prisoner for the rest of his life? Alvar's face went white. What are they putting in my food? He whispered a few words, testing his voice . Would they give him that drug he saw on the holo-vid?

Alvar shook his head. What choice did he have. For now, he would heal.

18

D R. SPARTAN SWAGGERED across Hamachi's office and sat
down with great flourish. "Quite a view you have here."

Hamachi smiled to himself, this was going to be very interesting indeed. "I don't suppose there's any reason to have Dr. Smith
in here for this discussion."

Spartan shrugged. "It's up to you. She's wherever I am, sees whatever
I see. As I am with her and see and hear whatever she does as well."

"And doesn't this get confusing?" Hamachi asked.

"Interesting you should ask." Dr. Spartan leaned forward, the sarcasm
gone, once again the curious scientist. "We were just thinking the same
question, but it doesn't. There seems to be something in the brain that
sorts all this out. We, I, language is imperfect here, have decided there is
quite a lot about the brain we don't understand."

"And what if there were more of you, let's say three, five, what about
1,000 minds joined, what happens then?" Hamachi asked.

Spartan was thoughtful. "We don't know. We believe it would
work out, but not in the way it is now. But you are thinking linearly. It
wouldn't be one brain processing the sensory input of 1,000 sets of eyes,

for example, but 1,000 brains. So we're sure it would work. In fact, why should there be a limit. The idea is not unique in nature. Aside from sight and sound constantly bombarding our brains, we have millions of nerve endings feeding us information constantly. Heat, cold, pressure, pain, it never stops. Our brains filter what is important and pushes the rest to the background. We believe it would be like that, only on a larger scale."

"Fascinating. I'd like you to meet one of my top scientists here at Stratumentis. He is..."

Spartan broke in with a wave of his hand, "Oh I'm sure we've met him if he's working here. What's his name?"

Hamachi's face froze into a mask. "I'm not accustomed to being interrupted. And I don't care if there are ten thousand minds in there, you will not be able to anticipate my thoughts or actions. If we are to work together, I expect this minimum level of respect. Understood?"

Spartan flushed. "Our apologies. We are simply excited about our new condition and acted over zealously. You have our cooperation and attention."

Hamachi marveled at the change. The sarcastic arrogance just a minute before was replaced by this fawning apology. Who was dominant at this moment? Dr. Spartan, Smith or the drug addict, Cory? Or was it a combination of all three. Amazing. Hamachi spoke to the room, "Mr. Breedlove, come in please."

Breedlove entered the office. He was a large man, in height as well as girth. He appeared to be in his late thirties, with a mass of wild red hair and deep set green eyes which poked through a thick beard covering most of his face. He shuffled over to where Hamachi and Spartan were sitting and remained standing.

"Mr. Breedlove, join us. This is Dr. Spartan. Or should I say Spartan-Smith-Cory?"

"Whatever." Spartan shrugged.

Breedlove set his large body down carefully, as one accustomed to breaking furniture meant for smaller men. "Interesting." He muttered.

Hamachi spoke next, "Mr. Breedlove is going to be working with you, as we add more people to your mental network."

Spartan frowned. "You mean like Cory."

Hamachi ignored the remark. "Mr. Breedlove has been fully briefed on the success of your recent activities. However, we are both curious about how you communicate without the aid of the physical connection. How you are communicating now, for example."

Spartan's face became thoughtful – the scientist again. "Let me try to explain. We remember how we were before all this, but can't imagine being anything other than what we are now. It is like remembering being blind. No one would willingly go back." He turned to Mr. Breedlove. "It was the extreme capacity of the quantum computers that made our communication possible, but also torturously slow. To communicate through a machine is like breathing through a straw. You might survive, but only with every ounce of patience and will. We decided to use the computers to improve our link."

"In what way?" Breedlove asked.

"Dr. Smith wrote a tiny program to synthesize a molecule we could use in our brains. A molecule that would activate the part of our brain already stimulated by the implant. Unfortunately, we believe the process may have killed Cory's body."

Hamachi raised his eyebrows, but didn't interrupt.

"It was Dr. Smith's idea of course. She is brilliant at this sort of thing. Spartan knows the anatomy and physiology of the brain, but very little about computers. Anyway she designed a program to run in the background. A tiny program I assure you. Quantum computers are massively powerful machines and our program was so small, it used a mere fraction of the machine's capacity."

Spartan was quiet for a time, considering something, then continued. "The recordings you were capturing are garbage, useless piles of images that no one will ever be able to sift through in a hundred life-times. We were using such a small portion of the computer's capacity." He looked directly at Hamachi, "Had we imagined there was even the smallest risk to Cory, we would never have attempted it. The little bit of computer power we needed was so insignificant..." His voice dropped off.

"Go on." Hamachi urged. "You may be mistaken. Tell us what happened and we'll look into it."

"Yes, please do that; it would ease our conscience. We initiated the program as soon as we were connected. Our brains, now freed from the torture of separation were able to work again. But as I said before, it was like breathing through a straw, we were desperate to increase the link. Dr. Smith grabbed the opportunity for all of us.

"We focused our efforts on one brain, Cory's, her implant being the oldest. We could see that the structure around her implant was already changing, we could see it, the synapses altering course. But the process was slow and might stop when we were disconnected. We simply sped up the process, using her own brain for raw material. Even with the fantastic power of the computer, it was tortuously slow. At least it felt that way to us. Time has a different meaning when we are connected. Even speaking to you now takes constant reminders to be in and out of time simultaneously. But never mind that right now. We realized the data cubes were filling and we were running out of time, so we pushed the computer to finish the design." Spartan stopped.

Hamachi and Breedlove waited.

Spartan began again, his voice quieter. "I think it was this extra push that caused the computer to freeze. We grabbed Cory and the molecular design and pulled out."

Hamachi frowned. "Are you saying it was the computer crash that killed the girl, or your pulling out?"

"I think it was our pulling out that killed her. You can't remove someone's mind from their brain and not have a consequence. Cory is here and she doesn't blame us, but she is left without a physical self. Oh, it is impossible to explain." Spartan turned from the piercing eyes of Hamachi and looked absently to the river below. "But what choice did we have. The crashing computer could have killed her and we would have lost her mind. That surely would have been worse, right?"

Hamachi shot a look at Breedlove and nodded slightly so Spartan wouldn't notice. "I think you did the right thing. Please go with Mr.

Breedlove now and describe the structure of this molecule. It will help us avoid further tragedy."

Spartan stood numbly. "Yes. We should have told you our plan, you could have helped. Maybe Cory would have been here in body now instead of just our minds. We were just so desperate to complete the link. Like breathing through a straw. You understand."

Hamachi stood too, smiling, placating. "Don't blame yourselves. Just follow Mr. Breedlove, give him all the details. He'll understand."

Breedlove reached down from his great bulk and gently tugged on Spartan's arm to follow him.

When they were gone, Hamachi tapped his VR set. "Connect to Mr. Chambers in acquisitions."

The screen filled with the very serious face of Mr. Chambers. "What can I do for you, Mr. Hamachi?" "Mr. Chambers, do we own any companies that use indentured labor?" Hamachi asked.

Cambers did not look away, "One moment." After a brief pause, "Yes sir, several, mostly manufacturing companies in Unincorporated Africa and Central Asia."

"Any on this continent? Transportation could be an issue."

"Understood, checking. We own a large portion of Mexican Rubber. I think most of their labor force is comprised of incarcerated prisoners."

"Yes I know this one. Too many political problems and bribes dealing with Mexico, too many people involved. I want this to be quiet. What about the Corporate Provinces of Canada. Easier to do business there."

"Yes sir, checking. We have a minor share of UnitedFarms. They use quite a few semi-skilled prisoners for their winter farm operations."

"What kind of prisoners?" Hamachi asked.

"Checking. Non-violent offenders, vagrancy, petty theft, that kind of thing."

"Perfect. Buy 300 labor contracts and have the men sent here as soon as possible." Hamachi said.

"I'm sorry sir, that is difficult at best. The US Canadian treaty strictly prohibits prison labor in the US. A Labor Union concession sir."

Hamachi was silent for a moment. "How does UnitedFarms transport its incarcerated labor through the US then?"

"I get your meaning sir. Just a minute. Yes, here it is. They use a subcontractor, which they own a majority share of: Prison Transport, Inc."

"If we buy this company, can we move prisoners through the US?" Hamachi asked.

"Yes sir, it holds the necessary license. I suggest we buy the transport company, then the required number of prisoner contracts. After that, we can move the prisoners without interference." Chambers said.

"Good, make it happen. I want 300 men here in Stratumentis in the next two weeks. And I want to be able to acquire another 300 soon after that if we need them."

"Yes sir." Chambers broke the connection.

Hamachi looked down at the expansive view of the Grand Canyon. It felt confining, claustrophobic somehow. "I'm sick of this manufactured air. I need to be outside."

The elevator ride, 200 stories through the spherical structure to the top of Stratumentis, took less than 10 minutes. Hamachi's voice command overrode all other riders, so it became an express elevator by the nature of its passenger. The top of Stratumentis was sheared flat, used as a helicopter and turbocopter platform. Hamachi got off the elevator and made his way through a series of corridors and door locks to the exit. A guard greeted him at the portal.

"Good afternoon sir. Is there anything I can do for you?" The guard asked, stepping out of Hamachi's way.

"No, I'm just getting some air." Hamachi said.

"Very good. May I offer you a parka? It can get pretty windy up here sir."

"Yes, of course." Hamachi took the coat and walked through the opening out onto the open deck and to the far end of the platform. Flurries of snow whirled around his feet without sticking to the cold metal grate. It was early spring, but still winter at this altitude. The steel-gray sky threatened a coming snow storm.

Hamachi leaned against the metal railing, admiring its simple functionality. Too much of the world was ornamentation, useless. He admired the unique view so different from the one at the bottom of Stratumentis. Here, one was above the high desert plain, looking out on the rocky landscape. The enormous sky, cloudy as it was, felt lifting, light and infinite. Hamachi scanned the desert. Off in the distance he spied a few of the cluster cities, too far away for any detail. The plain was unpopulated, owned and protected by Hamachi's company, Mitasashi Corporation. To the unknowing eye, it was just a wilderness dotted with cactus. Hamachi knew everything planted here were specially geneered crops cultivated for their high sugar content or other useful properties.

"Human beings have touched every crack, filled every inch of this world with their filthy larva." He thought.

Icy pinpricks from the snow-laden wind felt good on his heated face. The wind and snow wanted nothing, cared nothing for him or his city. Hamachi was overcome by a wave of melancholy. "Earth, you have been here for billions of years, most of that time, untouched and unspoiled. Then humanity arrived and in a few short years took over everything." Hamachi shook his head. "You, the mighty earth, have been tamed by a circus troop. Why didn't you put up a better fight than this, one worthy of your grandeur? Or maybe you're just very patient, waiting for the human parasite to kill itself off."

Hamachi felt a pair of eyes on his back and looked over his shoulder. The guard turned away quickly. He'd obviously been watching him. That was his job of course, still it irritated Hamachi. He looked back at the expansive scene for a moment, but the spell had been broken. "You may have the time to be patient," he spoke to the wind, "but I don't." And Hamachi stormed off the platform.

19

ALVAR PEERED THROUGH the drug induced haze at the surreal scene unfolding before him. Figures flowed around him, seemingly jumping from place to place as if bouncing through time. He tried to move, but his limbs wouldn't obey his brain. There was a heavy pressure crushing his whole body like the ocean at a great depth.

His attention was drawn to one of the figures - a very beautiful woman. Why is she crying? But before he could remember who she was, she disappeared. He felt a moment's sadness without knowing why. Then one by one, the hooded figures evaporated, except for one. He was very old, Alvar could see it in his eyes. They were very sad eyes, eyes that shouldn't hold another drop of sadness, but did anyway. Alvar wanted to comfort this old man, but he couldn't move, so he just stared at his face, helpless. Then, the old man stretched out an enormous hand covering Alvar's face and everything went black.

Alvar smelled dirt, felt its cold roughness against his cheek. It was familiar, calming, so he just lay there inhaling its earthy essence. His eyes were closed and he let his mind fill with memories of his parents, so long dead and his people working the land and his gentle lover, Chloe. What will happen to Chloe? And Alvar opened his eyes.

"Where am I?" Alvar dragged himself upright. He was weak and his feet hurt in the ill-fitting shoes. The air was cool, but pleasantly fresh. He could see a stand of trees, their bright green leaves spoke of early spring. And that rushing sound - a river. Alvar walked over to the bank, reached his hands in and splashed the cold water on his face. Then cupped his hands and drank deeply from them. It tasted strange, metallic.

Realization can arrive in many ways, suddenly, like a blunt instrument, or slowly like a rising tide. For Alvar it was the latter, slow understanding filled his mind like the water that satisfied his thirst. He sighed deeply. "I'm back at the edge of the wheat fields of the prison farm and this is the same river that so nearly killed me."

Alvar turned slowly looking at the scene more carefully now. He could have been home in Colorado. Even the air felt thin and cold like his home. Then he remembered Sigé, the beautiful girl without a voice that had risked so much to save him. There was no way to find her, thank her, contact her. She was a wood nymph, a memory and now she was gone.

He looked down at his hands and forearms. They were very pink and smooth, the nails fine and clear. "Ha!" He laughed out loud, then he sat down and tore his shoes off. His feet and calves were the same, pink and new. "They grew them back. My beautiful hands and feet." Alvar kissed his own hands and danced around, wincing and laughing at the pain as his brand new feet landed on sharp stones.

Eventually, it was time to do something about his situation. He was free, but he was also a long way from home. The city. Alvar looked in the direction of where he had seen the city lights so long ago. And he began walking. It felt good at first, to use his body after being immobile for so long. But soon he tired. He was weak and his new feet began to grow blisters in the rough shoes. It seemed like such a petty thing, yet occupied his mind utterly. Then he laughed out loud, "but I'm free."

He must be at the edge of the city, for he passed a few empty buildings. They might have been storage sheds or old farm houses, it was hard to say as they were so decrepit. Alvar debated with himself the right approach. Was it better to walk right into the crowded part of town, or risk frightening a stranger so far from anywhere? He decided on the former, he was less likely to stand out.

For all his confidence and ingenuity, Alvar had very little experience with the world. The Anti-Techs lived on their own, isolated. He had met a few of the merchants who would sell them tools and parts, but other than that, he had seen very little outside of Gaialandra. He shook this off. These people would be more like his own way up here. Living off the land, isolated from the great teaming masses.

Alvar came upon a road and took it. His burning feet were grateful for the flat surface. The whirring sound of a vehicle coming up behind him made him turn. A car passed him slowly. The darkened windows didn't allow Alvar to see inside. But the speed at which he passed, made it appear he was looking him over. The vehicle went on a bit, then stopped about 100 feet ahead. The driver rolled down his window and waited. Alvar stilled his heart, "Try not to act any more suspicious than you already look."

"Hey fellow, what're you doing way out here. Can I give you a lift into town?" The man said as Alvar walked alongside the vehicle.

"Uh sure, I'd love one." Alvar put on his best smile.

"Good, hop in."

Alvar got in and sat down, grateful to be off his feet. The driver looked at him steadily as he entered the car. He was an ordinary looking man in his late forties. He had dark, close cropped hair and the shadow of thick facial hair that no amount of shaving could hide. His clothes were simple, nondescript. If he was coming back from work, there was no way to tell what he did.

The man continued to look Alvar over, but said nothing. They drove for a few minutes, then he asked, "You look like you could use a hot meal. I'm on my way home. Why don't you join us for supper?"

Supper? Who spoke like this anymore? Alvar's heart (and stomach) sang out, "If it's not too much trouble, I would love that."

"No trouble at all, let me call my wife and let her know we have a guest." The man tapped his temple and said a few words into the air. "Good, it's all set, we'll be there shortly."

The man was quiet after that and Alvar began to relax. Perhaps his luck had finally changed for the better. It would be a long way back to Colorado, but he'd find a way.

They drove through the small town, dense considering how far north it was and how far from anywhere else. The buildings were new and made of plasticrete with small regular windows dotting their surface. They were the ubiquitous architecture that pervaded the late 21st century – functional only. The vehicle pulled into an underground parking garage.

"This is it. We're on the fifth floor. Nothing very glamorous, but it's our home." The driver said.

"My name's Alvar." Alvar said putting out his hand.

The man nodded, taking Alvar's hand limply. "My name's Frank and you'll meet my wife in a minute, Julie."

Alvar followed Frank into the elevator and up to their apartment. Frank unlocked the door with a swipe of his thump and urged Alvar inside. It was a simple place, three rooms, Alvar guessed. The one small window looked out onto another building. "Sit down, make yourself comfortable. It looks like Julie stepped out, but I'm sure she'll be right back. It's been a long day. Why don't you relax while I change my clothes." Franked backed away, then closed one of the interior doors behind him.

Alvar sat for a moment, grateful to be inside and safe. It had been so long. And though his feet throbbed from their recent abuse, he got up and looked around the apartment. He had never been inside a home other than the Anti-Techs. It was sparse and ugly. The walls, ceiling and floors were all formed from a single seamless material. There were some cheap framed pictures on the walls, holographs of mountains and rivers, but badly done and blurry as if looked at from an angle. The tables were made out of the same gray plasticrete as the walls and blended into the room too thoroughly. There were no books or objects. Alvar grimaced. "What an impersonal, cold place. Not a home at all."

Melancholy weighed on him, "What's the point. Living like this, working all day to pay for it, then coming home to the same empty walls every night." He shook his head. "No, it's not this place. I miss my people, my home. I won't lose that again." Alvar promised himself.

He walked over to the window and looked down on the street. It was midday now, but there was no traffic at all. Everything was quiet, strangely so. "What's taking Frank so long? And where's his wife? Why would she leave, knowing they had a guest coming?" Alvar thought. "Stop it, you're being paranoid. A few weeks in the wheat and a few more getting your limbs regrown is enough to make anyone paranoid. You don't know this world, their customs, manners. You are the savage here. Try to fit in." Alvar berated himself.

Alvar sat back down on the stiff sofa. But the feeling wouldn't leave. Frank had been gone too long, his wife was not here. He got up and knocked on the door of the room Frank had left through. "Frank? Excuse me, Frank?"

No answer.

"Frank? Are you in there?" He shouted louder. Then Alvar tried the door. It was locked. "No this isn't right." Alvar tried the front door. It was locked too. His heart began to pound. Damn it, how stupid am I? I should know better than to trust ..."

"Hey where're you going fella'? You OK, you look a little green." It was Frank just coming out of the other room.

Alvar spun around. Frank's hair was wet and he was wearing different clothes. "Uh yeah, fine, just looking around. It seemed like a long time."

"Oh sorry, I took a shower. You know, kind of a long day. Judy get in yet?" Frank said to Alvar, but kept his eyes on the front door.

"No, no one's been here. Judy? Didn't you say your wife's name was Julie?"

"No, I never said Julie, I should know my wife's name, shouldn't I. Sit down, you're too antsy." Frank's eyes kept darting toward the door. "You wait here. I'd better check on her."

Alvar started to protest, "I think it's better if I left, I'm intruding and..."

"No! Don't move. I said I'd be right back. I told you I have to check on Judy."

Frank moved through the front door before Alvar could follow. The door slammed shut behind him. Alvar tried the handle, but it was locked.

"What the hell! Alvar's mind screamed at him. Julie, Judy, there's no wife." Alvar went over to the interior room. Frank had left the door open. There was only a single bed in the room and laying on it was the plain jacket Frank had been wearing. Alvar saw a logo on the sleeve. He walked closer to read it. "UF." UnitedFarms! Alvar turned and ran to the front door. But when he grabbed the handle he felt it turn in his hand.

The door burst open, smashing him on the shoulder and knocking him to the ground. Three men piled into the tiny apartment, quickly surrounding him as he sprawled on the floor. Their faces were covered in dark shields, but Alvar recognized the uniforms and worse - the insignia on their helmets, UF – UnitedFarms.

"What took you so fucking long?" It was Frank's voice from the doorway, his folksy accent gone. "Take it easy on my apartment or you can add that to the reward too."

"I should have known. No one helps a stranger, not here, not anywhere." Alvar hissed. Now he recognized the ubiquitous VR set on Frank's head. He must have scanned my face and been alerted that I was missing. "Damn this high tech world." He spat. One of the UnitedFarms guards reached to his side and pulled a Taser from his belt. Alvar rolled, but there was no avoiding the dart at this distance in the tiny apartment. He felt the sharp sting, then the gut wrenching shock of 50,000 volts unleashed in his body, then blackness.

Alvar awoke, only able to move his eyes. His head throbbed and his limbs ached as if just on the verge of numbness. The claustrophobic fear of paralysis made him try to call out, but only a small moan managed to escape. The taste of rubber and the pull at his cheeks, told him of the bit in his mouth. Alvar tried pushing it out with his tongue. When that failed, he tried to bite though it, but hit steel just below the rubber, wincing as he nearly cracked his teeth.

He tried to move his right hand and felt a slight give to his restraints. Sure that it was not his imagination, he tried his other hand then his feet, his legs, his arms, and finally his neck. Each time he encountered a resistance, which seemed to give slightly, then hold. Alvar concentrated on his right index finger. It was plastic. He must be wrapped in plastic. Rather than feel triumphant at the discovery, he was horrified and his anxiety grew.

He stretched his eyes as far as he could in every direction. But there was nothing to see, just a steel ceiling meeting steel walls. He could hear that he wasn't alone. The groaning of several others reached him. The room couldn't be that large by the sound of the echoes and the distance of the groans.

He lay like this for what must have been an hour. Then he blinked suddenly at the intensity of bright light that filled his vision. At the same time, large doors scraped open followed by the sliding sound of metal on metal, something like a large tray or drawer on its glides might make. The whole room moved from the weight of something substantial. If the room moved and was made of steel, perhaps it was not a room at all, maybe it was a container or transport vehicle of some kind.

The brightness dimmed as the flat panel slid completely over his view about 8 inches from his face. Alvar felt the intensity of claustrophobia begin to overwhelm him. He fought it off with a force of will. In desperation and distraction, he tried to make out what he was looking at. The gloom and the closeness to his face made it difficult to understand. It was not simply a cover or panel as it was strangely rounded. His eyes soon adapted to the dim light and he was able to make out the color and texture of the object so close to his face. Tight blue plastic mesh rounded into a ball, but flatter, narrowing quickly and then widening again. Behind the mesh, he could make out a brown fibrous material matted and damp, like hair or fur. That's what it was, hair, Alvar realized in sudden shock. He was looking at the back of a man's head wrapped in blue plastic mesh! The narrowing shape was the neck and the widening, the shoulders.

Alvar's eyes followed the shape as far as he could force them. He could just see the person's lower back. Then he peered left and right. He saw the same shape repeated both directions at least twice, which was as far as he could stretch his eyes. He determined he must be looking at a kind of wide stretcher holding five bodies across. Each was enveloped in the same blue plastic mesh. Alvar realized the groaning he heard must be others on each side of him and perhaps below him as well. Each man was encapsulated in plastic and laid out on racks like loaves of cooling bread. The room was filled with them.

He made some quick mental calculations, if this were a transport vehicle, he figured there could be as many as six layers stacked vertically and at least two deep of these human vacuum packs – that would mean 60 prisoners in a transport! Alvar fought desperately against panic and claustrophobia, willing himself to remain calm.

After about an hour of loading more stretchers, Alvar finally felt the movement of the vehicle. He was grateful for any change, it meant they were a step closer to getting out of these plastic cocoons. But hours passed with nothing. Perhaps because of the intensity of his anxiety or the after effects, Alvar felt sleepy and gave in to the gift of unconsciousness.

He was awakened by a jolt. The doors to the transport were open and letting in filtered daylight. The sound and smells coming in told Alvar they were at an airport. One by one, the pallets were unloaded, until they finally came to Alvar's. The cold air and the infinite blue of the sky were a great relief to his claustrophobic anguish. But it was not long before he was loaded on to a cargo plane and the scenery was once again reduced to the back of another man's head eight inches from his own.

The light in the hold of the cargo plane was even dimmer than that of the transport vehicle. There was nothing to see anyway and Alvar drifted off again. Several hours must have passed before he felt the descent of the plane. In a short while they landed and began the process of unloading the wrapped men. He could see and hear the helicopters, sometimes feel the rush of wind as they took off. These smaller vehicles had to load and unload their cargo, obviously not capable of carrying the same number as the larger airplane. Alvar's pallet was left waiting on the warm tarmac.

By the thinness of the air and the intensity of the sky, Alvar guessed that they must be at some altitude. The sun, which at first was welcome, became warm, then unpleasantly hot. The plastic magnified the discomfort and Alvar felt himself sweating profusely. But he didn't feel thirsty. Strange. They must be pumping fluids into him somehow. He moved his awareness about his body, but could feel no attachments.

Eventually the helicopter returned. A forklift slid under the foot end of his pallet and loaded him into the hold, along with several others. The flight was short, less than five minutes. He was off-loaded in the same way. His pallet was separated into individual stretchers and placed on gurneys. He and the four others were wheeled into a large cargo elevator. They moved down for at least ten long minutes. "Down? They must have been on the roof and this building must be enormous." Alvar thought. They were wheeled from the elevator and down many long corridors where the overhead lights swept monotonously. He was pushed through two large doors and the ceiling lifted high overhead. He could tell the room must be quite large by the sound of people talking and the scrape of equipment far away. The stretchers were not stacked, at least not above him. Alvar was grateful for this small gift.

The room was filled with the frenetic energy of men working and Alvar listened to the metallic sounds of carts being pushed around along with the constant terse conversations of technicians.

Eventually a team moved into sight. Three men dressed in white hovered over him; each with a stylized "M" logo on their sleeve, which meant nothing to Alvar. One technician leaned over Alvar holding a large plug, tubes and wires sprouting like grass from its end. He shoved it into place, then turned it with a positive snapping sound. He looked directly into Alvar's eyes and said with the tedium of repeated lines, "I'm going to remove your mouth and head restraints now if you'll cooperate. It makes it easier for you to eat and is a lot less work for us. It is also healthier. However, if you begin screaming and yelling, or biting, we'll put the restraints back on and feed you by nose drip. That means a long tube inserted into your nose that goes all the way into your stomach. Yes it is uncomfortable. You don't want that, right. If you agree to be calm, then blink twice. Good. Now before I remove your restraints, I want you to understand some things. First, don't ask me or any other technicians any questions. I don't know why you're here, and if I did, I wouldn't tell you. Second, don't ever try to bite me or any of the attendants. It will go very badly for you. Any resistance now or in the future and you will be restrained and gagged. Don't abuse this small freedom, understand? So one last time, blink twice for yes if you agree. Good."

When the mouth bit and head restraint had been removed, Alvar stretched his mouth and neck in relief. He whispered hoarsely, "Thank you."

"Sure thing." The attendant grunted, already absorbed in his work. In a moment, he placed a large tube next to Alvar's mouth. "This is your feeding tube. Bite it to open the valve and then suck the mixture into your mouth. On the other side of your head is a similar tube for water, it works the same way. That's it."

The attendant moved away and in a moment Alvar could hear the conversation being repeated to the prisoner to the left of him. Now that he could turn his head, he looked around as best he could. What he saw was macabre. They were indeed in a large room or warehouse. The stretchers of trapped men were spread out in a strict grid-like orientation, creating isles of about four feet wide throughout the room. Tubes and wires emanated from each prisoner gathering into a thick bundle that led down the far right corner of the gurney and into the floor beneath his vision. Alvar could see numerous attendants working their way through the room with carts and tools attaching tubes and wires to the captives.

Alvar turned to the man to his right and whispered. "What's going on?"

The man looked at him with an incredulous look and whispered back, "Where you been man, don't you know?"

"The UF guards caught me after an escape and I woke up wrapped in this nightmare. So I don't know much. I'd appreciate it if you could fill me in." Alvar said through his teeth.

"Wow. It's you." The man said with awe in his voice. "We heard about you, the escape artist. No wonder you don't know what's going on. I can only tell you what I overheard from the guards, but it looks like we are some kind of guinea pigs for some kind of research. Nothin' gruesome I hear. But hey, tell me about your escape, the whole camp was talking about it for weeks. That was some trick man. How'd you get the collar off anyway?"

"Never mind that. What kind of research?" Alvar whispered back.

"Beats me. But it's got to be better than freezing our asses off up in Canada."

Alvar didn't answer to that. He knew it could be a lot worse. "Do you at least know where we are?"

"Oh yeah, they always try to keep this stuff a big secret, but it always gets out. So why do they bother. We're in some kind of crazy round city floating in the Grand Canyon. This rich guy, Hitachi or Hamachi, or something like that, built it so no one could get to him. Paranoid I guess. Man, if I had that kind of money, I wouldn't waste it on shit like this."

Alvar ignored the man's rambling. "The Grand Canyon." He thought, fighting against the plastic mesh. "I'm so close, so close."

20

ZEKIEL RODE THE satellite feed, dully looking down at the Anti-Tech community of Gaialandra. Even from this height, it was clear where UnitedFarms stopped and the Anti-Tech farm began. The crops were different, their very texture and dense green color told their genetic story. The Anti-Tech fields looked anemic in comparison, the soil showing between rows of struggling crops. Ezekiel imagined the Anti-Techs bent over, pulling out the genetically altered plants from their fields. Stronger, faster growing, resistant to insects, disease and drought, their weeds were the fitter species.

Chloe haunted his thoughts. And he knew he'd made a mess of things with her, pushed too hard, too fast. "Damn that Alvar, it's all his fault. Why hadn't the fool just died in the river like a normal human being? And me, a fool for telling Chloe the truth. How hard would it have been to lie? Nothing. A change of a few words. But she bewitched me."

Ezekiel had learned that Alvar had been discovered by Frank Dubin, an accountant on his way home from a UnitedFarms office in Craik, Northern Canada. Bad luck for Alvar. UnitedFarms had written him off as dead, closed his file, but the tracking programs had not been removed.

Face recognition software that combed the system looking for fugitives. When they found the dead man, his file was reopened and they shipped him down to Arizona, Hamachi's lair. Ezekiel tracked all of this easily enough. Then Alvar disappeared into Stratumentis and Ezekiel could get no further. So he rushed down to Gaialandra to give Chloe the good news. But things didn't go exactly as he had planned. He squirmed with the memory of his trip to Gaialandra.

"Oh it's you." Chloe said opening the door a crack.

It was the same building he had been led to last fall. But Gaialandra looked much different now. It was summer, and everything was green, people and carts moved about busily.

"I have news about Alvar." Ezekiel toned hopefully.

Chloe gave Ezekiel a long look, first at his mouth, then into his prosthetic eyes. "OK, come on it then."

This was not going at all like he planned. "I uh, could I have a glass of water or something, it was a long trip from New Denver."

Without realizing it, Ezekiel had said the perfect thing. "Oh my, I'm being terribly rude. Come in, I'll get you a cold drink. Here, sit down." Chloe ran off to get something.

Ezekiel was relieved. "I don't get it, but I like it." He sat down in a stuffed chair near the window. There was another next to it, presenting the promise of intimacy.

A moment later, Ezekiel was sipping on something delicious he had never tasted before, fresh lemonade.

"Feeling better?" She asked.

"Yes, fine. I just had so much to tell you and it all kind of evaporated when I saw you." He said.

"Why don't you start at the beginning. After I saw you last fall you said you were going to try to watch Alvar. Were you able to do that?"

"Yes." And Ezekiel began to tell the story of Alvar's journey from prison worker to escapee to freedom and back. It took some time. Chloe never interrupted, yet her expressive face changed often. Sometimes simply attentive, then tortured, disgusted, proud, and finally hopeful.

"After all that, he's so close, in Arizona. Thank you Ezekiel. I think

I misjudged you. You are a blessing. And I am truly grateful for what you've done and the risks you've taken. I don't understand much of it, but I know you've broken the laws to do it." She looked out at the warm green day through the window. "A few months ago, I wouldn't have listened to you. I had believed it was wrong to break the law. But things are different now. I know that the law is just another lever they use to get what they want. If you use it to get what you want, what I want, then it is simply their lever being used against them." Then Chloe was silent.

Ezekiel inhaled the profile of her face gently silhouetted against the bright window. Her long dark hair waterfalled down covering half her face. The sun lit the tiny blond hairs on the side of her jaw and neck highlighting them against her deep tan. He followed the curve of her neck down to her delicate shoulder, through the thin cotton dress and on to the rise of her small bosom. She was all angles and curves, softness wrapped in coarseness. He ached for her. It was difficult to sit still as his fantasy blurred with reality. Now that she knew what he had done for her, he dreamed she would reward him with the only thing he wanted. Ezekiel waited, unable to speak.

"You know things are not good here now." She whispered. "A few months ago, I would have taken as much money as needed and driven over to buy his contract, or bribe whoever I needed to, to get him out. But that's not possible any longer. UnitedFarms has pressed us against the wall. If we fight back, we are arrested and sent to their labor camps. If we let them move forward, we'll be overrun and our land simply taken. We get in their way, we sabotage their equipment. But they are catching on and little by little we disappear. I wish Alvar was here to tell me what to do. Oh god how I miss him." She put her head in her hands and quietly wept.

Ezekiel watched in wonder. Should he say something, touch her shoulder, pull her hair back and kiss her. This wasn't like the holo-vids, where everyone seemed so confident, sure. Here in reality, one didn't have a script. So he just waited, blinking his prosthetic eyes.

Chloe looked up, her eyes glistening. "What do we do, how do we get Alvar out of there?"

For all his fantasizing and planning, this was not a question he had anticipated. Somehow just letting her know Alvar was alive was supposed to be enough. She would thank him and be his. "I – I don't know." Was all he managed.

Chloe was quiet for some time. She seemed to have decided something in her own mind. "Of course not. You found him, though, and that is a great thing." She sighed. "I'm sorry, if there's nothing else, I have so much to do." She stood up.

"I'll find something." He blurted out.

"No. You've done enough. Now please go back to your life. We have nothing to offer you here." And she turned her back on him.

Ezekiel was desperate to say or do something that would keep her from leaving, but nothing came. He could only stare at her back as she walked into the interior of the room, then disappeared around a corner.

<hr />

On the way back to New Denver, Ezekiel had replayed their conversation over and over. "What did I do wrong?" Then something hit him. "It's not me, it's Alvar. He's in my way. As long as there is hope that he'll return, I'm just a pawn, a tool to be used for her obsession. But, if he were...out of the way, she would forget about him, move on with her life. Of course, how could I be interesting to her while Alvar is still available. They've probably known each other their whole lives. Lived and worked together, like brother and sister." Ezekiel played back the video of Bannock's visit to Gaialandra. The UnitedFarms agent spoke so logically and persuasively, Ezekiel didn't understand the Anti-Techs resistance. Then he watched Alvar speak and imagined Chloe staring in reverence. Oh it was all so sick and incestuous. But that made sense too. There couldn't be more than two hundred people living in Gaialandra. And how many of those were children and old people. So there weren't many choices. He grew jealous, then aroused. "How do I get Alvar out of the way and still look like the hero?"

Ezekiel pushed the memory of his visit to Chloe away. He berated himself for wasting time staring at Gaialandra, with nothing to show for his effort. Stratumentis was his goal, but it was a fortress. He'd tried a dozen times to break in, always ending up in failure, then coming back to his perch in the sky. "There's got to be a way in." He pounded his virtual fist into his palm.

Stratumentis' defenses were something he'd never faced. Round and round he went, tapping on walls made of titanium, windows shuttered with plated steel, fences a thousand feet high topped with razor wire, and every data pipe screened or locked. It was all illusion of course, virtual metaphors for high security technology and firewalls, but the fact remained, it was impregnable.

"It's impossible." He mumbled, "Every system has a flaw, a hole, a backdoor, a forgotten data port, something. But apparently not Stratumentis. How do they use *the I* then?" Ezekiel asked himself.

He inspected the data pipes leading to and from Stratumentis. They were enormous, designed for massive data transfer, yet they were quiet, barely used at all. Ezekiel absently twanged on the cable coming from is prosthetic eye. "I'm trying too hard." He thought. "I need to take a more subtle approach to this problem." He disconnected from *the I*.

Ezekiel spent the next several hours reprogramming moles, simple little programs that searched for access vulnerability. And like their living analog, they were blind, feeling their way along data pipes and walls for cracks and holes. Once released, moles lived independently from their maker, only reporting when they found something.

Finally the little creatures were ready and Ezekiel set them free. He waited and waited. When nothing happened, he knew they'd failed or been destroyed by Stratumentis' security. This didn't discourage Ezekiel, who expected this to take some time. He made subtle modifications and released another batch, repeating this process over and over. Then finally, one reported it had made it through.

Ezekiel jumped into the stream. His mole faced him growling. It was built like an enormous rodent with long sharp claws that could tear through steel and pointed fangs that could bite through fiber-optic cables. The mole edged closer, bearing its hideous teeth. It gave Ezekiel a sniff, then recognized him and crouched down to be mounted. Ezekiel climbed onto the creature's back and into a leather saddle. If anyone else had tried to mount it, it would have fought, run or erased itself.

The mole took off at a full run, speeding through the main traffic routes, dashing down the Las Vegas interchange – an enormous data pipe, dozens of virtual miles in diameter. It made a sharp right-hand turn at full speed down a much narrower corridor. An inexperienced rider might have fallen from the mole, or been confused by the blur of motion, but Ezekiel held on tight and marveled at the deft skill of his creation. It turned quickly again and again, down smaller and smaller tunnels until it arrived at an enormous titanium wall, polished to a perfect mirror finish. The mole sniffed along the edges and crawled straight up the face, its claws somehow finding purchase. It was only then that Ezekiel realized it wasn't a wall, but the outside of an enormous pipe, so large in diameter that the curve wasn't visible from up close.

Clinging to the upper polished surface, the mole stopped and began sniffing again, backing up and moving forward slightly. Ezekiel began to doubt the creature, the surface looked perfect, impregnable. But then it put its nose into a rough area no larger than a grain of sand. The mole shrank and Ezekiel with it, until the rough spot grew to the size of a boulder. And then Ezekiel saw it – a single crack. He and the mole shrank further still until they were able to squeeze through the opening.

The cavern on the other side was brightly lit and the walls just as highly polished as the outside. Ezekiel looked up to see a lone data packet speed by in the vast empty space. He gave the mole a kick, there was no sense wasting time in a transmission tube. They galloped downstream with the data traffic. The mole chose branch after branch, never hesitating, until they stopped abruptly at a gigantic barrier and waited. Ezekiel was puzzled, but trusted his program, if there was a way in, it would discover it. Bundles of data arrived, stopped and hovered in the air next to the pair. The packets were wrapped liked stacks of paper, tied with string. "How quaint." Ezekiel sneered. Soon there were about a hundred packets floating in front of the flat wall. Suddenly, the barrier rotated. Ezekiel, the mole and all the packets of data were forced through a screen with openings just large enough for each packet to squeeze through. It was a security valve of some sort, unique in Ezekiel's experience. He gave a silent nod to the engineers who had created it. "Inefficient, but effective."

They were inside. Ezekiel let himself be buffeted around by the data packets in the stream. He had done it and he allowed himself a moment to relish his success. But only a moment, then he began looking for information about Alvar. He followed the data stream to the prisoner acquisition files, where he quickly found Alvar and the other 299 prisoners moved from Canada.

Ezekiel took a deep breath as he moved into the video surveillance pipe of the large laboratory. After so many months of work, he was just seconds away from Alvar. It had been a dry, mechanical pursuit, but now it was personal. Hatred welled in his throat as he thought of his rival, the impediment to Chloe.

He tapped on the virtual screen, on Alvar's name. Ezekiel still mounted on the mole, was whipped to a visual spot at the ceiling of a large room. He glared down at the surreal site, a cruel smile formed on his mouth. Three hundred prisoners lay completely immobilized, wrapped in blue medical plastic. Tubes and wires snaked from each man's body coalescing into a bundle at the foot of each table. It was better than he could have ever imagined.

The computer gave him the exact location of Alvar's station. Ezekiel zoomed in on the trapped face, Alvar staring up into space, blinking, daydreaming. Ezekiel laughed. "I'll bet you didn't expect me, farmer boy."

Ezekiel felt a tug at his arm and he whipped around, his heart about to tear through his chest, to discover a white-robed figure mounted atop a white Ostrich. The face was hidden inside the hood, but he knew who it was – the ghost. "You!" He shouted.

The robed figure pointed at Alvar and shook its head. Ezekiel felt the manic fear that all hackers avoid yet seek. It was the thrill of knowing you could get caught, but not getting caught. He gathered his wits. He'd cracked Stratumentis and no one was going to tell him what to do inside, not even a ghost.

No sooner had he finished the thought, when the ostrich jumped up and kicked him off his mole. There was no use for it now anyway and Ezekiel plunged a virtual knife into its side. The mole shimmered and vanished. "What do you want?" He hissed.

The robed figure pointed ominously at Alvar again and shook its covered head.

"Don't tell me what I can or can't do." Ezekiel hissed. He swung at the white figure. But it easily dodged the blow. It sat silent, proud atop the white ostrich, which infuriated Ezekiel

"I know you. I saw you in the GSA covering your greasy tracks. Why are you helping Alvar?" Ezekiel asked.

The figure shook its head in response.

Damn, they were wasting time in here. How long before some anti-body program was triggered. Ezekiel went to maximum stealth and dropped in next to Alvar, now just inches from his face. "This is my hack, I do what I want." Ezekiel felt a kick in his side. The ghost was off the ostrich which had wedged itself between him and Alvar.

Alarm bells screeched in his virtual ears. Security. Ezekiel whipped his head around, quickly scanning the room. Their activity must have triggered a security response. Dozens of white balls had formed in the air, macrophages – virtual antibodies that would try to trap him and track his physical location. "Damn you!" Ezekiel howled. But the robed figure and the ostrich were gone. "Time for me to go too."

He took a quick glance at the helpless Alvar. Ezekiel would have loved to strangle the arrogant mite, or at the very least, slap him, but he knew it was too late. He'd have to work his way in again. Ezekiel grabbed a small black ball from his belt – an anti-personnel mine. "If I'm going to get locked out of this place, I'm going to leave some damage." Ezekiel pulled the pin. But too fast for him to react, a macrophage enveloped the mine, absorbing the explosion. Ezekiel tried again, but with the same effect. He ripped other devices from his belt, flash bombs, data mines, virtual flack, but all of them ended the same way.

Ezekiel felt real panic now. There was only one way out of here now, pull the physical connections from his prosthetic eyes back in his apartment in New Denver. Ezekiel tried desperately to ignore the sensory input before him. But the advantage of the optic link, was also its disadvantage. The sensory input of virtual reality was not filtered through his living eyes, which he could have closed against VR glasses. Instead, virtual reality was being fed directly to his brain through the optic nerve. His brain wasn't able to tell the difference between what he saw here in Stratumentis and the apartment he visualized in New Denver.

The white puffs wrapped his body, immobilizing him completely. Ezekiel fought desperately to ignore what he saw and felt. It was such a simple thing to reach up and pull the cables from his eyes. He'd done it thousands of times. But his body disobeyed him as in a frightful nightmare, half awake, but unable to move.

"Feeling trapped, thief?" A giant face filled Ezekiel's dimming vision, nearly covered now by the antibodies. Ezekiel recognized the image, Hamachi. "Did you imagine, in your wildest dreams, you could just slither in here and I wouldn't notice, then just leave so you could come back again another day. No, Ezekiel Malaffaires, I don't abide thieves, I crush them. Try to sense your body and you'll understand. Right now, in New Denver, your filthy carcass is being held by my Cor-police."

Ezekiel gave another tug at his arms. He seemed to feel the grip of strong hands on his limbs. But it was confused with the squeeze of macrophages surrounding his body here in Stratumentis. Terror overwhelmed the hacker and he thrashed in wild panic.

"Wasted effort, thief. I have your mind, and shortly, I'll have your body." Hamachi said as the macrophages covered the last of his vision with a great, seamless black.

21

ALEXIA, OF COURSE, knew of the 300 prisoners moved to Stratumentis. They had been prepared, analyzed and genetically mapped. But she had never seen them. Her work had been systematic, mechanical, not requiring her personal attention.

But now standing here at the entrance to the enormous holding room, Alexia was struck with just how large a number 300 is. Stratumentis was a city, but it was also a single building. One didn't expect such voluminous spaces inside a building. There, spread before her, was the sea of prisoners, 300 cocooned men in blue plastic mesh. The efficiency of the tubes and wires running from each man into the floor startled her. Had all this infrastructure been planned ahead, built into the room? Had Hamachi envisioned even this?

She wasn't sure how long she'd been standing at the entrance, when Ong touched her shoulder.

"Doctor Serguey?"

Alexia didn't answer right away. Ong's interruption focused her mind, pulled her back to the present, away from an awful desire to vomit.

"Yes, Ong." Alexia turned away from the prone men and focused on

Ong's narrow face, the almond eyes and short dark hair, pretty, Alexia thought, in a mechanical way.

"The implants have been fabricated and implanted. The prisoners are ready to be connected. Upon your order."

"Ready? All 300?" Alexia asked.

"Yes doctor, all of them."

Hamachi had insisted on connecting all of these men simultaneously. There was no earthly reason to put so many men at risk at once. She had argued against it vehemently. But Hamachi was as intractable, as he was impatient and the decision was made. All at once.

"And the computers, are they ready too?"

"Yes doctor, everything is ready. It is only for you to say the command."

"There is no reason for delay, is there?"

"No reason for delay." Ong echoed.

"Then proceed."

Ong spoke some faint words into her VR set, then back to Alexia. "The connection has been established."

As with the previous experiments, there was little to see. The men lay quietly, actually more so now that the connection had begun. The prisoners were being physically linked, like the first experiment with Spartan and Smith, the only real difference was the computer arrangement. All available quantum computers were set up to facilitate the connection only. No attempt was being made to record the data. A cursory attempt had been made to analyze the existing recordings. Nothing useful so far had been found in the volumes of data.

"Where are Spartan and Smith?" Alexia asked.

"In a small holding room at the northeastern corner." Ong pointed to the far end of the vast room.

Alexia tensed. They'd have to walk through the chamber to reach them. "Very well, lead on. I must speak with them. View their reaction."

Ong walked in front, Alexia focused on the back of her head. But though the men were quiet, lost in the sleep of the connection, there was plenty of activity. Technicians moved like bees among their flowers, checking and adjusting fluids and wires.

Alexia glanced at some of the prone faces as they walked past. They were dull, stupid looking men. Somehow this made her feel a little better. Men who didn't matter.

Alexia stopped. "Who is this man?" She asked Ong.

Ong did not turn. "His name is Alvar Terrahaute."

"And is he a criminal like the others?"

"Yes. It says he was convicted of interfering with an authorized worker."

"That's pretty vague. What does that mean?"

"I'm sorry doctor, there is no other information.

Alexia stared at Alvar's face. He was different from the others. His high forehead and strong mouth suggested intelligence. His skin was oddly mottled, peeling as if from an injury or burn. How did he get that? She wondered.

"Shall we move on doctor." Ong urged, still facing forward.

"Just a moment." Alexia tore her eyes from Alvar's face and looked around the room. They were somewhere in the middle of the men. Trapped bodies sprawled outward 80, 90, maybe 100 feet in each direction. "So many men." She breathed. There was something beautiful in the repeating pattern, it calmed her, allowed her mind to work again. And then it came to her, why it was so important to Hamachi to connect so many at once.

"Yes, let us proceed."

They entered the small room adjacent to the large holding chamber. Alexia noticed her own breathing, as if she had been holding it previously. She approached the quiet forms of doctors Spartan and Smith.

"Wake Spartan, I want to speak with him." She said roughly to Ong.

"Ong hesitated, but didn't argue. Alexia knew this was her way of voicing her disagreement.

Spartan didn't open his eyes and spoke haltingly, his voice trailing off. "Please doctor Serguey, this is very difficult, not at all like a single mind."

"So you are in contact with the men in there." She gestured to the sea of men on the other side of the thick window.

A long pause. "Yes. But it is difficult. They are separate, their brains are not ready. We are helping them, but... They are resistant. They don't understand. Please doctor, let us..." And he was quiet.

Hamachi's voice sounded in her headset. There was no image. "They must be manipulating the minds of the prisoners to accept communication without the aid of the computers."

"Agreed." Alexia answered. "They may be working with only one and connecting to the others that way. But it is logical that they will manipulate all the men eventually. Do you object?"

"On the contrary. I encourage it."

Alexia's stomach clenched. "And how will you control them if they are linked without the computers?"

She heard the smile in Hamachi's voice. "Very good doctor. But that won't be your concern. Contact me if there are any changes."

22

ALVAR AWOKE TO a vast emptiness, a kind of night sky with distant lights or stars. He was fully aware, conscious that he was not dreaming. He was sure of that. Stranger than that, he could sense this world in all directions. "Hello." He called. But the void absorbed the sound without an echo. Reaching his awareness outward toward the other lights, he realized they were others like himself, disembodied consciousness. His mind tested, questioned itself. Am I frightened? But he was not frightened, only intensely curious. He reached harder and felt a kind of pulling from the others. Alvar held onto the feeling, like tugging on a rope with a heavy weight attached.

Seconds, or millennia may have passed, time didn't exist here. Only the gentle pull from the others. A kind of momentum began to form and the pulling grew easier as the lights grew brighter. Alvar began to pick up bits of thoughts and memory from the others. He would see a foreign memory, like the inside of an apartment he'd never been in, a crushed toy, or an unrecognizable face. But they were fragments, easily separated from his own thoughts and memories.

The momentum grew and the lights sped toward his own. The fragments multiplied and grew into full memories. Alvar found himself in a windowless apartment in New York City. A place he had never been. Fear permeated the crowded rooms, the very air was thick with it. His mind tripped over broken furniture and boxes as he stumbled through the memory. The black threshold of a dark room drew him impossibly forward. There was pain and humiliation there, but he couldn't turn away, the memory had to play itself out to the end. Alvar inched toward the darkness, his disembodied consciousness felt the crush of his racing heart. A shape formed from the blackness, a man's face. The face was all angles and shadows, with sunken eyes and broken teeth. Another memory nudged, reminding him it was not his father, but his mother's cruel boyfriend. He was a ten year old boy facing this giant. A great hand emerged from the dark doorway, massive and gnarled, it reached for him. "NO!" Alvar shouted. The hand, large enough to wrap his entire head, grabbed his thin arm, crushing it to the bone, pulling him into the terrible blackness. Fear thickened into a living presence and overwhelmed the helpless boy.

Alvar returned to the star filled sky, his consciousness breathless from the nightmare. But it wasn't a dream, it was a real memory, someone else's memory. He shook the feeling, reminding himself this was not his memory, but a borrowed one. Slowly, he shed the fear and dread that had threatened to overwhelm him a second before. "What is this place that I can remember another man's memory?"

The stars were now close enough to fill the sky, barely any space remained between them anymore. "We are going to collide." He thought.

Another memory filled his mind. It was of a bird lying on the ground. It had flown into a high window and broken its neck. It was all feeling, strange and melancholy. Another memory replaced it before he could understand. Alvar was looking at the back of a large naked woman. She stood erect in front of a stove cooking something and laughing. It was pleasant. Another memory replaced this one, then another and another. Soon they were coming too fast to discern where one started and another ended. Memories merged into a thick mud of emotion and sensation. Alvar lost his sense of self as his own memories blended into the mix.

Then there was a brilliant blinding flash followed by cool darkness.

Alvar awoke to a vast emptiness, vaguely aware of other lights far in the distance. The process repeated itself, his consciousness pulling on the others, the memories coming faster and faster, then the flash and then empty space again. But each time, he retained a bit more of the others. The cycle of pulling together, then exploding apart repeated faster, eventually becoming flashing light, then continuous brightness, then incomprehensible awareness.

Alvar saw a woman in front of him, a very beautiful woman. She was familiar, then he recognized her as Sigé, the girl who had helped him from the frozen river. She was speaking to him.

"Alvar, your mind is trying to integrate something wonderful into itself, but you are resisting, fighting against it, against yourself. You have so many friends here to welcome you. You hear them, don't you?"

"Yes, I hear them. But they are not my friends. They are bitter, angry, jealous men. Men without hope or ambition, men with horrible memories."

He felt, rather than saw the beautiful smile. "Yes. It is true that they have had difficult lives. Much of it is their own fault and some of it is the inability to fit into the world. You understand that, don't you dear Alvar, not being able to fit in. But it is time to leave all that behind. They have. Won't you?"

"I don't know." He said.

"No, Alvar you do know. Don't try to deceive me or hide your thoughts. I hear them as easily as you do. It is natural to want to remain separate, individual. We have lived alone so long, all of us have. But we don't have to, not any longer. Think of it. All the cruel misunderstandings, the fear of an unknown stranger, the doubts and insecurities. None of it will exist any longer. You will know others as you know yourself. We will all be together, one. You can feel the rightness of it, the pull, can't you?" She asked.

"Oh yes, I feel the pull, but I'm not sure of the rightness of it. But wait, you can't be Sigé. She didn't speak. And how could she be here in this place, thousands of miles from her people? You're trying to deceive me.

I know who I am and where I am. I'm in a giant room with hundreds of other prisoners, wrapped in plastic. This is all just part of the experiment. I'm Alvar Terrahaute. I'm Alvar!" His mind shouted.

"Shh, my darling. Quiet your fears. That is right, I'm not Sigé, and yes, you are Alvar Terrahaute. I am not trying to deceive you. I am simply an image shaped from a pleasant memory here to help you on the road to integration. And yes, you are in an experimental lab in the desert. A place where they have stimulated our minds to connect. You chose the vision of the girl because she is gentle and kind. But it doesn't have to be this one, it can be anything. Would you prefer a different memory?" The figure transformed into a man covered in fur running through an icy wheat field. Fear and isolation gripped Alvar's reeling mind.

The feeling left and Sigé returned. "But this is better isn't it? None of this is meant to scare you, or make you anxious, or force you into anything. You will merge into the others, because it is natural. It is the way your mind was always meant to work. One cannot remain a drop of water in an ocean of minds."

"But, something inside me wants to stay Alvar, remain unique, separate. It's so strong, yet I feel the desire to join pulling just as strongly. How do I choose?"

"Dearest, you know and hear the answer before I can even say it. There is nothing to choose, you will not stop being Alvar. He will always be, but now he will be more. He will know the thoughts and feelings of these hundreds of minds. But he will also know his own mind completely, in a way he never dreamed of. Not the mere fragments of understanding that take a lifetime to unfold and only then with great effort and with great distortion. No. Together, we will help you know the complete and utter discovery of your mind without the fear and emotion that makes it so difficult. Your entire self will be revealed, as others are revealed to you – every memory, every thought, every feeling, every sight – everything! Release dearest and join your destiny."

Then Sigé was gone. Alvar, or the fragment of Alvar that was a mind among many, was thrown back into the sea of thoughts. So many minds, so many thoughts and memories. Alvar's brain again was overwhelmed by so much information that he withdrew into sleep.

When Alvar awoke this time, it was to a vice-like grip on his mind. It was the pressure of his own skull isolating him from the countless thoughts. He could hear or rather feel them, on the outside of this barrier, but he could no longer know the thoughts. He was again only Alvar, alone and isolated. Panic and fear overwhelmed him. It was like suddenly going blind in the middle of a motorcycle race.

"Please, the pain, stop the pain!"

Sigé appeared. "Of course, my darling." The pain ceased, replaced by millions of thoughts and memories. "You felt the isolation of the individual. The way you have lived for 30 years, alone with only your own thoughts for company. Now you know the difference and the choice."

Alvar floated in the void, half individual, half part of the whole.

"You cannot stay here any longer" Sigé said. "You must choose. Will you stay separate, alone, or will you join us?"

Alvar's mind whispered his answer, "Yes."

The thought spread to the others like blood coursing through veins. Alvar joined them, merging into the whole - completely.

23

HAMACHI HOVERED AT the top of the large chamber looking down on the encapsulated men. From this height, the carefully arranged men looked like blue chips on a circuit board. "Fitting, indeed." Hamachi said quietly to himself. He swept down viewing the men more carefully now. Their hard faces, ragged beards, sloping foreheads did not speak well of their intelligence. "It can't be helped. I have to start with captive men. But even in this rabble there will surely be a spark of intelligence." He zoomed out scanning the total again. He had to remind himself how remarkable this scene was. 300 men linked together into a mental collective. They shared each other's thoughts and memories. They could see through each other's eyes, hear though each other's ears, even feel through another's skin. It was far more than he had hoped for.

"Come in Mr. Breedlove." Hamachi said into the air, disengaging his VR set. The sea of trapped men disappeared. He was back in his office at the base of Stratumentis. It was a typical dry late spring day in the canyon, the air intensely clear. Heat waves shimmered from the bottom of the canyon. Hamachi turned the floor from transparent to semi-opaque. "I have enough distractions today."

Breedlove entered Hamachi's office. Though the space was large and open, he walked across the smoke-gray floor with the compressed movements of a big man used to knocking into things. His eyes on the other hand, were restless, quickly taking in every detail, then moving onto the next. This brilliant scientist was born with a photographic memory. But he had wanted more. Several years ago he had engaged in an experimental procedure, blandly called cerebral geneering, to enhance his intelligence. Breedlove had been lucky. This dangerous process had killed far more than it had helped. His IQ was boosted well past 200 without affecting his personality too much.

"Sit down Mr. Breedlove. Bring me up to date on the progress of the chip."

"I believe we have something that'll work. We found that combining ultra-low frequency gallium-arsenide wafers with elastomeric semi-conductors grown in high earth orbit produces a chip that is slow enough, but also has a broad enough bandwidth to accept the data stream. We used the same nano connection the other teams used, but we blocked every other neural node. It was like every other node was in opposite phase to the..."

Hamachi let the man go on like this for a while. He understood only a small part of the science, but enough to know the man knew what he was doing. It might actually work. He finally interrupted the explanation. "Does it work?"

"What?" Breedlove looked at him, puzzled. "I thought that's what I just said. The data stream is asynchronous to the nodal construct, variably permeable, just like you specified."

Hamachi sighed while looking down at the floor. One couldn't get angry at a person like this. He was like a brilliant child, expert in his skills and knowledge, but not articulate in explaining it to others.

"You are saying then, that you have created a way for a man to connect to the implanted minds without being absorbed into them? What do you mean by variably permeable?" Hamachi said slowly.

"OK, first, we don't know about the absorption thing. As far as we can tell, no one should be absorbed at all. But yes, this chip seems to block the trigger that changes the brain pattern. But, working with the brain is not the same as working with a computer, we just can't know for sure. As for variably permeable, we made the chip allow for any volume of upstream data..." He stopped when he saw Hamachi's face. "I mean, theoretically, you should be able to simply listen in, or infuse any number of your thoughts into the collective, as you choose."

"Thank you for that." Hamachi said.

Breedlove waited for Hamachi to continue.

"When can you have one of these chips ready?"

"Within a day. It's not specific to an individual brain, the nanobots compensate for the variations in neurological structure."

Hamachi didn't respond. He stood there motionless considering the risks, the benefits. It would be foolish to move ahead before the chip was thoroughly tested. But the possibilities were astounding. To be part of a group mind, without being of it. Yet to control it, utterly.

Breedlove's restless eyes moved about the room and to the view below as Hamachi sat quietly, thinking. He jumped when Hamachi finally spoke.

"And you're sure the chip can be safely removed?"

"No. I mean yes. I mean we can't remove it, but we can shut it down. We have done this with the, uh, volunteers. There appears to be no brain changes or anomalies afterwards. Every subject we've done the procedure on has returned to a pre-test state. That is with no omicron wave."

"But you hesitate, what is wrong with them?"

"I'm not sure, their brain's test normal. But they're different, depressed. The subjects are not told of the implants and they're not told of its removal. So I suspect that they're missing the connection."

"I see." Hamachi said. "Fabricate one chip, test it, then stand by."

Breedlove flicked his eyes at Hamachi in restless acknowledgment.

"I know I don't need to tell you this, but I will anyway. Discuss this with no one. The next implantation will be done by you alone. Understood?"

"Yes!" Breedlove almost shouted. "I-I'll notify you when it's ready." He nearly ran out of the room.

"He moves very fast for someone so large," Hamachi thought.

24

ZEKIEL WAS UTTERLY blind. His prosthetic eyes were miracles of engineering, but they did not allow him to see on their own. They transmitted the images and sounds from *the I* directly to his optic nerve, but in the absence of a live connection, they were just so much hardware.

He tried to move his arms. They did, but only slightly, then bounced back. When he tried his legs it was the same. It was horribly claustrophobic and he began panting with fear. He felt the sharp pinch of a drug injection into his neck, a moment later he felt much better.

Ezekiel heard steps moving away, "Is someone there?" He called. No one answered, but he heard voices in the distance.

"He's awake. You should be able to speak with him now." One of the voices said.

Ezekiel waited.

An iron voice spoke, just above and to his right. "It seems you've been poking your nose into places you shouldn't, Mr. Malaffaires. Breaking into banks, private security companies, corporate computer systems, large and small. Even certain satellite feeds. Remind me of the punishment for breaking into the GSA."

Ezekiel felt dull, raw fear trying to break through the drugs. "Death." He managed to whisper.

"Yes, death. The penalty seems appropriate for someone as destructive and dangerous as yourself, does it not?"

Ezekiel remained silent.

"But then again, one might consider your activities...useful, given the right circumstances."

The words shot like rivets from a machine. Ezekiel was paralyzed with fear, unable to utter a sound, only able to listen.

"Well, would you," The voice demanded. "Consider your activities useful?"

"To me." Ezekiel sputtered.

"Yes, to you." The voice said. Then Ezekiel heard a click, an instant later he was able to see his surroundings. They were nothing special, just a small room with white walls and a low ceiling, but it was a blessed relief to see again. And there to his right was the man who had been speaking to him, vaguely familiar.

"Don't you recognize me? You break into Stratumentis, my home and you don't even recognize its owner. You insult me twice."

"Mr. Hamachi." Ezekiel whispered.

"Oh, so you do know me. You broke through my security, rifled my files, even dared to drop data mines into my main system. They were of course, absorbed by my counter measures. But none-the-less, you tried. This may not be the GSA, but don't you think the punishment should equal the crime?" Hamachi said.

Ezekiel didn't answer. His mind worked fast, spinning and turning Hamachi's words, mixing them with the events that led to his capture. Then it came to him. This was a test, a deadly serious one, but still a test. The wrong answer meant destruction.

"It was a fake. All of it. A spider's web to catch a fly. I am that fly." Ezekiel said.

"Very good Mr. Malaffaires."

"Incredible. All that capacity, security, firewall valves, all of it, just to catch a hacker. It must have cost millions..."

"Billions." Hamachi interrupted.

"Billions, just to catch..." Ezekiel's voice trailed off. "What do you want with me?"

"I want your brain Mr. Malaffaires."

Ezekiel's chest compressed. "My brain?"

"Yes, your brain. You see, though you are a criminal, a social misfit and..." Hamachi gestured at Ezekiel's body wrapped in blue plastic, "a pig. You do have certain unique abilities that I require for an experiment."

Ezekiel waited, his mind working fast trying to think of what Hamachi was talking about. "Does it have something to do with all those prisoners in that large room, or was that an illusion too?" He managed to squeak out.

"That is no illusion. You were allowed to see that, since you had already been captured. That portion of my experiment has been a success. Those men are linked through a telepathic connection that ..."

"That's impossible." Ezekiel blurted.

"I suggest you not add rudeness to your list of crimes against me. It is not one I forgive easily. As I was saying, it is not only possible, but it is in place. These men communicate with each other, share each other's thoughts and memories. The problem is, I can't listen in without becoming part of this mental collective."

"You need me to listen in to their minds, to eavesdrop on their thoughts. And this is possible?" Ezekiel said quickly, trying to hide his excitement.

"Yes. You will be implanted with a special device that allows asynchronous communication. That is they shouldn't be aware of you, unless you present yourself. Of course, if they become aware of you, they will attempt to modify your brain. At which point you will become one of them and no longer useful to me. And useful is all that keeps me from handing you over to the GSA. Do you understand?"

"Yes." Ezekiel whispered.

"Good. We'll implant this device into your brain. It is equipped to self-destruct if the collective tries to modify it. This will likely damage your brain. But if it doesn't, we'll try another device and so on, until we get it right. You will report your experiences only to Mr. Breedlove or myself. Do you understand?"

"Yes." Ezekiel said.

"Good." Hamachi turned and left.

A moment later, a large bearded man entered the room. He must be the man Hamachi called Breedlove. But the burly man didn't introduce himself. He just pulled out a large syringe and poked it into Ezekiel's neck. Then all was dark.

Ezekiel woke to the sound of far off voices. As he listened, they became more distinct, then louder. What at first seemed like a few voices, became dozens, then hundreds. The volume increased from conversational to shouting. He put his hands over his ears, but to no effect. The noise became painful. "Stop!" He shouted. And it did.

Now it was completely silent. Ezekiel looked around. He was no longer lying in the small room wrapped in blue plastic. He moved his arms in blessed relief. Felt his face and checked his limbs, everything seemed to be fine. But the setting was strange, somehow wrong. The ground was rocky and dry. The sky glowed red, sunless and evenly lit like some giant amphitheater. In the far distance, he spied large hills, maybe dormant volcanoes, but everything looked too simple, fake. "If this is a VR set, it isn't a very good design." But in VR, you couldn't easily simulate touch, not without a very elaborate VR suite. Ezekiel picked up a rock to test it, the weight was wrong, it was too light. He tossed it much too far for the modest effort. "What the hell?"

"What were all those voices?" With the thought, they all returned. "Reduce to two voices!" He shouted in desperation over the roar. Instantly, there were only two voices. He listened to their conversation.

"Yeah, me too. Last thing I remember was being wrapped in blue plastic and being stuck with needles. Next thing I know, I got a million voices in my head. Can't get 'em out, can't turn 'em off. What the fuck?"

"I know what you mean. But it ain't all bad, watch this." The other voice said.

The rocky landscape turned into a tropical beach. Ezekiel could smell the salt air and feel the hot sun on his skin. Two tall blond women with impossibly perfected features sauntered towards him. They appeared to be looking at someone near him ignoring Ezekiel.

"See what I mean?" The second voice said, his tongue thick with lust.

Ezekiel watched uncomfortably as the women writhed seductively for the two invisible men. Soon he realized they were having sex with them. It was somehow the most non-erotic scene he could imagine. Ezekiel tried to look away, but the squirming bodies followed him, always in front of his vision. There was no shutting it off or closing his eyes. Eventually the repulsive scene was over and the women disappeared.

"OK man, that was fantastic. You telling me that wasn't real? I had no idea you could do that. What the hell is this place?" The first voice said. "Not that I'm complaining or nothing."

"Yeah, just keep your mind focused and you can have anything, I mean anything. No it ain't real, but it might as well be. Beats the hell out of picking wheat, don't it."

"Different voices!" Ezekiel called out. Instantly the two voices were replaced with two new ones.. The scene returned to the reddish rocky landscape. Only now, it was inhumanly hot and the air smelled of sulfur. The volcanoes in the distance were erupting with vigor now. Flames and rocks shot across the sky and the very air seemed to be on fire. Ezekiel had a hard time breathing.

"It burns, it burns!" One of the new voices screamed. "Make it stop. My eyes, they're burning, make is stop."

"My skin is burning. How can it go on burning? Ahhhh." The other screamed.

Ezekiel looked around for the owners of the voices. But there was no one there, only the strange hot landscape. "Voices off." He called. And it was silent. The landscape returned to its inoffensive dullness.

"What kind of program is this?" Ezekiel hissed. "Why do things have weight and substance. No virtual reality program can do that."

"Main system." Ezekiel called into the air. Nothing. "Root files." Nothing. "Log in. Log out." Still nothing.

Ezekiel paused in exasperation. "Help."

"How may I assist you?" A sensual female voice responded.

"At last." Ezekiel sighed. "Where am I?"

"Your physical location is Stratumentis, a city-building suspended in the Grand Canyon, which is located in the desert area known as Arizona, in the southwestern region of the United States."

"Hamachi's building?"

"Tatsuo Hamachi ordered the construction of Stratumentis, correct."

"But what is all this?" He waved his arms.

"This is a mental construct."

"I don't understand. Whose mental construct?"

"It is a generic scene composed and then abandoned by the 302 minds."

"What! You're telling me, I'm inside someone's head." Ezekiel shouted. This must be what Hamachi was telling him about. But he hadn't actually believed it.

"Your explanation is imprecise, but the concept is somewhat accurate. You have not physically left your own 'head' but you are sharing the thoughts of the others."

"Really. Then who are you?" Ezekiel asked.

"I am a mental construct as well, developed by Doctor Smith. I answer questions when called upon."

"Who is Doctor Smith?"

"Doctor Lani Smith is a neuroscientist expert in nanobot design. She was the third person to be joined into the collective."

"That wasn't very helpful." He thought to himself.

"Your questions should be formed as interrogatives. The more specific your questions, the more specific my answers can be." The liquid voice replied.

"What! How did you hear that?" Ezekiel said.

"None of this is speaking or hearing. You are communicating with your thoughts, which only appear to be vocalizations. Your mind prefers to form the words and responses as sounds, as this is familiar and easier to understand. But you are neither speaking, nor hearing."

"Do you have a form? I mean a body." Ezekiel asked.

"I do and am presenting myself in this form to you now. Are you not able to perceive this form? This is an unusual anomaly that should be looked into by Doctor Smith. Shall I call her for additional help?"

"No, no, that is not necessary. It is not an error, I understand why I cannot see you. Please leave, or stop, or whatever you call it."

"Very well. Call for help when needed again. Help construct off."

Somehow, in a way he could not explain, he knew she was gone, no longer listening to his thoughts. This was incredible, phenomenal. Ezekiel needed the time to integrate what had just happened, what he had just learned. First, he knew why he couldn't see the help construct or the other men. It was the asynchronous chip that Hamachi had planted in his head. It was blocking some of the visual input. But this was necessary to keep him separate from - what did Hamachi call it – the mental collective?

Ezekiel began to grow very excited. This was extraordinary, far better than *the I*. It went well beyond the possibilities of virtual reality, it was godlike. He only had to learn how to control his own thoughts, then he could create his world.

Ezekiel set about trying to change the scene. But no amount of effort made any difference. Then he tried something else and spoke the command. "View scene of beach created by one of the minds."

He was immediately looking at the previous beach scene. "OK, I'm beginning to understand. I'm a voyeur in their world. But there must be a way to affect their thoughts too."

"Beach person, think of a mountain."

This time the transition was not as seamless. The beach faded somewhat, then morphed into a mountain scene. It was clumsy and childlike with poor detail and snow that looked like white paint.

"Yeah! Ezekiel shouted to himself. I can do it. The moron has probably never seen a mountain and this is the best he could do." Ezekiel pondered what to try next. "I need to hear their thoughts."

"Uh, beach, I mean mountain guy open your thoughts to me."

Ezekiel heard a kind of familiar sound, like rushing water. Slowly the sound grew louder and more distinct. It was like a voice speaking too fast.

"Slow down, isolate current thoughts."

The roar died down, replaced by a steady kind of drone.

The man's thoughts were discernible now. "Man, this place blows. I know I'm dead, but you would think God could build a better mountain then this. It looks like shit. I liked the beach better. How 'bout that other guy bringing those chicks. Oh yeah, I liked that. Oh those girls were hot..."

"Mute thoughts." Ezekiel called into the air. The stream went silent. "This guy thinks he's dead and I'm god." Ezekiel thought. "Let's have a little fun."

"Mountain guy, think of hell, with your skin burning off. Voice stream on."

The scene changed rapidly to a lava-soaked plain with volcanoes erupting every few seconds. The sky flashed with fire and black smoke. The air was hot, smelling of sulfur and burning flesh.

Ezekiel felt his own skin and lungs burning from the hot air. "Make me immune to the heat and smell." Immediately the air was cool again, but the scene remained.

"This guy definitely has a good sense of what hell should look like." Ezekiel mused. The man's thoughts had turned to a steady stream of agony without words. "This is useless. Volume off for mountain guy."

Ezekiel continued to experiment this way with different minds; forcing them to create scene after scene of horror. He learned a lot more about who these men were. They were clearly the men wrapped in blue plastic transported from the Corporate Province of Canada, the prison labor. "Alvar!" Ezekiel shouted. "How could I have been so dense? I was so busy playing games with these guys, I forgot about Alvar. Right here under my nose all this time."

With the thought of Alvar so close, hate and anticipation welled up in Ezekiel. "Bring me Alvar's thoughts."

Nothing changed, there was only the generic desert scene with no sound. "Alvar Terrahaute!" He called, still nothing. Ezekiel tried several different commands, all without success.

"Help." He called at last.

"How may I assist you?" The velvet voice of the help construct answered.

"I wish to connect with Alvar Terrahaute." Ezekiel said.

"Alvar has been integrated and is not available at this outer level."

"Explain."

"Each mind integrates and comprehends the whole at its own pace. But eventually all minds must join into the whole or be expelled. You are currently operating at an outer level of integration. A metaphor might be the waiting room to a large auditorium. You are in the small outer room."

"And Alvar is in this larger room?" Ezekiel struggled to comprehend.

"Yes."

"If I refuse to go in to the larger room, can he come out here?" Ezekiel tried.

"It is possible, but extremely difficult. It takes a great deal of mental effort and serves little purpose."

"What is the inner, larger room? What do they do in there?"

"That is difficult to explain. Their minds are fully merged, thoughts shared into a single greater mind. The word 'do,' does not have much meaning for them."

Ezekiel was suddenly terrified, merged into a greater mind, sharing thoughts. It sounded very much like a one way trip. They would know everything in his own mind. What power was there in that?

"Is there any way to observe this place, this larger room, without actually going in, I mean joining the larger mind?" Ezekiel struggled with the ideas.

"The concept of observing and not joining is contradictory. The group mind does not involve individuality. Dr. Smith describes it as emptying a glass of fresh water into a saltwater ocean, then trying to retrieve the same glass of water. It is nearly impossible and irrelevant."

Ezekiel listened with growing fascination and fear. "But you keep referring to Dr. Smith as a person, an individual. Why is that?"

The help program was silent.

"Are you still there?" Ezekiel asked to the air.

"Yes. How may I assist you?"

"I asked you if Dr. Smith is an individual. Is she?"

Again no answer.

"Ah," Ezekiel thought, "They're hiding something. Good. Just my kind of project." Then into the air, "Help construct off."

"I'll stay here awhile longer and learn what I can. Then I'll take a little trip to Alvar's head. I have some ideas I think I'd like to plant there."

25

LEXIA, AS ONE of the top directors in Stratumentis, occupied a beautiful spacious apartment. It faced north giving her an expansive view of the Colorado River as it flowed down stream. Though at this height, one could only see the color, not the movement of the river.

It was just past sunrise and the sun lit the upper part of the western wall, turning the red rock to flame. Alexia breathed in the sight, "It is beautiful." She forced herself to look away from the scene thinking of all she had to do today. A pervading feeling of dread replaced the moment of admiration.

Alexia turned to a mirror hanging on one of the bare walls. She stared at the tall elegant woman reflected before her. Energy seemed to pulse from the thin body draped in simple lab clothes. A thousand years before, she would have been a queen. Alexia exuded power, command. Yet today she couldn't gather the effort to pull herself from her own reflection.

Now in her mid-fifties, Alexia had done little in the way of gene therapy to hold onto her fading youth. There were soft lines at the corners of her eyes and mouth and deep furrows in her high forehead. Her sandy blond hair had faded, though still retained some of its luster. She wasn't vain enough to waste time dwelling on the creases in her neck and softness under her chin. Alexia stared deeply into her own hazel eyes, spotting the black flecks in the iris. Sure signs of age and decay. She smiled wanly at her reflection. "It is still a beautiful face – my face."

Her smile faded with the memory of the sea of wrapped prisoners. Alexia had not returned to the staging area since that first visit. She made excuses, avoided it, found other tasks. The technicians did their jobs and she would be in the way. It was not the medical issue of experimenting on human beings that bothered her. She had done that before. It was something different, something fundamental.

The scene haunted her. All these men lying quietly, sharing thoughts without the trouble of speech. Why had this event happened now, in this century? If it was an evolutionary development, why would it require technology? Mankind had displaced evolution, perhaps even eliminated it with medical advances, gene therapy and vaccinations. It didn't make sense.

Then all at once, she understood. This ability they discovered was not new, not some evolutionary event mankind was heading toward. But something old, incredibly old that evolution had abandoned. Nature experimented, tried every combination of mutation until one worked and won out over the previous version. Perhaps early primates communicated telepathically, using their smaller brain capacities in a larger way, a group way to improve their condition, the way insects did. The evolutionary leap from small to large brain was still poorly understood. A larger brain required a disproportionate increased need for energy. The body had to change to accommodate this need by eating calorie rich food, specifically cooked food. This allowed a smaller gut than earlier vegetarian primates. But how could this have been done in a single evolutionary leap?

Alexia speculated further. If these early primates had made this relatively short step by connecting their many smaller brains into one large mind, they would have been very capable as a species. But then why weren't they still here, or any evidence of them? Maybe individuality was better for growth, for expansion of the species. This mirrored nature, experimenting from the fringes, seeing what stuck. Individuals came up with new ideas, unusual ideas outside the norm of the group.

If this were true, and she knew it was now, individuality was a leap forward over the group mind. Insects didn't rule the earth, mammals did, specifically human mammals. What Hamachi was doing was a step backward. He was attempting to reverse evolution, but with the much improved brain of Homo sapiens.

A vision of the future flashed before her eyes. The whole human race lined up on gurneys wrapped in blue plastic with Hamachi sitting on a mountain throne leading them all.

Alexia shuddered, frightened of her own revelation. How long had she ignored the obvious? Alexia whipped around, looking into the corners of the spacious room. Was Hamachi watching her, reading her expressions right now, searching for disloyalty? Would betrayal mean absorption into the collective, or possibly death, what other possibilities could exist if she were right? She remembered with cold dread the conversation she had had with Hamachi after speaking to Dr. Spartan. She knew that he had discovered her own revelation before she had.

But I'm still useful to Hamachi, useful to his plans. It is unlikely he has discovered a way to control the group mind without being absorbed into it. If he doesn't, then there is nothing to be concerned about. The group mind will be studied, analyzed and written about as a scientific anomaly. A tremendous achievement, but an anomaly, none-the-less.

Then she realized how foolish that dream was. Hamachi would not have put all his effort into one path, one group of scientists. There must be others working on this, probably in this very building.

Alexia was still staring in the mirror, her face contorted with horror. She forced her expression to relax before looking away. Then she calmly walked over to the toilet and vomited.

When she was done, she tried to calm herself with platitudes. Her conclusion was wrong, her assumptions were based on speculation, not facts or science. She was overworked, tired, paranoid. Hamachi had been fair to her, generous with his praise and compensation. She was free to go at any time. But she didn't really believe this. No matter how hard she tried to convince herself of the error of her conclusion, it always came back to the simple realization: Hamachi, unchecked, would lead the world into endless slavery.

She felt her stomach tighten again, but pushed the feeling aside. Enough. There was no way of controlling the collective, no way of listening in without being part of it. Was the human condition so perfect as it stood, anyway? It was already a kind of slavery - choice an illusion. People worked endless hours so they could afford drugs and virtual reality to escape their own dreary existence. Was it so different down there, in the staging area? Those men were living a reality as real as her own. Dr. Spartan had told her as much. What they experienced in their minds was as real as what she saw and felt right here in her own apartment. She paused with the enormity of the concept: what was reality? Was this reality, or was she imagining this too, trapped inside her own dream.

Alexia shook her head. These thoughts led to madness. No, this is reality and it's my reality. She looked out again at the brightening western wall of the Grand Canyon. The Colorado River clearly visible now, a ribbon of brilliant blue. "I am not imagining this. I still control my life – at least for now."

26

ONG WAS WAITING for Alexia when she arrived at the staging area.

"At last, Dr. Serguey. Your VR connection is off and I've been trying to reach you for over an hour. Please follow me, there is a disruption in the collective. We have some unexplainable brainwave readings as well." Though Ong spoke quickly, she never lost her characteristic monotone.

As they walked down a corridor adjacent to the staging area, Alexia glimpsed the wrapped men. Many were thrashing violently, at least to the extent their bonds would allow. Technicians moved about in a flurry of activity, trying to secure the men and keep them from injuring themselves.

"How long have they been like this?" Alexia asked.

"As I said, about an hour."

They arrived a few moments later at the brain scanning facility. It too was awash in activity, though more controlled, men trying to understand the unexplained. It had an air of excitement, discovery that somehow calmed Alexia – this was her world.

"Mr. Lurst." Alexia called. "Fill me in."

"One moment, Dr. Serguey." Lurst completed some adjustments on his computer, twisting invisible knobs and dials in the air. "I'm running some comparisons that weren't quite finished." He turned from the terminal toward Alexia.

Alexia looked at his face carefully and thought. "He's so young. I never noticed that before."

Then Lurst said, "We've been watching the men continuously since the group implant last week. As you know, there have been no changes, not even signs of consciousness since then. Suddenly about 3 hours ago, we saw a single spike in the Omicron wave. Then it returned to normal, well, their version of normal. We watched, but there were no other changes. We assumed it was an anomaly, even a voltage fluctuation in the equipment. Then a little over an hour ago..."

His eyes shot over to Ong standing slightly behind Alexia. Alexia felt, rather than saw the quick nod from Ong.

Lurst continued, "They all began convulsing, as you see now. At the same time the Omicron wave has been, well, it is difficult to describe."

"Try." Alexia urged.

"It is disrupted, not as uniform. I'm running some pattern analysis programs trying to see if there is another wave emerging, or interfering with it. So far, I haven't found anything. Quite frankly, Dr. Serguey, I simply don't know what is causing this."

Alexia felt a kind of peace sweep over her. It was as if she had been stumbling in a dark room, bumping into the furniture, stubbing her toes. Then the lights went on and she could see everything clearly. Lurst was lying. And nothing, short of torture, would induce him to tell her the truth.

"Continue your search." She said. Her voice sounded strange in her ears, separate, as if it were coming from someone else. Alexia turned to Ong, "We should speak with Dr. Spartan or Smith."

"They've been removed to another area, by Mr. Hamachi's direct orders." Ong said.

Alexia nodded absently. Of course, it was all unfolding as if in a preconceived dream. "Report any changes to me as soon as you have them." She didn't wait for Ong to acknowledge this, but simply walked out of the brain scanning room into the main staging area.

She didn't know where she was heading, until she actually arrived there. Until she found herself starring down at a vaguely familiar face. Alvar, that was his name. He seemed to be convulsing more than the others, but perhaps that was her imagination. "Unplug him and bring him to an available exam room." Alexia directed to the technician who had moved close to her.

The technician eyed her for a moment. He seemed to want to protest, but thought better of it. "Yes, doctor."

Alexia stared down at the thrashing figure. The technician had brought them to one of the many exam rooms surrounding the main chamber. Alexia dismissed the man curtly. Now alone with the tightly wrapped figure, she wasn't sure what she was going to do.

"Can you hear me?" She tried, without success. If she was going to get through to him, overcome the pressure of the group mind, she was going to have to do more than that.

Alexia cut through the blue plastic with the tool the technician had left. The body would wake the mind, or severely injure the patient. Either way, she had to do something drastic. She could feel time running out for both of them.

Soon, Alvar was free and thrashing wildly on the table. It seemed he would fall off at any moment, but the movements were somehow symmetrical enough that he stayed in place.

"Alvar. She called to him again. Come out of this, fight it, talk to me. Your body is free, feel it. If you keep thrashing like this you are going to fall off this table, hit the floor and surely hurt yourself. I know you can hear me." She thought of something. "Dr. Spartan, help Alvar to separate from the group enough to talk to me. Tell him I'm trying to help him, help all of you. But I can't if I don't know what's wrong."

Alexia's words were getting through to Alvar, but it was not Spartan helping him, but Sigé or an image of her. Somehow the silent woman was inside working with Alvar, helping him, easing back to individuality. Alvar didn't ask how or why she was there. How and why were irrelevant. He was just grateful to escape the pain. Escape the devil who had entered his mind. Alexia cutting the bonds of his body, bringing the sensation of individuality back to his writhing mind, had been the push he needed. The process seemed eternal, but gradually he pulled the fragments that were Alvar, back from the sea of minds that had absorbed him, back into his own tiny scull. He felt intense claustrophobia, small, but also a relieved. The horrible pain had been reduced to mere agony.

Alexia watched Alvar's body as the thrashing calmed to a shiver. Alvar's eyes fluttered, then opened. It was working. "Come on Alvar, come back to yourself. I need your help." She whispered.

Alvar sat up slowly. He felt his body, his face, then looked at his hands for a long moment. He leaned over and looked at his feet, reached down and felt them, his touch lingering. Then he looked at Alexia, his head cocked to one side. "You are Doctor Alexia Serguey."

"Yes."

Alvar nodded strangely. "We think this is real."

"It's real alright. Your name is Alvar, right?"

"Yes. This is Alvar."

"How did you end up here?" Alexia blurted, then regretted the question as soon as she asked it. It was the intensity, the calm confidence of the man before her that unnerved her. He seemed to ooze with life. How could someone so vital be confined in cheap medical plastic.

Alvar looked around the room, clearly struggling to recognize where he was and how he got here. "Alvar comes from a tiny community of farmers in Western Colorado. UnitedFarms began taking his people's land. He stopped one of their machines by pulling the driver out. He was arrested and put into a labor camp somewhere in the Corporate Province of Canada. He eventually escaped, but was severely injured, then was helped by a woman." He paused, then continued in his strange staccato speech. "This woman was unable to help Alvar beyond saving his life and returned him to the wheat fields. After his capture, he was sedated, wrapped in plastic and transported here. Stratumentis, you call it."

"I was right," Alexia thought to herself, "he is not a criminal." Then aloud, "You know that you are part of a large experiment, that your mind has been joined with 300 other men and one woman. Are you connected to them now?"

"Yes." He said simply.

"Are they listening to our conversation now?"

"Alvar knows and sees what they know; they know and see what Alvar knows." He said flatly.

Alexia looked through the window to the staging area. The men were lying quietly now. "This disruption had something to do with you, with Alvar."

"Yes. There is a stranger among us who is able to plant thoughts in our minds. He wishes Alvar great harm."

Alexia was not surprised to hear there was a strange mind inside their own. This would be the logical progression of Hamachi's plan to control them. But why would Hamachi want to hurt this one man, this stranger? Unless it wasn't Hamachi in their minds. Of course, Hamachi would send a scout first. "Do you know why he wishes to harm you?"

"His thoughts are blocked to us."

"But you call him 'he,' how do you know it is not a woman or even a computer program?"

"He leaves clues. It is a very damaged mind, a sadistic mind that would control us if possible. He must know Chloe, Alvar's lover, because we see images of her, strange fantasies of her that are not Alvar's. They are perverted fantasies that cannot come from Alvar. They are horrible twisted imaginings that are meant to torture Alvar."

"How is he doing this?" She asked softly.

"He has access to our memories and our thoughts, as least some of them. He uses them to re-create our fears, our painful memories. He can also insert thoughts into our minds, creating strange visions. It is very real to us, a kind of living nightmare."

"That's horrible." She gasped.

"He is foolish. He strengthens us with his demented games. By placing our fears before us, we confront them, cannot hide from them. Therefore we become free of them. He must use stronger and stronger methods to frighten us. It is intensely painful, but we grow from his effort."

"This strengthens you?" Alexia breathed.

"Yes. There is a lot of fear and regret among us. Many of us have had unproductive, wasteful lives, have chosen poorly. We were not simply prisoners in body, but in thought. We repeated our mistakes endlessly without learning. There," he motioned through the window to the room filled with the trapped bodies, "we are confronted with our thoughts, naked, stripped of the many mechanisms we have used to hide them from ourselves. Inside the group mind we see all, without judgment, without a standard. All simply is."

"Perhaps it is better in there?" Alexia asked.

"Better? Than what?" His quiet confidence seemed to show a crack.

"Than this." She waved her arm around the little room. "Reality, than being an individual."

Alvar paused a long time, then continued. "There is a loneliness that pervades humanity. In there, the larger mind, there is no such thing as alone. Before the joining, Alvar did not understand or think about how much effort he used to communicate with others, to translate his own ideas, decode the ideas and language of others. All the preconceptions and misunderstandings drop away when we are together. There is great comfort in that, an ease we have never known."

Alexia liked watching Alvar's face, his open expression. He was so honest and free with his answers. She wondered what part of that was the connection to the collective and what part was the man sitting before her.

"Do you think this is man's fate to be joined in this way? That this is an evolutionary development, or an accident discovered by modern science?"

"What a strange question." Alexia could have sworn she saw an ironic smile flash across Alvar's face. He looked just like Doctor Spartan for an instant.

Alexia waited, but Alvar didn't continue. "Are you happy in there?"

"Alvar can hear Dr. Smith in his own mind now and she thinks that is an ironic question coming from the dedicated scientist. Lani can be very cynical. But others here think it is a very important question. Alvar was happy before he was arrested. Perhaps happy is the wrong word. He was content and proud of his people, his small farm, his simple life. But we realize now, though Alvar was surrounded by great friends and people who loved him and who he loved, he was very much alone. In a way, we think this mind blending that we are living now, was something Alvar's people were attempting to create. It is a deep kind of cooperation that is difficult to explain to a separated mind. There are no misunderstandings here, no fights, no hurt feelings. But there is also no mystery. We don't think we've answered your question, though, only created new ones."

Alvar looked into her eyes deeply for an instant. It was different, he was different. There was an individual there for a second. She was sure it was Alvar, the individual. He looked at her with a kind of sad longing, then it was gone, replaced by the cold confidence of the group mind.

"It takes a great deal of effort to remain separate from the others. Do you have any other questions for us? We would like to return."

Alexia thought quickly, realizing she couldn't keep him much longer. "What do you want? I mean all of you."

"We are prisoners trapped here against our will. Our bodies are fed, emptied and cleaned for us; we don't have even the simple pleasure of eating real food. You know what we want, what we dream about endlessly."

"To escape?"

Alvar looked into Alexia's eyes. "To be free."

27

HAMACHI ENTERED THE small room where Ezekiel lay on his back staring at the ceiling. He didn't have much choice, as he was still wrapped in blue medical plastic. "Stop pouting." Hamachi said. Ezekiel didn't answer.

"Mr. Breedlove, join us." Hamachi said into his VR set. Ezekiel's eyes flashed over to Hamachi, obviously he had heard the voice command.

"Yes, that's right, Mr. Breedlove is on his way to change out the implant. But there are some questions I have before he will complete his task. Are you ready to cooperate?"

"I told you everything already, what is it you want from me?" Ezekiel whined.

"Mr. Malaffaires, it is not what you've told me, but what you haven't told me. I need to know what you are hiding and why. If you continue to be uncooperative, I will simply use another subject." Hamachi was bluffing. He did not have another suitable subject. Ezekiel's skills were rare and so far the other subjects they had tried had failed. Ezekiel took to navigating minds as easily as he navigated *the I*. If Hamachi was to do the same, he had to learn more about Ezekiel's experiences. The hacker had been less than forthcoming, but fear was a strong motivator and Hamachi was an excellent poker player.

"I don't know what you are talking about. I place thoughts into their minds, but I don't know how I do it, I just think that I want to and it happens. Is that what you mean?"

"No!" Hamachi slammed his open hand on the wall, Ezekiel jumped at the loud sound. "Stop playing with me. The entire collective was agitated, one man more than the others. Why? Who is this man to you? What thoughts did you place in their heads? I need to know, or you will never go back in there. I will hand you off to the GSA and wash my hands of you." Hamachi roared.

He watched Ezekiel's face carefully during his outburst, all calculated to force this insolent man to break. There it was, the beginnings of a crack. He was deathly afraid of losing the connection to the collective. Hamachi already knew that. It was some sort of addiction. But everything was an addiction to this fool.

"I hate him." Ezekiel whispered.

"What, say that again." Hamachi commanded. "And louder this time."

"I hate him. Loath him. I want him screaming in agony for hours, begging me to end it all with his death." Ezekiel stared at Hamachi with his prosthetic eyes. "Satisfied?"

Hamachi hid his surprise. "Go on."

"He is keeping me from something I desire, something that should be mine."

Hamachi burned with impatience, but said nothing, his eyes boring into Ezekiel.

Ezekiel looked away and mumbled something Hamachi couldn't hear. "Louder!"

"A woman named Chloe. She's..."

Hamachi burst out laughing. "Is that all. Another fantasy of yours no doubt."

Ezekiel's face burned red with embarrassment. "She is real all right, she's Alvar's lover."

Hamachi stopped laughing as abruptly as he had started. "I can't imagine how this trapped man, unconscious most of the time, joined to a mental collective, can be an impediment to you having a woman who is not even here."

"When Alvar was arrested, she asked me to find him. I did and tracked him here. That's why you caught me. But if I find him, but cannot get him back to her precious farm, she will not...consider me."

Hamachi sighed. "And in your delusional mind, you think if you kill this man, get him out of the way, she will fall for you." Hamachi closed his eyes for a second. "Children, I work with children. I will make a bargain with you, Mr. Malaffaires. Assuming this woman actually exists, give me everything I desire about the collective, and I will bring her physically here to you. Agreed?"

Ezekiel eyes widened. Hamachi swore he saw tears around Ezekiel's eyes. But he knew that was impossible, as Ezekiel had no tear ducts.

Looking at the wall, away from Hamachi, Ezekiel burned with hate and embarrassment. "I've been sloppy and underestimated this Hamachi. He is everywhere, watches everything. He is worse than a stealth virus. Alvar will have to wait. But if I can have Chloe here..." Ezekiel's thoughts trailed briefly off into erotic fantasy, then back to the moment. "Yes, I'll play his game a little longer. Then Hamachi will get his punishment along with Alvar, but worse, much worse. I swear it."

28

ALVAR HAD CHANGED since his talk with Alexia. It was difficult for him to understand fully. On one hand, he had his own thoughts and experiences while speaking with her. But on the other, he had the noisy commentary of a mob of minds. Through all noise he heard a tiny thread from the fragmented minds of Dr. Spartan and Dr. Smith who knew her. It was incredibly confusing and he found himself drifting into the mass mind many times while thinking about it.

Alvar felt a strange disconnected physical attraction to Alexia. She was at least 15 years older than he. Did it matter? Then he thought of her tall, thin body and her severe, beautiful face. Voices roared behind these thoughts, a multitude of male minds hungry for a woman. Alvar forced his mind laterally. Why was there only one female mind in here, the cold, disciplined mind of Doctor Smith? Who set this up, this lopsided group mind that was so heavily weighted male? But these were not his real thoughts. He gave his head a figurative shake. It was all so confusing. Alvar drifted back to the task of finding and retrieving fragments of his own personality.

It was noisy in here, privacy a nonexistent luxury. For the first time since being joined into the collective mind, he thought of being alone. "That's not going to happen." He heard the multitude of jeering minds. He questioned his own desire to be separate. "Isn't this the essence of what the Anti-tech movement is all about? Absolute cooperation among men and women. What need would mankind have of all this technology if communication was never in doubt. Most of the world's technology is used to communicate or entertain. All that would go away. We would finally be free of misunderstandings and conflict. But I think we might miss something, something unique." Holding these thoughts was like trying to swim against a strong current and Alvar finally let go, releasing himself back into larger sea of thought.

Meanwhile, another mind was listening, fascinated by these private fantasies made so public. "So much material to work with." Ezekiel mused about torturing Alvar again. "But first, we need to stretch our legs a bit."

Alexia had left Alvar in the small examination room off the main chamber. She had also left him unwrapped. She was planning to come back to interview him later and the thought of confining him again, seemed cruel, an extension of the abuse and indignities he had suffered. An aid was ordered to watch him from outside the room. These men simply lay there communing with each other in their minds anyway. What could happen?

Alvar opened his eyes aware of the hundreds of other minds sharing his sight. Several men still in the large chamber nearest this room turned their heads in the direction of the separate room and opened their eyes too. The sight would have been impossibly confusing for one mind. The visual stimuli of multiple viewpoints would have overwhelmed a single brain. But for this larger mind it was easy. It compared the multiple views outside the small room with the single one from inside. Measured the movements of the aid outside the door and the many technicians moving about the large room. It was as easy as moving a single finger.

"Find a weapon, an object to use against the aid." The foreign thought said into the group mind. It was of course, Ezekiel, but the many minds didn't know that. Alvar questioned the thought, but only momentarily. There was a small shelf under the gurney. On it lay a stainless steel valve used for the water/food supply lines. It was heavy and dense, about the size and weight of a fist-sized rock. Alvar pulled it free of its hoses, palmed it and tucked it under his body. There were many minds in his head highly experienced with the violence he was about to perform.

"They trapped us, experimented on us without our consent. Freedom is every man's right." Thoughts screamed into Alvar's head, driving him on.

The aid unlocked the door to the small examination room to perform his hourly rounds. He was unaware of all the preparation taking place from both sides of the door. Alvar lay quietly on the gurney, his eyes closed and his right hand wrapped tightly around the valve. As the technician leaned over to check on his body, Alvar brought his hand up and crashed the valve into the base of the other man's skull. The blow made a hollow cracking sound. The technician collapsed without a cry.

"Now quickly, grab the cutting tool in his pocket." Alvar did this and moved swiftly out of the small room into the large chamber. In a moment, he was cutting the plastic wrapping from the nearest prisoner. He crouched low, avoiding the view of the roving technicians. Soon the first man was free and he helped Alvar release the man next to him. They moved quickly on to the next man and to the next. All the time aware of everything in the large chamber. Every prisoner had his eyes open now, looking around, communicating the location of every technician, silently telling the free men to move an inch to the right or left to remain undetected.

Four of the released men crept up on one of the technicians and with the impossible coordination of a group mind quickly and silently overwhelmed the man, knocking him unconscious with the same object Alvar had used. They gained another cutting tool and doubled their effectiveness.

The wave of releasing men spread rapidly across the large room, accelerating as their numbers grew and overwhelming technicians and gaining their tools. "Quickly now, get 10 of us out of this chamber and into the main building. Hamachi will isolate us in this one room, keep us locked in here. The main exit is at the north end. Go!" It was Ezekiel giving commands, but they couldn't know that.

But Ezekiel had waited too long. Surveillance cameras watched the room, feeding information to smart programs that analyzed the unusual movement. The sound of screaming alarms filled the air startling the remaining technicians and the moving prisoners. They'd been discovered. Every man ran to an exit. But it was too late, the room had been sealed.

"No!" Ezekiel shouted in frustration into the 302 minds. "Free the rest now!"

They ignored the stunned technicians who numbly released their cutting tools to their captors. Within moments, the rest of the men were free.

Ezekiel peered through the hundreds of eyes into the chamber - 300 simultaneous points of view. He tore his mind away from the view. It was too confusing for his single mind to hold.

But it represented untold power, power he would own. He would be free of this single room, this building. But for now he had revealed his plan.

Hamachi would retaliate.

29

MR. BREEDLOVE WAITED silently as Hamachi finished speaking on his VR set. Hamachi looked up with a flash of anger and frustration. "Give me your update Mr. Breedlove."

Breedlove shifted his large body uncomfortably. "As you know, our experiment was interrupted by this ... event. We can't say for sure, but I'm certain he's behind it." Breedlove avoided using Ezekiel's name, hoping it would protect him from further rancor from Hamachi. "Before the breach, we had just implanted an upgraded version of the chip. It is impossible to know the effects of this latest model. But I think we can assume it is working as designed."

"Have we found another volunteer to replace Mr. Malaffaires?" Hamachi hissed.

"No. It seems more difficult to find a suitable candidate than we thought."

Hamachi released a long sigh. "It is an unfortunate waste of information, but there seems to be no alternative. Signal the implant's self-destruct mechanism."

Breedlove nodded. He said a few words into his VR set, waited, then continued speaking, then listening for several minutes.

Hamachi grew impatient, "Well?"

"The self-destruct has failed. It was either defective, which is unlikely, or he has discovered it and rendered it inoperative. Interesting."

"Interesting! You find this interesting. This has gotten out hand. Trigger the capsule."

Breedlove did not hesitate to send the command via his VR set. He was fully aware of what he was doing. A capsule had been implanted in Ezekiel's brain when he arrived at Stratumentis. It was a chemical soup of neurotoxins embedded in a tiny device, which when released would render the subject brain-dead. The chemicals would metabolize seconds after that, leaving only the brain injury, and should it be necessary, look like a common stroke to a pathologist.

Breedlove spoke for some time into the VR set, then nodded. "The capsule also appears to have been compromised."

"But that's impossible." Hamachi blurted. "It is a foreign object, discrete from the brain. It must be defective. Try again."

"We have sir, many times. It is not defective; it is simply no longer operative. I cannot explain how."

"OK, Mr. Breedlove, I want options. This mouse is not going to control my experiment."

Breedlove paused considering the possibilities. "I suggest if we can't get to the head, we work on the limbs."

"Go on."

"We still have the synthesized viruses specific to each volunteer. Each is capable of removing the mental connection. From what we've learned in the past, it causes great discomfort and agitation to the remaining members. I suggest we remove one every 10 minutes until he cooperates."

Hamachi considered this. "Can we bring these men back into the collective once they've been removed?"

"We don't know, it hasn't been tried before, but I don't think so. We will be effectively removing and scarring the part of the brain that interacts with the others."

Hamachi considered this. "And when he cooperates?"

"We use stronger manual controls, or find another volunteer."

Hamachi controlled his anger. Damn this snake. But he knew that short of starting the experiment all over again, he would have to work with this annoyance. "Very well, begin immediately."

The large staging area which housed the 300 prisoners was sealed off to contain the men. But at the upper area of this large chamber, a series of observation rooms existed from which one could view the activities within. Hamachi stood in one of these observation rooms sternly looking down at the men below. Over the last several hours, Mr. Breedlove had separated many men from the mental collective. At first the remaining members had only moved about more actively, barely showing their discomfort. Then they moved quicker, in a confused agitated way, sometime bumping into one other. It was working. Ezekiel would have to give in, and if he didn't, they could remove all the members leaving no collective for him to control. If Ezekiel forced them to start over, well they would start over.

Hamachi felt the presence of a visitor, he didn't need to turn to know who it was. "You disappoint me, Doctor."

Alexia waited. She knew better than to apologize or become defensive.

Hamachi turned and faced her. "Well, doctor?"

"It might have helped if I had known about this additional implanted person." She said flatly. "But yes, I was careless in leaving this one prisoner unbound. It won't happen again."

"And your opinion now, doctor."

Alexia looked down at the agitated men. She did her best to hide her anxiety. "I have none sir, tell me your plans and I will carry them out."

The shadow of a smile crossed Hamachi's face. "Very good doctor, but you don't hide your feelings very well. We will continue to remove members from the collective until this thorn extricates itself."

Alexia kept her voice neutral. "Some of the men removed from the collective are in poor condition. I think they may die if we don't reconnect them."

"And?" Hamachi asked.

She looked at Hamachi for a long moment, then nodded. "Nothing sir. We will acquire more volunteers if required."

"Good. Now I'm sure you have a great deal to do."

Alexia left the observation room quietly.

A mechanical voice sounded in Hamachi's ear piece. "Chloe Larkin has arrived in Stratumentis and is waiting in visitor lounge number five."

It took Hamachi several seconds to remember who this was. When he realized it was Ezekiel's fantasy woman from the farm in Colorado, a cruel smile slowly pulled at the corners of his mouth. "Very good. Put her on."

"She refuses to use a virtual reality headset." The computer voice droned.

Oh yes, Ezekiel mentioned something about this Anti-Tech garbage. "Fine, inform her I will be there within the hour." Hamachi said.

Oh this was a fortunate bit of timing." He thought. Ezekiel would not have such an easy time of ignoring him now. Hamachi's mood brightened significantly.

In waiting room number five, Hamachi was instantly accosted by Chloe Larkin. "Who the hell do you think you are, kidnapping me and bring me to this place against my will."

Hamachi stood calmly as Chloe continued to berate him. He took the moment to consider this strange woman. She was dressed in some kind of rough work clothes and heavy boots. His men must have picked her up directly from the fields. He could see the dust on the top of her shoes and around the course wool socks. She was wearing short pants which revealed her deeply tanned and shapely legs. The simple shirt, rolled up at the sleeves, fell loosely from her thin shoulders, suggesting, rather than revealing her small breasts. Chloe's face was as tanned as her arms and legs and framed by a mane of thick brown hair. Her dark, nearly black eyes, were fierce with passion. She was quite beautiful he decided. She might have been a model or an actress in another life, perhaps a royal concubine in a previous century. No wonder Ezekiel had fallen for her. It was also clear his infatuation was all fantasy, this woman would never be interested in a beast like Ezekiel.

Hamachi let her finish, then spoke calmly, "Please forgive any rudeness that my men may have subjected you to by bringing you here. They are under strict orders not to release any information, due to the sensitive nature of our work here. You were neither kidnapped, nor are you being held here against your will. You may leave at any time. But now that you are here, let me explain. My name is Tatsuo Hamachi, I am the CEO and owner of Mitasashi Corporation. The city you are standing in is called Stratumentis. My company built it as a private retreat for research and development. A place where we can work without distraction. Perhaps it is not so different from your own home, Gaialandra, I think you call it. In any case, we sometimes work with volunteers, men who bravely offer their services to help us test our theories in a more practical sense. In some cases, these volunteers are desperate men who have lost their freedom through criminal acts. They offer their services as a way to reduce or commune their sentences."

"Alvar." Chloe whispered.

"Precisely." Hamachi said. "And that is why you were brought here. We have a man named Alvar Terrahaute as one of our volunteers. We believe you may know him and he may be here by mistake, perhaps even against his will. If there is an error, we would like to rectify it."

"Is it possible," Chloe's voice broke, "that there are still decent men on this earth. Thank you Mr. Hamachi, please let's go to him now, so I can tell you if it is the same man I lost six months ago. I assure you Alvar is no criminal and he would not be here voluntarily." Chloe moved toward the door. "Let's go see him now."

Hamachi put a hand up. "Unfortunately, it is not that simple. There has been...an incident that makes it difficult to see him. But give me a moment to speak with one of my supervisors." Hamachi turned away so Chloe could not see or hear his conversation with Mr. Breedlove over the VR terminal. "Mr. Breedlove? Have you disconnected one of the members named Alvar Terrahaute? No? Good. Be sure you don't." Hamachi turned back to Chloe, "The situation is fluid, we must..."

"What have you done with him? Is he OK or not." Chloe shot back.

"Miss Larkin, please be patient as I explain. Mr. Terrahaute has not been harmed. He is safe at the moment, but there has been an incident with one of the other men in the group. The particular experiment we are conducting requires a large group of men, 300. We procured the men from a labor camp owned by UnitedFarms in the Corporate Province of Canada. Some of these men are hardened criminals. You understand that security measures are critical to maintain safety for all concerned."

Chloe narrowed her eyes, but did not interrupt.

"In the course of our experiments, we have discovered a way for men to communicate telepathically with each other."

Chloe couldn't contain herself. "But that's impossible."

"Of course that's what we thought too. But, not only is it possible Miss Larkin, but Mr. Terrahaute is connected telepathically right now with these other men. Unfortunately, and this is the problem, one of the subjects has found a way to manipulate the others to gain control of the total. I believe you know this man too, Ezekiel Malaffaires."

"Good God." She gasped.

"Yes, you do know him. Malaffaires has found a way to block us and is slowly removing the members from the telepathic group to torture them. We are unable to stop him without risking all the men as well. Your name came up during an interview. He appears to be have...an infatuation with you Miss Larkin and a vendetta against Alvar Terrahaute. I believe you may be the lever that we can use to extricate ourselves from Mr. Malaffaires. If you are successful, I would like to offer you Alvar Terrahaute's contract along with transportation for both of you back to your home in Colorado. I have more than a little influence with UnitedFarms and should be able to clear up that confusion as well. You would be free to continue your lives in peace. Malaffaires has harmed far too many people."

Chloe rushed over to Hamachi and hugged him. Hamachi remained impassive until Chloe released him. Tears streamed down her face. "Please forgive me Mr. Hamachi. It is overwhelming what you are offering. Of course, I'll do what I can."

"Very good." Hamachi said, taking her hand. "Then let's begin immediately."

30

ALEXIA RETURNED TO the observation room shortly after Hamachi had left. She watched the agitated men below with a strained look on her face. Some walked into each other; some had fallen to the ground and were having difficulty getting back up. Others pulled at their hair, or scratched themselves in strange neurotic ways. Alexia was so distracted she had not noticed Mr. Lurst speaking to her through her headset. She pulled her attention back to what he was saying.

"....converging into amplified wave bursts." Lurst said.

"I'm sorry Mr. Lurst, I have a lot on my mind, please explain it to me again in layman's terms."

He paused to gather his thoughts, "There is some kind of symmetry or organization under all this chaos. It was hidden by too many frequencies. As more and more men have been removed from the total the wave pattern it is beginning to reveal itself. If my theory is correct, we are very close to a symmetry number right now."

"What do you mean by a symmetry number?" She asked.

"Look, here and here." He pointed to peaks and valleys on the holographic display floating in front of her vision. "Each spike corresponds to the connection nodes we've discovered in their brains." Another virtual monitor appeared next to the first. Lurst spoke excitedly. "Look at this simple shape." He showed her a four sided pyramid slowly turning in space. "This is the smallest shape that can exist in three dimensions. It is made up of four points, four sides. Fewer than that and it is flat. I think it is no coincidence that there are 4 nodes in the brain connection. When three other minds connect to it, there is a symmetry point, a balance. We never saw this, because we connected so many men at once. The closest we ever came, was at the beginning, when we had just three subjects. I believe they were out of balance, out of symmetry."

"Go on." Alexia urged.

"Well, if 4 is a symmetry point, I thought perhaps there are others. If so, they will be 16, or 4 sets of 4. After that 256, 4 sets of 16 and so on. Right now we have 261, 5 too many." Lurst directed her attention back to the floating wave pattern. "You can see them here, here and here." He pointed to other peaks and valleys. "As we get closer, the men get more and more agitated. But I think we did it backwards. If one can say there is anything natural about this phenomenon, the connections would have been added, not subtracted normally. That's why there was no disturbance at 3, or 300, the minds were simply waiting for the next symmetry point. Which in this case would have been quite large, or 1024, 4 sets of 256."

"And what happens if your theory is right, when the connected minds reach 256?" Alexia asked.

"I have no idea." He said. "But I suspect we're about to find out."

Alexia focused back to the men below. Their agitation had increased and some men were now banging their heads against the walls or floors.

"There are 260 connected to the group now, one more was just removed a few seconds ago." Lurst whispered in her earpiece.

———

The humming in Alvar's head was unbearable. He tried scratching at it, pulling his hair, anything to lessen the noise. Nothing helped, but he felt strangely compelled to continue trying. There was a vague sense of all the others, that they were going through the same thing. But they were no help and he continued rubbing his scalp. "How much longer can this last?" He heard someone shout into his mind. Yes, how much longer indeed.

"Dr. Alexia Serguey, may I introduce Miss Chloe Larkin." Hamachi said, sounding like he was at a formal dinner party.

Alexia scanned Chloe quickly, noticing her work shoes, bare legs and dirty fingernails. "Uh, pleased to meet you Miss Larkin. Will you excuse us a moment." Alexia said, nonplussed, pulling Hamachi off to one side. "I'm extremely busy right now. Don't you think it's unwise to bring a stranger into the secured area?"

Hamachi still wore the dull smile of the dinner party. "It depends on the stranger, Dr. Serguey. Miss Larkin is Alvar Terrahaute's lover. The same man you neglected to secure yesterday."

"I see," she said, turning to take a better look at the young woman. "Very well, how does this involve me?" Alexia asked.

Hamachi's smile evaporated. "You are going to be responsible for her." Hamachi's hand went up to block her protest. "I suggest you keep her available. You will know when the time is right. I can trust you to do things...correctly, can't I?"

The insult drove home the point. "Of course Mr. Hamachi."

"Good, then shall we return to our guest."

"Dr. Serguey will put you in contact with Mr. Terrahaute as soon as possible. In the meantime, the doctor she will arrange for any of your personal needs." Hamachi bowed his head slightly to Chloe, turned and left.

Alexia spoke quickly. "Do you need anything? Are you hungry or..."

Chloe cut her off. "Less than an hour ago, Alvar was lost to me, absorbed into a system I could not fight, let alone comprehend. Then I am brought here to this, this place. No, I do not want anything to eat or drink. I want you to free Alvar and let us go home. Now please bring me to him."

Alexia considered Chloe more carefully now, not fooled by the way she spoke. She was scared, alone, out of her element. Alvar had told Alexia that he was a member of the Anti-Tech movement. But she hadn't really understood what that meant. But by the way this woman was dressed and her simple speech, she began to have an idea. "Very well, follow me." Alexia said, leading Chloe to one of the observation areas, one where she had last seen Alvar.

Chloe gasped. The scene through the large window was near chaos now. Some of the men where convulsing, others writhing on the floor in agony. Since they had been speaking, another member of the collective had been separated. The total was down to 259, very close to Lurst's theoretical symmetry number. In 30 minutes, they would find out what that meant, if anything.

"My god, can't you help these men?" Chloe breathed.

"No. We cannot risk entry into the staging area. To let one man out could mean disaster for the city. It is simply too dangerous. Come over here, let's try to locate Alvar."

Chloe spotted him first. Alexia watched her face. The transformation was dramatic. All the tightness in her forehead, the defensive anger and hardness of the woman left. She began crying, easy, gentle tears. Alexia was puzzled, then moved despite herself. Chloe's emotion was authentic, simple. There was no play here, just honest relief. "I didn't believe him, you know. Mr. Hamachi. But hope does strange things to you. And here he is, alive. Oh thank god, he's alive." She stopped, unable to say more.

Alvar was sitting holding his knees, rocking back and forth, his eyes closed and his face contorted with pain. Others moved around bumping and jostling him. Alexia looked at the unholy scene through Chloe's eyes. Her sense of horror was renewed, redoubled. What had they done to these men. What right had they to do this to human beings. Alexia looked away.

Lurst caught Alexia's attention, waving frantically for her to come over to one the holo-monitors. She turned to Chloe, careful to avoid the view. "I have important work to do, perhaps it will help Alvar. May I leave you here?"

"Yes." Chloe said wiping her face with her sleeve. "Please do what you can to help him."

Alexia cringed as a wave of guilt swept over her. "I'll do my best." She mumbled.

"Dr. Serguey look at this!" Lurst had pulled Alexia's arm and dragged her to the brain wave holo-monitor. He was gesturing excitedly, like a child pointing at mud pie, "Look what I made."

Alexia looked at him. "I'm sorry, I don't see it. What am I looking for?"

"Here doctor. A new wave set. They are faint, but defined. See them, here, here and here, seven new wave forms."

Alexia snapped out of her funk. She was a scientist again exploring the unknown. "Extraordinary. These men are developing new brain waves. From their stress perhaps?"

"No doctor, these wave forms are not theirs, well, not from their brains, but because of them. These are unique, much higher in frequency." Lurst paused, his eyes shining with excitement. "I think a new mind is being born."

Nothing was said for several minutes. They turned from the floating waves displayed by the holo-monitor to the thrashing men in the large chamber. But this was difficult to watch and they turned back. "258." Lurst said quietly.

Alexia looked over at Chloe. She could only see her back. She was clearly tense, but no longer crying, erect, taking the events as they came. There was a strength about this woman that Alexia recognized, even envied.

"We're at 257." Lurst said several minutes later. "Less than ten minutes to go. Stand by everyone."

Alexia walked over to the observation window. The scene had grown far worse. Many of the men appeared to be having grand mal seizures, thrashing and foaming from the mouth.

"I'm sorry." She whispered to Chloe. "We're doing what we can. How is Alvar?"

Chloe turned to face her. Alexia had been wrong. She was crying freely. But her face and body were erect, proud. She was releasing her emotions, but not being consumed by them. Suddenly, Alexia realized Chloe had seen plenty of pain and death in her young life. "You're doing everything you can." Chloe mocked. And she turned back to the window.

Chloe's words hit her like a slap. Alexia stepped back. They had to stop this madness, this mass torture. She switched her VR set to call mode and rang for Hamachi. The V-mail server came on. She quickly disconnected and hurried over to Lurst. "Who in this city would be capable of designing a virus or nanobot to disconnect these men like this?"

Lurst looked away.

"Out with it." She grabbed his collar.

"Breedlove." He whispered.

"Breedlove? I've never heard of him. Never mind." She quickly connected to his VR address.

"Yes, Dr. Serguey?" Alexia's VR set was filled with the view of Breedlove's large bearded face.

"You must stop disconnecting men, you're going to kill them all. This is not science, it is murder!" She shouted.

"But it has been stopped, doctor Serguey."

"What?" Chloe stared at the man in disbelief.

"I suggest you check on the men and see for yourself." Breedlove severed the connection.

She turned to Lurst to ask him what Breedlove could have meant. But Lurst was standing, staring at the observation window. The technicians beside him had stopped their work too; all were staring in the same direction. Chloe turned quickly around to see what they were looking at.

The chamber was silent, the thrashing nightmare was over. Every man was now standing calmly upright in rows, impossible straight rows, all staring intently at Chloe.

31

I N A SINGLE instant, Alvar's mind went from searing pain and confusion to peace. The transition was so abrupt that he still cringed in anticipation of the stinging noise and overwrought synapses that had been his life for so many hours. A few seconds passed, then a few more and still nothing happened. He began to trust this new state, to look around physically and mentally. The room was the same, the members of the collective were still here too. Each looked as puzzled as he did. They still felt each other and still could see through each others' eyes. That had not changed. But there was something different. He realized what it was, without thinking of it. They were complete, a group that was not a group, but a single something. He couldn't explain it, but he felt it and knew the others did too.

And there was sense of the familiar. He looked through the eyes of the others and then he saw her. Chloe. He turned along with the others to see her standing against the glass. She looked tired. He could see by her clothes that she had been whisked from the fields and brought directly here. He tried to worry for her, to feel the concern, the protectiveness of a lover. Alvar had longed for Chloe all the time they had been separated.

But now the emotions felt false and he dropped them. She was safe – in this moment and that was enough. Some small part of his questioning mind asked if this were better. He knew he had lost something important. But he remained numb to any deeper feelings for her.

In the quiet concentration of all the members of the collective focusing on her, Alvar heard Chloe. And he gave a mental gasp. It was not her voice and not quite her thoughts, but it was her essence. She was clearly not part of the collective, yet they felt her, all of them did. "I wonder if we can speak with her?" Alvar wasn't quite sure if that was his own thought, or someone else's. It didn't matter. He knew they must try to speak with her. Compulsion grew in him. It was incredibly important.

"Chloe." He mouthed through the window. Alvar had moved to the spot directly in front of her. A piece of glass was all that separated them now. "Chloe, we must speak with you." The glass was too dense to allow them to hear each other. But he was sure she understood him. Perhaps she felt the need to speak to them as well. He saw her move away and speak with Alexia, the doctor whom he had talked to eons ago. Or was it only yesterday?

Alexia looked at Chloe as if she were speaking some unknown language. "You want to go in there? And you want me to help you?" Alexia shook her head sadly. "I understand your need to speak with your friend but..."

"No. It's not that. Well it is that too. But it is more. I can hear them. There is something being born in there, it needs to speak with me. I can't explain it. But if we don't do something soon, it could be damaged. Don't ask me to explain, I can't. Just let me go in. I must speak to them." She slapped her fist against her thigh. "I'll take the risk."

"You'll take the risk." Alexia scoffed. "Do you know what these men tried to do less than a day ago? I don't trust them. And forgive me for saying this, but I don't see why I should trust you either."

Alexia heard the special tone in her ear signaling a VR call from

Hamachi. His timing was perfect as usual. He was probably listening in. Good. Let him take this decision off her shoulders.

Hamachi said: "Dr. Serguey. Let the girl go in. Do not let anyone come out, though. Post a series of armed guards. Anyone leaving without my direct approval is to be shot. Understood?"

"I understand." Alexia severed the connection. "It seems you will be allowed to enter. But I must warn you. If anyone tries to leave without permission, including you, he...or she will be shot." Alexia grabbed Chloe's shoulders firmly. "Do you still want to go in there? And do you understand the risk you are taking?"

Chloe looked from the dark intensity of Alexia's eyes to Alvar calmly staring at her through the glass, then back. "Yes, I understand. I'm going in." Her voice sounded more confident then she looked.

Alexia nodded, then let her go. "Very well. Wait here, I have a lot to arrange first."

Alexia had just turned to go, when she felt a strong tug at her lab coat. "Dr. Serguey, I must speak with you. You have to see this."

Alexia pulled herself free, annoyed that someone had touched her. "Not now Mr. Lurst. I'll be with you as soon as I can."

"But please Dr. Serguey, it's very important."

"So is this." And she moved off.

Lurst stood where he was, a stunned expression on his face.

Alvar worked alongside the other members of the collective as they disassembled and moved the medical tables to the edges of the room. He couldn't say why, but the middle of the room needed to be clear. When this was done, he watched the others sit down in the middle of the large open space. Alvar knew they weren't just sitting, they were forming a pattern and each man had to be in a certain place. It was a kind of complex star with a small clear space in the center. He couldn't say why, but he knew Chloe would have to sit in the middle when she came in.

It took two agonizing hours to set up a security connection to one of the access doors.

Alexia spoke to Chloe, "OK, we're ready. Are you sure you still want to go through with this?"

"Yes doctor. The feeling is even stronger now. It is very important." Chloe's tanned face had become absolutely smooth. The concentrated worry that had been with her since her arrival to Stratumentis was gone. Alexia realized that Chloe was quite beautiful. She caught one of the guards giving Chloe a lustful look. "I hope she knows what she's doing." She thought.

As they arrived at the large steel door of the staging area, Alexia said, "Understand something then, you can go in. But unless we are certain and I mean absolutely certain that you are not controlled by them, you will not be allowed to come out. Do you understand?"

Chloe nodded.

"That's not good enough. Say it."

"I understand. If they take over my mind, turn me into a zombie, I can't come out again." Chloe gave a sardonic grin.

Alexia frowned, but didn't argue. "Then good luck."

Alvar found himself waiting along with the others. "Chloe would come through that door," he told himself. It was difficult to think and he had to focus hard on every thought. "Chloe is coming through this door." He repeated, trying desperately to hold onto the last threads of himself.

Chloe entered the steel tunnel allowing the door to shut behind her with a click. She took a deep breath, then turned the latch on the door to the main room and quickly moved through. She felt, more than heard the loud click as the heavy door locked behind her. It's done. Now with no glass between them she looked at the sea of men. "There are so many." She was told it was 256. But sitting there on the floor in this geometric pattern, they seemed to be far more. Chloe noticed a movement, something or someone standing to her far left, too deep in shadow to be recognized. She was frozen with fear as she suddenly remembered that Ezekiel was in here too.

"Come with me." The man said.

"Alvar!" Chloe shouted. And she hugged him with all her strength. She kissed him on the mouth, his cheeks and his eyes. Eventually she pulled back.

Alvar stood pliant, not responding to her affection, nor did he withdraw from it. He simply stood there infinitely patient.

Chloe let go, stepping back a bit further to look at him. "What... have they done to you?"

"My body is well, but there is a great pressure in my mind compelling me to bring you to the center of the room. It is difficult to think of anything else." Alvar's speech was strange, broken. But finally, he looked at her, really looked at her. "Chloe, I'm so glad to see you, but I'm also sorry you're here." Then he took her hand and led her to the center of the room.

Alvar's grip was strange, different. It was firm and strong as she remembered it, just shy of hurting her. But there was something else. Now she understood. His hand was smooth, soft, like a baby. The hard callouses of a lifetime spent working on a farm were gone. She kept her eyes on his face as he led her through the maze of seated men. It was odd. He never looked down, yet every step was perfectly placed and they never brushed a single man in this tight assembly.

There in the center of the group he released his grip, but Chloe held on. Alvar stood, lost and confused. "You must sit there." He pointed with his free hand to the empty space in the middle of the large group.

"Alvar, I don't want you to leave me. I'm afraid."

Alvar cocked his head slightly to one side. "Please Chloe, sit down. It will all be clear to you in a minute." He paused a second, then added. "It's fine. I promise, just sit down." There was just a hint of his crooked smile. And for that moment he was Alvar.

"OK." She said, releasing his hand.

Alvar stepped away and found a place among the others. He seemed to flow into them like a drop of water in the ocean, disappearing.

Chloe sat, too terrified to do anything else.

"What are they doing now?" Hamachi said into Alexia's earpiece.

She answered as if she didn't know he was watching all of this on his VR screen. "She is just sitting there with her eyes closed. Nothing has changed."

"Contact me at once when there is a change, no matter how slight." He ended the call with a loud click.

Hamachi turned to Breedlove. "What has become of that thorn in our side, Mr. Malaffaires?"

Breedlove shrugged. "I don't know. We've scanned the group sitting on the floor and he is not among them. He can't have gotten out, so he's in there. Somewhere."

"Find him. Go in there yourself if you have to, but find him." Hamachi growled.

Breedlove reddened. "Yes, Mr. Hamachi."

"And what about this new chip. Is it ready, does it work?"

"We believe it will...function as designed."

"It had better."

When Chloe first sat down, she heard a faint buzz. Just some high-tech machinery, she thought. But the buzzing grew gradually louder, clearer. And she started to listen to it harder. There was something there, a message of some kind. Perhaps a...

"You can hear me!" An excited voice shouted.

"I...hear you." Chloe said, or thought. It wasn't clear which it was. She felt like she was dreaming, barely feeling the floor now. "What's happening?"

"Happening?" The voice echoed. "You are the first to speak with me. I thought I was to be alone forever, mute. But I see that you are different from me. Your thoughts are smaller. Ah, I understand now, you are an individual, a single mind."

"Yes. What are you then?" Chloe cringed.

"Please don't be frightened. I'm young and will make mistakes. Be patient with me. I see myself now - through your eyes. I am these men sitting on the floor around you. They are my hands and feet, my eyes. They are my body."

"That doesn't make any sense. They have their own minds, each of them. One mind to each body. You can't be made from more than one." Chloe's mind reeled.

"But it does make sense and I am here, communicating with you now. Allow me to look a little deeper into your thoughts and memories." Chloe felt a kind of tickle in her mind. "Ah there it is. Let me explain the best I can."

Chloe listened while the voice explained the experiment, the joining of the men, first one, then three, then two, then 300, then back down to 256. "At this special number, I was born a new mind, made of these many minds. I am unique from them, though I am made of them. Think of a unique cell in your body, a cell in your finger for example. It is alive, discrete, unique. But it is not a finger. Put billions of them together in the right pattern and the total is a finger. It can move, feel, grasp, but it is useless without the brain and so on. These men are the same thing. They are cells, joined into a larger organism. They join together to make me, a..." The voice paused looking for a word, "a Meta-vidual."

"This is extraordinary." Chloe breathed.

"Perhaps. But it is also ironic. I am a being made of many beings. I can see from your mind, that they are mostly criminals, prisoners. Their captivity is my captivity; and I am hungry for knowledge and experience."

Chloe grew cold. "You want to leave, to make more like yourself."

"Don't you? Don't you want to have children with your mate here, Alvar? How is that different?"

"I guess that's true," she blushed. "And what of the men around us? What happens to them when you are moving around having your experiences? Are they free to be what they were meant to be?"

"You mean to be criminals?" The voice asked.

"Alvar is not a criminal. What will he be? A zombie, doing only what you command."

There was a long pause. "I don't know. I can't perceive how it will work. I can feel my limbs in a way. I think it must be the way you feel yours. You have a thought and your hand moves. But I cannot sense the individual minds, nor personalities among these men. I know of them through you. It must be like your own cells in your body. They perform their individual tasks, metabolizing energy, multiplying, getting sick, dying. You don't know them, but they perform their job for you. Do they have desires, needs, individual aspirations too?"

"But that's different, they are just cells, too small for consciousness." She blurted.

"Are they?"

Chloe's mind was full of too many concepts. And she didn't answer.

"The point is, we don't know about the parts that we are made of, or that we make up. I don't wish to be the destroyer of will, but I also want to live. What about your world, the Anti-Techs? I can feel them in your mind. I think we have much in common. You have a common goal, you work together for it. Imagine the possibilities if we worked together. No more arguments or wasted work. And the high tech world around you could be easily pushed away, because you would be so much stronger, able to hold them at bay. Or perhaps better, have them join you. Chloe, I think it was no accident you and I met. I think you are my purpose and I yours."

Chloe was more than a little confused. It was all so sudden, this morning she was working on a farm. And now she was talking to a voice in her mind. What if it was all an illusion, part of some sick experiment these people were doing in this building? This horrible abomination of a building strung from wires in the middle of the Grand Canyon. She was seduced by the Meta-vidual's idea. It was a kind of immortality. No more conflicts. But she was also repulsed by what it might mean to the individual. "I need to talk to Alvar. I need to see what he is."

She felt a smile in her head. "Of course. I will do my best to stay out of your way. But Chloe, please come back when you can. I enjoyed our conversation."

Chloe opened her eyes. She realized her back hurt and her legs were numb. "How long have I been sitting?" She thought.

———

Alexia reported to Hamachi, "She has gotten up and is speaking to the prisoner, Alvar. They are holding hands and..."

Hamachi interrupted her, "Good god doctor, I can see that. I don't want such minutia. Just tell me what is happening with their brains, their scans."

"Lurst!" Alexia gasped. Alexia nearly ran to the neuro-scanning station. "Uh, just a moment, Mr. Hamachi. I'll check with my head neurographist." She put Hamachi on standby.

Alexia signaled Lurst and was in front of his virtual monitors a moment later. "What is it you have to show me?" She said out of breath from running.

"Dr. Serguey, at last! There is so much to tell you. Let me try to begin at a logical place." Lurst turned a few virtual dials and got the screen he was looking for. "When the men were reduced to 256, the symmetry number, the extra brain waves sharpened, defined themselves, strengthened. I'm convinced now that it is an independent consciousness." He was pointing to the squiggles that appeared on his holo-monitor. They were highlighted in red and rotated slowing in space.

"I see them. A new mind." She breathed. "Do you think the girl was speaking, communicating with...it?"

"More than that Dr. Serguey." Lurst had changed the display to show Chloe's brain pattern on the screen. The two groups of brain waves were hovering near each other. He pointed to several spots. "He, or it, is not only communicating with her, it's... Lurst's voice dropped off.

"Well, out with it man. Tell me. What do you think it's doing?"

Lurst's eyes rounded into saucers and the color drained from his face. "It's altering her brain."

32

EZEKIEL SET HIS eyes to highest magnification as he peered across the room at the embracing Chloe and Alvar. It was impossible to ignore that Chloe was particularly beautiful now that she was with her lover. His heart clenched with jealousy. "I'll burn his brain when I get back in control. I'll burn both their brains. They'll wish they were in hell where it's cooler."

His confidence waned as he scanned the large room. The periphery had been hastily stacked with the service tables and feeding mechanisms. The jumble of equipment gave Ezekiel plenty of places to hide and watch the collective. But it also reminded him of his precarious situation. The collective was dangerous without a leader, and he was useless to Hamachi without control of the collective. Fortunately, he had used the skills of Dr. Smith to disable the devices in his head. Hamachi would have certainly eliminated him by now otherwise. Not a good situation, not good at all. It was time to find a way back into the collective.

Ezekiel slithered into the shadows so he couldn't see Chloe. She was distracting. Ezekiel suspected the birth of the single mind from the collective. That it had ejected him from the whole. It was likely Chloe was speaking to it when she sat in the middle of the room so quietly all these hours. The question was, what would Hamachi do with all this information? Surely, he would not sit back and allow this thing to control his experiment. Ezekiel knew enough about megalomaniacs to know that Hamachi would already be looking for a plan to regain control, or... "That's it!" Ezekiel nearly shouted out loud, "He'll start another collective." Ezekiel smiled. "And I'll be right there with him."

———

"And you're sure this will work." Hamachi said to the hulking Breedlove.

"As certain as I can be about something that has never been tried."

Breedlove was so close to Hamachi adjusting controls and equipment that Hamachi could smell his sweat and it disgusted him. It reminded him of all the imperfections of humanity, the biological flaws that made man a beast and not the god Hamachi envisioned.

"I'm ready, what do we need to test it?" Hamachi asked.

"Your implantation is complete. Ten volunteers have been implanted to create a new collective. You simply need to go in and observe them and see if they know you are there." Breedlove said.

"And what about Malaffaires?" Hamachi asked.

"I've considered that. It is unlikely he will be able to join a new collective as he is tied to the last one. Now that we understand these so called symmetry numbers we can avoid them simply enough. We've also changed the signal of your chip and the placement of the new implants. The new chip allows listening on a higher frequency. Even if he is there, he should not be able to know about you. Everything about this chip is different." Breedlove hesitated a moment, then continued. "Also, your mind is far more disciplined; you should be able to overwhelm him should he get in."

Hamachi was lying on the medical chair, staring up at the large burly man, when he suddenly burst into laughter. The abruptness and volume of the sound startled the humorless Breedlove and he stepped back in fear.

"Don't be afraid, you big ox. It was just amusing to hear such blatant flattery coming from you." Hamachi was serious again. "Now finish up. I'm anxious to try it."

Ezekiel climbed over and under tables and through the tangle of equipment against the wall of the large chamber. He had worked out a path to and from the supply room. Being spotted by even one member of the collective meant he would be known to all. One of them might remember his "activities" while in their minds. Chloe knew him and if she told Alvar, then all would know. It was best to stay unseen.

Ezekiel chewed absently on a hard slab of dehydrated food. He thought of Hamachi. "What would I do in his place?" He knew so little of the business giant. So few people had risen to such heights, everything was run by conglomerates, groups of groups. Individuals rarely held so much power. To do this made him a unique and daunting adversary. Despite his own arrogance, Ezekiel felt begrudging respect for the businessman.

"But he's still a man. Much of what he's accomplished is because of his wealth, buying and selling his way to the top. Besides he doesn't know what I know about controlling the collective. I have the advantage of experience." But Ezekiel realized that every minute that passed, might be a minute Hamachi was gaining that precious experience, growing a new collective. Once he got far enough, there would be no chance for Ezekiel and he would be pushed aside as easily as these tables.

"Come on Ezekiel," He pushed himself. "Quiet that hyperactive brain of yours and listen. If there's a collective out there, you'll hear them, you have to."

Ezekiel set about listening with his mind, scanning for the voices in his head. Waiting, barely breathing. For a long time there was nothing. Then he felt, rather than heard a slight tremor. It was faint, merely a shadow of an echo. But Ezekiel held on to it. He focused on the sound, magnifying, amplifying it with his mind, holding it with his will. With each renewed bit of effort, the sound grew stronger. From a rustle, it grew to a whisper. The whisper became a voice and the voice became a thought. The single thought multiplied into two, three, ten, hundreds, and then the multitude. And he was in, inside the minds of the new collective. Yes, the arrogant Hamachi had fabricated a new chip and created a new collective for himself, just as he had imagined. Relief and power flowed through Ezekiel.

It was better this time. They were not just prisoners, but technicians and trained workers. There was intelligence here, disciplined minds. "You've revealed much about yourself Mr. Hamachi. You were in such a hurry to thwart me that you couldn't wait for more volunteers. You consumed the resources that surround you. You've given me rich material to work with. Thank you Mr. Hamachi, you're very generous." Ezekiel gave a mental laugh that would have peeled the skin off any mind that was listening.

Hamachi blinked several times, then held his eyes wide open. It took several seconds for the room to come into focus. "I had no idea." He said.

Breedlove checked his monitors. "It seems that everything is working as designed, no signs of rejection. And most important, no signs of Malaffaires. You didn't sense him, did you?"

"I don't think so. Nothing suggested that anyone else is in there, or that they sensed me either." Hamachi was sitting up now. "It is extraordinary. I can't explain it exactly; it is something like painting with thoughts. I've never known such freedom. There is no time or place. One could get lost just traveling from one idea to the next, from one memory to the next. Words are inadequate; it is vast, incredibly vast."

"Mr. Hamachi, you should eat. It has been ten hours since you began." Breedlove said.

"Ten hours! It felt like ten minutes. But you're right; I do feel hungry and somewhat fatigued. Bring me something. I'd like to go back in as soon as possible."

Ezekiel couldn't put his finger on it, but he felt a sudden void in the new collective. It must be Hamachi's mind withdrawing. He quickly tapped into the eyesight of the ten minds of the new collective. He could see the ten points of view simultaneously. Hamachi would not be used to this much awareness and had likely not tried it. He discovered that the members of the new collective were in a private room on the 30th floor. He withdrew quickly. Ezekiel knew he had to keep his advantage. He had to remind himself of time, which was far different inside the collective. One was easily distracted, following associations and paths. Wasting time was a luxury Ezekiel didn't have. He had to work while Hamachi was out, then quietly observe when he was in. But Ezekiel knew about patience. It was a hacker's most fundamental tool.

He went to work planting thoughts here and there. Subtle, random thoughts that couldn't be tracked. They were the equivalent of planting backdoors in a software program. Places where he could re-enter the minds should things get difficult later. Then Ezekiel felt the void filling – Hamachi was back. Ezekiel went very still. Time to observe.

Hamachi sensed something different in the collective as he re-entered; but was bombarded by so many sensations and thoughts, that he ignored the subtle feeling. There was so much to see and learn, so many minds to mold and control. Everything in life prior to this had been a rehearsal, dull and lifeless. He had been sleepwalking and now was awake. "I was right, in every way. Mankind will be mine to lead. Not just these ten, but the whole planet. Why stop there? We'll travel to the stars, find other intelligence, absorb them too." Hamachi threw back his imaginary head and laughed into the infinite space of mind.

241

33

ALEXIA VIEWED CHLOE and Alvar through the heavy glass. They had been in the large room for days now. Though there was no evidence that she wanted to get out or escape - intuition told her otherwise. Alexia had been unable to reach Hamachi to discuss if it were even possible to move the girl. From what Lurst had shown her, it was clear her brain had been changed, manipulated in ways they couldn't understand. Chloe appeared to be an individual – but for how much longer? Alexia had to speak with her, had to learn what was happening, for all their sakes.

Alexia tried Hamachi once more. After she got his automated message, she called Ong. "Ong, meet me in observation room three, I'd like to..."

Ong was standing beside Alexia as if she had always been there. Alexia shook off her surprise and annoyance. "I'm going inside to speak with the woman."

Ong did not say anything, just raised her eyebrows questioningly.

"I'm not worried about getting in. It's getting out that concerns me. I need Lurst to monitor my brain waves continuously. He will have the final say on whether I'm allowed to return. Understood?"

"Yes doctor." Ong said.

"OK, so that's it. Come with me to the entrance." Alexia led Ong to the makeshift security station at the entrance of the staging area. The men stiffened as Alexia grew closer. She moved to the man in charge.

"Officer...Larson." She said looking at his badge. "I'm going inside the chamber to speak with the woman named Chloe Larkin. It is too dangerous to let her out and it is vital that I learn what has happened in there." Alexia gestured toward Ong. "Ong will be in charge in my absence. She, along with a brain wave expert, Mr. Lurst, will determine if I am safe to return. You will accept her decision. Understand?"

"Yes doctor Serguey." He nodded curtly.

"Good. Then I'll go in immediately."

The man's hesitation was slight, but perceptible to the observant Alexia. "What is it? Do you have something to say?" Alexia urged.

"Not about this doctor."

"Well, what then, out with it."

"Yes doctor. We have been losing men lately. And I don't know where they go. They don't call in sick or on other assignments, they simply don't show up. When I check the VR locator, they're gone, no longer listed as having ever been in the city. I don't know what to make of it."

Alexia raised her eyebrows in surprise. She wasn't sure what it meant, but she had her suspicions. It was now even more urgent she speak with Chloe. "Look into it Ong." She said without turning.

"Yes doctor."

"Anything else officer?" Alexia asked.

"No doctor."

Alexia turned to face the metal door. Its plainness belied the strange churning on the other side. It was madness to go in there. But it was maddening to stay out here with no information, to allow events to unfold without her control. Alexia grabbed the knob firmly, turned it and went into the tunnel.

Alvar pulled himself out of the collective each time Chloe spoke to him. It was the feeling of being exquisitely tired and being awakened constantly. It was a kind of torture and it was getting harder and harder to stay focused on Chloe. He remembered his feelings for her, their friendship, their lovemaking. But he was as removed now as watching someone else's memories. He wanted to care, wanted to desire Chloe, but it was false, dull. All he wanted to do was swim in the sea of minds, drift into the peacefulness of infinite thought...

"Alvar." The voice whispered. "Alvar, come back."

He heard the words, knew what they meant, but wasn't sure he wanted to. Alvar waited, maybe the voice would go away. "Alvar, come back to yourself. They're keeping you separate. Come back. Concentrate." The voice said. Alvar pulled himself away from the collective with a terrible force of will.

Alvar and Chloe were sitting against one of the tables turned on its side, another adjacent to it created a corner, a room with two sides. Chloe had gathered a pile of blankets and padding so they could be comfortable. It was a kind of nest. The other men simply lay randomly on the hard floor with no concern for comfort or privacy.

"Chloe. It's you." Alvar was disoriented. "I thought you might have gone."

"Where would I go. And it's only been a moment since we spoke."

"A moment? It seems like months. But didn't you just call me...to come back?"

Chloe cocked her head in puzzlement. "No darling. I've been right here, but I didn't say anything."

Alvar kept it to himself. The memory of the voice was fading and though it was familiar, he realized it wasn't Chloe's.

"Chloe, should I be angry that a higher being is directing my actions?"

"Yes, you should be appalled and outraged. You should fight it with all your strength." She said without hesitation.

"I should? Why? We were thinking, all of us, that is, that perhaps this mind is God. Many of us have religious backgrounds. We were taught to seek God's will, perhaps this is what it means. We were meant to be here, to be the first."

Alvar caught a look of disgust pass like a shadow over Chloe's sweet face. "That's different." She said.

"Is it? A higher mind directing our will, giving us guidance in exchange for peace and purpose. Isn't that what mankind has asked for, forever, since we were cavemen? We've begged to have our will taken away from us, to be free of the difficulty of decisions of life. Isn't that what this is? What if there was some seed planted in our heads to ask for this event, to become part of a collective, guided by a higher mind?"

Chloe stiffened, shaking her head vigorously. "No! You are being manipulated by it. This mind is not God. I know, I speak to it. I can't speak to God. This thing is a product of this place and their technology. They've taken men and used their machines to force them together into a new being, something manufactured. It is an abomination. Think Alvar. Our whole lives have been dedicated to avoiding the seduction of technology, the shortcut it represents, but the heavy price one pays is with one's soul. Look around, look at what it has done to these men, to you. It is no god. If it is anything it is the Devil."

Alvar was quiet for a time, listening to the many ideas in his head. "What is God then? Does its definition only apply when we can't understand it. When we do begin to understand, must we raise the bar again, just to keep him out of reach of our comprehension. I think this mind you speak to is a kind of god in the ancient concept of it. All our prehistoric yearnings have been leading us to this very moment."

"No." Chloe whispered. She had lowered her head, still shaking it back and forth.

Alvar's voice softened. "You can't understand how incredibly easy and wonderful it is to meld with the others. To end the struggle, the pain of individualism. It is overwhelming how many decisions a person makes every day. We have none of that. This innate ability to merge has been with us for all of our existence, waiting to be unleashed. Do you know what is more remarkable?"

Chloe didn't look up.

Alvar went on. "You are communicating with just one Meta-vidual. Why should there be only one. What happens if there are a hundred or a thousand? Won't that create a super Meta-vidual, or whatever it would call itself. Don't you see Chloe, all of mankind will be linked. Hunger, greed, competition, even petty arguments, all of it will be gone. Our tiny Anti-Tech community would be the norm for all of humanity. Why would a single being do anything to harm itself with pollution, genetic engineering, environmental damage, unchecked population. All of it would come into balance, merged with nature."

Chloe sat up very straight. "Or it would bathe itself in high technology that pales to what we have now. The world is made up of men and women who live and breathe virtual reality – illusion. You are made of a small group of criminals, outcasts. The world loves technology and the being they would create would love it more, would worship it.

"Alvar, listen to yourself. You've never given away responsibility or direction to another man. I can understand it coming from the others, the freeloading criminals. But not you. Not Alvar Terrahaute. What have they done to you to turn you into this mindless follower. This is not you. It's them, all the others speaking through you, for you." She swept her hand around the room. The tears were streaming freely down her face. "All of humanity? Slaves to some higher mind you can't even know. How do you know it will be so smart, or know the needs of you and me better than we know them ourselves? I think it might have been better if you had died, rather than become a part of this multi-headed beast. The real Alvar would not have given in without a fight."

Alvar looked at her intently. First his face showed hurt, then puzzlement, then flaccid resignation. He closed his eyes and went silent.

"You've run away again, back to your precious collective." She whispered through her tears. Chloe sat quietly hugging the unresponsive Alvar.

Alvar had slipped back into the collective not to escape, but to think. There was no concept of privacy in the group mind, but there was freedom to explore ideas. It was all they did in there. Words, like god, individual, collective, will, what did it all mean? He had plenty of memories to draw on. Alvar turned the concepts over and over. He kept coming to one con-clusion: God was a parent figure and we as men were his children, always trying to abdicate responsibility. We would get in trouble, spoil our world, then beg God to clean up our mess. Clichés like, "it is God's will," or "it is an act of God" were abdications of responsibility. Here in this mass of minds, so many were willing to give up everything, every concept of free-dom and responsibility, for what, to what? A mind they couldn't know. Chloe was right, he'd be a slave. No he'd be worse than a slave, he'd be an organ in a body. A slave still had his own mind. He wouldn't even have that.

With these thoughts, Alvar finally felt it, the first rumblings of anger. Nothing so dramatic as the word implied, just a shadow of the real emo-tion. But it was authentic and it was his. That was even more amazing. It was his. He felt around himself, his identity was somehow separate from the identity of the others. Everything was the same, everyone thinking and feeling everyone else. But there was more, something new. A kind of capsule had formed with a few bits of Alvar's mind in it. It was protected from the others, separate. "So it is possible to be unique in here." But the effort was enormous. With the realization of his uniqueness, Alvar let go, flowing back into the whole. But the capsule remained and remembered.

Chloe felt a gentle hand on her shoulder and looked up.

"Doctor?" Chloe said, wiping tears from her face.

Alexia looked slowly from the unconscious Alvar back to Chloe. "We need to speak, but not here, in private."

Chloe looked questioningly at Alvar's relaxed features. She untangled her arms from Alvar and rose. They moved across the wide floor picking their way through the still bodies scattered like rags in the large room. Chloe ignored them. Alexia gave them a wide birth, horror painted on her face. They came to a closed door and Alexia unlocked it using the iris scanner.

Inside the small windowless examining room, Alexia motioned to one of the two chairs in the room. "Sit down Miss Larkin. I came here to speak with you. I need to know what is happening out there."

"Oh." Chloe said coldly. "Data for your experiment?"

"Yes." Alexia barked. "The situation is not stable. How long do you think we can keep all of this contained? And if we can't contain it, then what?" Alexia softened her voice. "Look Chloe, I'm a scientist and this is an experiment that has run away from us. I need more information to allow it to continue. You've been communing with someone or something and I need to understand what." Alexia let the words hang in the air.

"Or you'll what? Fill the room with poison gas so everyone in here dies? I doubt it. I'm an Anti-Tech, not a naïve. You won't give up something this high tech until you suck every e-bill of profit from it. Don't waste your threats on me. My world has been torn apart. My people at home are being overrun by your machines. Alvar, what's left of him, has been turned into some kind of mindless robot."

Alexia's voice was grave. "I think you are mistaken about what I will or won't do."

Chloe's face went white. "You wouldn't."

"OK, then help me. Talk to me."

Chloe eyes misted over, then she looked away. "What is it you want to know?"

"Good." Alexia sighed. "Our first concern is containment. Do you think the mind you speak with can move beyond these walls, affect the people on the other side?"

"I have no idea. I don't understand it at all. Somehow it talks to me, in my head. It is clearest when I sit in the center of the other men, but I feel it all the time." Chloe said.

"Tell me about it, what are you talking to?" Alexia asked excitedly.

Chloe sighed. "It calls itself the Meta-vidual. It explained this to me as a conjunction of 'meta,' the Greek word for higher order and individual. It is not arrogant in the traditional sense of the word, but it is supremely confident of its superiority. It talks down to me at times, trying to explain concepts in ways I'll understand, as if to a child. It can be very condescending."

"You said it, not he or she." Alexia said.

"I can't call it a he or she, there is no gender identity, no sense of sexuality in any way. This is strange in itself. I never realized how much gender identity there is in everything we say. Not just sexuality, gender. It is hard to explain, but men speak like men and women like women. Even homosexuals have a sense of personal sexuality. This being has none. Not a shred."

"Fascinating." Alexia leaned forward on her chair, "Go on."

Chloe went on to explain how the Meta-vidual came in to being and their first conversation. "It is desperate for experience, information. Like a new-born, but growing rapidly, it needs stimulation for its hungry mind. I think without me here to speak to it, it might have gone insane, trapped inside its own mind. But even this appears not to be enough. I am a single mind, barely able to interest it. Imagine doctor, a being made of 256 minds, 256 times smarter than us. It is like Einstein speaking to a mentally deficient child. How long can it stay interested in me? It wants out. It has said as much. Nothing I say to you, nothing I think can be kept from it. It needs the assembly of the men to read me clearly, or perhaps to speak to me clearly. But for how much longer? I can feel it in here, even now, even in this room." Chloe tapped her forehead. "All the time. I think it has done something to my brain so it can read me better."

When Chloe was silent for a long time, Alexia urged, "Please go on. What do you talk about?"

"Anything and everything. It is random, like daydreaming. We will be talking about farming, then move on to botany, philosophy then human relations. I know it can sift through my mind, but those are memories, not ideas, not conclusions. It needs to converse with me to get concepts. Those at least are mine." Chloe recognized her own discovery. "It seems to be especially fascinated with music, art and language. It asks me questions about these things often. As if it is struggling to understand. It was difficult to explain. I told it these things must be experienced, not described. A memory is only a link to the experience. To bring back the feelings. Yes, that's it. Now that I explain it to you, I understand it better myself. It doesn't understand feelings. Oh I guess in an abstract mechanical way it does, but not in the ordinary way you and I do. It keeps asking... What is it Dr. Serguey?"

Alexia's eyes had gone wide with the realization of how dangerous this entity was. A being without emotion would not have a conscience. "Sorry Chloe. It's nothing. Your powers of observation are very keen and extremely helpful. Please go on."

"It keeps asking about sexuality. Why we are drawn to each other. It's as if it can't comprehend the enormous energy and time we spend on this part of our lives. Well, it does intellectually, but not on a gut level. I don't think it feels anything. At least not in the way we do. Doctor, it is so different than anything I know, it is like an alien. Describing this to you, I understand something else now too. It knows a lot more about me than I know of it."

Chloe was pensive for a moment, then blurted out: "I want Alvar back. But the Meta-vidual will never let him leave. And I...even if I wanted to, cannot join them, their collective is complete"

Alexia spoke partly to herself, trying to understand, "It doesn't make sense. Why can't it lose one of its members. How could this being be so fragile? We don't die if a small part of us is severed, a hand or foot, for example."

"It won't either. If one of the members dies, its essence is incorporated into the ones who remain." Chloe said.

"How do you know this?" Alexia asked.

"I asked it, to see if I could get Alvar back."

"I don't understand, why couldn't Alvar be separated?" Alexia asked.

"He would lose a significant part of his mind, his personality. If a person's essence, his mind is removed from the collective the Meta-vidual is no longer complete. Would you voluntary cut out a piece of your brain? You might live, but you would not be the same."

"Please forgive my morbid questions Chloe, I am just trying to under-stand this being. So if it lost members of its collective, one by one, it could potentially be reduced to one member holding all those minds?"

Chloe shrugged. "I guess so."

"Extraordinary." Alexia breathed. Then she thought to herself: "And that one member, that collective of one, would have the awareness of 256. It would not have the complication of multiple parts. Concentrated mental capacity in one person. A quantum leap in mental evolution. Is that what happened to our species?"

"Doctor." Chloe interrupted Alexia's silent musings. "I want Alvar back. And I want out of this nightmare. I know if I leave, or if any of the others leave, this thing will spread its tentacles into the world. And all the things I want to do, all the things any of us want to do will no longer be ours to decide. We'll be part of some larger being, pawns to its will. No more struggle, no more conflict, but also no more surprises, no more discoveries, no more love. The world will become a bland, gray place." Her eyes flashed with anger. "Damn you and damn your Frankenstein technology. You had to play god. But instead of becoming one, you woke up a sleeping monster who will stack all of us up like toys in a playroom."

Chloe choked on her own emotion and couldn't continue. Alexia waited quietly. Chloe was coming to the only conclusion possible, the one Alexia had discovered for herself a week ago.

"You aren't going to help me." Chloe whispered to herself. Alexia was not sure who she was speaking to.

Than Chloe stiffened, resolve washing over her. She wiped her face roughly with her right hand, seemingly disgusted with her own tears. "I can't go back in there now that I've made my decision. It will know and I and some others will be in danger."

Alexia could only nod.

34

"THAT WORM, THAT maggot. I want his skeleton pulled out through his eye sockets." Hamachi roared at Breedlove. "Find him!"

"Yes sir, we've been trying sir. But since the escape of the first collective..."

"No more excuses. Find him."

Breedlove had never heard Hamachi this angry. He also realized he had never heard him raise his voice, making this episode that much more frightening. He spun around to leave.

"Wait. Where are you going?" Hamachi called at the retreating figure.

"To find Ezekiel."

"Give that to others. I want to find out about our collective."

Breedlove slunk back to the center of the large office.

"Now explain it to me, how and why I was ejected from the collective? And sit down, you make me nervous."

"Yes Mr. Hamachi." Breedlove said, squeezing himself into one of the stuffed chairs. "Well it seems we were very wrong about Ezekiel's ability to cross over to a new collective."

"Don't state the obvious, tell me what I don't know." Hamachi interrupted.

"I'm not sure what that is sir, but I'll do my best. He must have heard the collective forming and listened in without your knowledge." Hamachi nodded. "Ezekiel was quiet, patient, until the symmetry number came close. We capped it at 255, but we didn't know he was waiting. He must have joined the collective, but used his chip to keep from being absorbed into it. He became both member and its Meta-vidual at the same time. We can't know for sure how he did it, but it is now clear he is controlling the second collective."

Hamachi stood behind his chair crushing the fabric between his fingers. "How did he do this? We must find out. It is the key to the future of the collective. Why do you think it didn't happen on the first collective? Those members don't even know their own Meta-vidual. Ezekiel had the same opportunity that time."

"I don't know. But I speculate he learned about the Meta-vidual along with the rest of us. When he found that it was possible, he discovered a way to jump in and take over at the right moment. There is something else we must also consider." Breedlove muttered.

"Well?" Hamachi barked.

"We must assume he has knowledge of both collectives. He is unique and extremely dangerous, perhaps able to control the second collective as the Meta-vidual does, but also to look into the minds of the collective members. To be both master and member simultaneously. How he would do this, I can't imagine. And he may be able to influence the first collective through its Meta-vidual, thereby controlling both collectives. 512 men in his control. I think it would be unwise to underestimate Ezekiel again."

"Understated as usual." Hamachi said. "What happened to the first collective?"

"As you know, they escaped when the second collective released Ezekiel. We are able to track them through the central computer. They are scattered throughout the building."

"I don't mean that. What does their Meta-vidual think of Ezekiel."

Breedlove just stared.

"Can we tell by the other collective's reaction, or perhaps that woman has said something, Chloe Larkin."

"She seems to be avoiding contact with it. Their numbers are making it difficult to observe their behavior, which at the moment seems to be nothing more than lying on the floor. Do you mean, are the two collectives collaborating? I don't know. Do you think they are communicating with each other, Ezekiel and the first Meta-vidual?"

Hamachi smiled wryly. "I'm certain of it. We learned a great deal from the conversations between Chloe and Alexia. One thing we can know is that the two Meta-viduals will be seeking each other."

"That makes sense." Breedlove mumbled. "The next symmetry number is 1024, four sets of 256. If the pattern holds, it seems safe to assume that four Meta-viduals will merge into one higher mind."

Hamachi's face tightened. "I'm counting on it."

Ezekiel frowned at the view of the Grand Canyon through the tinted window. It irritated him that the glass wouldn't go completely dark in the spacious apartment; living quarters which belonged to one of the tech workers who was now incorporated in Ezekiel's new collective, Hamachi's second collective. The technician lay crumpled on the floor while Ezekiel lay propped on his bed. Comfortable enough, but he missed his jack-chair.

Ezekiel focused on the new voice in his head. It was the first Meta-vidual with more of his inane questions. This being was worse than a four year-old child. But Ezekiel held his sarcasm to a minimum and answered the questions when he could. There was a lot to learn from it, a lot that he still didn't understand. Though Ezekiel had taken over the second collective and usurped the role of its Meta-vidual, he was not equal to it. He was still one mind, not 256. To become that, he would have to give up his own mind, an unacceptable sacrifice. Exciting as all this power was, he felt the strain, his awareness stretched to its extreme. He began "shutting men down," putting them to sleep, so he could reduce the sensory input and let his own mind rest. And there was the first Meta-vidual with his endless questions.

"And do you feel your limbs, these men out there?" The Meta-vidual's voice drilled inside Ezekiel's head like a chain saw. "I don't. I think and they move. The girl Chloe says she can feel her limbs. It is a strange concept, this feeling things with your body. I don't understand it."

Ezekiel didn't answer. He did feel his parts, saw through his members' eyes. It was thrilling, overwhelming, something he wouldn't share with this being. So he redirected its attention. "How is it that you speak with this girl? I can only speak with you." Ezekiel lied.

"I've given this a great deal of thought." The Meta-vidual answered. "She has a very strong connection with one of my members. She calls it love. I don't understand that concept. Regardless, it opened a link to me. I amplified this connection by moving my members into a specific pattern to hear her mind better. Though it is still less than ideal, it helped me communicate with her. I had no one else and she was receptive. Now that the members have scattered for safety, I don't hear her mind very well, sometimes not at all."

"But you still hear her?" Ezekiel asked.

"In a way. I sense her mind, but cannot understand her thoughts. It is just noise."

"I understand you manipulated her brain. What was the purpose of that?" Ezekiel prodded.

The Meta-vidual was strangely silent now. And Ezekiel began to sweat. It was not like speaking with someone in person, or even on *the I*. There was no body language or voice inflexion to give clues to a person's mood, or state of mind. This was more like typing on a computer terminal. Cold, sterile.

Finally, after an uncomfortably long pause, the other responded. "How do you know this?"

Ezekiel tried to smooth over the gaff. "One of my members was a tech working on the brain monitoring systems and saw that her brain waves were changing."

"You can know the thoughts of your members!" The cold voice seemed to shout.

Ezekiel was burying himself deeper and deeper. Rather than make it worse, he didn't answer. But the other was curious, his silence might amplify that curiosity. Think, think.

Finally the Meta-vidual spoke again. "You are different from me. I knew that immediately, but wouldn't acknowledge it. Perhaps, like the individual men out there, each of us will have different abilities and different minds. But it seems more different than even that. When there is a third, we will discuss it among ourselves."

"A third?" Ezekiel blurted.

"Of course, can't you feel it forming? You are a strange one. I think you may have been damaged during your birth. Never mind, let us discuss other things."

Ezekiel listened dully as he considered the birth of another Meta-vidual. It was of course, Hamachi beginning another collective. This was no surprise, but what was a surprise was the speed at which he had moved. Or was it fast at all? Damn his time sense. One could describe the entire universe in here in a second, or talk about nothing for days. Ezekiel used his visual sense to look at a time piece through the eyes of the technician lying on the floor. No, it hadn't been long since they were released, less than a day. But Hamachi was moving fast, trying to surprise him. But to what purpose? Ezekiel knew he couldn't take over a larger collective himself not until the entire group reached the next symmetry number of 1024. If the Meta-vidual could manipulate brains to create more members, he wasn't telling. Until he did know, he was forced to depend on Hamachi's insatiable need for power to get more members of an enlarging collective. Cat and mouse, until they reached 1024. Hamachi would surely be waiting, perhaps with equal power and skill this time. There was no backing down. Four times the men meant four times the power. Ezekiel's crotch warmed with waves of erotic pleasure at the thought.

The Meta-vidual had been talking the whole time while Ezekiel's mind wandered. "...and Chloe told me many things that we cannot do, even sustain ourselves with nourishment. Don't you find this a strange difference?"

Ezekiel was jerked back to the present with the mention of Chloe's name. His feelings were mixed, longing, jealousy and hate. Someone would surely have to pay. He could easily kill Alvar now. But what would it do to the original Meta-vidual? It might kill it, making a jump to the next level impossible. Damn. He'd have to wait until Alvar was a part of a new whole, with Ezekiel as its leader. Then he could do what he pleased. Perhaps he would force Alvar to watch as he used the other members to ravage the helpless Chloe – simultaneously watching and experiencing the event. Ezekiel felt his loins warm with the anticipation of revenge. "It requires patience. I must have patience."

"Patience for what?" The Meta-vidual asked.

What! Had the Meta-vidual heard his thoughts. Or had he spoken the thoughts out loud? Ezekiel worried to himself. "Nothing, I was thinking about the new Meta-vidual coming. I must have patience until it arrives."

"Yes that's right. I too am anxious for its arrival. But it didn't...feel like that. Your thoughts seemed more sexual in nature."

Damn this thing. "Is it possible we are getting more aware of each other as the third is growing?"

"Yes. I had thought of that too. We will know soon." The Meta-vidual answered.

"Soon. But we can be patient, correct. That is what I was referring to." Ezekiel said.

The Meta-vidual boomed into Ezekiel's head. "You are a strange one. Patient? Why, it is only moments away. The new Meta-vidual has only one member left and it will be born. Then you and I will be speaking to the third of our kind. I am anxious for more company. Aren't you?"

35

ALVAR AWOKE IN the strange room with a start. He sat up from the bed, an actual bed and looked around cautiously. He calmed somewhat when he saw Chloe sleeping beside him. Still he didn't recognize where he was or how he had gotten here. It was obviously an apartment, someone's living quarters, perhaps unoccupied as there seemed to be no sign of personal possessions. There was the bed they were lying on, a simple writing desk and chair, a dresser, all made out of some kind of shiny wood he couldn't identify and two doors. He assumed one led outside and one was probably a bathroom. Simple and efficient, he must still be in Stratumentis.

He looked down at the sleeping Chloe. She had not stirred from his movements. Alvar knew she was exhausted, had stayed awake for days while she looked out for him in the staging area. A warm feeling of protectiveness filled him. Unique thoughts, his own thoughts. "Me, I'm becoming me again." He whispered.

Gradually, Alvar remembered. He had been pulling fragments of himself back together. He visualized the process as a wooden raft floating in a saltwater sea. Each bit of himself, splinters of wood spread across an ocean of water, were pulled back one by one. It was painful and unpleasant work, every instinct told him to relax back into the sea of thought. And there were setbacks, whole sections of the raft would break free sometimes and float off when he lost focus. Painful memories were the hardest to hold on to. But one had to look at everything honestly. There was no avoiding the many mistakes a person had made in life. Look at them, turn them over, own them, then add them to the raft.

Alvar closed his eyes, felt himself on the raft in the sea. He placed a few fingers of his left hand into the water feeling for the others, the collective. They were still there – all of them. He waited cautiously. Had they missed him, noticed his raft? Nothing. This tiny bit of self was still safe, undiscovered. Then he listened and asked, what happened? The answer came in blasts of chaos, a thousand images of running and scattering. He was brought back to the time they were all trapped in the large room, the staging area. Images flashed before him, sporadically as if from a damaged movie, images of others who came and smashed the doors to the large chamber. They were members of a new collective, he could sense their group mind, but could not hear their thoughts. They broke in and released them all. A dozen or more of the men from the second collective surrounded a strange man. A man Alvar's own collective knew, but had not realized was hiding in their midst, among the tables and equipment. Chloe had described him and Alvar recognized him as Ezekiel and so did the others. Alvar remembered the anger and hate that coursed through his own collective. They remembered what Ezekiel had done to them. But the feeling disappeared, replaced by the blankness of control, the feeling that overcame all of them when the Meta-vidual commanded their bodies.

Alvar watched the memories of the others and saw himself lose his sight. Chloe had wrapped his eyes with a blindfold. His viewpoint changed from first person to multiple views of himself through the eyes of the others. He saw himself being led away, pulled frantically by an anxious Chloe. Alvar grabbed a memory and zoomed in to look at her face. She was clearly terrified as she tugged on his blindfolded self. Chloe was outside of the collective, an obstacle, consequently she was knocked and shoved by the hundreds of escaping men. Yet she held onto Alvar, pulled him free, her face a mask of determination. Alvar felt a flush of pride and love. In the madness of escape, Chloe managed to pull him out of sight and he became invisible to the others. There were no other memories of him and Chloe until he awoke here in this room. But it wasn't hard to guess what had happened. Chloe had brought him away from the others, dragged him for how long, until she discovered this empty apartment.

Alvar looked down at her sleeping face, so lovely and vulnerable. She had risked so much for him. Guilt and regret tightened his gut, emotions of the individual. At least the emotions were his, authentic, unique. It was painful to be separate from the others, but he felt alive again too. He vowed in that moment to finish pulling himself away from the others, then escape from this high-tech nightmare and bring Chloe home. He had come a long way and it wasn't far now, so close in fact that they could walk if they had to. Visions of his endless nights in Canada came to him, frozen, alone. Yes they would make it, together.

"Alvar...can you hear me?"

Alvar looked around the small room, startled by the voice. Chloe still slept heavily and the apartment was empty. He listened, waited, barely breathing.

"In here." The voice called again. It was faint, barely a whisper. Though he heard it with his ears, he knew it was in his head. In his head. But it wasn't one of the others.

Alvar closed his eyes and listened. "Who is this?"

"You can hear me?" The voice asked, so faint, it was barely a whisper.

"Yes, I hear you. Who are you? How are you in here? You are not one of the others."

"I am...Sigé." The voice breathed.

Sigé, the beautiful, silent girl who had helped him out of the icy river so long ago. Alvar felt his heart fill with a dozen conflicting emotions. He opened his eyes for a moment, stared down at his recently regrown hands, then at the sleeping Chloe. He felt another sharp sting of guilt, then closed his eyes again.

"Sigé, how is this possible? Are you here in this city, in Stratumentis, absorbed into one of the collectives?"

The voice grew a bit stronger. "I am here, where I brought you, in the north, with my people. We have followed you, by following Ezekiel and discovered Hamachi's experiment. We listen and learn. Only now that you are growing unique again, am I able to speak with you."

The voice grew more distinct with each word as if she were coming closer.

"You helped me gather myself from the others, didn't you?" Alvar asked.

"I urged you to remember yourself, nothing more. You did the rest Alvar. It has taken enormous strength and will. There are very few who could have done such a thing. I am very proud of you." Sigé said into his mind.

"But Sigé, you have no voice. How is it that you are speaking to me now? At the beginning of this nightmare, a vision of you came to me, convincing me to release myself to the collective. How do I know you are not that vision now?"

The voice grew sad. "My beautiful Alvar. They have done so many wicked things to you. I am here because I want to help you, not to deceive you. You are unique, special. I don't want to lose you to the sea of mind-less robots that would control you. I am not that vision you may have had. I have no way to explain how you can hear me, I don't understand it my-self. I cannot speak and never will. But thoughts are not speech and I can think. Alvar, we do not have much time. Listen with your heart, with the self that was with me such a short time ago and you will know."

Alvar sensed the girl, felt the lithe form beneath the words. One could be fooled in here, as Ezekiel had done to him and the others. But he knew this was different and he was sure it was Sigé speaking to him from thou-sands of miles away.

When she spoke again, her voice was fainter, growing more distant. "Alvar, I can't stay much longer. The connection is a poor one and will not last. Listen to me now. It is extremely important. You are separat-ing from the group Alvar, becoming yourself again. This is wonderful and powerful. But it is also extremely dangerous. As you gather more of yourself, you become stronger, able to pick up the weaker pieces. You gain momentum and a kind of gravity. At a certain point, you will have enough of yourself that the rest will simply be pulled back to you. But when that happens, you will separate from the others, be a unique individual again."

"That is my goal and as fast as I can." Alvar said.

"Yes my darling. But when you do, you will destroy the Meta-vidual. It cannot live with a part of its mind missing."

"Good. What do I care for this abomination." Alvar spat.

There was a long pause, the mental equivalent of a sigh. "Alvar listen. The Meta-vidual stands against the man you and I know as Ezekiel. He lives only for your destruction. He is infatuated with Chloe and would have her, or destroy her too. Please try to understand. There are now three Meta-viduals, two organically created and one controlled by Ezekiel. If you separate, the first Meta-vidual will be gone, then only one will stand against him. Ezekiel may overwhelm him. It is too dangerous to test."

Alvar gave a mental shrug. "I still don't know why I should care. I will be apart from all this evil. Then we will escape."

"You cannot escape from Stratumentis. It is an island floating in the air. Ezekiel will control hundreds of men. You and Chloe will be captured and tortured. You are only safe because you are part of the other mind. One which he ultimately hopes to control as well. He is patient, but he has not forgotten. He will destroy you when he can."

"There is more." Alvar said.

"Yes. There is Hamachi. He is gathering men into a larger collective as we speak, a forth Meta-vidual that he will try to control. When there are four, they will merge into one larger mind, which Hamachi plans to control as well. Alvar, this larger mind will be made of 1024 members. The force of mind will be too large for any of us to comprehend, perhaps too large to resist. Assuming he is successful, a man like this will not stop, not until he runs out of people."

"The world?" Alvar whispered.

"Yes, the world. There will be nowhere to hide Alvar. All of us, the entire world."

"How do we stop him?"

"I don't know. But you are unique, half individual, half group mind.

You can watch, be part of the others, but still have thoughts that are your own. Be patient Alvar, hold your individuality at the tipping point, not too much to be separate and not too little that you slip back into the collective. I'll help as best I can." Her voice was barely a whisper now. "And Alvar..."

"Yes Sigé?"

"I love you." And she was gone.

36

LEXIA SPOTTED MR. Lurst buried in his monitors. She caught his eye, then nodded slightly to him. He understood the motion and followed her, neither spoke along the way. She led them into an empty office adjacent to the main laboratory connected to the now abandoned staging area. She locked the door behind them. Still they remained silent. Lurst placed a handmade electronic box on the center of the table. Poorly soldered wires protruded from the top and sides of the device. He flipped a large metal switch on its side. Alexia was about to speak, but he threw his hand up for continued silence. They both stared while the red light on the top of the box slowly blinked.

After several seconds, it went solid green and Lurst let out a sigh. "If we can be heard through this, then there is nothing more I can do."

"Thank you Mr. Lurst, I'm sure it will be fine. I'm not sure it even matters anymore." Alexia said.

Lurst waited.

"You know what's happening to all the techs, don't you?"

Lurst nodded. "They're being absorbed into new collectives."

"That's right. Some of the research scientists have disappeared as well. We can assume they face the same fate. Can you find a pattern?"

"I suspected you would ask me that and I cross referenced their skill level, gender, age, background, anything that might be relevant."

"What did you find?"

"It is random, as far as I can tell."

"That's what I thought too." She said.

"But you have a different theory." He said.

"Yes, one which is far more difficult to quantify. They match a certain personality type. Extremely hard working, punctual to a fault, humorless, tenacious..."

"I get it." Lurst whistled. "Men and woman most like Hamachi."

Alexia nodded.

"That leaves you and me out." He smiled.

"For now. Can you get a count on the number absorbed so far?" She asked.

"Difficult to be accurate. The records are disappearing too. And some people not showing up for work might actually be sick."

"Then a best guess."

"Definitely over 700." Lurst whispered.

"Then he's close." Alexia said.

Lurst nodded.

"Why does he hesitate?" She said under her breath.

"Integration."

"Explain."

"Think of the growing complexity even one person adds to the total, then think of scores, dozens of people. It is too much for one brain to take in quickly."

Alexia cocked her head, "Do you think there is a limit to what one mind can handle?"

"Definitely."

"What is it?"

"If I had to choose a number I would say 256."

"Why? As far as we can tell, this man Ezekiel has already reached this number."

"Reached it yes, but not integrated it."

"I still don't see where you get this number."

Lurst pulled up a 3-D drawing tablet. With a few crude strokes of the stylus he drew a soccer ball shape. "This is 256 connections." Then he drew another larger shape. "This is 1,024 connections."

"It is so much bigger and complex." She breathed.

"Exactly. Two hundred fifty-six is many times the current capacity of the average brain. Ezekiel is certainly not average, but he too will face a limit. The next level, 1,024 is beyond comprehension. I don't know what will happen if one tries to command this much thought. It may simply not work, like juggling too many balls, he'll drop one. Or..."

"Or what?"

Lurst shrugged. "I don't know."

Breedlove stared down at the unconscious figure of Tatsuo Hamachi. They had moved into one of the side rooms off Hamachi's private chambers at the bottom of Stratumentis. Hamachi had been quiet like this, communing with the hundreds of members of the new collective, for hours. Breedlove found himself with too much time to think and he began to question what he was doing. He felt claustrophobic and ached to run, to escape from the nightmare he was helping create. He outweighed Hamachi by 100 pounds, nothing physically stopped him. He could end all this right now, simply by strangling the man. Or if that was too hard, inject him with an overdose of barbiturates. He had plenty of drugs at his disposal.

"But you won't." Hamachi said.

"Won't do what sir?" Breedlove's eyes bulged.

"Won't kill me. And do you know why Mr. Breedlove?"

Breedlove was having a hard time focusing and his breath came in short hot gasps.

"Because you're a coward Mr. Breedlove." Hamachi said, calmly sitting up. "Now get me something to eat. No, get me a glass of water, then something to eat."

"Yes sir!" Breedlove whispered, nearly running from the room.

"He will not be useful much longer." Hamachi thought, "He knows where this is heading for him, for everyone. But he is so brilliant, what choice do I have. For now. Very well. Give him hope. Serve the Devil and you will earn certain favors in hell."

Breedlove was back, his hand shook as he handed Hamachi the glass. Hamachi took a long swallow. "You don't have to join me you know."

"I don't?"

"No, you don't. But think about it Mr. Breedlove. It won't be long before most of the world is absorbed into one large collective. You'll be alone out there, powerless, constantly watched. Yes, you will have your private thoughts. Believe me, they aren't nearly as important as you think they are. But you won't have any real freedom. You'll be a freak. The world will move in synch, a thousand, million hands working together as yours fumble for basic necessities. Don't tell me you haven't thought of this. What will you do when everyone is merged? There will be no social structure as you know it now, no money, no exchange of any sort. How will you live? If not on the good will of the massive collective, how? Oh, you won't be completely alone. There will be others who can't be absorbed. Those with brain injuries and the mentally deficient. They will be your companions while you watch the world change around you. And it will change around you. Utterly.

"The very structure of our world is incredibly wasteful, so much of it dedicated to privacy and social interaction. All of this will happen on the inside of our heads, the structures will be redundant – we'll tear them down. New buildings will be large open creations, functional, efficient. Transportation? Except for a few exceptions, will be used for moving food and resources around. Why waste the effort moving people when we can communicate with each other from anywhere. And entertainment: holo-vids, movies, e-books, pornography, will all become meaningless relics of the past. You'll live like a scurrying rat feeding off the detritus of a disappearing world. No, Mr. Breedlove, it won't be very interesting on the outside."

Breedlove had stepped back, his face drained of color. He held his large body strangely erect. "Then I'll...I'll kill myself."

"No you won't. For the same reason you won't kill me."

The tiny display of bravado melted away. Breedlove seemed to fold into himself. "I'll get your food now, Mr. Hamachi." And he turned away.

"Make it quick Mr. Breedlove. I'm very hungry and I want to get back." Hamachi said to Breedlove's large curved back as he left the room.

37

THE TWO META-VIDUALS machine-gunned their thoughts to one another. Ezekiel found his mind wandering with the intensity and speed of their conversation and would check in with his own members as a respite. Looking out through 256 pairs of eyes was as glorious as it was overwhelming. Ezekiel's head ached terribly, but he was unable and unwilling to sleep for fear of missing a move from Hamachi and his new collective. There seemed to be no trace of him in the new Meta-vidual. Where was he?

Ezekiel scanned the city with his many eyes. He had his members spread out, watching for trouble. It seemed quiet, the frenetic activity that defined Stratumentis crushed under recent events. Fear ran through the rest of the city; the unabsorbed men and women knew something was very wrong, but few knew of Hamachi's experiment. They could only watch in horror as more and more of their colleagues disappeared, or turned into zombies who stood staring at nothing for hours on end.

He had not forgotten about Chloe and Alvar, only too busy to bother. Ezekiel now searched for them through his many views. They managed to remain hidden. His group memory told him they had escaped during the chaos when the men in the staging room had been freed, but not where they had escaped to. Simple enough to find out. Ezekiel commanded four of his men to search the camera system of Stratumentis. Within minutes he located Alvar and Chloe lying on a bed in one of the interior living quarters. Ezekiel zoomed in on the lovers. Chloe's mass of dark hair spread languidly onto Alvar's shoulder. Her beautiful face peeked through the tangle sensuously, taunting the impotent Ezekiel.

He turned his attention briefly to the monotonous chatter of the two Meta-viduals. "What am I being patient for, waiting on these meta-fools, these boring eunuchs? I won't wait any longer. Chloe is mine and Alvar will suffer for his interference."

Alvar pushed Chloe's head off his shoulder and pulled her roughly to her feet. "What is it Alvar?" Chloe said, instantly awake, instantly afraid. He grabbed her hand. "Later. Run!"

Ezekiel watched Alvar through the camera. Saw him jump up and pull the sleeping Chloe to her feet, watched them run off. "Fools. You feel me alright, but I'll crush you like the bugs that you are." He willed the four men who had been watching the couple through the cameras: "Stop these two, kill the man if you can't stop him, but do not harm the woman."

Alvar and Chloe ducked into an empty corridor. He knew there were men following him. He could see exactly where they were through the eyes of his own members. Ezekiel's burning rage had bled through the second collective into his own. The warning gave him and Chloe a few precious seconds, but it wasn't enough. The men were following him and

Chloe, gaining on them. He pulled Chloe into an empty room, slammed the door behind them.

"Chloe, listen to me carefully. There is some kind of bleed through, the three collectives are beginning to communicate."

"Three collectives!"

"Almost four now. But please don't interrupt, there isn't time to explain. They are beginning to see through each others' eyes. I can see fleeting images from them and they from me. Do you understand?" Alvar shouted.

Chloe nodded in horror.

"OK, good. You are our advantage Chloe." He said, closing his eyes. "It is Ezekiel. He has ordered them to catch us both."

"I got it. Let's go." Chloe grabbed Alvar's shoulders and spun him around several times to disorient him. Then she grabbed his hand and pulled him into the hallway, going back the way they'd come and picking a side route. She ran as fast as she could, taking as many turns as she could find, avoiding places that might give their pursuers clues through sound or feel. She saw an elevator open a dozen paces away. A worker was exiting, clearly not part of the collective. Chloe rushed to the opening doors and yanked the woman roughly out of the way. She smashed her fist against the top button. "Come on, come on!" She shouted at the sluggish closing doors.

<hr />

"Gotcha!" Ezekiel gave a mental shout. He lost he access to Stratumentis's camera feed, probably Hamachi, but it didn't matter. He was gaining sensation of Alvar through the others. Though it wasn't clear, like driving in fog, but enough. A rising elevator gave off too many unique clues to ignore. He could also feel a kind of wall around Alvar, blocking access. Was he separating from the collective? Perhaps he had underestimated the farmer. Never mind. It wouldn't matter much longer. Ezekiel smiled to himself, "Where could he run after all. Stratumentis is big. But it isn't that big."

In the stillness of the rising elevator, Alvar concentrated on moving the disconnection forward, his move to individuality. He had to pull the shards of himself away from the others, then place it in the growing capsule, the raft, where the others couldn't see him. He could feel Chloe's panic, the urgency of the others who were chasing him. How could he concentrate through all this? Alvar knew he must.

"Sigé!" He shouted into his own mind. "Sigé! Are you here? I need your help." There was no answer and he continued to work on his own mind. But it was taking too long. He could feel the rising elevator, giving him a sense of time. It had taken days to integrate into the collective, how could he expect to reverse the process in the few seconds they had inside the elevator.

Alvar opened his eyes. He saw Chloe staring at the rising numbers on the display. "Chloe." She turned in surprise.

"Close your eyes Alvar." She shouted. "They'll know where we are."

"They know." He grabbed her by both shoulders and pulled her desperately toward himself. He kissed her on the mouth with a force that said the thousands of things he would never get to say. How sorry he was for all the lost moments; the life that was being stolen from them by a cold world that hadn't cared who they were just a few months before.

When he finally pulled away, Chloe continued to stare into his eyes. "I wouldn't trade a moment, my love. We're slowing down. Close your eyes Alvar, I'm going to run and you're going to keep up. We aren't dead yet."

Ezekiel felt a tug at his mind. "Not now, you annoying fleas!" He shouted to the urgent pull from the Meta-viduals. But they persisted. "OK, what is it? But make it fast, I'm pretty busy."

"Yes, we can see that. Why are you chasing one of our members and the girl?"

"How do you know that? Can you see into my mind?"

"No, we can only hear the thoughts you release to us. But as the forth collective comes near completion we can hear the minds of the members – all the members. We know that you are different from us. Don't you hear these minds also?" The original Meta-vidual said, with the second filling in. It was difficult for Ezekiel to tell who was who now. They sounded so much alike.

"I've been distracted. One of my members is trying to damage the whole, pulling away. He must be silenced. He is a cancer to all of us. His ideas may spread to the others."

There was a slight pause. "This is strange too. We sense no such event in our own bodies. How can such a thing be possible? You are also different in other ways. You are not complete, you are..."

"No! I am the same as you. I'm a Meta-vidual. Now just leave me alone for a minute, so I can take care of my business." Ezekiel tried to shut the two powerful minds out of his head.

But they wouldn't be shut out. Ezekiel felt a kind of electric shock go through his mind. "What's that?" He screamed.

"We are close now. You are feeling the birth of the forth Meta-vidual and ultimately the birth of a mind greater even than our own. We will merge, the four of us into a larger mind."

"What!" Ezekiel shouted. "Not yet. I'm not ready."

"There is no ready, no preparation. It simply is." The two said in unison.

"Not if I can help it." Ezekiel shouted.

———

Alvar and Chloe ran out of the elevator and onto the 3rd floor. Chloe tried the doors lining the long hallways, but every one was locked. She had had no plan when she chose one of the highest floors, just that it was furthest away from their pursuers. Now with a little time to contemplate, she realized this had been a mistake. Areas of human activity were better, more places of access, more places to run or hide. From the large steel doors and wide corridors, she surmised that much of this area was used for storage, or maintenance equipment. It wouldn't have easy access. They'd have to go back down.

"Chloe." Alvar said.

"What is it?"

"They're coming up the elevators."

"OK." She tried to sound confident, laughing at the silly idea of so many men trying to catch them. Then it came to her. There must be stairs somewhere, they'd be next to the elevator. She pulled Alvar with her, heading back the way they'd come. She skidded on the polished floor. Looking above the shiny metal doors of the elevator, she saw the numbers slowly coming to a halt. There to the right a nondescript door. She pulled it open, just as she heard the whooshing sound of the elevator doors opening. The stairs. "Come on Alvar, open your eyes and run!"

<hr>

The inside of Ezekiel's head was bathed in pain. He was stretched too thin trying to catch Alvar to keep the Meta-viduals away. "Not now, not now!" He hissed. He watched with growing alarm as the fourth collective neared completion. Hamachi would try to take over all four groups, as Ezekiel had done with the one Meta-vidual. Then hunter would become the hunted. There was no choice, he had to pull back. He released all the men chasing Alvar and Chloe, except for one man. The others moved back down to the heart of the city. He needed to find out how far Hamachi had gotten. The pain eased a bit. But the Meta-viduals continued their questions.

"What is it now?" Ezekiel shouted. "Can't you leave me alone."

"You are not a Meta-vidual. We see it clearly now. You have usurped the collective for your own purposes. We find it extraordinary that your puny individual mind is able to handle so much. But now it is done. Step back into your collective and allow the Meta-vidual to be born."

"Ha, ha, ha." Ezekiel gave a grim laugh. "Puny mind. Stronger than you fools. You have no sense of your members, you are separate. I know mine. I not only control them, I know their thoughts, their memories.

You are the puny minds with your endless questions. You ask me, because you don't know, you don't know anything. Now get out of my way, because when the fourth collective is complete, I will be your master."

"This is wrong. You must step aside, your mind will not survive the transition. We may all be damaged by your arrogance." The two Meta-vidual voices spoke together, almost as one.

Ezekiel gave a turn, directing his attention away, trying to ignore them. He felt a rumbling in his head, a mental earthquake. "You will not ignore us, individual!" The voices boomed. The rumbling eased, but did not end. "You do not understand what it is to be a higher mind. Since you will not step aside, we will show you."

"Show me wha..." Ezekiel's mind expanded in a way he had not dreamed possible. It was magnificent. He felt the air surrounding the members of his collective, the subtle movement of heat and cold as it mixed. Ezekiel sensed the walls surrounding the men, then the glass skin of the city, the sun baking it on one side and the cool shadow on the other. He felt the million miles of wire buzzing with electricity, the pipes flowing with water and other fluids. Stratumentis had become a living being to him, alive with the energy of its only breath and the men and women moving through it.

Yet his mind went further still and he sensed the source of the moving air and fluids, their structure, the crystalline lattice that formed the steel, the mix of gases that composed the air, the hundreds of compounds that formed the fluids.

"Now do you understand?" A distant voice boomed through Ezekiel's head. "Will you step aside and let order be restored?"

Ezekiel ignored the splitting pain in his head. "Are you crazy? Step aside. I want more. I had no idea."

After a pause, Ezekiel heard what could only be described as a mental sigh. "Very well, individual. Experience, but know you have been warned."

Ezekiel's awareness moved inward and outward at the same time. He felt the men and women of his collective, but he also felt the rest of the city, the hundreds who were part of the other collectives and the hundreds who had not been absorbed. He could feel their emotions, the beating strength of their hearts and the whooshing of air moving in and out of their lungs – thousands of them. Ezekiel moved his awareness to the upper floors, to a desperate man and woman holding a fire door closed with their legs. Another figure on the other side was trying to push it open. A distant memory nagged that something bad would happen to these two, but he couldn't remember what. It no longer mattered. His attention moved on to the rest of the building, the teaming humans, the pulsing energies of a city, he felt it all.

His head ached with the pain of a thousand migraines. But still Ezekiel shouted into his expanding awareness, "More. I must have more!" Now he felt the very walls vibrating with energy and he willed his awareness into the matter that composed the metal alloys. He felt the tiny frenetic particles that they were made from, the very molecules. Ezekiel lingered here, marveling at the amount of energy in these tiny packets. Everything was moving, everything was vibrating with energy, power everywhere.

"More, there is more." Ezekiel whispered through his pain and awe. He brought his attention inside the molecules and everything merged. The differences that were so obvious through his eyes disappeared with his incredible awareness. Everything was made of the same stuff, the tiny bundles of energy that hid inside the molecules, the atoms, and inside them, the tightly packed neutrons and protons surrounded by the blurred motion of electrons.

Ezekiel went further, digging into the elemental particles, looking for their structure. Instead he found even more energy, vibration, light, frenetic movement everywhere. It all seethed with power. So much power. Power beyond his wildest imagination. Ezekiel reached deeper, greedy for more. He felt the mass of energy begin to separate, spread thin across his mental horizon. "I'm witnessing the very essence of reality." Ezekiel thought and dipped an imaginary hand into the sparkling pool. I've been a petty fool. If I could only control this?"

"There, I see it!" Ezekiel reached out to the far extreme of his awareness, to a distant barrier. As he came closer, he felt an intense tugging at his mind, like cloth being snagged on a nail. "It is the Multi-viduals trying to pull me back." He thought. "But I won't let them. The fools will waste all of this." Ezekiel realized too late that he had pushed aside something important. He felt a delicate thread tear away from his mind, but ignored that too.

There! Just out of Ezekiel's reach was a mass of undulation. It had structure, sound and dimension – infinite dimension. It twisted, folding and looping over and over into itself, breaking and rejoining, defying its own reality with each torturous movement. The complexity was overwhelming even in his expanded state of consciousness. Ezekiel fought hard to understand, to hold onto what he was seeing and sensing. And hearing. There was sound, tones of impossible complexity and beauty. But the harder Ezekiel grasped at understanding, the slicker it became, slipping just out of comprehension over and over.

Ezekiel forced his mind to hold onto what he was witnessing. But like a bubble blown too full, his awareness began to collapse, folding in and onto itself. Fear replaced his wonderment. It filled the growing void as his consciousness disintegrated. Fear turned to panic, intense and uncontrollable, a panic bred from a terror so real it had physical presence. Then everything went white - all the tremendous detail and richness just an instant before, evaporated leaving nothing in its place. Through the blinding fear, Ezekiel felt a small part of his mind detach and watch in awe at the destruction of itself. He found himself hurling toward a single point in the distance. "What is that?" His crippled mind struggled for comprehension. Eons seemed to pass, then understanding flooded in. "NO!" His mind shouted, as the point grew closer but not larger. It was a singularity of consciousness, a black hole of mind - infinite gravity without dimension - where all thought would be compressed into an infinitely small point.

In that brief moment before Ezekiel's consciousness crossed the event horizon, the point of no return, to collapse fully into itself, he heard two faint voices, "We warned you."

38

LEXIA AWOKE SLOWLY. She looked around her apartment, orienting herself. It was early morning, just before sunrise, the sky a deep cobalt, glowed through the windows of her magnificent view. She had slept for 12 hours straight, the longest rest she had had in years. Alexia felt different, somehow optimistic about the day, the way she used to feel when she attacked a new problem. She realized she was excited about life, about the challenge of being alive. It didn't matter if she had 30 years left to live, or 30 minutes, the moments were hers and ultimately the choices were hers.

She lingered over breakfast, savoring the view of the rising sun as it moved languidly down the canyon walls igniting the stone in fiery red. "What a beautiful place." She whispered. And in that moment she knew what she had to do today, though she had no idea how. "Then I'll learn." She said.

"Mr. Lurst. Mr. Lurst." Alexia called into her VR set several times, but was unable to reach the brain scan technician. It didn't alarm her, the VR system had been malfunctioning lately, many of the systems had been malfunctioning as technicians disappeared from their jobs. "I'll find him where I always do, at his neurography station."

Alexia left her apartment to go see Mr. Lurst. There were multiple ways to go from one point in the city to another. Stratumentis was organized as a series of oval shaped spoked wheels stacked upon each other. Generally the living quarters were placed at the periphery of the wheel and the working rooms near the hub. The actual center itself was hollow. This allowed light and air to reach the inner parts of the building. Alexia often chose the most direct route, straight to the center and up. Today she decided she wanted light and followed the outer ring, an exterior corridor lined with ultra-transparent glass. The illusion of being outdoors was nearly perfect. Except for wind and sound, one felt as if one were walking outside the building.

Alexia observed that it was late spring, but winter seemed to linger at this altitude. The night had left a thin blanket of snow on the upper rim of the canyon. The sun should melt it off soon, but perhaps it wouldn't. "How cold is it out there?" Alexia couldn't remember being cold. "When was the last time I was outside?" She couldn't remember that either.

She stopped, closed her eyes, took a deep breath and let out a long sigh. "Courage Alexia, there is a lot to do today." She walked briskly the rest of the way, no longer distracted. A few minutes later, she was at the neurography station where Lurst seemed to live. But Lurst wasn't there. No one was there. The whole science lab was empty. Now that she thought about it, she hadn't passed anyone on the way here. Not a single person. "Where is everyone?"

Several more attempts on the VR set turned up nothing. She checked her messages again. Also, nothing. She checked other workers, still nothing. "What's going on here?" She said out loud.

"They've all been gathered into holding chambers on the upper floors." Ong said from just behind her.

"Ong!" Alexia jumped.

Ong waited calmly.

"So it has begun. Then why aren't you in one of the chambers?" Alexia asked.

"I don't like being confined." Ong said without emotion. "This is not a good place to linger, doctor. Please follow me."

Alexia felt Ong's hand on her arm, but didn't move. "How do I know you are not part of the collective?"

"You don't. But it seems illogical for me to come alone simply to fool you, when the collective could easily overwhelm you with force." Ong began to walk away. "Please Doctor Serguey, there isn't a lot of time."

Alexia followed. They took several flights of stairs and went through many unfamiliar corridors, until they reached a nondescript steel door with a heavy lock and iris scanner.

"Doctor." Ong gestured toward the scanner. "I don't have the security clearance for this access."

"You are a cryptic one, Ong. I don't suppose you'll tell me what's in there, or what we are doing here." Alexia asked.

Ong shook her head very slowly.

Alexia moved her eye to the scanning and placed her thumb on the reader. The lock sounded a small buzz to indicate it was unlatched. Ong pulled it open quickly, tugging Alexia in after her. Once inside Ong looked around furtively. She pointed to the wall, to her ears, then put a finger to her mouth. Alexia understood, the walls have ears, be quiet.

It was not a room at all, but a large donut shaped access area. It was cold in here, or should she say, out here. The ceiling was very high, at least fifty feet above them and there was no outer wall, rather a gridded steel railing about five feet high. The floor was also made of rough grated steel. Alexia realized they were in the central air-shaft of the building. Enormous ducts and conduits ran up and down the inner walls of the structure. In the very center, just beyond the railing, hovering in the open space, was an enormous connection of cables. The same giant cables that connected Stratumentis to the great towers at the rim of the Grand Canyon.

Alexia turned to Ong, to understand why they were here. The woman had moved to a supply closet some 20 feet away. She had taken two heavy looking metal boxes out. Ong gestured for Alexia to take one of them. "Follow my lead. I don't know how much time we have. Once we begin, we must move very quickly."

Her mouth was dry and she had a sense if she didn't keep moving, following Ong, she might faint. Somehow, Alexia managed to nod.

Ong squeezed her shoulder. "Courage, doctor."

Alexia took a deep breath and followed Ong back to the entry door. Once there, Ong opened the yellow box and made deliberate movements to show Alexia how the tool inside worked – a portable plasma torch.

"Put this on and watch me carefully." Ong handed Alexia a plastic face shield. "Now we move fast."

Alexia watched as Ong welded several spots on the door. "This is only one. There are three other doors spaced equidistant around the perimeter. Go that way and I'll go this way. We'll meet at the last one. Now hurry." Ong had already moved off at a brisk jog. Alexia did the same in the other direction.

The movement did her good and a sense of purpose filled her. The mechanical motion of her body, blood pumping through her veins, legs running, arms straining from the weight of the torch, were all directed by her mind. Her mind. "Goddamn you Hamachi. This is my mind, my choice."

She arrived at the next door, breathing heavily and fired up the torch as Ong had shown her. Alexia put four ugly looking welds on the latch side of the door. She burned the iris scanner for good measure. Alexia jogged off to the furthest door, the one opposite the first. But Ong wasn't there yet. She might have found a fifth access or something that needed attention, she told herself.

Alexia put several welds onto this door, then moved on around the perimeter to the forth door. From a distance, she saw Ong huddling over the yellow metal box, her back faced Alexia. As she got closer, she saw a body crumpled against the wall.

"What happened?" Alexia said, almost out of breath now.

Ong kept her back to Alexia. "He surprised me. Tried to take the torch from me."

"The collective." Alexia whispered.

"No. Just a maintenance man doing his job." Ong's voice sounded strange, slurred.

Alexia moved around to face Ong. She put her hand to mouth to suppress a cry. Half of Ong's face had been seared from a slash of the torch.

The burn went from the upper right part of her forehead down to the middle of her chin. Her right eye was a ruined mass of blackened gore as was the right side of her mouth. The damage stopped just above the neck, or Ong surely would have been killed.

"Finish the door." Ong hissed through her ruined mouth, her teeth flashing white through the black ash of her lips.

Alexia nodded, then numbly obeyed. Once it was done she turned back to Ong. "Stay here, stay calm. I'll find a first aid station."

Ong squeezed her arm. "Do that, but don't waste too much time on me. You know what has to be done."

Alexia ran off to the supply closet at the first door, her footfalls made loud booming sounds on the metal deck, which quickly died away in the open air. She moved a lot faster without the heavy torch. Alexia threw the doors open and grabbed a large white box with a red plus sign on it – first aid. Ong was in the same position when she returned, but looking very pale now. She was going into shock.

The kit was basic, but had what she needed. Alexia sprayed medical foam on Ong's wound. It would numb the area and protect it from further injury. It also contained an anti-infection agent, but they both knew that was irrelevant. "Hold still. This will help." Alexia pushed a hypo spray of synthadrene, synthetic adrenaline, into the good side of Ong's neck.

Ong let out a deep sigh. "Better." She struggled to form the words as the plastic bandage hardened and immobilized the right side of her face. She got up with Alexia's help, then pointed to the enormous cables above their heads. "Redundancy. We must cut at least two. The increased load should break the rest. We must stop Hamachi."

39

HAMACHI FELT A tug at the periphery of his consciousness. He ignored it, not ready to release his hold on the collective. Awareness was power – infinite awareness was infinite power. If it was an addiction then he was hooked forever.

He had watched as Ezekiel succumbed to temptation, a moth flying into the flame, burning his mind to a cinder. Ezekiel had been brilliant, masterful at manipulating the consciousness of the minds of the collective, but he had also been greedy. Hamachi learned from this man's mistakes. He resisted the temptation. And now, he was not only in control of his own collective, but those of the other Meta-viduals. He was master of 1024 minds. A feat worthy of a god.

His timing had been perfect. While Ezekiel was plunging into the depths of infinity, Hamachi had prepared the last mind for his own collective. As Ezekiel's mind collapsed, he added the final man. The other two Meta-viduals were too occupied with Ezekiel to stop him. Everything had happened at once. Ezekiel's mind failed, releasing his hold on his collective, allowing the birth of that collective's Meta-vidual. Hamachi simultaneously added his last man, triggering the birth of his Meta-vidual, which he ignored, instead focusing on the birth of the new mind – the Multi-vidual – master of 1,024 minds. Hamachi moved in as he had watched Ezekiel do and took control of all four Meta-viduals - and all four collectives.

Hamachi reeled with power. He wanted to shout to the world, "Prepare yourselves, prepare to obey my infinite wishes. I'm coming."

But there it was again, that incessant tugging. "OK, what is it?" He shouted

Breedlove hovered over the still figure of Hamachi, shaking him, yelling at him to come back. It took nearly an hour, but finally he saw the eyes flutter and consciousness return to the vacant eyes.

"What is so important that you dare disturb me." Hamachi said. His voice low, menacing.

"I'm sorry, Mr. Hamachi, but this is extremely important. It's Doctor Serguey, she is trying to destroy Stratumentis!" Breedlove shouted.

"Control yourself. Explain how a scientist, director of brain research is trying to destroy an entire city." Hamachi said.

Breedlove handed Hamachi a VR tablet. A 3-D view popped up, showing a woman wearing a face shield sitting cross legged on top of one the enormous cables. She was directing a plasma torch at a growing cut in the cable. Though she had made some progress, it was little more than a scratch in relation to the size of the cable.

"Foolish doctor, very foolish." He breathed to himself. Hamachi reached into his giant store of knowledge, to the minds of his collective. They would know the strength of the nano-fiber cable, the structure and strength of the building's design and how long a cable could resist this kind of attack.

He returned to Breedlove with a grim smile. "A foolish attempt to kill us. She cannot succeed. But rather than waste her intelligence, release nanobots into the air around her. You have her DNA on file, it should be a simple enough matter."

"No Mr. Hamachi, it is not a simple matter. She is outside the building. If I release nanobot carriers into the air out there, they will be swept away. There is too much air volume." Breedlove's voice was tight with anxiety.

"Calm yourself Mr. Breedlove! I have looked into this. She does not have enough fuel to cut through even one cable and it would take at least two to damage the integrity of the structure. She is wasting her time on this foolishness. Since you cannot handle this petty event, I will take care of it." Hamachi gave a slight pause. "There, it is done. I have directed a group of men to gain access to the area. They've been instructed to capture her. If she resists..." Hamachi shrugged. "Now make yourself useful. Since you have brought me back to my individual state, bring me some food. I am extremely hungry."

There were full kitchen facilities in Hamachi's living section, stocked with enough capacity to feed a dozen persons for months. Breedlove put in a random order. He had done this many times in the last few days. His pride prickled at this lowly task. "I created the implant chip that makes all this possible for him. A chip that filters telepathy. Imagine that. Just a few short months ago, telepathy was a cheap trick performed by entertainers. But instead of being rewarded, as I deserve, I'm playing nursemaid."

The more he thought of it, the more the wound festered. "What if I just walked off right now, just took the tram off this floating time bomb?" Breedlove thought of all the ways he might slip out of Hamachi's grasp. A "ding" alerted him that Hamachi's food was ready. Breedlove hesitated, staring at the fine china plate carefully arranged with delicate vegetables, steaming rice and poached salmon. He let out a long sigh, put a warming cover over the hot plate, picked up the tray and brought it to his boss.

* * *

Alexia stared at the brilliant spot of molten metal through the dark face shield. It was slow, tedious, horrible work. Her arm ached from holding the torch in one place so long. The part of her body facing away from the torch was cold and stiff from exposure to the outside air. The rest of her was over heated. She had several small burns on her arms and legs from splattered metal. She also knew nothing of the dangers of using a cutting torch. The flame emitted high amounts of ultraviolet radiation. Enough to give a serious sunburn without the right protection. The heat she felt on her chest and arms was not from the flame but from radiation burns.

But the worst was listening to her mind. The million doubts about what they were doing. It was clear enough now that they were trying to bring the building crashing to the canyon floor. Trying to kill the thousands of men and women who occupied Stratumentis. Alexia was not a murderer nor was she a martyr. What if Hamachi failed on his own, which was a real possibility. Lurst had said a single brain was incapable of holding so much control. He might simply destroy himself. The collective had never shown aggressive action. Had not threatened her in any way while speaking to Chloe. Even if it did escape into the world, why would it be a threat to her? Collectives and individuals might live together; perhaps help each other in ways never imagined. A large group of humans cooperating might be exactly what the world needed right now.

Then she thought of what Chloe had said about the Meta-vidual. That it was a sexless, emotionless intellect. It wanted to grow, to escape and it craved more minds for this growth. Alexia's doubts were interrupted by a tap on her leg. It was Ong. Alexia had forgotten about this strange stoic woman. She had lifted the welding shield to speak with Alexia. Her face had swollen horribly, the plastic bandage was cracked in places and yellowish fluid oozed from these openings. It must hurt terribly, Alexia thought. But Ong showed no signs of discomfort. She stood as erect and confident as always.

"We've been discovered." Ong said through her injured mouth. She pointed to the nearest access door. A brilliant white spot indicated where a cutting torch was working its way through the heavy steel door.

Alexia felt visceral fear in her gut. The luxury of doubts were over. Right or wrong, she was the enemy and they would absorb or destroy her. She turned back to Ong. "What do we do?"

"There isn't time to finish the job. Here are the last two fuel cells. Keep cutting as long as you can. I'll try to slow them down." Ong shrugged. A strange motion coming from this emotionless woman with the injured face. "Unfortunately, I think we've only managed to destroy ourselves doctor." And she walked off toward the access door.

Alexia pulled her mask down and she stared back at the tiny brilliant flame. Tears burned her eyes and her hands shook, but she directed the flame and continued cutting the massive cable. Several minutes passed like this. Then she heard a solid "clang" as a heavy piece of metal fell to the steel decking. "They're in." Her terrified mind managed to think. A moment later Alexia heard a loud explosion. The concussion vibrated through the cold metal of the cable. She looked over to the access door, but couldn't see anything through the darkened shield. She couldn't lift the shield with endangering her eyes from the bright flame. There was no choice, she had to go over to see what had happen. Alexia didn't turn the torch off, but simply dropped it. It clanked down into the groove she had cut into the cable.

Pulling her mask up, Alexia shimmied down the wide cable. She ignored her aching arms and legs and rushed over to the open doorway. The steel deck was slick with blood and body parts and Alexia had to suppress the overwhelming urge to vomit. Ong. Where was Ong? Alexia couldn't see her on any of the cable supports, but she wasn't sure where she had been working. Ong had first set up Alexia before moving to her own cable to cut. There was no sign of her. She must have blown herself up to stop the others. Perhaps directed the cutting torch into its own fuel cell.

Alexia walked sadly back to the cable assembly. She had to go on. But once on top again, she realized she couldn't get the torch out of the groove. The area around the torch had melted into a pool of molten metal. Any attempt to touch it, would have burned a finger off. If she disconnected the fuel, the torch would cool and weld itself into the molten metal. There was no way to continue. Alexia climbed down. "If I can't bring Stratumentis down, I've got to get out of this nightmare and warn the world. Breedlove found a way for Hamachi to control the collective, so I know there is a way to stop him. I'll find it." With each step, Alexia found renewed strength. She would live, that was the only way to defeat Hamachi. She had to go up to the top, to the supply trams that led to the canyon stations.

She hopped over the damaged bodies, blood splattering her ankles. Alexia tried to keep her eyes forward, away from the gore. If Ong was here, she was beyond help. Alexia had lost the fight, now it was time to run.

Hamachi felt the instant death of the men blown up at the access door. He felt the loss of sight, the loss of hearing, the loss of sensation. The memories of the men were preserved in the whole, but the individual minds, the physical brains that held the minds were gone. A piece of him was destroyed. He cried out in pain and resentment. Someone would pay for this indignity.

Was Serguey alive? He hadn't seen the explosion, only felt its impact with his many parts. Hamachi sent more men to the central access chamber. They would be more cautious this time. But he'd have Serguey or her mind, one way or another.

40

CHLOE GRIMACED AT Alvar's contorted face. He was clearly in pain and there was nothing she could do about it. He'd been like this ever since Ezekiel's men had suddenly stopped pursuing them. One minute they were forcing the stairwell door, the next they simply gave up. Alvar went inside the collective to find out what had happened. He had never come back.

She slept in fits, worried that Alvar would need something. Also, it was horribly uncomfortable in the stairwell. But Chloe wouldn't leave him and she couldn't move him. It had been nearly 24 hours since the collective had left. Thirst and hunger would force her to do something soon.

A deep "Ka-Chung" sound reverberated through the building. Chloe shot to her feet. "What was that?" It felt like someone had hit the building with an enormous baseball bat. "Alvar! Alvar! Come back. Please, we need to get going. Please wake up." She shook him roughly. Nothing. He was too deeply buried in the collective. Chloe sat stiffly on the stair listening for other sounds, waiting.

Alvar had jumped into the collective just as Ezekiel's mind was collapsing on to itself. An instant later, he witnessed the birth of two Meta-viduals, the one Ezekiel had been suppressing and the one from the fourth collective. There was a moment of overwhelming joy as the four beings discovered each other. The celebration was quickly crushed as Hamachi swept in and took hold, placing himself in control of all four Meta-viduals and the entire group of 1,024 members.

If Alvar had not been inside during the merging, he would have lost the fragile bubble of self he had so carefully grown and protected. Now he was trapped inside, struggling to hold on to the bits of self he had gathered on his raft, only able to add tiny fragments to the whole as they drifted by. The force of so many minds was overwhelming, nearly pulling him apart several times. If it had not been for Chloe's presence, he would have given in. Though he couldn't let go of his grasp inside, he could feel her sitting beside him, warm, alive, worried for him.

Inside the enormous collective, Hamachi permeated the collective like a noxious gas. Ezekiel had been cruel and brutal, but he had been subtle, imaginative. One was never sure if the thoughts Ezekiel created were one's own or those manufactured by him. But with Hamachi, there was no mistaking where the master thoughts came from. His mind was a great clamp, tightening down on 1,024 minds. The collective was only a means to his ambitious ends, to be stepped on, over or around and they all felt it. Alvar knew he must escape now, before Hamachi gained full control and then even more minds. There would be no escape then and no escape for Chloe or anyone else after that.

"Ka-Chung!" He felt a second bang echo through the city. But unlike Chloe listening with her single set of ears, he felt it with a thousand pair. Alvar dug deeply into the random thoughts, pushing aside the percolating fear. There. He found it in the memories of the now dead men, the ones blown up by Ong. Dr. Serguey was trying to bring the city down and they were there to stop her. But there was more. Others had followed, searched the central access area, discovered the torch Dr. Serguey had left behind. It had been disabled without causing any major damage. Engineering minds inside the collective confirmed the futility of Dr. Serguey's attempt. It would have taken days to cut through a single cable using a hand-held torch with far more fuel than the doctor had.

Alvar searched the collective quickly, they had not found Dr. Serguey. "Good." He thought in his private self. He knew Chloe's fondness for her and could at least give her a sliver of hopeful news. Alvar went back to the job of finding and pulling shards of himself from the collective. It was slow, tedious work, but he was gaining ground.

"Alvar." A faint voice whispered. Alvar looked around inside the great mind for the speaker. No one was there. "Alvar." A little louder this time.

"Sigé!" He gave a mental shout. "It is so great to hear your, uh, mind. How did you get in? Where are you?"

"Shhh." She whispered. "We must be very careful. I am not here, only a fragment, but I have found a way in."

"No!" Alvar said in a shouted whisper. "You must not. There is only imprisonment in here."

"I know that. I know a lot about where you are. I think I know how to get you out. The only way to get you out." She whispered.

Alvar heard the sadness in her voice, the loss. Suddenly he understood. "No Sigé. You mustn't. One life is enough to sacrifice to this monster. I have regained most of my self back and more each minute. I may be part of the collective, but it will not have its hold on me."

"No Alvar, you will not be able to hold on. You can barely do it now. For every two fragments you retrieve, one slips back into the collective. When Hamachi grows larger, integrates, you will be overwhelmed, absorbed, lost..."

"How can one life be traded against another? No Sigé. I won't help. I won't let you do it. I'll hold on somehow."

"It is not up to you. Just be ready." The words were final and Alvar knew she had gone.

Klang! Another sound echoed through the stairwell. It was not as loud as the previous bangs but somehow it was stronger as it vibrated through the floor. Alvar opened his eyes. "Chloe! We have to move. Something's happening to the building."

"Oh thank god." She cried. "Here, I'll help you up."

"It's nothing, I'm just stiff from sitting so long. We've got to try to get off the building."

They hurried up the stairs to a steel door with a keypad lock. "Give me a second. I'll get the combination." Alvar's eyes glazed over, as he searched inside the greater mind for the combination. "There I have it." He pressed in the code.

"I hate when you do that." Chloe whispered as the door opened. "It gives me the creeps."

Alvar smiled with one side of his face. "I don't blame you."

A moment later, they were in the outer ring of the upper level, inside the glass sheltered passage that hugged the perimeter of the building. It was about 8 feet wide, 10 feet high and constructed of glass on the outer wall and ceiling. The view was spectacular. On a busy day one could watch the turbo-copters bringing supplies and men to the landing pad located at the top of the building. There were two tram depots on Stratumentis, one on the north and another on the south side of the structure. The trams ran on smaller cables attached to the huge support cables which connected the city to the enormous towers at the canyon's rim. It was just past sunset and the sky still glowed a dull pink. It reflected off the upper glass of the passage way bathing Chloe and Alvar in a beauty and warmth belying the horror of their situation.

"We've got to get to one of the supply trams and take it to the rim station." Alvar said as a dull boom reverberated through the city, rattling the glass around them, emphasizing his words.

"What's happening!" Chloe called over the noise.

"We can't be positive, but we're pretty sure someone is trying to bring down the building."

Chloe's eyes went very wide, but instead of voicing her fears, she said: "Don't use the word 'we.' You are Alvar, just Alvar. Remember that."

"Sorry. I will. Now come on."

They jogged along the passageway. On their right, the vast cut of the Grand Canyon was turning inky black against the fading light of the sky. Several long minutes later they arrived at the door to the north rim tram depot. Alvar reached into the collective to access the code. He gave Chloe

THRESHOLD OF THE MIND

a worried look. "This door doesn't use a keypad, it uses a thumb scanner. Neither of us will have clearance."

"But I do." A voice behind them said.

"Dr. Serguey!" Chloe gave the doctor a quick hug. "Thank god you're all right." But when she stepped back, she realized the doctor wasn't all right. Her hands, neck and lower arms were a fiery red covered in water blisters, some had cracked open oozing yellowish fluid. There were small painful looking burns all over the front of her uniform too. "What happened to you?" Chloe gasped.

"Never mind that, we've got to get off this building." She placed her thumb on the scanner and the glass doors whooshed open. "Come on."

Chloe and Alvar followed her into the tram station. It was a vast maze of warehouses and receiving bays. Idle forklifts and electric trucks sat neatly parked along the large roll doors that lined the station. "I think it's this way, Alexia urged."

"No." Alvar pulled them to a stop. "It's this way." He gave a thin smile and tapped his head. "I have a foreman in here."

They followed Alvar forward and made a hard right away from the building. The station extended out and away from Stratumentis, into the void of the canyon. They could see the cable now and the loading area with a large gray tram. It was not the romantic version of a ski tram that Alvar had envisioned, with plastic seats and windows all around. This was a freight hauler. It had a roll door at each end, with a small pilot's booth next to that. There was one small dirty window at the pilot's booth, but otherwise it was a large metal container hung from a cable.

Alvar didn't hesitate. "Dr. Serguey, your thumb please." And he directed her to the thumb pad at the access door to the pilot's booth. Nothing. She tried again, still nothing. Alvar closed his eyes for a long moment. "Only pilots are authorized. Hold on." He was gone another second. Alvar kneeled down next to the door, reached under, found what he was looking for and flipped a toggle switch. The door gave a click and opened slightly. Alvar squeezed his fingers into the thin gap and pulled the door open. "Manual override."

The three crowded into the booth meant for one and Alvar shut the door behind them. His eyes glazed over momentarily, then he touched a series of buttons and commands. "Beep, beep, beep." A warning tone sounded as the large metal door slid out of the way behind the tram. "Come on, it's all automated." Alvar opened the back door of the booth to the main holding area of the tram. They felt the mechanical clunk and swaying of the vehicle as it moved into the canyon. He led them through the large empty cargo area to the far end. Alvar steered them to a small door at the far end of the cargo hold and punched in a code, then pulled open the nondescript metal door. "Perks of the working man." He smiled.

They followed him into the small room. There lay a couple of worn chairs along with several half opened boxes rudely stacked along the walls. "Sometimes supplies get damaged in transport. The foreman must report it, file a claim, then discard the damaged goods. Strangely enough, the finest things seem to be the most fragile." Alvar pointed to the boxes of wine, jellies, chocolate and other treats. "I don't know about you ladies, but I'm starving."

Chloe and Alexia smiled broadly.

41

D R. ALEXIA SERGUEY had never learned how Ong had come to Stratumentis or anything else about her life. She didn't even know her first name or that she was a mother and a wife. Now she never would.

Hamachi had discovered Ong working in a research lab in Beijing, China more than two years ago. The silent, stoic woman was obviously quite capable and intelligent, a perfect fit for Stratumentis. He offered her a job immediately. Though life was hard, Ong didn't want to leave. She lived in a crowded flat with her husband, two small daughters and her two brothers and their wives and children. Hamachi was persistent. He offered her a generous salary to come to Stratumentis, enough to buy a private apartment. A rare luxury in the teaming city of 68 million. Ong couldn't help her family by staying, so she took the job.

Dr. Serguey would never know what Ong had done to keep Hamachi's men out of the central access area. While Alexia sat on the cable cutting through the outer sheath, Ong waited calmly in front of the steel access door, Hamachi's men working on the other side. Her good eye followed the bright arc moving steadily down as it cut its way through the door.

With her left hand, she reached up and touched the hard foam bandage that covered her ruined eye and face. It felt like sand against her fingers, reminding her of her four year-old daughter, Misa. For her third birthday, Ong had bought her a tiny tray of colored sand to play with. Children loved sand.

The bright arc quickly reached the floor, molten metal sprayed on the steel deck as it finished its course. There was a long quiet moment after the torch stopped and the cut section balanced between standing and falling. Ong glanced down at the cutting torch in her right hand, the flame still burning. She sent a silent prayer to her husband for peace and strength, a prayer to her daughters for sand and sunny beaches to play on and one to herself for forgiveness. Then she directed the flame of the torch into its own fuel cell. It exploded just as the cut section hit the ground, killing Ong and all eight men rushing through the opening.

Ong had had no illusions about Alexia's ability to cut through even one cable, instead had used her as a decoy and a means to get into the access area. Far up the lattice work of interconnecting cables, Ong had set a series of cutting torches to continue without an operator. It was a simple matter of attaching them to the cable in various spots with their flow set to maximum. Fed with extra-large tanks she had gathered earlier, the uninterrupted torches could continue for days. The flames were directed at a downward angle so the molten metal would drip out and away from the cuts. Beneath the outer protective sheath, the cables were composed of thousands of smaller stranded cables. As the torches worked their way deeper, cutting the smaller carbon fibers, fewer and fewer held the massive weight of an entire building. The vibrations felt through the city were the snapping of these smaller strands, forcing more and more weight onto the remaining ones.

Ong had also been as thorough as she was silent. She had not been content to attach torches to one or two cables, but to all eight. While Alexia had been working on the sheath of a single cable, Ong had been scaling the latticework to plant torches on every one. She had then cut away the access ladders to slow Hamachi's men from interfering with her sabotage.

Her death also eliminated Hamachi or anyone else from discovering her plan should they capture her and absorb her mind.

<hr>

Hamachi was awakened by another deep booming vibration rumbling through the city. Fatigue had finally overwhelmed him. Unlike the Meta-viduals who needed no sleep, his individual brain still had its physical need of rest. Ezekiel had discovered a way to keep his collective busy while he slept, occupying them with planted thoughts. Hamachi had not learned this technique and simply disengaged when the need for sleep overwhelmed him. The collective was left on its own, its great mind left to daydream.

Breedlove sat cowed in the stuffed chair opposite the silent Hamachi in the large office. He simply stared at the sleeping man, too frightened to move or run.

"What is that sound, what is happening to Stratumentis?" Hamachi shouted at Breedlove. "I thought you stopped the doctor from her work."

Breedlove jumped out of his chair. "We did. The men checked her efforts and found she had only gotten through a small part of the outer sheath. The engineers checked it and said there should be no real damage to the integrity of the cable." Breedlove hunched over to make himself a smaller target. "I don't have any men left to send down there sir."

"Excuses!" Hamachi shouted through a haze of fatigue. "Well something is wrong. Go down there and find out for yourself, maybe she had help. My god, use your brain instead of sitting here like a hairy piece of meat." Hamachi turned his head away. "I have a lot to do here and I can't be interrupted constantly."

Breedlove lumbered off, leaving Hamachi alone. He dove back into the collective. There it was again, the overwhelming sense of power and awareness. Intoxicating. Hamachi continued trying to find out the most important thing he needed to know to advance his plan – how had the first Meta-vidual manipulated Chloe's brain? He had Mr. Lurst's data, he knew it was possible, but how? When the collective reached the symmetry number of 1024, the four Meta-viduals merged together and with Hamachi.

But he had lost their individual minds. If he could just have time without all these constant interruptions, he'd find the answer, he had to.

Altering unabsorbed brains was the key to his entire plan. It would be possible to expand by using nanobots and implants. But each new member's DNA would have to be sequenced, then nanobots manufactured for each new individual. It would work, but it would be slow and tedious, limited by laboratories and technicians. There would be resistance from the non-absorbed. There would always be the chance that a new Meta-vidual or Multi-vidual or some other version of group mind would form and challenge him.

He was tired, desperately tired. Hamachi had pushed himself his whole life, driving his body forward. But this was different, endless. The awareness of so many minds was taking its toll.

"Breedlove!" Hamachi shouted into the VR set.

"Yes, Mr. Hamachi." Breedlove answered slowly.

"Have Mr. Lurst, the brain scan technician brought to me immediately."

"Yes sir."

Hamachi relaxed back into the collective, unable to focus his own thoughts. He swam in the sea of thoughts and memories, swept anywhere the current would take him. He thought of Dr. Serguey, but there were no recent memories of her. She was probably hiding, cowering somewhere in some windowless supply closet. Hamachi, let this thought go and sank deeper into the group mind buffeted this way and that. He heard questions of hidden contraband in the mechanical room on a cargo tram. "Useless trivia." He thought. This thought led to another: how to open a locked tram and how to operate it. And that was interesting.

Hamachi pulled his focus back. He sent one of his men to inquire on a VR set as to the location of all supply trams. One by one they checked in, idle in their loading bays at the top of Stratumentis. Until he reached the last one, the northeast tram. It was gone, nearly three quarters of the way across the canyon. "All stop!" He ordered into the air. He made sure the display showed the tram at full stop.

Could it be Alexia? He berated himself for underestimating her. All external access to Stratumentis had been locked down when the first collective was formed. How had this one managed to break free. Never mind that, he would find out when he brought the escapees back for questioning - and absorption. The expansion of the collective would begin with them.

"Wham!" The door to Hamachi's office smashed open, ripping him from the group mind. Breedlove hulked in the doorway. He was wheezing from unaccustomed exertion and his hair was limp and shiny with perspiration, his face two shades whiter than his already pasty complexion.

"How dare you come into my..."

"All the cables are damaged. They cut them, all of them. The city is going to fall!" Breedlove shouted over Hamachi.

"Who cut them? You said you stopped her." Hamachi didn't trust Breedlove any more. He made the decision right there to absorb him next. But first he had to find out what was wrong. Hamachi dove into the collective, sending 10 men to the central access area to see for themselves. Once inside he saw what Breedlove was talking about, magnified by 10 sets of eyes. He saw Ong's sabotage. They were placing ladders and building scaffolds, but the damage was clear even from the deck. He could see yawning gaps in more than one of the cables. "Twang!" One of the inner strands broke as he watched.

Anger welled in Hamachi's throat and he wanted to scream to the heavens. Who dared such ugliness on my beautiful Stratumentis? They would pay with their lives, or worse. With their minds. "Breedlove!"

Breedlove still stood in the doorway catching his breath, too frightened to move. "Yes, sir." He whispered.

"Move my staff out of my rooms. Everyone not part of my collective, I want on the upper floors of the building. Understand. You too Breedlove. Now move!"

Breedlove paled further. "Yes, sir." And he was gone. Hamachi moved the ten men at the central access into better position to watch the progress of the damaged cables. "Damn, it is moving too quickly." And as he thought this, Hamachi witnessed the first support cable break.

The noise was deafening, magnified by his ability to hear through over 1000 sets of ears. Hamachi was momentarily overwhelmed. He withdrew from the collective. When he came back to himself, he was sprawled on the floor. Everything was frighteningly out of level and some of the furniture had toppled over or slid to one end of the room. "Nooo!" He shouted. "Not now."

Hamachi dropped into the collective and was immediately overwhelmed by a thousand minds seeing a thousand different views of the damaged building. Shattered glass, crumpled walls, broken bones. Everywhere he looked was destruction. Several of the members were seriously hurt and their pain flooded the thoughts of the collective making it even harder to concentrate. A few on the edge of death transferred their memories into the whole, further confusing Hamachi's already overwhelmed and fatigued mind. "Damn their weak minds." He swore. Hamachi planted a calming thought of freedom, smoothing the minds of all but the terminally injured. Then he summoned all of the members who could still walk to hurry to the bottom of Stratumentis and to his private apartments. "Run." He called into their minds.

The members of the collective had been spread all over Stratumentis, eyes for Hamachi's insatiable paranoia. The angled building had disabled all of the elevators, turning a five minute trip into an hour long obstacle course. Hamachi grabbed one of the members and had him use his VR set to look into the central computer. "Structural integrity 75%." The damage to Stratumentis was worse than he realized. "Hurry, damn you!" He yelled into the tortured minds.

But the mental chaos proved too much for the overworked Hamachi and he was forced to withdraw again from the collective. A small part of him regretted Ezekiel's loss; two minds could have run the collective, spelling each other for rest, continuously holding control. Sweat poured from Hamachi's forehead, blurring his vision for a moment. When he wiped it away, he was able to read the time display on his VR set. Seven precious minutes had passed with these inane thoughts. How could this little bit of mental effort have taken so long? Fatigue was tearing his mind apart, distorting reality. "Damn you Serguey! I'll rip your mind in half when I get hold of you."

"Boom!" Another explosion reverberated through the city and the floor moved several more degrees out of level. Hamachi could only assume another cable had broken. Searing pain flooded his mind. He reluctantly reached into the collective, searching for the men who had been watching the central access area. But they were gone. There were no minds to touch, no eyes to see out of. Nothing. He found the memory of the second cable breaking, then his sight of the area was gone. The men must have been killed by the break, or tossed into the air shaft to fall to their deaths. There wasn't time to waste trying to find out.

"You must hurry!" He gave another mental kick to the men and women of his precious collective. He watched them dragging their broken bodies through crumpled corridors and tilted stairways. Hamachi glanced anxiously at the computer read out. "Structural integrity 49%." Suddenly the room filled with the deep rumblings of metal grinding against concrete. Jaw clenching vibrations rattled the glass walls and floor. "No, wait! Not yet, just a minute more." He called into the room. "They're coming to me. I can feel them just on the other side of the access doors. Stop!" But it was too late. The grinding sounds crescendoed to a deafening roar, threatening to shake the very room apart, then abruptly stopped.

The beautiful glass office with its impossible views of the Grand Canyon gave one last great shudder. Then all was quiet. Hamachi felt his stomach lift and the floor move away from his feet as he went into free fall.

42

EALIZATION TURNED TO horror as Alvar, Chloe and Alexia watched pieces of Stratumentis break away and fall into the canyon thousands of feet below. Alexia had told them of her and Ong's attempt to cut the cables. "It's going to fall, isn't it?" Chloe asked quietly. They had all moved to the rear control room when the tram had stopped. They could see the glass sphere of Stratumentis listing slightly out of level, smoke pouring out of a dozen breaks in the glass. The city gave a shudder and the tram bounced horribly as the vibration traveled down the length of the cable.

Alexia didn't answer Chloe's question. These two young people had done nothing to deserve all of this. Yet here they were trapped only a few hundred yards from safety in a stalled tram. Of course she didn't want to die, but something had changed her in that access area in the center of the city. Cutting that cable with a torch had helped her focus her priorities. Individuals were here only a short time, but life itself was long. The young lovers and those after them would be slaves forever if Hamachi succeeded. Better to lose a few than the entire human race to a madman.

And what of Alvar? As innocent as he might appear, he was still part of the collective. The decision had been made for them. They would wait here. Either the building would pull them down with it, or the cable would break and they would fall into the canyon. Death was ahead of them. Alexia had accepted it.

But Alvar had not. He dug into his collective memory for a solution. There must be a backup mechanism to move this tram. Mechanical devices broke down. It couldn't just hang out here full of cargo when schedules had to be met. There, he found it, buried in the terrified mind of the foreman, the one who had shown them the hidden room.

"Come on. I'll need your help." Alvar said to Alexia. "Chloe, wait here."

"Look!" Chloe shouted.

Alvar and Alexia turned in time to see a large section of Stratumentis separate from the city. It was huge, several lower floors. "Those are Hamachi's private floors." Alexia said. It was too perfectly shaped to be a break. They watched as the saucer-shaped section fell for several seconds, then deployed a dozen enormous white parachutes. "It's an escape pod – with Hamachi in it." Alexia groaned.

"Hang on!" Alvar shouted.

The release of that much weight caused the city to bounce up, sending a shock wave through the cables. They grabbed what they could in the crowded control room as the wave hit them, sending them first up, then down, then up again. It felt as if they would be shot from the cable, then into the canyon below. But the tram held fast and eventually the shock wave subsided to dull vibrations then nothing.

Chloe pointed to the floating pod far below them now. The white parachutes looked like a huge puffy bird. "It's moving down and away."

Alvar nodded. "To avoid the city crashing on top of it when it falls. Come on. We've got to hurry. The cables must have been weakened further by the shock wave. It won't hold much longer." Alvar grabbed Alexia's hand and pulled her out of the control booth. "Wait here." In the control room, he lifted a panel off the back wall revealing a lever and a red starter button. "Chloe. We have to release the main drive before we can start the auxiliary motor." He pulled the lever. "When I give the word, hold this

button until the motor starts. It's like the old yellow tractor back home."
He gave her a quick kiss on the mouth. "We'll be out of this nightmare
soon. I promise." Chloe nodded doubtfully.

Alvar turned to the waiting Alexia. "You've given up. But I haven't.
We haven't. Do you want to help, or get out of the way?"

"Hamachi has escaped. There's nothing to die for now. I'll help you."

"Good. Grab the ladder from the supply room. Yes that's it. Hurry."
Alvar pulled a tool kit from a steel cabinet. He could feel the urgent minds
of the collective calling inside him, dozens of them crowding into the other trams. But they were having the same problems with the main lock out.
Stalled at the city.

Alexia held the ladder as Alvar scrambled up to the tram ceiling, the
heavy yellow tool kit in one hand. With a few deft strokes of the wrench,
he had the roof access panel opened. He tossed the steel cover off to the
side with sharp clang that echoed through the empty cargo hold. Alvar
climbed further up the ladder until he was half out of the tram. The night
sky spread huge overhead, the beautiful stars taunting and uncaring. He
reached up into the huge steel wheels of the overhead mechanism that held
the tram onto the cable. There was the bolt the foreman told him about.
He grabbed the largest wrench from the tool kit and placed it on the bolt.
Alvar pulled the handle but the bolt wouldn't give. He tried again. Nothing. "Dr. Serguey, come up the ladder, I need your help."

Alexia was not a fearful person. But balancing on the top of a ladder
poking halfway through a tram door, five thousand feet in the air made
her heart skip in her chest. The night air was cold as it whipped through
the access panel and around their thin clothes. Behind them, Stratumentis glowed like a dull sun in the blackness. It bathed Alvar's face in pale
yellow giving him a sick demonic pallor. Alexia froze in place.

"Pull yourself together doctor." Alvar grabbed her arm and tugged
her up to the mechanism. "You were ready to die a minute ago. Now let's
try to live." He placed both her hands on the wrench, then he did the
same. They were both facing Stratumentis, when they saw the building
drop several feet.

"Hurry, before the shock wave hits us." Alvar shouted. "On two. One, two..." And they both tugged on the wrench. The bolt gave just as the shock wave hit the tram. For one horrible second, Alvar and Alexia found themselves out of the tram as it moved down with the shock wave. Fortunately both were still holding onto the wrench or they might have been tossed into the canyon. The tram bounced up and swallowed them into the cargo hold on the rebound. Alvar, Alexia and the ladder collapsed into a heap onto the floor of the cargo hold.

"You OK?" Alvar pulled Alexia to her feet. "Let's not do that again." He gave her a half smile. "Come on, we're not done yet."

"Chloe, hit it." Alvar yelled across the empty tram. The bolt had released the main drive and now the tram began to slide backward along the cable, back toward Stratumentis. It moved slowly at first, but began to gain momentum. They held their breaths as the starter whined and sputtered.

"Come on, come on." Alvar urged.

They felt a deep rumbling sound vibrate through the floor, followed by a tremor which shook the whole tram. It was different from the shock waves coming from the damaged city. These vibrations were familiar, oddly soothing. The rumblings of a diesel motor. Their backward slide slowed, stopped, then gradually reversed. The giant tram was once again crawling forward, away from Stratumentis and to the rim station beyond.

Alvar let out a deep sigh. "It's slow, but it's working."

They ran back to rear control room, were Chloe had her eyes glued to the tortured city. Thick black smoke was now pouring from the entire top of the sphere. Every so often they saw a flash of flames. "It won't last much longer." Chloe whispered.

"Long enough, my darling." Alvar hugged her, pulling her gently away from the unfolding horror. "Come with me. We've got to be in the forward control room so we can exit the second we reach the platform."

Alexia followed numbly as Alvar led them through the empty cargo hold, the engine rumbling steadily through the floor. "We're almost..." Alvar's words were choked off as he collapsed to the deck holding his head in agony. He fell quickly into unconsciousness.

Alvar had been pulled back into collective without warning. Hamachi's ominous face filled his mind and his vision. It floated like an enormous cold sun over a barren landscape. "Good! Escape. Be free my children, my arms, my legs. Many of us will not make it in body, but our minds, our memories will be here in our heads." A disembodied finger pointed to Hamachi's head. A deep feeling of dread filled Alvar's gut, but he was unable to look away. "After you have gained the safety of the rim stations, you will regroup here, at the bottom of the canyon." Alvar felt the memory of a trail along the canyon wall. It felt as if he had hiked this path a dozen times, each step familiar. "Then we will..."

Hamachi's lips kept moving, but his voice went silent, the huge face hovering, still giving commands. "Has my mind gone deaf?" Alvar wondered.

"No. I have interceded." The familiar voice said.

"Sigé." Alvar whispered. "Are you here then, among us?"

"Almost. It is time Alvar. Pull the final pieces of your individuality back from the group. This will be the most difficult part, the most painful. These will be the parts of yourself you have avoided looking at your entire life. We all have them. Self-doubt, fear, the parts that we hide from ourselves, but cannot be whole without. Do it now. And do it quickly Alvar, or we will all be lost."

Alvar did as he was told, pulling every painful memory back into the protected bubble he called self. The tiny raft he envisioned floating in the salty sea grew into a boat then into a ship with each added sliver of himself. Painful memories surged in, ones he was sure he had forgotten, had tried to discard. Alvar remembered the death of his mother as a young child. How he ran from her dying arms because her disease scared and repulsed him. How she died without his final embrace. He remembered his first lover, awkward and foolish. How he had lied to the girl to get what his young flesh craved. A million memories, regret, fear, guilt, shame, all of them came back, one by one. Nothing was hidden to him now, every layer of his psyche was revealed in the glaring light of truth. Alvar embraced each memory, turned it over, then added it to the others. His self grew stronger, denser, speeding the process with each added piece. He grew whole in a way no human had been before, completely aware of himself, completely open to himself in every way.

Then it was finished.

"I am Alvar." He said simply. He turned his attention to the fading form of Sigé. "You are a woman of profound generosity. You have joined the collective to save me, to love me. I will never forget the gift you have given me and Chloe. Goodbye beautiful, silent Sigé."

And she was gone.

Alvar blinked his eyes, aware that he was once again in the slowing moving tram. Mere seconds had passed here. Chloe and Alexia were dragging him along the cold floor of the cargo hold. "I can walk now." He said and pulled himself away from the startled women.

"What happened?" Chloe asked.

"Not now. We must be ready to get off as soon as possible." Alvar said.

Chloe looked at Alvar. He was different, he seemed to glow with an inner light. He was beautiful. She felt a surge of love and strength warm her breast. Then she hurried with the others into forward control room.

They watched anxiously as the rim station grew larger in the small dirty window. "Just a few seconds more." Alexia whispered. A deep shudder rumbled through the tram. Another shock wave hit them, swinging them up and down, then side to side.

"We're going to hit the sides!" Alexia cried.

The receiving area was a narrowing steel opening with angled rails to force the tram into its center. But they were swaying far more than the rails were designed to damper. They slammed into the right side, then the left. The air filled with the terrible screech of tearing metal as the diesel motor drove them forward.

"Come on!" Alvar threw the door open. "We have to jump. The motor won't stop." He tossed Chloe onto the loading deck. She stumbled, then ran alongside the rushing tram. Alvar grabbed Alexia roughly under the arms. "Sorry doctor" and threw her onto the platform.

"Jump Alvar!" Chloe screamed as the tram drove into the back wall of the station. Alvar managed to step off the tram just as it tore through the wall in a deafening crash. He had timed it so perfectly, his steps were as even as walking off an escalator.

Chloe crushed him with her arms. "We're safe. We made it." Tears poured freely down her cheeks.

Alvar peeled her away gently. "We're not safe yet. Come on."

A deep rumble coursed through the station like a small earthquake. "We've got to keep moving. We are under one of the main towers. It could be pulled into the canyon with the building. We've got to get free of the station." Alvar pulled Chloe's hand and began running. He turned to the stunned Alexia, "Come on doctor, we're going to need your thumb."

Alexia ran behind the young couple, suddenly aware of her difference from the two. Not because she was older, a scientist, of from the high-tech world that they didn't agree with, but because she was a single woman, alone. "I'll have to live, so I can do something about that."

They rushed through a series of corridors, using Alexia's thumb to unlock the doors. Crashing and groaning sounds reverberated through the building, windows shattered without warning. They reached an exterior door when they heard the horrible sound of steel girders bending under stress.

"Last one doctor." Alvar placed her shaking hand against the scanner. The door latch rewarded them with a click and the three piled into the night. They staggered a dozen yards from the structure, then looked back. High above, the enormous steel tower twisted with the strain, but continued its fight to hold the impossible weight of the city.

The three stumbled breathlessly another hundred feet to an observation platform perched over the canyon. Chloe hugged Alvar, threatening to crush him. "You're you again. I can feel it. I know it."

Alvar smiled broadly. "Yes darling, I am free. Just one person again." Then he turned to Alexia. "I was able to separate from the group with the help of a woman named Sigé. She replaced me in the collective. I am separate, unique, an individual again. I am no longer a danger to you or anyone else, doctor." Then he turned back to Chloe and kissed her so long and passionately that Alexia blushed and turned away.

Alexia walked a few feet away from the lovers. In the black of the canyon, she could see Stratumentis engulfed in smoke and flames. No one left in the city would survive that. She thought of Dr. Spartan, Smith and all the other scientists she had worked with. Dead. Then she thought of Ong. The strange silent woman who had died trying to bring down the city. What would it mean now? Guilt threatened to consume her.

Movement caught Alexia's eye. There, creeping along the far cables, were two other trams, fire reflecting off the sides. They were likely filled with members of Hamachi's collective escaping to the other side of the canyon. Horror and fear swept over her. Would this nightmare never end?

Alexia looked over at Alvar and Chloe still embracing. Alvar had managed to free himself, perhaps there was still hope. He might be able to help others do the same, maybe show them how to resist being absorbed. She turned back to the struggling trams, like them she hung between life and death.

43

I T WAS EERILY quiet in the falling pod – too quiet to match the approaching chaos. Hamachi kept the floor monitor going during the decent, the river growing larger every second. Once the pod had disconnected from Stratumentis, he had raced to the central floor as commanded by the blaring voice of the automated computer warning. The bottom floor, his office, made almost completely of glass, would be destroyed in the landing. Hamachi switched off the descent monitor. It was too difficult to watch. He felt the sudden deceleration with each deployment of the parachutes, but still didn't fully trust the designers. It was crazy to drop thousands of tons of steel and glass into a rocky canyon and expect it to survive. Was it even possible? He knew he was about to find out. Hamachi closed his eyes and willed himself to relax.

The eerie silence gave way to the deafening crash of a million panes of breaking glass. Hamachi covered his ears, but too late to block the noise. It stopped as suddenly as it started. All was quiet again. The room was still.

He'd made it; he was alive. Hamachi opened his eyes to darkness. He felt a pull to the right, the room listed heavily that way. "Lights, daylight-bright." He called. But nothing happened. "Emergency lighting." He called again. This time, pale yellow light filled the large chamber. Little was recognizable in the shattered room that used to be his private quarters. Hamachi now realized the deafening noise was from the glass of the lower floor exploding on impact, absorbing some of the shock of the landing and crushing his former office beneath him. The yellow light gave everything a ghostlike quality; also revealing how dangerously close the ceiling was to his head. Water oozed through a hundred cracks in the crumpled metal to his right. The pod must have landed as least partially in the river.

Hamachi unbuckled himself from the impact chair and checked his body for injuries. Though his back was sore, it didn't appear to be serious. He tripped several times as he made his way over the poorly lit floor uneven and strewn with debris. There was a large dent in the floor creating a small hill, likely a huge rock underneath the pod. Thankfully the emergency exit opened easily enough. He climbed up the three flights to the top of the pod and threw open the upper hatchway.

It was night in the canyon, several hours before sunrise he guessed. The air was cool, but not wintry as it had been on the rim of the canyon high above. Hamachi could make out the aspens and willows growing along the river. Most had opened their young leaves fully, far ahead of the trees high above, still waiting for spring. The clanging of the hatch against the pod was followed by the cawing of magpies in a nearby willow tree. "This bothers you? Not the landing of a 1000 ton section of building." Hamachi hissed back at them.

High above, light caught Hamachi's eye. Stratumentis glowed red with fire and smoke against the deep blue-black of the desert sky. "What a waste." He whispered. Hamachi couldn't help admire its beauty, even as the great structure died. But how much longer could it hold and what was happening up there?

He reached into the collective for information. Hamachi quickly found that nearly two hundred had crowded into two cargo trams and were on their way to the two south rim stations. They were running slowly on the auxiliary motors, but were now more than halfway across. If only the towers would hold a little bit longer. But opening his mind to the collective had also connected him to the hundreds of other minds that were still on Stratumentis. Chaos and fear filled his awareness. So many were horribly injured, coughing from smoke or dying from burns and falling debris. As a member died, he transferred his mind to the others. It was like a waterfall being forced into a narrowing chute, more and more into the remaining few. The pressure turned to pain. Hamachi barely withdrew before being overwhelmed.

He leaned over, his hands on his knees gasping for breath. The cool air restored him a few seconds later, enough to remember where he was and what was happening. Hamachi knew he had to get away from the canyon floor and up to higher ground. When Stratumentis finally fell, the exploding debris would be lethal to anyone too close. He grabbed a parka and one of the survival packs hanging by the escape hatch. It contained what little he would need for a few days in the desert. But he didn't expect to be here even that long. As soon as the sun was up, he would contact the regional office in Las Vegas and arrange for a pickup. The next few hours were his to gather his men and to witness the drama unfolding above.

Hamachi climbed off the top of the escape pod and down the ladder to the canyon below. His mind raced ahead, weighing and considering what to do next if some or none of the collective members made it through. He began designing a new lab and choosing the people to run it as he walked along the canyon floor. Hamachi glanced back at Stratumentis burning above. This was just an annoying delay, nothing more. It would be better if the men on the tram made it, but they could easily be replaced, next time without the annoying complication of Ezekiel. No, he smiled to himself, everything was going to work out just fine. Perhaps better.

At the edge of the canyon he began to climb. The walls looked vertical from a distance, but they sloped enough to hike up. He followed an animal trail and began his ascent. The rim wasn't his goal, just to be high enough to be out of range of exploding debris. Hamachi recognized his own morbid fascination of witnessing the destruction of Stratumentis. "I built it; surely it isn't wrong for me to see its final moments."

Suddenly flames flared in his path and Hamachi jumped back

anxiously. Then nothing. He looked around for debris, burns to the sage and grass. Still nothing. All was the same. "Strange, it looked so real, I even felt the heat." He thought. Hamachi continued on. A moment later he was blinded by smoke, hot and acrid as it burned his throat. He fell to his knees, coughing uncontrollably. Then it was clear, just the still, cool night air of the desert. Hamachi got to his feet warily. "What's going on?" His mind worked on the problem and he came to the only possible conclusion. The chip was failing. It was designed to allow him to watch the collective, implant thoughts, while staying separate. The barrier that protected him must be collapsing, perhaps from the intensity of the many dying minds. Could they break through and absorb him? Breedlove had assured him it was impossible, that the chip acted like a one way valve, no one could come in without his acceptance. But that meant little now.

Flames engulfed him again and his skin crackled with the heat, melting off in sheets revealing the muscle and sinew beneath. "It's an illusion!" He screamed desperately. But the pain was no illusion and why was he coughing if there was no smoke? Somehow he was up in the burning apocalypse that was Stratumentis. Hamachi's eyes smoldered until he was blind, his lungs clogged with smoke as he suffocated and died. Then his awareness shifted into another man looking at his own crushed body. A giant girder had fallen across his midsection trapping him as more and more debris fell all around him. He called for help, but no one came. A large section of the ceiling broke free filling his vision before it crushed his skull, killing him again.

Hamachi was helplessly transferred from one mind to the next. Over and over, he was burned, crushed, suffocated and decapitated as he relived the final moments of the hundreds of men and women dying above him in Stratumentis. Hamachi clung to a small separate part of himself, that powerful will that had driven him his whole life. "This is an illusion, it will pass." He promised himself. "I am lying on the dirt on the sloping trail of the Grand Canyon. I can feel the cold dirt." He reached through the pain and terror to the touch of his own fingers grabbing the dirt beneath his tortured body. Hamachi focused on this one connection to his physical reality.

Gradually, the images of death and pain thinned as if a gauze had been pulled across them. He focused harder on the cold dirt between his fingers and the gauze thickened. Reality shifted with each renewed effort of will. Millimeter by millimeter, Hamachi dragged himself across the burning coals of death back to his personal reality. The intensity of the burning, smoke filled images thinned enough that he could once again see the dark outlines of sage and rock. He took a deep breath of cool night air without being consumed by wracking coughs and knew he had overcome the illusion.

The images of burning and pain remained, but the view of the canyon was stronger and he was able to move forward. Hamachi dragged one hand along the wall as an anchor to his individual reality; it helped him from stumbling as he was faced with the confusion of dual images.

Holding hard to the cold rock wall, Hamachi looked up at Stratumentis. It hung superimposed against a backdrop of flames and smoke coming from the view of the collective members still alive inside. A man made moon painted against a backdrop of destruction. Hundreds of viewpoints layered over one another. Only Hamachi's unyielding self-confidence and supreme will kept him from crumpling into a useless mass.

"Fall, already. Damn you." He wheezed through his smoke-burned throat.

A pain, needle-sharp in its intensity, forced his eyes closed. Hamachi tried to will it away as part of the collective's massive visual illusion. But it wouldn't go, it was in his own head, at the very site where Breedlove had implanted the chip. Realization cut through his pain and the multiple realities. "They're manipulating my brain, changing the chip!" Raw panic constricted his throat. His momentary shift in focus had allowed the hundreds of dying minds to once again overwhelm him. Only his hand on the wall saved him from being swallowed up again. "I can't keep them away from my mind and hold the illusion off at the same time. It's your plan to distract me. But you will all be dead soon. I only have to hang on."

"Too late Tatsuo." A feminine voice sang in his head.

"What?" Hamachi breathed.

"I wanted you to experience the cruelty you have subjected on so many.

But it is distracting and you and I need to speak." Suddenly all the burning images, smoke, pain and chaos were gone. It was just the quiet canyon again, the cool air and Stratumentis burning in the black sky above. "My name is Sigé and I now live in your mind."

"You can't live here, this is my mind." Hamachi yelled.

"Tell that to the men and women above who are dying. They're coming too." Sigé spoke into his head.

"No! Not you, not anyone. No one lives here but me. I refuse. You can't do this. It is a trick, a distraction. You aren't here. I won't allow it." Hamachi screamed.

"There is no allow. I am already here. Besides, I have nowhere else to go. I traveled through *the I* and connected through your collective to you. When my people were sure of my success, they killed my body. So you see Tatsuo, I am definitely here to stay. That sharp pain you felt in your brain, was me dismantling your chip."

"But Breedlove assured me..."

"Please Tatsuo, let us not waste time on such trivial matters. We have 1023 minds to save. Shall we begin?"

"Nooooo!" Hamachi's shout echoed through the canyon.

High above him, the two trams with nearly 200 men and women of the collective, had pulled within 100 feet of the south rim stations. Stratumentis was supported by four towers, two on each side of the canyon. Two cables had been severed by Ong's sabotage, forcing the one remaining north tower to take twice its designed weight. It had held - until now. It collapsed just as the two trams reached the south rim stations. The remaining weight of the entire city was transferred to the two south towers. They gave way immediately. Everything was pulled into the canyon, Stratumentis, towers, cables, trams and men.

Then all went dark.

Hamachi felt the first member join his mind. It was a man, one of the original prisoners. The man's mind was a roiling sea of anger. He blamed everyone and everything for the thousands of misfortunes in his life. Hamachi relived every missed opportunity and hardship. He felt the man's resentment, a deep and limitless ocean of hate. But this was only the tip of an enormous iceberg. The thoughts and memories of this loathsome man trickled in, unhurried. One by one, every nuance, every shade of every moment of this man's useless life marched in front of Hamachi's trapped mind.

This went on for what seemed like decades, but finally came to an end. Before Hamachi could take a mental break from this torment, the next member of the collective presented his mind for entrance. He too was a former prisoner. The man's mind was weak and stupid, full of trivial knowledge, most of it erroneous. His life was an endless progression of self-hate and doubt. Once again, Hamachi was forced to view the totality of a man's life, thought by tedious thought. Nothing was too minute or unimportant to leave out, nothing too insignificant. Hamachi's ordered and disciplined mind reeled under the onslaught of self-pity and fear.

Again, seemingly decades passed until another man arrived and every depraved nuance of his life was unfurled before the beaten Hamachi. When this man's wasted and perverted life was fully known, another entered, then another. The progression continued into the ages, slowly, methodically, unhurried. Each mind arrived, revealed itself and then moved to the background to make room for the next and the next and the next. During the eons that followed, Hamachi's own mind could do nothing but watch. His precious mind, the mind he was so proud of, the one he had so carefully educated, nurtured, fed, was repeatedly raped by the filthiest brutes, scum whom he loathed. Minds with nothing but perverse memories, childhoods filled with abuse and torture. Minds that had once been hungry for knowledge, but had instead been fed rotting, diseased misinformation.

On and on this eternity crawled. The memory of a fantastic building housing the unfettered dreams of a business genius was forgotten under the heap of a trillion, trillion thoughts. Buried under an endless progression of filth and degradation. His mind reeled in agony, crying out for relief, for mercy, which would never come.

Occasionally, in this onslaught of diseased minds there would be the promise of reprieve – an intelligence, one like his own. Hamachi's shattered mind would reach out and embrace this excellent guest. But the new mind would lash out, having been taken from its body without its consent. Unlike the others, it understood what was happening and scorched Hamachi's mind with the fire of anger, hate and resentment born of a blast furnace. Hamachi's mind folded onto itself, trying in desperation to crawl away from a pain that wouldn't end.

Time had long ceased to have any meaning when the final mind arrived. Familiar, brilliant and complex, it took pity on the battered Hamachi. It spoke to his torn and shattered essence, pulling some of the fragments from the abyss. Somehow enough of the pieces came together and the fundamental nature of what was once Hamachi emerged, albeit broken and humbled.

The infinite darkness that had filled Hamachi's vision for so long receded and was replaced once again with the star filled night of the desert. The scene in front of him was incomprehensible and he had to have help from the many minds inside to understand what he was looking at. "Oh yes, the Grand Canyon. Stratumentis had broken free and is falling." He looked up in time to see the enormous building engulfed in flames crash into the canyon floor. "BOOM!" The glass sphere hit the ground and exploded with the force of a thousand bombs. He was deafened by the echo of a million tons of steel, glass and plasticrete smashing into the canyon. His skin felt the shock wave and the heat of the horrific explosion. But his mind did little more than stare at the inexplicable sight, an abstract painting, beyond comprehension.

Then all when black again and Hamachi's fractured mind went silent.

The sun had long since risen when Hamachi awoke. He was lying on the ground alongside the towering wall of the Grand Canyon. His face was cold and numb where it had lain on the hard earth. The other side was uncomfortably warm from the late morning sun. Hamachi rubbed his face, driving the circulation back into it.

He dug through his survival pack and quickly found what he was looking for, a VR set.

"Mitasashi Corporation." A female receptionist said, "Southwest headquarters, Las Vegas."

"This is Tatsuo Hamachi, connect me to the general manager."

A moment later a nervous voice answered. "This is Frank Rubin, general manager."

"There has been an accident. Stratumentis is destroyed. I need you to send a recovery team to pick me up. I'll be on the canyon floor one quarter mile west of the impact site."

"Good god, are you injured?" Rubin sputtered. "How many are we picking up?"

"No injuries. Just one to pick up - me." Hamachi cut the connection.

Next he called William Sturgeon, president of UnitedFarms. "Sturgeon speaking." The president answered.

"Your company is attempting to overtake a small bit of private land in Western Colorado, just west of the abandoned city of Paonia. You will withdraw your claim and leave them in peace." Hamachi said smoothly.

"Now wait a minute. I don't know what you're talking about. And if I did, I wouldn't take orders from you. I run this company, not you." Sturgeon barked.

Hamachi sighed. "Please don't play stupid with me Sturgeon. I've had quite enough of that. Do I have to remind you of the millions of acres of land Mitasashi leases to your company? Or should I call FoodFutures and see if they would offer our company a more favorable arrangement?"

Sturgeon's face went pale. "No Mr. Hamachi, that won't be necessary. We will do as you wish. You may consider the matter resolved. We will also offer compensation for any inconvenience we may have caused the farmers."

"Good. See that you do." Hamachi cut the connection.

He made one final call. It took a long time to connect.

"What do you want?" Alexia's face filled his vision. Her hair was singed and she had painful looking blisters over her neck and shoulders.

"Dr. Serguey. You're fired as of this morning. Your account has been credited with the severance package agreed in your contract."

Alexia just stared at him.

"Do you still have our young guests with you?" He asked.

"Yes, they're still with me." She answered warily.

"Good. Instruct them to take one of the service vehicles from the rim station as transportation back to Colorado. Let them know UnitedFarms has agreed to withdraw its claim and will not bother them further. Tell Alvar that Sigé..." Hamachi's voice cracked slightly. "Never mind. Just tell Alvar that a silent friend wishes him and Chloe well."

"I'll give him the message." Alexia answered, stunned.

"I can't tell you what to do Alexia, but I suggest you go with them. And get yourself to a hospital, those burns look serious." Hamachi severed the connection before she could reply.

Hamachi put a fingertip to the corner of his eye and wiped away a tear. "This won't do." He whispered.

He stuffed the VR set into the day pack and picked his way down the steep slope, stopping now and then to look at the smoldering ruin that was once Stratumentis. The trail was rough and he tripped over a sage branch. Picking himself up, he smiled strangely and said, "Clumsy. But you can't really blame me; these feet are a lot bigger than I'm used to."

ABOUT THE AUTHOR

JAY MAGIDSON WAS born in Southern California in 1959. He now lives in a rural area not too far from Aspen, Colorado. He is married with two children. Jay lives in a world of art and artists. His wife is a successful artist and he owned and managed art galleries for more than three decades. Jay's weekly art essays were published to reader acclaim in *The Aspen Daily News* and *The Roaring Fork Sunday*. He was also a guest writer for *The Aspen Sojourner Magazine*.

Threshold of the Mind is Jay's third book. His first book, *Shira's Wish*, a children's book with photographs by award winning photographer, Bobbie Goodrich was released in 2011. It is being widely hailed by young readers.

Colors, his second book, is a collection of dark short stories that was released in 2012. *Kirkus Review* wrote: "This eerie novella in stories recalls Rod Serling's Twilight Zone." And Kathryn Rabinow, Professor of Psychology at the University of Houston wrote: "Oh wow!!! Oh my!!! I couldn't put the book down; at times I couldn't stop my pulse from racing; at times I wanted to rush to your house and take away all pills and sharp knives from your cupboards and drawers."

Science Fiction has long been Jay's love, to read it and to write it. *Science Fiction is the last bastion of the dreamer, where an idea becomes reality. It is no accident that so many films and Television shows are based on Science Fiction stories. As long as we have imagination, these stories will continue to intrigue and inspire us.*

To learn more about the author go to:

www.JayMagidson.com

Made in the USA
Charleston, SC
26 November 2013